DO NOT FORSAKE ME

ROSANNE BITTNER

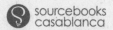

sourcebooks
casablanca

Published by Sourcebooks Casablanca, an imprint of Sourcebooks,
Inc.
P.O. Box 4410, Naperville, Illinois 60567-4410
(630) 961-3900
Fax: (630) 961-2168
www.sourcebooks.com

Printed and bound in Canada
MBP 10 9 8 7 6 5 4 3 2 1

For my kind and patient husband, who puts up without my company for hours, days, and weeks at a time when I am working on a book. He knows how much this one meant to me. And for Sourcebooks and my editor, Mary Altman, who gave me this chance to finally write a story I've wanted to write for the last twenty years. We both fell in love with Jake Harkner.

One

WITH A REPORTER'S EYE, JEFF TRUBRIDGE STUDIED Marshal Jake Harkner as the man rode into Guthrie with four prisoners in tow, three of them looking mean but defeated, their faces bruised and battered. The fourth man was obviously dead, his body draped over a horse and wrapped in a blanket tied tightly with rope.

Harkner put two fingers to his lips and gave out a loud whistle.

"What's that for?" Jeff asked a man standing next to him.

"The marshal always signals his wife when he's comin' in," the man replied. "She always comes to greet him."

Jake Harkner looked every bit like Jeff's vision of a notorious outlaw turned United States Marshal serving in the raw, new, and unorganized territory of Oklahoma. Oklahoma was ripe for men who preyed on Indians and settlers alike. It was a place where such men could hide in No Man's Land, the name given to the western half of the territory because the government still couldn't decide what to do with it. It was a place few men dared to tread...except for the likes of Jake Harkner, who was familiar with lawless country and lawless men.

Jeff savored the opportunity to observe Harkner without having to approach him directly...yet. He searched for the right words to describe the man who'd made a name for himself in all the wrong ways yet had become nothing short of a hero in the eyes of the common man. How did someone who was at one time so lawless and ruthless become so well liked?

Notorious reputation, he quickly scribbled on his ever-handy notepad. *The way he carries himself—still a tall, slim, solid, hard-edged man with a look about him*. What was that look? *Danger*. That was it. *Like nitroglycerin—one wrong move and it explodes*.

He liked that word. *Nitroglycerin*. Jeff carefully mingled into the crowd that followed the marshal toward the jailhouse. It was obvious some of them just wanted to be near Harkner so they could brag about knowing him. Fact was, Jeff wouldn't mind having bragging rights himself, except his would be that he was the only man who'd convinced Jake Harkner to let him write a book about him. So far the man had refused all other requests to write his story, but Jeff was determined. Still, now that he saw the man in the flesh, his resolve was weakening.

The man wore the signature duster of a U.S. Marshal. The spring morning was heating up, and as he rode in, he removed the coat, reaching around to lay it over his horse's rump. Now Jeff could see his weapons—the Colt .44 revolvers holstered on each hip, a Colt Lightning magazine rifle and a sawed-off ten-gauge shotgun resting in loops on either side of his saddle. An extra cartridge belt hung across the man's chest, and a third handgun rested in a holster behind the marshal's back.

Jeff knew what kind of guns Harkner wore because he'd already spoken to Guthrie's local sheriff, Herbert "Sparky" Sparks, and had interviewed several others in town. He'd arrived two days earlier to discover the marshal was not back yet from his latest manhunt.

During his wait, he took advantage of various citizens' eagerness to share stories about the man. Aware that people tend to exaggerate such things, Jeff was not about to rely on hearsay. He wanted only facts, which was why he needed to hear the story straight from the marshal himself. Countless men had gone down under his guns, including—most shocking of all—Jake's own father.

Jeff desperately wanted to know why. He intended to get to know the man some had nicknamed the Handsome Outlaw, but it wasn't going to be easy. He needed to talk to Harkner's family too, but had so far stayed away. The fact that Harkner even *had* a family was amazing, considering the things Jeff knew about him. How did a man so notorious end up having anyone?

What he observed now only confirmed that his quest for a story had been worth the trip. Harkner was back from No Man's Land—a place most men feared to tread. Those prisoners still alive were in a bad way. All rode with hands tied to saddle horns with rope that was then looped up under their horses and tied to their ankles under the horse's belly. One had a bloody bandage around his forehead, with dried blood on the side of his face. Another wore an eye patch and looked ready to fall off his horse. The third prisoner just hung his head but occasionally gave Harkner a dark look of hatred. The left sleeve of his shirt showed a huge bloodstain. All were filthy—hair matted, faces showing several-day-old beards as well as cuts and bruises. Had Jake Harkner put those there?

Jake's son, Lloyd, a deputy U.S. Marshal, was nowhere to be seen, and Jeff wondered why. He'd been told that Lloyd had ridden out with Jake to track down these criminals.

"Lloyd okay, Jake?" someone from the crowd called. Apparently Jeff wasn't the only one wondering. "Where is he?"

"He's fine," Harkner answered. "He stopped off at the Donavan place."

Jeff took more notes and wrote a brief description of Jake's clothing—denim pants, dusty boots, black bib shirt, black wide-brimmed hat from which his nearly black and slightly wavy hair hung just past his shoulders. From what Jeff could tell, there was just a touch of gray in it despite the man's age. He wore a brown leather vest with a six-point marshal's badge on it...and those threatening guns. Jake Harkner was still a very handsome man, but hard lines about his dark eyes spoke of a man who'd led a very rough life. Everything about him spelled toughness—a man with not a soft spot on him. He kept a cigarette between his lips now as he answered more questions. The scene reminded Jeff of the pied piper, as the crowd following Harkner kept growing. Suddenly, a stocky young man exited a saloon not far from the jailhouse and called out, "Jake, you bastard! I don't see my pa! Is he the dead one? Is that my pa's body draped over that horse?"

Jake didn't even look at the young man. "It is," he answered casually.

"You murdering sonofabitch!" the young man screamed. "I should kill you!"

It looked to Jeff as though the young man meant exactly what he said. Harkner continued to ignore him as he stopped in front of the jail.

"How'd you do it, Jake?" the young man screamed. "Did you put your gun in his mouth and blow his fucking brains out? Ain't that the way you usually kill a man?"

"Mind your business, Brad!" someone in the street yelled. "Your pa was no good, and you know it!"

Two more young men came out of the saloon and flanked the one called Brad. All three just stood watching for the moment, but the air was tense and people backed away. Jeff suddenly felt too hot in his neatly tailored suit, and he unbuttoned the top button of his shirt, wondering if bullets were about to fly.

Then...there she was. He'd never met her, but the woman hurrying down the street from the other end of town had to be Miranda Harkner. She'd apparently heard her husband's whistle. The look of both relief and concern in her eyes said it all: even after many years together, the woman was still very much in love with Jake Harkner.

Jeff had expected a heftier, older-looking woman, but the woman hurrying down the street now had a lovely, slender shape and looked far younger than what Jeff figured she must be—somewhere around forty-five years old. She wore a well-fitted yellow checkered dress, and her ash-blond hair showed no hint of gray.

So small! he quickly wrote. *I expected a stout and somber woman; she was somehow bigger in my imagination. How does such a tiny woman handle a man like Jake Harkner?*

The rugged, dangerous-looking Harkner finally halted his horse when he saw the woman coming. He dismounted and removed the extra belt slung over his shoulder, hanging it around his horse's neck. He threw down his cigarette and walked up to her. It struck Jeff then how tall Jake was, perhaps six feet and two or three inches. He towered over the woman, who looked past him at the men he'd brought in, then warily eyed the young men standing on the boardwalk near the jail. Jeff snuck closer, straining to hear.

"Where's Lloyd?" the woman asked with a worried look.

In a surprisingly gentle move, Jake put an arm around her shoulders and led her a few feet away. "He headed to the Donavans'. He'll stay there the night, I expect. He was anxious to see Katie again."

The woman smiled and they said something more to each other. Jeff could hardly believe it when Harkner leaned down and kissed her cheek before grasping her arm and gently steering her aside. "Stay out of the way till I take care of Brad Buckley," he warned. "I don't want you to get hurt."

So, Jeff observed, *the man's wife can change him from a cougar to a kitten with one look.* It was becoming clear that this book also had to be a love story. How strange that a man like Jake could love anyone. Even more strange that someone could love Jake Harkner, especially someone as lovely and seemingly gracious as Miranda.

"Hey, Jake, I bet the Buckley and the Bryant boys wish they hadn't gone up against the likes of you, *señor*, huh?" The words were spoken by an older Mexican man named Juan López.

Jake waved him off as he tied his horse in front of the jail, removing both his shotgun and rifle from the saddle. "Juan, you talk too much," he told the man. "Take care of the horses once I unload these men, will you?"

"*Sí, amigo.*"

"*Estoy ansioso para poner en orden este asunto y regresar a mi esposa.*"

The old man grinned more. "Ah, *señor, lo comprendo.*"

The conversation answered one of Jeff's questions: Jake Harkner did sometimes speak in Spanish. Jeff didn't understand what was said, except that he knew *esposa* meant wife. Supposedly Harkner's mother had been Mexican, and one rumor was that Harkner's father had killed the woman. No one knew any details, and all had advised Jeff never to ask Harkner about it…or if he'd really killed his own father. The subject was apparently closed for the man, and Jeff swallowed at the thought of trying to bring it up. He watched Harkner hand his shotgun to his wife.

"Get farther back," he warned her. "I'll be finished here in a few minutes, and I'm tired as hell. You should go back to the house. I'll be along."

"I'm not going anywhere until that young man across the street goes back inside. I don't like the looks of this, Jake."

Jake sighed. "You just be careful with that shotgun. It's still loaded."

Sparky came out of the jail then to greet Jake. "Damn it, Jake, you have to quit rounding up so many of these no-goods. You're crowding my jail."

Jeff caught a quick grin on Harkner's face. *The man actually smiles!*

"Sorry about that, Sparky. Want me to shoot a couple of them to give you more room?"

Sparky guffawed at what Jeff hoped was a joke, but he wasn't so sure Harkner didn't mean it.

"Send a wire to Edmond and have them send a wagon up here for this bunch," Jake told the sheriff then. He handed over a bank bag obviously stuffed with money. "This has to be returned to the bank in Edmond. And when you send that wire, tell Sheriff Kennedy there that they'll need extra men to take this bunch back to Edmond. A marshal from Oklahoma City can take them from there. They'll likely be hanged or sent to the federal pen in Michigan. I'll come around Monday to sign papers."

The marshal took another cigarette from a pocket inside his vest as Jeff dared to step even closer. He rolled up his shirtsleeves against the warming temperatures, and Jeff noticed that although Harkner was in his midfifties, his forearms showed hard muscle. *Handsome Outlaw is very fitting*, he noted. He watched the man light his cigarette. As he did so, the marshal glanced at Jeff, and the look in his dark eyes was stunningly suspicious and threatening. Jeff stepped back a little and nodded to the man. Harkner's eyes said it all: he didn't like strangers watching him. His eyes showed a combination of curiosity, distrust, and a warning to stay out of his way as he looked Jeff over, summing him up. Obviously not impressed and sensing no danger, he gave him a brief nod and turned away.

"Stay back like I told you," he told his wife. "Go around behind that wagon." He nodded to a freight wagon parked just a few feet away.

Rather reluctantly, Miranda walked closer to the wagon, still holding Jake's shotgun. Jeff scooted a bit closer to her as Jake walked back to the men he'd brought in. The young man on the boardwalk let out a blistering tirade of threats and insults as Jake untied the dead body and yanked it from the horse, letting the body fall to the street. It landed stiff and still bent.

"Somebody take care of this one," he ordered. "Take him over to the undertaker."

"*Murderer!* That's what you are, Harkner! A murderer with a badge!" Brad continued screaming. "Everybody knows you're nothing more than an outlaw with permission to kill!"

Jake walked back to the other three men, Guthrie's Sheriff Sparks walking with him, holding his shotgun ready as Jake untied each man and jerked him off his horse, in spite of their injuries. He seemed to be ignoring the young man on the boardwalk, but Jeff suspected he was very much aware.

"Someone go get my son-in-law to take a look at these men," Jake spoke up. A young boy ran off.

Son-in-law is a doctor here in Guthrie, Jeff wrote. That was something else he already knew. It was so hard to imagine Jake Harkner had a lovely daughter who was married to a doctor. They had a son named after Jake, or so Jeff had been told. Jake's own son, Lloyd, also had fathered a little boy.

A grandfather. Jake Harkner is a grandfather. I can't seem to put the two together—the grandfather and the mean-looking cuss I am watching right now.

Brad continued to harass Jake. "Harkner, you can't throw my pa down like so much garbage! I'll kill you for that!"

The crowd quieted. People backed even farther away. Jeff glanced at Miranda Harkner and saw the worry in her eyes. How many times had she been through something like this?

"You want me to arrest that smart-ass kid, Jake?" Sheriff Sparks asked him.

Harkner watched Brad a moment. "No. Just get those three prisoners into the jail. Brian will be here soon to take a look at their injuries."

Sparks sighed. "If you say so."

"Juan, come take these horses over to Tobe's," the marshal ordered, and the old man eagerly obeyed. He led all five horses away, and Sheriff Sparks herded the three prisoners into the jailhouse, nudging them with his shotgun. Jeff's heart pounded with anticipation as Harkner, still carrying a repeating rifle, walked closer to the angry young man on the boardwalk.

"Your pa robbed a bank and killed two men," he announced loudly enough for all to hear. "Then he took refuge with some innocent ranchers, and he and his men defiled their fifteen-year-old daughter. Did you expect me to feel sorry for him? I threw your father down like a piece of garbage because that's what he *is*."

Brad's eyes spit fire. "Anything my pa did ain't no different from things you've done *yourself*," the young man sneered, "including defilin' women. Somebody should have shot you dead a long time ago, Harkner, and I aim to do it *today*!"

People mumbled.

"Sweet Jesus," a man near Jeff muttered. "You stupid ass. You lookin' to die?"

Jeff shot the man a glance and happened to spot a very nice-looking young man with a doctor's bag standing near the marshal's wife. He put an arm around her. *The son-in-law.* Harkner's wife didn't take her eyes off of her husband for one second as he stepped even closer to the much younger and very stocky man who had challenged him.

"Your father already tried shooting it out with me," the marshal told his accuser. "You can see how that turned out."

The two men behind Brad backed away.

"You'd better back off, Brad," one of them told his friend.

"Your friends are talking sense," Harkner told him. "Fact is, I'd suggest all three of you lift your guns and drop them. Sheriff Sparks can hold them for you until you cool off."

One of them obeyed. "I don't want no part of this," he muttered as he unbuckled his gun belt and let it drop. He hurried around behind Brad and jumped off the boardwalk.

Jeff watched, spellbound. He'd never expected to see Jake Harkner in action today.

"I'm really not in the mood for this, Brad," Harkner told the young man. He threw down his cigarette and stepped it out. "You're young, and you don't want to die yet—and I don't want to be the one responsible—so why don't you hand over that gun and go home?"

"You don't scare me, Harkner."

Jeff couldn't imagine why any man would want to challenge Jake Harkner this way. In fact, the second man behind Brad also backed away, putting his hands in the air. "Leave me out of this," he told Jake. He turned and ran back into the saloon, leaving Brad standing there alone, sweat stains on his shirt.

The marshal stepped even closer, still holding his rifle in one hand. "Last warning, Brad. I'm goddamn tired and don't want any of this. Be on your way."

"You worried, Harkner? Age catchin' up with you?"

The air hung silent. "You don't want to find out," Harkner answered. "And I really don't want to kill you. You're no older than my own son."

"Yeah? I'll bet he loves his pa like I loved *mine*! That's where we're both different from *you*, ain't we, Harkner? We *loved* our fathers!"

Miranda Harkner gasped. "Oh my God," she said softly.

No one expected what happened next.

In one quick movement that gave Brad no time to react, Harkner slammed the butt of his rifle into the younger man's chest with a violent punch that sent the kid flying backward. He landed against a stack of barrels, which crashed and rolled over the boardwalk and into the street. The marshal kicked more barrels aside and slammed the rifle butt across the side of Brad's head. In a flash, he swung his rifle around and pressed the barrel against Brad's forehead.

"Don't do it, Jake!" Jeff heard Miranda Harkner say softly.

Jeff was sure Jake would pull the trigger right then and there and blow the young man's brains all over the boardwalk. The stunning attack had been so quick and vicious that Jeff felt a sudden need to urinate in his fear.

"You're goddamn lucky we're in town and I have to abide by the law, kid!" Harkner growled. He moved the rifle aside and fired it into the boardwalk, right beside Brad's ear.

Everyone jumped at the gunshot, and a couple of women screamed and ran into a store. Harkner reached down with his free hand and grasped the younger man by the shirtfront. He jerked him up and slammed him against the remaining barrels, sending more of them flying. "Thank your God you're still alive, kid!"

Brad stood there shaking and sweating. He opened his mouth, and Jeff realized the young man couldn't breathe.

The blow to his chest had probably knocked the air out of him.

"Take his gun, Sparky," Harkner ordered the sheriff, seemingly unaffected as Brad's face started going white with the struggle for air. A huge split in the skin at the right side of his face bled profusely, and the whole side of his head was already turning purple.

The sheriff ran up and took Brad's gun from its holster. Still using only one arm, Harkner threw Brad violently off the boardwalk and into the street. "When he can breathe again, somebody help him up and take him over to the jail," he ordered.

Brad rolled over with an ugly gurgling sound. He held one hand to the ear that had taken the brunt of the rifle shot, blood dripping into the dirt from the gash at the side of his face. Harkner glanced up then, his dark eyes boring into Jeff's. Jeff stood there frozen in place as the man stalked closer.

"You've been watching me. Who the hell are you and what do you want?"

Jeff swallowed. "I...my name is Jeff Trubridge, and I'm...I'm a reporter...from Chicago. I didn't mean any harm." He held out his arms, his small pad of paper in one hand and a pencil in the other. "I don't even own or know how to use a gun."

Harkner glanced over at Brad, who was now crying as he got to his feet with the sheriff's help, then crumpled to his knees again. The marshal turned back to Jeff. "I'm not in a very good mood right now, Trubridge, so whatever you want, it will have to wait a couple of days."

"But—"

"*Monday!*" Harkner growled. "Tomorrow my wife goes to church, and I need some time with my family."

"Yes, sir." Jeff was glad to realize the man actually meant to hear him out. He felt a now-painful need to urinate as he watched the marshal walk away. His wife approached him with a devastated look on her face. Jeff could see the love there and realized her concern was over how Brad's remark about fathers might have hurt her husband. Jeff started after him, but the young man with the doctor's bag put out his arm.

"Leave him alone," he warned. "This isn't a good time. Surely you can see that."

Jeff faced the sandy-haired and very handsome young man of medium but sturdy build. The doctor's blue eyes showed deep concern and something else. Love? For his father-in-law? Jeff found all of it hard to believe—his wife's loving concern, the doctor's, the friendly manner in which Sparky and the Mexican spoke with Jake Harkner... "Are you Jake Harkner's son-in-law?"

"Dr. Brian Stewart, and I have some prisoners to tend to. I want your promise to stay away from my father-in-law the rest of today, though. The man has been on the trail for over three weeks, and I suspect he's damn tired. Combined with what just happened, that isn't a good mix for a man like Jake."

Jeff watched Jake and his wife walk up the street. "Will his wife be okay?"

"What?" Brian looked at him as if he were crazy.

"Well, Jake Harkner is in one hell of a bad mood. Is she safe?"

Brian grinned and shook his head. "Mister, I don't know everything you've heard about the man, but Jake would slit his own throat before he'd raise his hand or even his voice to that woman. She'll be just fine. Times like this, she's the only one who can calm him down. That woman has my father-in-law wrapped around her little finger so tight, he couldn't cut himself away with a bowie knife."

It struck Jeff again how badly he needed to urinate. "I, uh, I need to find a privy."

Brian chuckled. "Yeah, Jake does that to a man

sometimes." He nodded toward a building across the street. "There's a privy over there behind that store."

Jeff nodded, embarrassed. "Thanks." He hurried away, stepping around barrels that still lay in the street and thinking how there was nothing old or soft or weak about Marshal Jake Harkner. He was every bit the notorious, hardened ex-outlaw he'd expected. He had to urinate so badly that he unbuttoned his pants as he half ran to the privy, and he'd barely made it inside before his bladder let loose, spilling out pent-up anxiety and fear along with urine.

He wondered if any man had literally wet his pants when faced down by Jake Harkner.

Two

RANDY SET JAKE'S SHOTGUN INTO A WALL RACK NEAR the kitchen door. The tight feeling in her chest and stomach that plagued her every time her husband left on a dangerous mission was only just beginning to ease up. As each weapon was set down or unbuckled and untied and laid aside, she felt a little better. Shotgun—rifle— spare six-gun—gun belt and its two .44s. "Are you really all right?" she asked Jake.

He unbuckled the gun belt after untying the holsters from around his thighs. "What do *you* think?"

Randy put her hands on her hips. "I think Brad Buckley weighs well over two hundred pounds, and you threw him off that boardwalk like he was five years old. Should I find some liniment for that left shoulder?"

Jake scowled. "That kid called me an old man. Are you agreeing with him?" He hung up his gun belt and locked the back door, then faced his wife, folding his arms. Randy was smiling.

"I'm just being realistic, and I know you have a lot of pain from old wounds, Jake Harkner."

He looked her over in a way that always made her feel beautiful as well as weak, even after twenty-six years together. "Woman, I've been gone three weeks, so right now, no pain of any kind could stop me from stripping you naked and having my way with you."

Randy walked closer, rubbing her hands over his muscled arms. "And you are trying to change the more important subject here. I don't like what happened out there in the street. Brad Buckley isn't going to let this go."

Jake firmly embraced her. "Well, right now he's hurting really bad. He's not going to be a bother for quite a while. The fact remains, I killed his father, worthless as the man was, and Brad's not going to forget about it anytime soon. I know that." He leaned down and kissed her lightly. "But right now, I don't want to think about him. I just want my woman and some sleep—and I smell fresh-baked bread."

"Yes, you do," Randy answered with a smile. "I had a feeling you'd show up today. I've reached the point where I can almost feel it when you're close, so I made some for you early this morning. I also made that beef stew you like so much. When I heard your whistle, I felt very proud that I'd predicted correctly."

"Lady, you know me too well." Jake turned and hung up his hat, then sat down and put out a foot. "Help me get these boots off."

Randy eyed him slyly, knowing what was coming. She straddled his leg and began tugging, then laughed when he placed his other foot on her rump to support her as she pulled off the boot. He repeated the gesture with a stockinged foot and wiggled his toes teasingly as she removed the other boot. Randy jumped away when the second boot came off.

"I'll eat later," Jake told her, "after I take care of my appetite for you."

Miranda grinned as she turned to the stove to stir the stew. "You should be too tired."

"For you? Never."

"Is Lloyd really okay? I wish he'd come back with you. Little Stephen misses him so when he's gone."

"He's fine. By now he's turning on the charm for Katie Donavan Lamont. I told him it's time he made up his mind. Our son needs a woman in his life, and Stevie needs a mother. You can't be doing it all."

"I hope he listens to you. I like Katie very much, and she needs a husband as much as Lloyd needs a wife."

In the next moment, Jake's arms came around her from behind. He leaned down and kissed her neck. "God, I miss you when I'm out there. I worry about you, Randy. I don't like not being close enough to watch out for you."

Randy turned and wrapped her arms around his middle, relishing his strong embrace. "I hate it too, because I'm always afraid you'll never come back."

"Oh, I always find a way to come back and keep making life miserable for you."

Randy looked up at him. "It would be miserable *without* you, and you know it."

Jake met her mouth with a deeper kiss, pressing her tightly against him. He moved his lips to her brow. "We might have to forget about dinner. Once I'm through with you, I *will* be too tired to eat. Will Stephen stay at Evie's tonight?"

Randy breathed in his masculine scent. "Of course, but they will have a time keeping Little Jake confined. He asks about you at least ten times a day when you're gone. That boy lives to be around his 'gampa,' though you need to stop cussing around him, Jake. He's picking up some of it, which upsets Evie."

"I try, but the kid is a little hellion."

"Like grandpa, like grandson. The boy knows no fear, and he's going to make Evie crazy. But, yes, both boys will be with her and Brian tonight. They understand we need time alone when you get back, although it embarrasses me a little that they know *why* we need some time."

Jake kept his arms around her and walked her backward out of the kitchen. "Why does it embarrass you? You're my wife."

Randy laughed lightly. "Because they are our daughter and son-in-law, and they probably think we're too old for this."

"Oh, I think they *both* know me better than that." He kept urging her toward the bedroom. "I don't even need to wash up first."

"Oh? You do smell awfully good for a man who's been on the trail for three weeks, Marshal Harkner. And I notice that this time you came back clean-shaven, except for what looks like a hint of a beard only a few hours old." Randy planted her feet and grasped his arms. "Maybe you'd like to explain that."

Jake grinned—the handsome smile that always made her want him. "Lloyd and I took turns watching the prisoners last night while we each took a bath at Dixie's brothel in that shantytown west of the Donavan place."

Randy stepped back and looked him over. "Is that so?"

"That's so. The women there were more than happy to help out."

Randy folded her arms. This was all part of their old game; Jake loved when she played the jealous wife, loved pretending to have to talk her down. "I'm sure they were. And of course you slept there."

Jake unfolded her arms and pushed them behind her back. "Of course I did. We *both* caught a few hours' sleep in real beds. It felt good. We kept the prisoners hog-tied in a barn and a Mexican who works there tended them for us."

Randy held his gaze. "You *slept* there."

Jake pressed her tight against him. "Sure did…all alone. Woman, you know better than to think I'd ever betray your trust." He nuzzled her neck.

"What I know is that women look at you like you're chocolate candy—even the decent ones in town. They wonder what it would be like to belong to Jake Harkner."

Jake kept her arms behind her as he continued walking her backward to the bedroom doorway. "Then I guess they'll just have to keep wondering, won't they? Including the ones at that brothel. Hell, I've been around whores since I was six years old, Randy Harkner, and you know it. You also know there is only one woman for me, and you're it." He shut the bedroom door. "Then again, when I'm gone for so long, maybe it's me who has to worry about *you*, working for that fancy widowed lawyer in town. The man is eight years younger than I am and not bad-looking."

Randy hesitated, then pulled the combs from her hair as he unbuttoned the front of her dress. This wasn't part of their usual game. "Peter Brown is no Jake Harkner."

"Yeah? I've seen how he looks at you, and Lord knows he has a lot more to offer a woman like you than I ever had in my whole life."

Randy sobered and grasped his shoulders. "Jake." She watched his eyes. "I hope you're joking."

He lost his smile as he ran his hands through her hair and pulled it over her shoulders. "Maybe I'm not. He's smart, educated, lonely, has money—"

"And he's not *you*." She finished unbuttoning her dress and pulled it off. "Nor would he want to have to answer to you, of all men. I only work for him when you're gone, Jake, and that's because I'd go crazy if I didn't have something to keep me from thinking about what could be happening to you. If you think for one minute—"

He caught her words on his lips. He held her close with one arm as he used his other hand to pull one strap of her camisole over her shoulder, then pushed her playfully to the bed. "It's the same here," he said gruffly. She sat down on the edge of the bed, and Jake knelt down in front of her to unlace her camisole. "When I'm away from you, I never once stop thinking about the woman I love and want to come back to so bad I think I'll die from the need of her."

He opened her camisole and leaned closer, nuzzling her cleavage. Randy closed her eyes and grasped his hair as he moved his lips back to her throat, then to her mouth again, devouring her lips. The man had a way of erasing the years, always bringing her to the first time they'd made almost savage love in a wagon on their way to nowhere.

Then, reluctantly, he pulled away, beginning to undress and sliding back into their old game. "I stopped for that bath so I wouldn't have to waste time with one when I got home to you," he told her.

"That's a fine excuse," she teased. "And why didn't you have one of them cut your hair?"

"I like letting *you* cut it."

"Well, it's past your shoulders."

"Maybe it makes me stronger, like Samson."

Randy smiled. "I think the only Bible passages you remember me reading to Lloyd and Evie are the ones that were about battles and wars."

Jake grinned. "Those were the only exciting parts. Now, wiggle out of those slips and anything else that's in the way, woman. Right now, *you* are Delilah."

Randy gladly did as she was told, thinking how her husband was still a fetching man, his body hard, his dark hair showing no sign of thinning. He remained amazingly strong for his age, but she hated the scars that told of the rough life he'd led—especially the scars put on his back by his father. Those were the deepest scars of all.

She moved under the covers.

Jake frowned. "Why are you hiding under those blankets like a bashful young girl? You know I'll rip them off of you."

Randy sighed. "I *do* feel more bashful as I get older. I'm not the skinny young woman you married, Jake."

He shook his head and grinned, moving under the covers with her. "Woman, I don't believe you just said that. You've gained, what, maybe all of ten pounds in all these years? And that's weight you *needed* to put on, because you've always been too thin." He pulled her close. "You still feel damn good to me, and in all the right places." He moved a leg between hers. "And you know damn well that there isn't a more beautiful woman in all of Guthrie…in all of Oklahoma, for that matter."

"And you have been away so long that anything would look good to you."

He nuzzled her neck. "Well, maybe it's the same for you. I'm not getting any younger."

"There isn't one thing old about you, Jake Harkner."

He pushed up one breast, kissing at her cleavage.

"See?" Randy commented. "For some reason, my breasts get bigger every year."

Jake broke into laughter, hugging her close. "Is that supposed to upset me?"

Randy couldn't help her own laughter then. "I'm sure you got quite an eyeful at that brothel."

"Yeah, but I *own* these breasts. They're molded to my hands…and my mouth." He relished each breast as though something delicious, then moved his lips to her neck. "You look damn good, and it's not just because I've been gone, and you *know* it."

"Just so long as you're not tasting any other breasts," she teased.

He met her mouth hungrily, his words spoken amid deep kisses. "If I wasn't so needful of being inside you right now, I'd be tasting a lot more than your breasts."

Randy's smile faded to pleasure as his hands began searching all the places he knew awakened her womanly needs. She couldn't help thinking how nice it was to be married to a man who knew every way there was to please a woman. He kissed and licked behind her ear, then spoke softly.

"Who do you belong to?" It was a ritualistic question he always asked before making love to her.

"Jake Harkner," she answered, the words mumbled amid a searching kiss.

"And I'm just claiming what's mine."

Randy closed her eyes and breathed in the scent of him, leather and fresh air and…man. She couldn't think of another word for it. Just *man*. They were so much in unison…mind, body, and spirit. Jake Harkner knew every inch of her body intimately, knew exactly what she did and didn't like. She in turn took great satisfaction in giving this man who so sorely needed to be loved everything he wanted.

She drew in her breath as his fingers toyed with places that belonged only to him, and in moments she felt the erotic explosion from her deep need for him. She groaned with the sweet ecstasy of the orgasm. He pushed her arms over her head then and gently pinned her there, taking her under his command as he always did in bed, filling her with a love and passion that had not lessened over the years. They could never be sure how long this would last because of the dangers he faced, a worry that made them devour each other as much as possible when he was here with her.

He moved inside of her then with the need of a man long without his woman. Randy knew that though this man had once known many women, she was without question his only love, as he was hers. Over their many years together, their desire for each other had not changed. He always made her feel young and daring and beautiful, and she took him with a desperate need to make sure he was really here and alive and unhurt.

She felt the pain then…the odd pain that came and went lately. It hit deep in her belly, but she ignored it—it always went away after a moment, just as it left her now. Soon there was only pleasure again.

Jake groaned her name as he filled her with stunning thrusts that told her his desire for her was as strong as ever. A second, even more intense orgasm made Randy arch up to him with hungry desire. Jake reached under her hips and filled her until he could no longer hold back his own orgasm.

They lay there quietly for several long seconds, wrapped in each other's arms in glorious joy that all was well and they were alive and still able to enjoy each other this way.

"I missed you so much, *mi esposa. Tú eres mi vida.*"

"And I missed you holding me. I love your arms around me. I feel so safe and loved when you're here."

He kissed her several times over—her mouth, her neck, her breasts, her belly, the hairs between her legs, back up to her lips—and soon he was ready for her again, pushing deep inside her with an aching need to be sure he'd pleased her after over three weeks apart. They groaned together with their climax, then Jake wilted beside her. They took a moment just to enjoy the quiet, the feel of naked body against naked body, to listen to each other's soft breathing, to stroke each other lovingly. Finally Jake rolled away from her with a deep sigh. "God, I hate this job. I hate not being here to watch out for you every single day."

"Evie and I get along fine when you're gone."

"But you're Jake Harkner's wife and she's Jake Harkner's daughter, which means you're always in danger, and so are the grandkids—all because of me."

"Jake, stop it." Randy put an arm across his chest and nestled into his shoulder. "You were in prison for four years, and we were just fine."

"You had Jess York to watch out for you. And it was different with me locked up. Most thought I'd stay in prison the rest of my life, but I'm out now, and a target for those who want to lay a claim to fame through me."

She kissed his neck. "You've just been through a lot

and it's got you on edge, that's all. We're safe here in town, and Evie has Brian."

He rubbed his eyes. "I suppose. Damn, I'm suddenly really tired, Randy," he told her, the weight of the last three rugged weeks and the pain of Brad Buckley's remark clearly taking their toll. "I'm sorry, but I need to sleep. I can't even get up to eat any of that stew you made."

Randy pulled the covers over them and snuggled against him. "For heaven's sake, Jake. Do you think I wouldn't understand how tired you are? It's all right." She kissed his chest. "I love you. Thank God you're home safe and sound and Lloyd is all right."

He closed his eyes. "He's fine." His words came in a lazy mutter. "I love you."

Randy settled against his shoulder, and in moments he was breathing deeply in an exhausted sleep. She lay still, enjoying the feel of his warmth in her bed again. The sun wasn't even completely set yet, but it didn't matter. She knew Evie would make sure no one bothered them. The stew would simmer on the cookstove for several hours. There was no need to do anything with it right now. It was enough to just lie here with her husband beside her.

Remarks like Brad Buckley's earlier today brought forth pieces from Jake's past that he might never be able to put behind him, memories that evoked pain and rage. And because she didn't want to worry him, she kept silent about the pain in her belly. It was nothing. It would go away. The Jake Harkner who lay beside her now was a far cry from the man he became when he put on guns and badge and walked out the door. He needed this peace. He didn't need something new to worry about.

Three

LLOYD TROTTED HIS HORSE CLOSER TO THE DONAVANS' cabin, hoping Katie was home. He'd always liked her, and the part of him that wanted more kept arguing with the deeper part of him that missed Beth so much that he'd almost lost his mind when she died losing their baby eighteen months ago. The only thing that kept him from returning to a life of drinking and despair after her death had been his father, who'd literally slugged him and hog-tied him one night. Jake and Sheriff Sparks had dragged him into a jail cell and left him there until he sobered up.

A lot of long talks with both his parents had brought Lloyd around, but it was mainly Jake who'd managed to get through to him, reminding him he had a son to live for, a son he never wanted to disgrace...the way Lloyd once felt his own father had disgraced him. He never wanted those same hard feelings between himself and his son, Stephen.

Now he had to face the fact that he was a widower with a six-year-old son to raise. He'd loved Beth desperately, but she was lost to him. Stephen was his whole life now. The boy stayed with his grandma Randy when Lloyd and Jake had to go out on a manhunt, but he couldn't expect his mother to keep doing all the raising. The woman had been through hell over years of living with a wanted man who'd ended up in prison and now lived the life of a U.S. Marshal. A loving grandmother she was, but she needed some peace.

Lloyd knew deep inside that he needed a new wife,

someone who would be a good mother to Stephen. Beth would want that too. Katie Donavan Lamont had those qualities, and it didn't hurt that she was beautiful. He'd been seeing her a few months now, had taken her to the spring dance in Guthrie and stolen a kiss or two, but memories of Beth had held him back from allowing serious feelings, and his job often kept him away for days or weeks at a time, making it difficult to develop a closer relationship. Still, he was pretty damn sure Katie would marry him if he asked.

"Lloyd!" Patrick Donavan came out of the cabin to greet him as Lloyd halted his horse at a hitching post.

Lloyd nodded as he dismounted. "Hello, Pat."

"Sure 'n' you came at a good time, boy!" Lloyd had to grin at the man's strong Irish brogue. "The wife and Katie just took a couple of pies out of the oven. Come on in. You look tired. You been out riding with your pa again?"

Lloyd towered over the much shorter but very stocky man as he tied his horse. "I have," he answered. He loosened the rawhide string that held his long hair away from his face. "I left Pa back at Winter Point. We had quite a shoot-out with some bank robbers who'd holed up in No Man's Land—Jack Buckley, two of the Bryant boys, and Brad Buckley's uncle, Stu Forbes."

He pulled his hair back better and retied it, thinking how he really should cut it. But constantly being on the trail made it difficult to keep a decent haircut, so he'd just let it grow, and now it was midway down his back.

"We chased them out of there, and they took shelter at a ranch west of here," he continued. "The worst part is, they attacked the rancher's daughter in the worst way. You can imagine the rage that put in Pa's gut. By the time he and I got through with them, they were in bad shape. Jack Buckley is dead. I knew Pa could take them on into Guthrie on his own, so I rested up a bit and decided to take the fork and stop here before I go home."

"Sure 'n' I'm glad you decided to visit," Pat answered. "We'll feed you good and put you up for the night. You can get all the rest you need before going on into town. We're heading into Guthrie tomorrow ourselves. You can ride with us. We'll feel plenty safe with the likes of a Harkner man along."

Lloyd shook his head as he followed Patrick into the house. "I didn't come here to eat your food, Pat."

"Ah, boy, it's not a problem. The wife will be makin' a good supper soon." Pat reached up and patted his shoulder. "When Katie saw it was you comin', she tore off her dirty apron and hurried up to the loft to fix her hair." He gave Lloyd a wink. "Come on in."

Lloyd grasped his arm and gently pulled him aside. "Hold up, Pat."

Pat frowned and folded his arms. "What is it, son?"

Lloyd removed his hat and glanced at the doorway, then back at Pat Donavan. "Actually, sir, I came here specifically for Katie. I should tell you I've decided to ask her to marry me, if you approve."

Pat's face lit up like the spark of a match. He grasped Lloyd's hand and began shaking it vigorously. "Of *course* you have my approval!" he answered. "Sure 'n' my Katie girl has a very fond eye for you, and it's time for the both of you to move on from mournin' those who are gone. You're both too young to be livin' in the past."

A quick pain stabbed at Lloyd at the memory of losing Beth so soon after finding her again after years apart. "Yes, sir. Just don't say anything when we go inside, please. After we eat, I'll ask Katie to step outside with me. I don't want to rush in there and cause a commotion, and we have a lot of talking to do first."

Pat was grinning from ear to ear. "I'll try my best, son. This is such good news. When the wife finds out, she'll be beside herself."

Lloyd just grinned and shook his head as Pat took his

arm and urged him to the door. "Come! Come! The wife will be happy to see you. She and your mother are such good friends, you know."

Lloyd stomped dust from his boots before going inside. He actually felt a little nervous. The last three weeks on the trail were the closest he'd come to allowing himself to think about Katie seriously enough to consider marriage. His father had urged him to commit to taking another wife. He wanted Lloyd to be happy and settled again.

Katie Donavan Lamont was only twenty-one years old, but she'd already lost a husband at nineteen to a hunting accident and buried a newborn baby lost to cholera. She was no wilting flower, but a woman who'd known hardship and loss, just as Lloyd had. It only made her more attractive.

The Donavans were part of the new influx of settlers who'd come to Oklahoma from St. Louis in the land rush a couple of years earlier. That land rush had a big hand in the troubles out here, where new settlers were pushing out Indians of numerous tribes who had themselves been forced to Oklahoma with promises of this being Indian country forever. As usual, the government had broken its promise, and now Oklahoma was filled with angry Indians, eager new settlers, and a host of outlaws who'd come here because there was very little law…until Lloyd and his father had come on the scene.

He followed Pat into the house, where Clara Donavan greeted him warmly. She immediately urged Lloyd to sit and poured him a cup of coffee.

"You must need a good rest," the very robust woman told Lloyd. "We'll put up your horse for you."

"Thank you, Mrs. Donavan. My father took some prisoners in to Guthrie, and I came this way to check on things here. Neighbors say they've had trouble with rustlers."

"Well, we've not had problems so far, but it's good of you to stop."

"Your pa probably figures you'll stay the night," Pat Donavan added as Clara set some sweet cream and some sugar in front of Lloyd. "He won't worry because he knows how well you can take care of yourself."

"He's an able young man, that he is," Clara added, "just like his pa. A man would be a fool to go up against this one, that's sure."

Lloyd felt a little embarrassed at the compliments. He drank some coffee as he caught sight of the skirt of a green checkered dress at the top of the loft ladder. Katie came down the ladder, and just as she reached the bottom of the steps, the door opened and nineteen-year-old Tommy Donavan came inside.

"Lloyd! I thought that was your horse," he said, coming in and shaking Lloyd's hand. "I had my little brother put it up for you."

Lloyd felt a bit shanghaied by the Donavans. "I could have gone back tonight," he objected. "But I have to admit, I'm pretty worn-out." He glanced sidelong at Katie. Her lovely red hair was pulled back neatly at the sides and hung down long and lustrous. Her eyes were as green as a grassy valley in the spring, and right now her cheeks were crimson with what Lloyd knew was embarrassment over her parents' too-obvious solicitude.

"Hello, Lloyd," she said softly. "Thank you for stopping by."

"Just thought I'd follow up on some rumors about rustling," he told her, sticking to the excuse for now. Still…he saw an expectancy in her eyes.

She held his gaze in mutual understanding, putting her hands to her cheeks as though to cool them off. "Mother and I just finished baking some sweet-potato pies. Would you like a piece?"

Lloyd nodded. "Sounds fine." He forced himself to

turn his attention to Pat. "Got any ideas who might be giving your neighbors problems?"

"The same idea you probably have. Indians. The sneaky devils are upset over settlers moving in on what's supposed to be theirs, but how are we supposed to ignore free land, Lloyd? The government says we have a right to be here, so here we are."

Lloyd took note of Katie's slender fingers as she set a piece of pie in front of him. "Thank you," he told her, giving her another smile. "It's a good thing I don't come out here too often. I'd be fat in no time from you and your mother's cooking."

Katie's eyes sparkled with pleasure. "I'm sure your mother is a good cook too. I've heard your father rave about her bread and fried chicken."

Lloyd laughed lightly. "Yeah, that's true. I swear he loves that bread Mom makes as much as he loves the woman herself."

"Ah, and anyone can tell how much your folks love each other," Pat added.

"I tease him about that all the time," Lloyd joked.

Katie turned away to cut more pie, and Lloyd thought she might be embarrassed at their frank talk. "Pa and I have a pretty good connection with most of the Indians in these parts, Pat," Lloyd told him, changing the subject back to rustlers. "Pa thinks it's maybe a few Indians bribed with whiskey and guns who are doing the rustling for white men. It's hard to keep up with everything that goes on in this godforsaken country. We don't get a lot of help out here. The government keeps promising to send soldiers, but so far we haven't seen any. We've been out three weeks just hunting down the riffraff we brought in today. We could call in other marshals, but Pa likes to work alone, and the others have their hands full in their own territories—let alone the constant hunt for the Dalton gang."

"Aye, it's a hard and dangerous job."

Lloyd sobered. "It was Pa who killed Jack. He has a son who lives in town named Brad. He's a no-good himself, and he'll be really angry when he sees my pa bring his own father in draped over a horse. I'm a little worried about him making trouble."

"Well, I expect it's not something your pa can't handle."

Lloyd swallowed a bite of pie. "I know that. It's just that he's my father, and I owe him. He's taught me so much, Pat, and I can't help worrying about him."

"Aye, it's because you love him, boy. It's only natural."

Lloyd finished his pie. "Well, things are fine for now. After a few days' rest, Pa and I will go talk to what's left of the Bryant family."

"Sure 'n' you should stay together. Neither one of you should be goin' over to visit that bunch alone. There's too many, and I don't doubt some of them have no problem shootin' a man in the back."

"Now, now, let's not speak of such things at the table," Clara scolded. "Lloyd, I hope you don't mind sleepin' in the barn. We'll make sure you have nice clean hay and a blanket to put on top of it."

"I've slept under far worse conditions," Lloyd answered. "For the last three weeks, I've been sleeping on the ground most of the time."

"And always havin' to look out for dangerous men and wild Indians to boot," Pat added. "We worry about you and Jake both, Lloyd. My Katie there, she worries too."

"Father!" Katie scolded, looking embarrassed. She turned to set a kettle on the cookstove. "It's just because Mama and Lloyd's mother have become good friends that I worry," she added. She cast her father a chiding look, though she was obviously blushing again—something a woman of her complexion could not hide.

Pat grinned. "Finish that coffee, son," he told Lloyd.

"I've got a couple of horses I'd like to show you. Maybe the government would buy them for you and Jake. Nice big geldings, they are. Men your size need good, sturdy horses, that's sure."

"I'd be glad to take a look at them." Lloyd finished his coffee. "Great pie," he told Clara. He glanced at Katie. "I, uh, I'd like to talk to you alone after I look at those horses, Katie, if you don't mind."

Katie's cheeks flushed again, and Lloyd wondered if she blushed like that when a man was making love to her…a not unpleasant thought at all.

"Of course," she answered. "I have to wash up and change, so take your time with the horses."

Lloyd nodded, then put on his hat and turned to go out. Pat and Tommy followed, and Katie watched the screen door close.

"He's a lonely young man, that one," Clara told her daughter. "I am thinking it's a good sign that he wants to talk to you alone, darlin'."

"Oh, Mother, I don't think he's ready to change his situation just yet. And I wish you and Father wouldn't keep pushing the issue. It's embarrassing."

Clara shrugged. "Some men *need* a little push. And that one…well, girl, could you ask for a more handsome and able man?"

Katie sighed. "I can't argue with that."

"Yeah, well, his father is awful handsome too. Lloyd is a fine mixture of Jake and that lovely Miranda, but mostly his pa, with that tall, strong build of his and those dark eyes."

Katie looked at her mother. "And he leads a very dangerous life. I've already lost one husband, Mother. I'm not sure I want to end up with a man who could be shot in the back the day after he marries me."

"He's an able man, Katie, and isn't sharing a man's bed again, even if it's for just a little while, better than never sharin' that bed at all?"

"Mother, sometimes I can't believe the way you talk!"

"Just don't be forgettin' there isn't one thing about that young man that wouldn't make a good husband. Sure 'n' I wish he would cut that hair, though."

Katie watched Lloyd head for the barn with her father and Tommy. "I like it long," she said softly.

Four

JEFF TRUBRIDGE WAITED JUST OUTSIDE THE JAIL DOOR while Dr. Brian Stewart tended to the prisoners' wounds. Jeff heard one of them yell that he didn't want to be touched by "that sonofabitch lawman's son-in-law."

"Suit yourself," Stewart answered. "I guess that means you don't even want anything for the pain?"

"Hell, yes. Give me some laudanum or somethin'."

"I won't give you anything until I check your wounds," the doctor answered.

"It's your damn father-in-law who should be layin' out there in the street wounded or dead," another grumbled.

"Shut up and let the man clean up your wound," Sheriff Sparks yelled.

Jeff cautiously stepped inside, nodding to the sheriff.

The rather hefty man sat behind a desk, his boots up on the desk itself. "You still skulking around town, kid?"

Jeff sat down across the desk from Sparky. "I've only been here two days...staying at the Guthrie Inn. The *Chicago Evening Journal* gave me the job of coming out here to report on how things are going in Oklahoma after the land rush and all, especially since Oklahoma is thinking about statehood."

"Yeah, well, there are some Indians bandin' together, tryin' to make it their own country, separate from the United States. Did you know that?"

"Yes, sir."

"There are a lot of hard feelings going around—Indians that fight each other and fight the settlers, lawless men like that bunch in there thinking they can do whatever they want because there *is* no law out here except locally, like here in Guthrie. Whatever men like Harkner and his son can do out there in No Man's Land helps keep the peace, but that's a tall order. And I know your real motive, Trubridge. You want to interview Harkner himself."

"Harkner ain't no lawman!" one of the prisoners shouted. "He's no better than the rest of us except he's bein' paid for bein' a vigilante outlaw. That's what he is. A vigilante outlaw wearin' a badge. Report *that*, kid!"

Trubridge made some notes. "May I sit here until the doctor leaves?" he asked Sheriff Sparks. "I'd like to talk to him because I'm thinking about more than an interview. I'd like to write a book about the marshal."

The sheriff looked him over. "A book about Jake?" He laughed. "Kid, that's wishful thinking. Others have tried. A few wished they hadn't. And as far as sitting there goes, it's fine with me, as long as you're not armed."

"I assure you, I've never touched a gun in my life. What's your opinion of Jake, Sheriff?"

The hefty man grunted as he took his feet down from the desk. "He's a mean sonofabitch, and *mean* is probably an understatement. But he can be a damn good friend, once he's figured out you're worth it. He's the kind of man you want to have your back if you're in trouble, but also the kind of man you don't want to cross—something Brad Buckley found out earlier today. And my advice to you is to tread lightly. Jake doesn't like people poking into personal affairs or bothering his family."

"I'll keep that in mind."

Sheriff Sparks grunted again as he stood up. "Good luck to you, kid." He lit some oil lamps as the sun began to set behind the western landscape. Jeff wondered how soon Guthrie would get electricity. The town was amazingly developed already, for being so young, but having grown up in Chicago, Jeff felt like he'd walked back twenty years coming out here.

"You all right in there, Doc?" the sheriff asked Brian.

"I'm almost done."

"I'll tell you about Harkner," one of the prisoners yelled to Jeff. "He's a murderin' sonofabitch! Killed his own pa, they say!"

"Shut up, Marty!" Brian told him. Jeff watched the doctor jerk extra hard on a bandage he was tying around the outlaw's arm. The man cried out, and Brian finished tying the bandage. He dug a brown bottle out of his doctor's bag and handed it to the man called Marty. "Take a swallow of that—one swallow!"

"What about poor Brad over there?" another asked. "The kid is in a bad way."

"I already checked him over. I think his breastbone is cracked. The only reason he's not yelling from pain is because it hurts too much even to breathe."

"You tell that father-in-law of yours that we're gettin' out of this jail, and when we do, he's gonna have to start watchin' his back twenty-four hours a day, seven days a week," Marty told the doctor. "He done put my eye out a few months ago, and if that ain't bad enough, now he's killed my best friend."

"He deserved it," Brian answered as he put supplies back in his bag.

"Harkner ain't got the right to be judge and jury! He'll pay! He won't be safe *no* place now! Same goes for his kin! Even if we don't get the chance to get him for this, Brad will! He ain't gonna forget what Jake did to him, or that Jake killed his pa!"

Brian took the brown bottle from him and corked it. "Jake should have shot you dead, Marty. Be glad you're breathing. You should thank him."

"*Thank* him? He wounds men and then brings them back here for his son-in-law to patch up so's the government can turn around and send them to prison or to *hang*! Pretty good setup, ain't it? Even *you* make money off it. I'll find a way to get you too. You've got a good-lookin' wife, Doc, and her bein' Jake's daughter makes the thought I'm havin' even sweeter."

Brian put the bottle of laudanum back into his bag. "You touch my wife and Jake will have you begging for death when he's done with you, and you damn well know it. And I have ways of making wounds hurt even *more*! You remember that, you worthless sonofabitch."

"Whoo, you touched a nerve, Marty!" the one called Stu joked. "Doc Stewart don't often cuss."

"Why don't you give some of that painkiller stuff to poor Brad over there?" Marty grumbled to Brian.

"He can't even sit up to drink it. If he starts choking, it will lead to coughing, which will in turn bring him unbearable pain," Brian explained. "He could even vomit and gag to death, so he's got to just lie there and not move for a few days." He rose and asked Sheriff Sparks to let him out of Marty's cell.

Sparks rose and took a ring of keys from where they hung on the brick wall of the jail, then came over and unlocked the cell door, immediately pulling his six-gun and holding it on the prisoners until the doctor exited and Sparks again locked the door.

"Hey, you want to know somethin' else about Harkner?" Marty shouted to Trubridge. "He cheats on his wife! He's supposed to be a great family man. Bullshit! On our way back, he stopped off at a brothel—got a bath and a shave, and you can bet he got somethin' else, 'cuz he slept there the whole night! I wonder what that perfect wife of his thinks about that!" He laughed. "How about you, Doc? Your father-in-law cheats on your mother-in-law when he's out there supposedly doin' good work for the government. And he's gettin' *paid* for it!"

Brian Stewart glanced at Jeff Trubridge, ignoring the remark. "I told you not to bother Jake any more today," he told Jeff.

Jeff followed Brian out the door. "I understand. Maybe *you* would talk to me?"

Scowling, Brian faced him. "Anything you want to know, it's Jake's place to tell you, not mine."

Jeff studied the well-built, good-looking young man who stood about five feet ten inches but had electric-blue eyes. "You're married to Jake's daughter, right?"

"I am. And Jake Harkner is one of the finest men I've known, so don't be thinking I'm going to tell you horror stories about the man." He turned away again. "Not that he doesn't have any horror stories to tell you himself."

Jeff kept pursuing him as he walked. "Did he really kill his own father?"

"That's a very touchy subject for him. I'd be very careful asking him about it. You'd better get his wife's permission to ask any questions at all first, and even then, you'd better get to know them pretty well before you even touch that subject."

"What about what that man in there said—about Jake stopping off at a brothel on his way home? I thought he was supposedly a devoted husband."

Brian stopped again, running a hand through his hair. "He probably stopped for a bath and a shave so he wouldn't come home a filthy mess. His son probably did the same thing. That doesn't mean they did anything more than that."

"But…"

"Look, Trubridge, you are asking the wrong questions of the wrong man. All I can say is you have to really know my father-in-law to understand how he could spend time at a brothel without cheating on his wife. People just like to make more of it than it is."

"Would he tell his wife?"

Brian grinned. "Of *course* he would. One thing the man isn't is a liar and a cheat. And Randy wouldn't miss the fact that he was clean-shaven when he got here. He usually comes back with a couple-week-old beard. She knows Jake Harkner better than he knows himself, and there's no pulling the wool over her eyes when it comes to that man. Now leave me alone and don't be hounding my wife, either. Evie is staunchly devoted to her father and won't answer one single question from you unless she knows her father and mother have approved."

"But...how did you and Evie Harkner meet?"

"In Laramie, Wyoming, where she and her mother lived while Jake was in prison there. Randy Harkner helped me with my practice. I actually tended to Jake once, when his jailers beat the hell out of him. He'd landed in the prison hospital with cracked ribs and pneumonia. If it weren't for my wife and her mother's relentless hounding of the prison warden to be allowed to see him and let me treat him, Jake would have died." Brian turned and kept walking again. "I swear, Randy Harkner would have shot the warden herself just to land in prison so she could be with her husband."

"Those are the kind of things I need to know!" Jeff told him excitedly, keeping up the pace. "I want to write a book about him, Dr. Stewart."

"I heard you tell Sparky."

"But I want it to be the *truth*. I mean the *real* truth. Wouldn't you and your wife and Jake's wife and his son all want that? I don't write sensationalism, Dr. Stewart. I want the West's famous settlers and lawmen and outlaws documented correctly. A hundred years from now, people should know how it all really happened."

Brian sighed and faced him again. By then they stood in front of a whitewashed frame house. It wasn't completely dark yet, and Jeff could see rosebushes lining the front of the porch, just like at Randy Harkner's house, which was only two doors down.

"Mr. Trubridge, I'd like to believe you," Brian told him.

"You can! I've even brought samples of my writing to prove my credentials to Jake."

"And he'll tell you it's Miranda you'll need to deal with, not him. If he lets you write a book, it will be because Randy says it's okay. Out there on the trail, he's in full command. But when it comes to things like this, it's like I told you—my mother-in-law *owns* that man. And if you do anything to offend her, you'll have Jake to answer to. Now it's been a really awful day, and my wife is holding supper for me. You wait and talk to Jake's wife, though even if she approves, I can't guarantee Jake will open up even one iota if he doesn't want to. If you can figure out how to get through to that man, more power to you." He started to walk away again, then turned a final time. "And by the way, if you intend to hound Jake like this, you'd better make sure there is always a privy nearby." He laughed lightly and headed for the front door.

Jeff stood watching. The doctor went inside, and he could hear a child's voice yell "Daddy!" as another slightly older child called out, "Uncle Brian! Is my dad back?"

"He'll be here tomorrow, Stevie. He stopped at the Donavans'."

The lovely silhouette of a young woman graced the doorway, and then the door closed.

Jeff sighed with frustration. He walked up the street to what he'd been told was Jake Harkner's house. Across the street was a small stucco home he'd learned belonged to Lloyd. The whole family lived a stone's throw from each other.

Jake's frame house was lovely, painted yellow with white trim. There was a white picket fence around a lawn, and rosebushes that probably took a lot of work to keep green in this unholy, dry, still barely settled country.

Notorious outlaw lives in a house that totally belies the kind of man who dwells within. He had no doubt all the neatness and frills were due to Miranda Harkner. Jake certainly didn't seem the type who would care about such things. Right now, the house was dark and quiet. Jeff couldn't help wondering what went on behind closed doors with a man like Jake Harkner, but from what he'd seen in the street, the man was very attentive to his wife. He hurried back to his hotel room to scribble more notes where there was more light.

Visited a brothel on his way home. He is a man of confusing contrasts but one who appears to be very much loved by his family...and his wife. I am trying to determine why.

Five

LLOYD WASN'T QUITE SURE WHY HE FELT NERVOUS. He'd been seeing Katie off and on for most of the winter and into spring. If nothing else, they'd become good friends. Still, this was different. This was total commitment. What he wanted to do meant truly moving on from memories of Beth, and those memories were still painful. He watched Katie approach the wooden bench where he sat waiting a few yards beyond the horse barn. He'd told Pat where he'd be and asked him to have Katie come out to talk.

God, she was pretty. Fact was, Katie Donavan Lamont had pretty much every quality any man could want in a wife. She'd changed into a pink dress, and the color made her red hair look even more beautiful. She reminded him of flowers, all pink and green and red and white and colorful. The dress fit her slender waist in a way that told him the body underneath would feel good next to a man at night, and he'd ached for that kind of companionship for a long time now. He'd been with a couple of the whores at Dixie's place a time or two, but that was different. That was just physical relief. He longed for the kind of love his parents shared...longed for the total satisfaction of taking a woman because he ached for the woman herself, not just the thrill of sexual pleasure. A man and wife ought to share hopes and dreams and souls.

Katie stopped a few feet away. "Father told me you were waiting here to talk."

Lloyd rose and reached out his hand. "Come sit down by me." He squeezed her hand gently as she sat beside him on the bench. "You look really pretty in pink."

Katie smiled and looked away. "Thank you."

Lloyd hesitated, keeping hold of her hand. "I guess you probably know what I want to talk about."

Katie put her other hand over his. "Maybe. But I don't want to make a fool of myself, so you'd better tell me yourself."

Lloyd couldn't help a smile. "Well, I thought a lot on this trip…about how a man is better off with a good woman by his side." He squeezed her hand. "I see a lot of strength and understanding in you, Katie, and we've already grown close, close enough that I…I'd like you to be my wife. I know our whole situation is a little different, both of us being widowed…the danger of what I do. But this job won't last forever, Katie. And I have other skills. I'll always provide for you every way I can. I have quite a bit of money in the bank that I inherited from my wife's estate. Her father was a pretty rich man, but…" He let go of hand. "Damn it," he said in a near whisper. "Katie, that's not why I loved her. I don't want you to think—"

"It's okay," she interrupted. "I know what you're saying."

Lloyd noticed her hands were clenched tightly in her lap. "I'll understand if you say no," he told her. "God knows I'm like my father in a lot of ways, which means I won't be the easiest person to live with. But Pa is a real good husband, Katie, and a great father. And the grandkids are crazy about him. I can be that way too."

She grasped his hand. "Lloyd, you don't need to sell yourself to me." She faced him, tears in her eyes. "I do have concerns, but you've been nothing but sweet and attentive to me, and I never saw a more handsome man in my whole life, and I know what a good father you are to Stephen, and a loving brother to Evie...and you're so devoted to your folks. I see the love in you, Lloyd, and I know..." She looked away again. "I know what losing Beth did to you. I just worry I could never truly replace her."

He turned sideways, grasping her arms and making her look at him. "Katie, I'm not asking for a replacement, or promising mad, crazy love, at least at first. We're an awful lot alike, you know. We've both lost so much. I can't take the place of your first husband, just like you can't take Beth's place, because we're each different people than they were, so we just have to learn to love each other for just that...who we are...right here and now. Trying to replace someone else can't work. And we can't move on together if we try to do that."

Katie nodded, turning her gaze downward. "I miss my little baby girl so much that sometimes I cry into my pillow till there aren't any more tears. I want another baby, Lloyd. I need to *hold* another baby. And Lord knows I can't have that till I marry again. I hope you want more children."

"Hell, we can have all the babies you want. I'd like my Stephen to have sisters and brothers...and he needs a mother. But he's no baby, Katie. You'd be walking into mothering a half-grown kid. Do you think you can love him like a mother should?"

She faced him again. "Of course I can. Stevie and I are already good friends. You've brought him out here, and he's come along with us other times. We've picnicked together and fished together and...well, he's such a good boy...easy to love. If I care about his father enough to marry him, I'll care about him too. I already do."

Lloyd turned away, resting his elbows on his knees. "I have to be honest. I think my being a deputy U.S. Marshal will be harder for you than anything else. It's asking a lot of a woman to put up with what I do. My mother has to, because she and Pa were already married when he became a marshal. Neither one of them wanted it, but it was the only way Pa could finish out his prison sentence. It's dangerous as hell, Katie. And the fact remains, I don't *have* to do this, but I promised myself I'd not let my pa handle this alone. I expect he probably could manage, but I vowed a long time ago to always have his back like he's had mine. But this kind of life is not something easy for a woman to put up with. You need to consider that."

Katie toyed with an embroidered flower on the skirt of her dress. "Lloyd, I've already thought about that a lot, and I'm willing to try. I was talking with my mother earlier about…about how I've already lost one husband, so I wasn't sure I could be with a man who could take a bullet in the back the day after we marry. But when I was changing my clothes just now, I thought how you must be so lonely, and how hard it must be to come home to an empty house, and how we shouldn't turn down a chance at happiness because of what *might* happen. I'd be proud to call you my husband, Lloyd."

He stared at a butterfly that had landed on a nearby weed, thinking how delicate and colorful it was…like Katie. "There will be times when I'm gone and you won't know if I'm alive or dead, Katie. My mother said once it's the waiting that drives her crazy. She lives to hear my pa give that whistle that he's coming back."

Katie rose and walked a few feet away, folding her arms. "Lloyd, the only thing that bothers me is…well… it's kind of like you're serving Jake's sentence with him."

A gentle breeze blew her hair away from her face as Lloyd met her gaze. "When my father went to prison, I abandoned him and my mother and sister…rode off and turned to the outlaw way myself out of spite. I never knew about Jake's past, and it hurt so bad to find out the way I did, because up to then, I worshipped the ground he walked on. By the time he got out of prison four years later, I'd got myself into a big mess with a bunch of outlaws who meant to kill me, but Pa, he came after me. He got into a big shoot-out to save me. After all my hatred and rebellion, my father never stopped loving me, Katie. I'll never forgive myself for judging him like I did, or for abandoning him and my mother and sister for so long. Pa's no angel, that's for sure, and he did do a lot of bad things when he was young, but things happened that led him to all that. He's a real good man down deep inside. He'd argue that one till he's blue in the face, but that man knows how to love better than most men do. Just don't ever tell him that."

The remark brought a smile to Katie's lips. "He kind of scares me sometimes."

Lloyd returned the grin. "Heck, haven't you noticed how my mother can put him in his place? He practically worships her. You don't have to be scared of Jake Harkner, Katie, especially not if you become family. Family is the most important thing on this earth to him. He thinks Evie has wings and my mother is the Madonna herself." He rose, walking closer to her. "The fact remains, Katie, that I will never again abandon my father. He and I have had our bad times, but that man would die for me, and me for him. You have to understand that I won't quit this job until he's free of it himself."

Their gazes held.

"Tell me what you're thinking, Katie," Lloyd said. "Be honest. There's more you want to ask."

"Your father has a temper, and you're just like him, Lloyd Harkner. I'm not blind to the fact that you can both be pretty ruthless. That means making a lot of enemies…let alone the fact that there are surely men out there who'd like to say they killed a Harkner."

"Pa has lived with that his whole life, and he's still here, isn't he? You have to trust that we're pretty good at taking care of ourselves. That's what I meant earlier when I asked if you can live with that part of me, because it will be the hardest part." He put his hands on her shoulders. "I've given this a lot of thought, Katie. And in you, I see strength and beauty and everything it takes to be a good wife and mother. I'm only twenty-five and you're four years younger, and look what all we've both already been through. We each need somebody strong at our side. And we're too young to be putting up with life alone." He leaned close and kissed her forehead. "And Stephen thinks you're great. He even told me once I should marry you." He brushed her cheek with his lips, and she turned her face upward, inviting his mouth to search her own in a gentle kiss. "Marry me, Katie," he said softly before kissing her again. "Marry me." Another kiss. He left her mouth, lifting her and pressing her tightly against him, her feet off the ground. "Marry me." Another kiss...delicious, heated, hungry. He enjoyed the feel of her firm breasts against his chest. He wanted to touch them, taste them.

"Yes. I'll marry you," she told him between hungry kisses. "But give me some time to get used to all this before we're...more physical?" More kisses. "Be patient with me, Lloyd. Our love has to grow."

"I know that." He set her on her feet and reached into his pocket. "Here. I got this in Cimmaron City. I didn't want to buy it here in Guthrie because of gossip. I figured somebody might tell you I'd bought a wedding ring. Do you like it?"

Katie looked down at a gold wedding band in his palm. She smiled. "It's lovely!"

"Try it on. You do it. I shouldn't put it on your finger till we actually marry. Just make sure it fits. I had a girl at the place where I bought it try it on her finger because her hands were pretty and slender like yours."

Katie turned around. "Don't look." A moment later,

she turned back around. "It fits just fine." She handed back the ring, and Lloyd put it back in his pocket.

"Wear the dress you're wearing now. I like you in pink. You look perfect just the way you are." He ran his hands into her thick auburn tresses. "And I like your hair down like this. I want you to look just like this when we wed."

Katie smiled lovingly. "All right. But you have to promise not to cut your hair. I like it long."

Their gazes held again in excitement, anticipation, hope.

"Then I won't cut it." He kissed her again. "I'll be good to you, Katie. I'll support you and love you the best I can. I know this seems kind of like a marriage of convenience right now, but I wouldn't take you for my own if I didn't think we'll grow deeper in love every day." The pain of losing Beth stabbed at him again, but he truly did want to love again, wanted a woman in his bed and his heart. He fought feelings of guilt for knowing he didn't love this lovely woman the same as he'd loved Beth, but maybe that was natural. The fact remained that he couldn't stand the thought of any other man having her. A girl as pretty and kind as Katie Donavan Lamont wouldn't last long without other men trying to woo her and take her for a wife. He'd go crazy knowing some other man had her in his bed while he was still struggling to move on with his life.

He'd make this legal and make her his own, the sooner the better. The rest would surely come in time.

"Marry me tomorrow, Katie. We'll go into town. We can get there before church lets out. We'll corner the preacher and have him marry us."

"*Tomorrow?*"

"Sure! I'm not taking the chance that you'll change your mind. Tell me you'll marry me tomorrow."

She wrapped her arms around his neck, and they

kissed again. "I will," she answered when he finally left her lips. "I'll marry you tomorrow."

Lloyd kissed her again, devouring her mouth eagerly. She was sweet and willing. Their love would surely grow.

Six

THE MORNING CAME ALIVE CLEAR AND BRIGHT, AND warmer than normal for May in Oklahoma. Birds sang, and Jeff Trubridge watched what seemed like half the town heading for church, some coming into town from outlying ranches and settlements. They came by horseback, in buggies and farm wagons, and some just walked from homes closer in. He saw Brian and Evie Stewart leading two little boys by the hand. He knew the younger boy, maybe three, was the doctor's son. The older boy, perhaps five or six, had to be Lloyd Harkner's kid.

Then he saw them—Jake and Randy. Jake wore his guns. Surely he didn't intend to wear them into church! Probably not, because he also was not wearing a suit. He wore denim pants and a dark blue bib shirt with no vest and, from what Jeff could see, not even his badge. His hair looked shorter, cut to just above his shoulders. When the younger grandson with Evie and Brian turned and spotted his grandparents, he smiled and ran back to Jake.

"Gampa!" The kid reached up and Jake lifted him onto his shoulders.

"You're getting almost too big for this, Little Jake," he told the boy. "Grandpa is getting too many aches and pains to lift such a big boy."

After what Grandpa did yesterday? Jeff found that hard to believe, but surely the man did have aches and pains. One of the questions he wanted to ask was how many times Harkner had been shot.

The older boy also noticed his grandparents and ran back to Jake, hugging him around the hips in spite of the guns he wore.

"Careful! Careful!" Jake told him, gently pulling him away and tousling his hair. He lifted the smaller boy from his shoulders and knelt in front of the older boy. "How's my youngest deputy?"

The boy hugged Jake around the neck. "Where's my dad, Grampa?" he asked.

Jake hugged him in return, patting his back. "He'll be along sometime today, I expect."

"Is he hurt?"

"No, your daddy is just fine. I promise."

Randy scolded Jake for messing up the boy's hair. "Honestly, Jake, Stevie's hair is unruly enough. Evie probably spent ten minutes just getting it to stay in one place." She stopped and smoothed the boy's thick, dark hair as best she could.

"A kid his age shouldn't worry about his hair," Jake answered. He rose and deliberately messed it up with a wicked grin. The boy giggled and ducked away from his grandmother when she tried to fix his hair again.

"Jake Harkner, just for that, you won't get any of my bread for dinner later."

Jake grinned. "You've threatened to withhold more than that a time or two."

His wife pushed at him. "Please. People can hear you, and we're on our way to church, for heaven's sake."

"*You're* on your way to church. I'm not."

Randy gave him a disappointed look, and Jake seemed to regret the remark. He reached out and put an arm around her. "Okay, I won't mess his hair up again."

Randy moved an arm around her husband's back and they stayed that way until they reached the church.

Jeff took notes. *Incredibly stark contrast to yesterday. The man brings in four killers and rapists, then beats on a young man half his age and throws him into the street, and today he's playing with his grandsons and walking to church. He looks so relaxed today.*

He looked up then, watched Miranda say something to Jake when they reached the church steps. She told both boys to go inside with Evie and Brian, but first Evie walked up to her father.

"Daddy, please come inside."

Daddy? Jeff had trouble picturing Jake Harkner being called Daddy.

"Baby girl, it's just not going to happen. Church is for angels like you and your mother."

"But *you're* an angel too—maybe an *avenging* angel, but you have every right to go inside."

Jake leaned down and kissed her cheek. "You know how I feel. Go on now. They are already starting a hymn."

Evie glanced at her mother, who put an arm around her and cast Jake a pleading look before going inside. Latecomers greeted Jake on their way in, and one older, heavyset man jovially invited him to join them.

"I'll wait out here like I always do," Jake told the man.

The older man kept hold of his hand a moment longer.

"Jake, you know you're always welcome."

Jake nodded. "Maybe so—maybe not."

The older man patted his arm in what Jeff thought was an amazingly kind gesture that Jake actually didn't seem to mind. The man turned and went inside the church. Jake waited until the front door closed, then went to the steps and sat down. Moments later, everyone inside began singing the hymn "Rock of Ages."

Jeff waited a moment, studying Jake, thinking how lonely he suddenly looked sitting there on the church steps.

Let me hide myself in thee…

Did he think he wasn't good enough to go inside?

Let the water and the blood, from thy wounded side which flowed…

Jeff took a deep breath for courage and approached him. He couldn't resist this chance to talk to the man, even though he'd been warned to talk to his wife first. After all, Harkner seemed in a better mood today, and he was rested up from his encounter with the outlaws he'd brought in. Jake caught sight of him right away and watched him closely as Jeff pointed to the steps. "May I?"

Jake removed his hat and ran a hand through his hair, then put his hat back on. "I don't own the steps, Trubridge. Go ahead and sit."

Jeff sat down, leaning against the wooden railing. "You're not going inside?"

Jake took a cigarette from a shirt pocket. "No." He lit the cigarette.

"May I ask why? Your whole family is in there."

Jake rested his elbows on his knees. "I'm beyond salvation, Trubridge, and my final destination sure as hell isn't heaven. I don't think the good Lord needs someone like me defiling his place of worship."

"Your wife doesn't believe that, does she?"

Jake smoked quietly for a moment.

"I was wondering when you'd show up again. Brian told me you were snooping around the jail last night and asking him a lot of questions. I told you to wait and talk to my wife first."

So, you intend to change the subject. "Oh, I will do just that. The reason I went to the jail was to see what those men had to say about what happened. Your son-in-law just happened to be there."

Jake took a drag on the cigarette and took it from his mouth as he exhaled. "And I'm sure the men I brought back had some glowing things to say about me."

Jeff grinned. "Oh, they are very fond of you."

Jake actually laughed lightly. Jeff was struck by how different he looked when he smiled. A damn handsome grin it was, and it seemed to change the whole nature of the man. "Yes," he answered. "They said you're the most wonderful man they've ever known, and they're glad you made them see the wrong in what they did."

Jake laughed again. "Trubridge, I don't want to like you, but I kind of do." He looked Jeff over. "I'm a pretty good judge of men, and something about you says I can trust you."

Jeff nodded eagerly. "Oh, you can!" He removed his wire-rimmed glasses and cleaned them with a handkerchief. "I'm sincere in wanting to do this right, Jake. I put in my notes last night what an enigma you are."

"Enigma?" Jake shook his head. "Well, number one—I never had any schooling, so I wouldn't know what that word meant if it weren't for my wife. She schooled our kids most of their lives because we usually lived where there *weren't* any schools. I guess while she was teaching them, I was learning more myself. And number two—I guess you're right. I can't figure my own self out, let alone somebody else understanding me, so *enigma* is a pretty fitting word."

Another hymn. "Amazing Grace."

…that saved a wretch like me…

Jake quieted for a moment and seemed to be listening to the words. Jeff waited.

"I guess my wife understands me better than anyone." He smoked quietly for a moment, then cleared his throat. "So, what did those men really say about me? As if I can't guess."

Jeff adjusted his spectacles. "They pretty much called you every name in the book. Some were so bad, I can't even bring myself to repeat them."

Jake grinned again. "Well, sticks and stones may break my bones…"

"Yeah, I guess you've heard it all."

"And a lot of those names apply, which is why I'm not in that church."

"Aren't you a little worried about revenge?" he asked. "Those men said if they ever get loose, they'll come after you…and I'm afraid they also threatened your family, your daughter in particular. That really roused your son-in-law."

Jake cast him a dark look. "That true?"

"Yes, sir. The one called Marty made the threat."

The look in Jake's eyes made Jeff wish he hadn't said anything about it.

Jake looked away again and smoked silently. Jeff waited until the man spoke again on his own.

"Jeff, my daughter is an absolute contrast to me. She's as close to an angel as anyone. Marty Bryant is welcome to come after me anytime. If he does, he has half a chance of living through it, because I'm supposed to behave like a lawman." He stared at his cigarette as he rolled it between his fingers. "But if he goes after one member of my family, especially my daughter"—he watched a wagon go by—"the badge comes off," he finished. "I've done some rotten things in my life, but none of it would compare to what I'd do to that man if he ever touches Randy or Evie. Hurting a woman is unforgivable in my book."

Jeff swallowed. *Because of your mother?*

"I've been a target most of my life, Trubridge," Jake added. He seemed to be weighing his words then. "I'll tell you something about revenge. I've enacted revenge of my own, and I've been the brunt of it. Either way usually ends bad, and revenge doesn't take away the hurt, or the ugly memories. Sometimes it creates even more ugly memories. But a man can't help going after it anyway."

Jeff wanted to ask specifics but decided it was way too soon to press the man for more details.

"Tell me what keeps you and your wife together," he dared to ask instead, hoping to lighten the mood. "Twenty years or more, I'm told."

"Twenty-six."

"From what I've observed, the two of you couldn't be more...well...different."

Jake finally grinned again. "Different is an understatement," he told Jeff. He thought a moment and Jeff waited, deciding he'd get farther by keeping his mouth shut than by opening it at the wrong time. One wrong question and the man would probably throw him off the church steps.

"I actually tried once or twice to get rid of her—for her own good, not because I didn't love her. I expect maybe I love her *too* much. The damn woman won't leave me. She's stuck by me through things that would make most women scream and run away, but not Randy. She's everything a man hopes to find in a wife, and why in hell she picked me, I'll never understand...never."

Jeff scribbled some notes. "Maybe she saw the good in you."

Jake didn't answer right away. He took one last draw on his cigarette, then stepped it out while inside the preacher carried on about sin and salvation. "Some people see things through a rosy glow, I guess," Jake finally answered.

"And some see very clearly, Marshal." *I see you, Jake Harkner. There's a part of you that wants to go into that church.* Jake glanced sidelong at him, and Jeff knew it was a warning. He decided to move on to something else.

"Tell me something, Marshal. How in heck do you know when to draw on somebody...or I guess I should ask when you know he's going to draw on you. Do you watch his gun hand?"

Jake shook his head. "Never." He looked straight at Jeff then with an unnerving glare. "You watch his eyes. Only his eyes, Mr. Trubridge. His eyes will give him away every time. And I've never drawn first on a man in my life. I don't need to."

"How do you think you've managed to stay alive this long?"

Jake watched another wagon rattle closer into town. "Haven't you ever heard the term *too mean to die*?"

"Well, they say the Earp brothers were too mean to die, and they were federal marshals too. Did you know them?"

"That was in '81, and I was still a wanted man living under an assumed name in Colorado. No, I didn't know them. A lot of lawless men are a product of the Civil War and its tragedies. My reasons were far different. I did meet Jesse James and Cole Younger a time or two on the Outlaw Trail in Wyoming, back during a bad time when I had to leave Randy for a couple of years." He lit yet another cigarette. "That's a period in our marriage I don't like to talk about. That woman has been through a lot of bad times because of me." He sighed. "At any rate, Lloyd and I and several other U.S. Marshals have taken part in tracking some of the Dalton gang here in Oklahoma Territory, but they've been pretty elusive."

"No other famous outlaws ever challenged you?"

Jake shook his head. "There's a kind of code among us, I guess. No love lost, but most men like that don't go around drawing on each other. It's the filthy worms who don't really know what they're doing, like the Bryants and Buckleys, who are stupid enough to go challenging someone with a reputation. They want to make their own name famous, and they usually die trying."

The wagon Jake had been keeping an eye on pulled up under a huge shade tree just a few yards from the church, and a young man on a big roan gelding rode beside it. Jake immediately dropped the conversation and rose to hurry toward them. Jeff stayed back and watched as the younger man dismounted and walked up to Jake. The two men embraced.

The son, Jeff thought. Other than the harder lines on Jake's face and the fact that the younger one was a bit meatier from younger muscle, they could have been twins.

"Good to see you back, Son," Jake told him. "I was a little worried about the Bryants, seeing as how two of their relatives are sitting in jail."

"I didn't see hide nor hair of any of them on the way in."

"Jake, sure 'n' it's good to see you!" the hefty man driving the wagon shouted.

Jake walked up and shook the man's hand. "You too, Pat. You're a little late for church."

"Ah, it's pretty hard to make it on time, comin' all the way from my farm." Pat turned and helped his even heftier wife down from the wagon. "We're not really here for church this time anyway, Jake. We have some good news, but I'll let Lloyd tell you. I left my two sons at home to keep a watch. They both said to wish you well."

"And I thank them for that."

Jeff watched as Lloyd walked up to the wagon and lifted a very pretty, redheaded young woman down from the back of it. He leaned down and kissed her cheek, then told her to stay put for a minute. He took his father's arm and walked closer to the church. "We need to talk," he told Jake.

Jake put his hands on his hips. "Something wrong? I thought you said you didn't run into any trouble."

Lloyd grinned. "No—nothing like that." The younger man glanced at the church. "Mom and Evie inside?"

"As always."

"Well, as soon as the service is over, maybe we can have the preacher hang around."

Jake grinned. "Hang around?"

"Yeah." Lloyd glanced over at the redheaded young woman, then back at his father. "Katie and I have decided to get married, and the sooner the better. Soon as services are over, we want the preacher to stay and marry us."

Jake's grin widened. "It's about time." An eager handshake turned into another embrace. "I'm damn glad for you, Lloyd. You be good to that girl," Jake told his son. "She's sweet through and through."

"You don't have to tell me that." Lloyd sobered.

Jeff looked away but kept his ears open.

"It's not like Beth, Pa."

"Of course it isn't. But you're both far too young to go the rest of your lives without love and family, and that girl is crazy about you. Anybody can see that."

"Yeah, well, there's also the job. She says she can handle it, but I'm not so sure."

Jake glanced over at Katie to see her mother placing some flowers in her hair. "She's strong, Lloyd. It will be hard at first, but she'll manage." He looked back at Lloyd. "Besides, this job won't last forever. And I've told you more than once that you don't need to do this. I'm the one who has no choice. Maybe now is the time for you to—"

"No! You know how I feel about that. Do you really think I could let you ride off into backcountry alone, where most of the men you're after would love to put a hole in your back? It's not going to happen, and Katie knows that, so stop trying to make me quit."

Jeff glanced sidelong at the two of them. Jake walked a few feet away for a moment, clearing his throat and lighting another cigarette. "Then I guess I'll have to do my best to make sure Katie doesn't end up a widow for a second time," he told Lloyd.

Lloyd put his hands on his hips, and Jeff picked up on the distinct feeling that both men were trying to treat lightly much deeper feelings. "I guess you will," Lloyd answered.

Jake came closer and shook his son's hand firmly again. "I hope you'll be as happy as your mother and I are. Living with a Harkner is hard on a woman, Lloyd, so you have to be *extra* good to her when you're at home."

"I know. I will be."

Jake left him to go and greet his soon-to-be daughter-in-law. Lloyd just then caught Jeff watching and listening. "Who the hell are you?" he asked. Apparently the younger Harkner could be just as intimidating as his father.

"Oh—Jeff Trubridge, Mr. Harkner." He rose and came down the steps, putting out his hand. "I've been making friends with your father—came out here from Chicago to do a story on him."

Lloyd's eyes narrowed. He didn't shake his hand. "A story? What kind of story? My pa doesn't like people snooping around his personal life, and he sure as hell doesn't 'make friends' with just anybody. I highly doubt you can call him friend yet."

"Oh, I'm—I'm well aware of that. I'm just waiting for the chance to talk to your mother—all of you, in fact—so I can make it clear what I want to do. I'm told your mother is the decision maker in the family."

Lloyd just scowled at him. "My mother is the decision maker on a *lot* of things. Does she know about this?"

"I…I'm not sure."

Jake came walking back then with his arm around the lovely young redhead who'd come in on the wagon. Jeff realized she must be Lloyd's wife-to-be. She looked at bit taken aback by Jake's embrace and was blushing profusely.

"Lloyd, thanks for bringing another beautiful woman into the family," Jake joked. He looked down at Katie. "You will soon be my son's wife, Katie, so you will be loved like a daughter. And Randy is going to be thrilled about this. Church will let out soon. I can't wait to tell her." He leaned down and kissed her cheek, then shook Pat Donavan's hand when the man joined them.

Lloyd reached out and put an arm around Katie, then nodded toward Jeff. "Is that kid okay?" he asked Jake. "He said he's writing a book about you. You've never allowed that before."

"I haven't decided for sure yet. It's all up to your mother. And I have a few questions for this kid before I answer any more of his, but yes, I think he's okay." He turned his attention back to Lloyd and Katie. "Good Lord, you two make one hell of a handsome couple," he commented. He pushed back his hat. "Let me tell Randy about this myself as soon as church lets out. Let's walk over to that shade tree by the wagon while we wait."

Jeff waited impatiently, wishing he could hear everything being said. He watched Jake's interaction with the Donavans and his soon-to-be daughter-in-law…his relaxed attitude around his son. He noted how happy Lloyd looked, but more interesting was Jake's demeanor. Seeing him merely as a family man, anyone who didn't know him would have trouble believing the kind of past the man had led, or how ruthless he could be. Jeff still couldn't quite get over that.

Finally the church doors opened, and Jake left the others to hurry up the church steps. He leaned against the railing, still smiling. Jeff rose and stepped aside as people began pouring out of church, many of them again greeting Jake on their way out, some warmly, some looking away nervously, a few women actually casting him fetching glances.

Jake's smile faded then when his wife finally exited… on the arm of a well-dressed, graying, but well-preserved man who made ready to help her down the steps.

Who the heck is that? Jeff wondered.

As soon as the man saw Jake standing there, he let go

of Randy Harkner's arm and put on a smile, holding his hand out to Jake. "Jake!" he said jovially. "You should have come inside."

Jake grasped his hand in what Jeff could tell was an unnecessarily firm handshake, keeping hold of the man's hand a little longer than necessary. "Good to see you, Peter."

The man he'd addressed looked a little nervous. "Preacher Zilke gave a very good sermon."

Jake finally let go, and Jeff noticed Peter flex his hand a little, as though it hurt.

"I heard the sermon from out here," Jake answered. "And last I knew, my wife was a pretty able woman... able enough to get down the steps without your help."

"Jake Harkner, don't be rude," Randy told him as more people exited the church.

"It's all right," Peter answered. "I'm sure your husband is still feeling the strain of the last three weeks." He held Jake's eyes the whole time he spoke. "I saw you ride in yesterday, Jake. I'm glad you made it back in one piece."

Jake took Randy's arm. "Are you, now?"

Peter nodded. "I most certainly am. I wouldn't want to see the look on your good wife's face if you *didn't* make it back, and that's the God's truth." Peter didn't back away, and Jeff suspected Jake respected that. It meant Peter was likely being genuine and wanted Jake to know it.

Jake held his eyes a moment longer. "And a good wife she is."

"Jake."

It was one word, spoken by Miranda. The look she gave Jake said it all. She was warning him to be polite.

Jeff smiled at the simple, quiet command. The woman could stand right up to Jake Harkner. Jake immediately softened and actually smiled. He met Randy's eyes then.

"Maybe your good friend here would like to stay and watch your son marry Katie," he told her.

His wife's face lit up and Jake nodded toward the Donavans' wagon in the distance. Randy turned to see Lloyd standing with his arm around Katie. "Lloyd!" She hurried down the steps and out to greet all of them, embracing her son and then Katie.

Jake kept his eyes on Peter a moment longer. "Thanks for giving her something to do when I'm gone. She needs that. Just make sure it's only work you offer her."

Brown shook his head. "Jake, get the chip off your shoulder. That woman is so devoted to you it's ridiculous. And you know I highly respect her. I most certainly would like to stay and see Lloyd get married, if you really mean that. All Randy talked about while you were gone was getting those two together."

Evie and Brian walked out of the church, and young Stephen made a beeline for his father.

"Daddy! Daddy!"

Lloyd swept the boy into his arms, and Jake watched as Evie and Brian also walked out to greet the Donavans. "Some family, aren't they?" He looked back at Peter.

"I never had children, Jake," Peter answered rather wistfully. "You're a lucky man."

Jake studied him. "Well, I'm sure you are more deserving of a family than I am." Jake put his hat back on and walked down the steps toward his family.

Jeff decided to step back from things for a while. This seemed like something too personal—Jake's son getting married and all. It was Sunday, a family day. He turned his attention to Peter. The look of love in the man's eyes was startlingly evident.

Well, well. This was interesting. Peter apparently felt a strong affection for Mrs. Jake Harkner. Jeff turned away and started back for the Guthrie Inn. Within a block of the church, he noticed three well-armed men on horses, eyeing Jake and his family. None of them looked friendly.

"Hey, kid," one of them called out to Jeff. "You there—four-eyes, in the fancy hat!"

Jeff knew he'd better stop. He looked up at them. "What?"

"You a friend of Jake's?"

"I'm just a reporter from Chicago."

"What are you doin' in Guthrie?"

Jeff swallowed. "Just business."

"What's all the commotion over there?"

Jeff shrugged. "I guess Jake Harkner's son is getting married today."

The man who'd asked the questions guffawed. "Well now, ain't that just sweet, Gordy? Lloyd's gettin' married. Ole Jake's family is growing. Can you beat that? Jake Harkner, the family man."

The one called Gordy grinned. "Warms the heart. Once Harkner is dead, there'll be one more pretty woman added to his family for us to pick from."

"You'd better take out the son too," the third man spoke up. His eyes were a cold, faded blue…emotionless. "I hear he's just one step down from his pa when it comes to using a gun."

"It's Jake's daughter I'd like to get my hands on," the one called Gordy commented. "I'd just as soon be able to keep Harkner alive and let him watch. That would be worse to him than a bullet in the gut." He stuck out a booted foot and gave Jeff a shove, just hard enough to make him fall on his butt. "You tell Jake that Gordy says hello," he said.

The three men turned their horses and headed closer into town. Jeff turned to see Lloyd and Katie hurrying up the steps into the church, probably to catch the preacher before he left. The whole family and Peter also went inside. They left one of the double doors open, and Jake leaned against the doorjamb to watch. He didn't move one foot past the threshold.

Jeff didn't want to be a bother hanging around during a family marriage, but he thought he should at least tell Jake about the three men. He edged closer, hating to interrupt.

"Marshal," he spoke up quietly.

Frowning, Jake turned. "Not now, Trubridge."

Jeff waved him over.

A rather disgruntled Jake came down the steps. "What do you want? Give us a couple more days and you can come and talk to my wife when things calm down."

"It's not that." Jeff looked back toward town. "Marshal, when I headed back to town, some men stopped me. They were watching you, and they…made threats. One even said to tell you that Gordy says hello."

Jeff watched Jake Harkner the family man fade as Jake looked past him toward town. In one quick moment, he'd become the man Jeff saw ride into Guthrie just yesterday.

"How many?" Jake asked.

"Three. Do you know who they are?"

"You bet your ass I know them." He looked back at Jeff. "Trubridge, you're starting to come in handy." He gave Jeff a sly grin. "Thanks." He brushed at dirt on the front of Jeff's suit jacket. "What happened to you?"

"The one called Gordy kicked me down." Jeff brushed at dust on his rear end.

Jake stiffened. "I'm damn sorry about that. Now you know that if you intend to write a book about me, you might be walking into more problems than you expected."

"I don't mind. And I appreciate our conversation on the steps."

Jake looked him over, and Jeff noted the smoldering anger in his dark eyes.

"That doesn't mean I'm letting you write that book, Trubridge."

"I know, sir."

Jake glanced past him toward town. "Thanks for the information. We'll talk again later. I will obviously be pretty busy the rest of the day." He nodded to Jeff and walked back up to the church doorway, glancing back toward town yet again before resuming his position at the doorjamb to watch his son get married.

Jeff headed back into town. He'd walked about three blocks when he noticed the horses the three men had been riding, tied in front of a tavern. Loud voices and laughter drifted past the saloon doors, and Jeff stayed out of sight as he moved a little closer. He heard someone say something about not shooting a man on the Sabbath. A round of laughter rang out then, and Jeff decided he'd better get away from there quick.

Seven

RANDY REMOVED HER DRESS TO CHANGE INTO SOME-thing more comfortable. It warmed her heart to hear the noise in the house. She'd invited the Donavans to dinner along with Brian and Evie, Lloyd and Katie, and the grandchildren. Evie was helping cook Sunday dinner, and everyone else was visiting, the grandsons running in and out of the house, the screen door to the kitchen slamming every time they ran through again. The house was actually too small for so many people, which only made the bigger gathering warmer and more exciting, especially after a wedding.

She unlaced her corset and removed it, then put on a different camisole that fit better. She hurried, wanting to get back to helping in the kitchen. She began tying the camisole, her back to the bedroom door. The door opened then and she turned to see Jake coming inside.

"Jake, close the door!"

He grinned, coming closer. "Need help with that thing?"

Randy turned away. "I need help with stuffing myself into it, that's what I need."

Jake came closer and reached around her, moving his hands inside the camisole to fondle her breasts.

"Jake Harkner, get your hands out of there! The whole family is right outside the door."

He nuzzled her neck. "You're the one who said you needed help," he teased.

Randy wanted to be angry but found herself laughing. She tried to pull his hands away. "Jake, that tickles."

The camisole fell open, and he ran his fingers over her ribs and back over her breasts, making her laugh more. "Stop that! I mean it. I have to change and go help Evie."

"Evie is a great cook. And Lord knows Clara Donavan is too. They don't need your help."

"Really, Jake, please stop." She tried to be serious, but she couldn't help more laughter. Jake moved his hands to her shoulders and gently massaged them. "I just thought, since those things were getting so big, as you claim, I'd help you out."

Randy laughed more as she situated herself into the camisole and began tying it again. "Honestly, I don't know who is the child in this house, Little Jake—or you. You're fifty-six going on sixteen."

Jake grinned, walking over to sit down on the bed. "If I was sixteen, I wouldn't give you the chance to dress at all. You'd be naked and in this bed."

Randy finished lacing the camisole. "By sixteen, you'd probably slept with heaven knows how many women."

He stretched out on the bed. "Yeah, well, there is nothing like the woman who truly loves me, although I still can't figure out why she does." He drank in the sight of her as she started to put on her corset again. "You're still a beautiful, beautiful woman, Randy Harkner. Leave that thing off. Why in hell does a woman small as you need to wear a corset?"

"It's just proper, that's all."

"Leave the damn thing off."

"People will know."

"No one will know but me, and if you leave it off, it means a lot less work for me getting you out of it later."

She smiled and tossed the corset aside, glancing at Jake. Just the way he looked at her sometimes made her feel beautiful and loved. She noticed the sly grin on his face. "You're in a mood today."

He sat up again. "I'm just happy for Lloyd."

She smiled. "I am too."

"Do you really need to go right back out there?"

She gave him a warning look. "You know I do." She hurriedly took a more comfortable cotton dress from her wardrobe and pulled it over her head, letting it fall down over her petticoats. "And you really were rude to Peter Brown today. Don't think I missed the fact that you wanted to break his hand."

He sobered. "I wanted to do a lot more than that."

Randy sighed, putting her hands on her hips. "He's every bit a gentleman, Jake, and he was genuinely glad you made it back all right. He's a good man."

"I figured that out by the look in his eyes. I want to *not* like the man, but I think he's sincere—sincere in how he feels about you, but also sincere in never trying to move in where he doesn't belong. I guess part of me wants him to stick around so he'll be here for you when the day comes that I *don't* make it back."

"I hate it when you talk that way. You could at least say if, not when."

He shrugged. "It's a fact of life."

"And you tried to hand me off to Jess York a few years ago, if you will remember. You practically ordered me to settle for Jess and abandon you when you were in prison. I didn't forsake you then, and I didn't forsake you before that, when you disappeared for two years after the Kennedy shoot-out in California. God knows what you were up to all that time hiding out with outlaws and no-goods and painted women." She smoothed the skirt of the dress.

"Randy."

She met his eyes.

"This thing with that reporter, it's bringing up old memories, isn't it?"

Randy shrugged. "I guess."

Jake rubbed at his eyes as though weary. "All I did was

try to protect you and the kids," he told her. "You know that's why I left. I wanted to forget you, which is the only reason I…pretended you didn't exist, but I couldn't go on without you, and now you're stuck with me."

She smiled. "And you're stuck with me, Jake Harkner, like it or not. Now get over here and button the back of this dress."

She turned around, and Jake got up from the bed.

"And no funny stuff," Randy warned, laughing again.

"Yes, ma'am."

"I mean it, Jake."

"I know." He leaned down and kissed her neck as he buttoned the dress.

"Jake?"

"Just a kiss because I love you."

"What did you do with your guns? I don't want either of the grandsons to find them."

"Everything is locked in the gun cabinet in the dining room, and all the ammo is in the lockbox on top of the icebox, and even you don't know where I keep the key."

Randy caught sight of him in a mirror. His sudden shifts in mood worried her. She knew every look, every mood, every tone of his voice.

"What's wrong, Jake?"

He didn't answer right away.

"Jake?"

"Nothing." He finished buttoning her dress. Randy turned, grasping his arms and feeling tense muscles.

"You made a point of piling all us women and the grandkids into the back of the Donavans' wagon to come over here from church. You pretended like we were making a game of it—telling Stevie and Little Jake to see which one of them could keep his head down below the sides of wagon the longest. The sides of that wagon are a good two feet high. What were you protecting us from?"

He sighed, studying her eyes. "Bo Buckley and Gordy

Bryant are in town, along with one other man. I'm not sure who the third one is. He might be a hired gun."

"And naturally they are very unhappy about having relatives sitting in jail, wounded and waiting for a prison wagon."

He leaned down and kissed her. "Just be careful the next few days. Try to stay home. Peter Brown doesn't expect you to work when I'm home, so you don't need to be out walking around. Tell Evie to do the same. I'll go over to the jail tomorrow and check things out and try to find out how soon that prison wagon will get here."

"Do you think they'll try to help their brothers escape before it does?"

"Men like that will try anything."

"Well, Lloyd needs a few days alone with Katie, which means that if something new comes up, you'll go riding off without him."

Jake stepped back, putting out his arms. "Randy, this is me—Jake. In all these years, what have I not been able to handle on my own?"

"You came pretty darn close to not handling Kennedy's bunch."

He shook his head. "There were *seven* of them. They all died, and we didn't. What does that tell you?"

Randy rubbed at her temples. "Oh, Jake," she groaned.

Someone knocked on the door. "Dad, come on out of there," Lloyd yelled through the door. "What the heck is going on?"

"What do you think?" Jake joked, in an obvious attempt to brighten his wife's mood and erase the worry.

"Katie and I are supposed to be the newlyweds, Pa, not you and Mom," Lloyd answered.

They could hear Evie and Brian laughing in the background.

"We'll be right out," Randy called to Lloyd. Then she

let out a short scream when Jake suddenly picked her up and carried her to the bed.

"Let's give them something to talk about," he said, climbing onto the bed with her.

Randy laughed and jumped off the bed, hurrying to the door and opening it.

Lloyd stood there leaning against the doorjamb with his arms folded.

"Could you two stop long enough to come and eat with the rest of us?"

Randy re-tucked a pin at the side of her hair. "It's all your fault." She leaned up and kissed Lloyd's cheek. "We are very happy for you." She hurried into the kitchen. Lloyd grinned when he heard Evie teasing their mother about behaving herself.

"Tell your *father* to behave himself, not me," Randy answered. All three women laughed.

Lloyd turned to watch his father climb off the bed. Jake walked over to a dressing table and picked up a comb, running it through his hair.

"Last I knew, you were the *old* man of the family," Lloyd teased.

Jake put down the comb and faced him. "Don't make me have to hurt you to prove I'm not as old as you think."

Lloyd closed the bedroom door. "You want to go out there in the street and prove it?"

Jake took a cigarette from his shirt pocket and lit it. "Hell, no. I wouldn't want to embarrass you."

Lloyd laughed. "You wish."

"Believe what you want, if it makes you feel better, Son."

Lloyd sobered. "I know when you're keeping something from me, Pa. I saw a worried look on your face when we came out of the church, so don't try to cover it up by joking about other things. What's wrong?"

Jake took a drag on the cigarette. "Nothing I can't handle on my own." He headed for the door, but Lloyd planted his hand against it.

"We don't keep secrets anymore. Remember?"

Jake scowled. "You're as bad as your mother. She noticed I crammed all the women and kids into the back of the Donavans' wagon on the way back here."

"Yeah, well, I noticed too. The kids and probably Katie thought it was just a game, but we knew it wasn't. What were you protecting them from?"

Jake kept the cigarette at the corner of his lips and walked to a bedroom window, pushing a curtain aside as though to check what might be outside. "We have a couple of visitors in town," he answered, telling Lloyd what he'd told Randy.

"Did you actually see them?"

"No. That reporter kid I introduced you to saw them when he left the church. He came back and told me he saw three armed men watching me and talking about our happy family. One of them called the other Gordy."

Lloyd scowled. "Shit."

"Yeah, well, it might turn out to be nothing." Jake faced him and took the cigarette from his lips. "Just keep an eye out. I'll go check things out at the jail tomorrow, and then I'll find out if those bastards are still around—find out what they're up to. In the meantime, you enjoy your new wife and spend some time with her and Stevie. This isn't anything I need help with."

He started toward the door again, but Lloyd grasped his arm. "Pa, I'm here for you and you know it. Don't do something rash."

Jake broke into a grin. "*Rash?*"

"You know damn well what I mean. What happened yesterday? The preacher told me he was glad you were alive and able to enjoy the wedding. I believe his words

were, 'after that run-in Jake had yesterday with Brad
Buckley.' What happened between you and Brad?"

"The kid was just a little upset that I brought his father
back draped over a horse. Wouldn't *you* be?"

Their eyes held for a few quiet seconds. "I reckon
I'd want to kill the man who brought my father back
that way."

Jake nodded. "And there's your answer. The only
difference is, Brad proceeded to remind me that at least
you and he *loved* your fathers."

The room hung silent and Lloyd closed his eyes. "Jesus."

Jake took a drag on his cigarette. "Now let's go eat.
Your mother doesn't like me smoking in here—says
it spoils the rose scent she puts in the sheets or some
such foolishness."

"You didn't shoot Brad, did you? Did he draw on you?"

Jake opened the door as Lloyd stepped aside. "Let's
just say he didn't get the chance, and right now he's in
a bad way. If you want to know any more than that, ask
your mother. She was there."

Jake walked out, and Lloyd felt a renewed hatred for
the grandfather he'd never known. Any reference to the
man and the fact that Jake had killed him brought out a
dark rage in Jake, who preferred to pretend his father had
never existed.

Eight

RANDY AWOKE TO DIM MORNING LIGHT AND THE smell of peppermint. Something tapped her nose, and she opened her eyes to see a stick of red-and-white candy in front of her face. She turned to face Jake, and he licked one end of the peppermint.

"Remember the first time we did this?" he asked, putting the candy into his mouth and offering her the other end.

Randy grinned. "I believe you were forcing yourself on me."

He took the peppermint from his mouth. "I don't recall you fighting me off." He put the candy back into his mouth.

"You're just as much a devil now as you were then." Randy put the other end into her mouth, and they both chewed on the stick of candy until their lips met.

Early-morning lovemaking was, for Randy, the best kind. Both of them were warm and relaxed. Already naked, Jake nuzzled her neck then as he pushed her gown up past her waist. "How about getting this gown out of the way?"

Randy frowned in mock irritation. "If you insist." She raised her arms over her head and sat up so he could pull the flannel gown all the way off. He kissed her neck and breasts as she lay back down and admired his solid frame. When things were quiet and peaceful like this, Randy had no trouble relaxing to his touch as he explored and massaged all the right places.

Some of her women friends hinted that they seldom did this anymore…but they weren't married to Jake Harkner, and they didn't have to live with knowing that tomorrow their husband could be shot down. She did wonder, though, if any of those women allowed their husbands to go as far as Jake did now, making her wilt under his desire to taste her most secret places. She had once never thought she could be this intimate with a man, but intimacy meant everything to Jake, who liked to make love in every sensual way there was.

She closed her eyes and breathed deeply as he worked his magic with licking kisses to what he called her "sweet-ness," and she knew she could never have allowed this with any other man. There was something about being together for years that made their lovemaking almost worshipful, an extension of a much deeper relationship that required a union of soul and spirit and not just bodies. She groaned as he circled his tongue magically until he brought her to a deep climax that made her need him inside her. He moved to her breasts, her neck, her mouth, her sweet juices still on his lips. She welcomed him between her legs to give him pleasure in return.

"Who do you belong to?" he asked softly as he licked behind her ear.

"Jake Harkner."

The man knew damn well how to make a woman want him, and her desire had not waned with the years. The first time they'd done this satiated an almost violent desire for each other. Perhaps it was because back then, Randy knew deep down this man was forbidden, just as he knew he had no business bringing her into his life—yet neither of them could resist the other and had never been able to since then.

He moved inside of her with a deep groan, and she arched up to greet him. There was always a kind of desperation to their lovemaking, as though they needed to make sure this was still real and perhaps cling to the moment in case this never happened again. She thought Jake seemed more ardent and a bit more demanding than usual, ramming himself deep and hard in a faster than normal rhythm while holding her bottom in a tight grip.

She relished the masterful way he had of making a woman feel ravished and adored, but again came the pain. She said nothing because she knew with secret dread what his urgent lovemaking meant. There could be trouble today. She didn't want to think about it herself, but it was there between them...always. His life surged into her with more force than normal, and he relaxed on top of her then, keeping hold of her bottom. "I'd like to stay here all day," he told her.

"Then stay," she answered. She grasped him around the neck. "I love you so, Jake. Stay here today."

I'm scared, but not just for you. I'm scared of this pain.

He sighed as he kissed her deeply before moving off of her and settling beside her. "If I stay, someone might come to the door, and you'd be embarrassed to be caught still in bed."

Randy nestled against him. "I don't care."

Jake frowned, leaning up to study her eyes. "What's wrong? You seem upset about more than me going out this morning. Is there something you aren't telling me?"

Randy looked away. "No," she lied. "It's just that you've been back only two days, and already I can see there is going to be more trouble."

"And you don't usually talk this way. You know I can take care of myself. What else is wrong?"

"Nothing."

Jake leaned down and kissed her eyes. "You don't fool me, Randy Harkner. I know you too well. I have to leave now, but I want some answers when I get home later." He kissed her again, a long, soft, delicious kiss of promise and devotion.

Tell him, a little voice nudged her. *Tell him. He needs to know.*

No! came a reply. *Don't get him upset before he leaves. It will go away. At least wait until he gets home.*

"*Yo te amo, mi querida,*" Jake said softly.

"Make love to me again," she asked. She wished his gaze were not so discerning.

"Randy—"

"Just make love to me again. Something doesn't feel right about today. If you won't stay home, then make love to me again."

Jake sighed, leaning down to kiss her near her ear. "Randy, tell me what's wrong."

"Just that. I'm scared for you."

He kissed her again, and in moments he moved inside of her again. For Randy, it was like a joining of the souls. Every thrust seemed to claim her, body and soul, reaching into her deepest places and branding her from the inside out. She returned his kisses desperately. How would she ever live without him? In spite of another pain gripping her belly, she pulled at him as she felt his release, then wrapped her arms tightly around his neck yet again and clung to him.

"Don't go, Jake. Don't go to the jail today."

"It's all right."

"Get Lloyd first. I don't trust the Bryants."

"Randy, I've handled a lot worse. I'll be fine."

"Hold me a little longer."

He moved his arms under her back, staying on top of her. "I'll press the air out of you."

"I'm okay. I love being this close, love your arms around me. I want to keep you right here today."

He kissed her several times over. "I'll be back before you know it. I really have to go, baby. This damn job requires it."

A tear slipped out of her eye. How could she tell him

about this pain…or tell him how afraid she was of what it could be? He needed all his wits about him.

He put a hand to the side of her face. "I love you, Randy. I wonder sometimes if you truly know how much."

"And I love you more than that."

He kissed the tear. "I wish you'd tell me what's *really* wrong."

"I guess I'm just used to Lloyd always being with you. Don't go out there alone."

"Hey, I didn't have Lloyd for all those years that were the worst, before he was born and when he was just a kid. I think I can go sign some papers at the jail just fine on my own."

"You know what I mean. And sometimes I get these awful, ominous feelings."

He frowned. "Twenty-six years of living with me is wearing on you, that's all. Someday, *mi querida*, I'll be done with this job, and all this worrying will be over." He kissed her once more and climbed off the bed. He went to the washstand, and Randy studied the now-faded scars on his back.

"Will you please go get Lloyd first?"

"No. Let him and Katie enjoy their time alone. They need time to adjust. They are both still in mourning over lost loved ones, but I think they'll find real love and be really happy. At any rate, little Stevie will be wanting to go home this morning and spend some time with his father too. Lloyd should stay home with him. He can't go running off, wearing guns and worrying poor Katie, on their first full day of marriage."

He poured water from a pitcher into the washbowl, then leaned down and splashed his face. "I expect all three of them will go out to the Donavans' soon to get some of Katie's things. If they do, they'll probably stay the night there." He washed the rest of himself and pulled on knee-length long johns and denim pants, then a white shirt.

"I'll shave later or tomorrow. I'm anxious to get out there and see what's going on." He buttoned his shirt, leaving it open at the neck. "By the way, that reporter might want to talk to us later today. His name is Jeff Trubridge and he writes for the *Chicago Evening Journal*. Whether he writes a book about us is all up to you."

Randy lay back down. "I don't trust anyone to do a decent job writing about you, Jake. And you have never before acted as though you would even consider such a thing."

He tucked his shirt into his pants. "Something about this one is different. I kind of like the kid. I think he's more sincere than the others, and I suspect he's pretty talented. I told him the decision was yours, not mine." He ran a wide belt through the loops of his pants, then reached for his gun belt, which hung on the bedpost, where he always kept his guns at night. He buckled the gun belt.

Randy's stomach tightened a little, watching him strap on the guns. She never quite got over the dread of what each new day could bring. It was bad enough that there were still men out there who would love to say they shot down Jake Harkner, but becoming a federal marshal had only added to his list of enemies.

"Jeff is the one who warned me about the three men in town." He tied the holster straps around his thighs. "So I feel I owe him. I told him he could come to the house later today. I'll look him up when I go into town." He straightened and faced her. "What do you think?"

She pushed her hair back from her face. "I trust your judgment. You read a man pretty good."

He walked over to the dressing table and picked up a comb and ran it through his hair. "I was just thinking—if it was handled right—a book could mean extra money for the grandkids. If my sorry-ass life leads to a book that means they can go to college and make better lives for

themselves than I ever did, then it might be worth it. I'd
put anything we make from it into a trust fund for you
and the grandkids. We'd have to sign some kind of contract that says we have the right to approve of the thing
before it gets published—something like that—make sure
it's not just a bunch of dime-novel bullshit." He pulled
on his leather vest, his badge already pinned to it.

Randy sighed and got up, pulling on a robe. "I can
already see a dark mood setting in, Jake."

"I don't like having to look at Marty Bryant. I want
to kill him and I can't. Maybe I'll get lucky and he'll
give me an excuse." He opened the bedroom door and
started out.

"Jake, don't you want breakfast?"

"No. I'll just grab a hunk of bread on the way out
and get a cup of coffee down at the jail." He walked
over to the wash pan and picked it up. "I'll go dump
this. There's a clean wash pan below the shelf. I'll rinse
this one and scrub my teeth at the pump in the kitchen."

"Wait." Randy walked closer and stood on her tip-
toes to kiss him. "I'm telling you, I don't have a good
feeling about this. Lloyd would understand if you went
to get him."

"No. Sparky will be at the jail."

Their gazes held.

"Jake, don't lie to me."

He turned away. "Just stay in the house today, will
you? At least until I say it's okay to go out. I'll come back
and let you know if Trubridge is coming over later. If we
do this, I'll let you answer most of his questions. I have
no doubt he'll ask about things I'd rather not talk about."
He opened the bedroom door and left.

Randy poured some fresh water into the second
washbowl and began washing. She heard Jake pumping
some water in the kitchen, knew he was scrubbing his
teeth with baking powder. He still had nice teeth, still

had that handsome smile that unnerved her. She found it amazing that in all his father's beatings, he'd managed to keep from getting some of his teeth knocked out. Then again, he could have lost baby teeth that way, since he was beaten as far back as a child can remember.

She shivered at the unwanted vision.

"Randy," he called from the kitchen.

She went to the bedroom door and looked across the dining room to where he stood in the kitchen doorway. "What is it?"

"You promise me one thing, and I damn well mean it."

Her heart fell even farther. Something was up. "What?"

"I said to stay right in this house. That means even if you hear shooting. Don't you dare go running out into the street, you hear me? If you're needed, someone will come and get you."

"Jake—"

"Promise me!"

She felt the tears wanting to come. "I promise."

Shotgun in one hand and rifle under his arm, he gave her a grim smile. "Don't worry. I know they're around. That makes all the difference." He walked out.

"Jake—" she said softly. She hurried to the door, pulling aside the lace curtain at the oval window there. She watched Jake emerge from the pathway beside the house and walk through the front gate and into the street. The pain came again, this time so bad that she doubled over. She knew she should ask Brian about it, but Brian would tell Evie, and eventually it would get to Jake, and she just couldn't bring herself to tell him. She grimaced from the pain and closed her eyes, praying the same prayer she prayed every single morning. "God, be with him."

Nine

Jake walked into town, thinking how Guthrie had mushroomed over just the year and a half since he moved the family here. Born out of the land rush, the town was a grand mixture of clapboard, stone, brick, and frame homes and buildings, and already boasted several banks, barbers, supply stores, feed stores, pharmacies, a lumber company, restaurants, doctors, lawyers, and of course, saloons.

Brian was in the process of urging the other doctors in town to help with fundraisers and petitions to create a property tax that could be used toward building a hospital. It pleased Jake greatly to know what a good man Evie had married. They were perfect for each other, two people who saw the good in others and were both interested in healing pain and saving lives. Jake still wondered how he could have had a hand in creating such a gift to the world as Evie was.

He headed for the stables where he kept three horses. Every day he had the owner, Tobe Baker, saddle one of them so it would be ready in case he had to ride out of town quickly.

"Mornin', Jake!" Tobe greeted him. The old man stood barely over five feet tall and had to tilt his head back to look up at Jake. "I hear your son married the Donavans' daughter yesterday."

"Sure did." Jake leaned against the doorjamb, watching the street. "Saddle Prince for me, will you?"

"Sure thing."

Jake studied his surroundings. It was early and things were quiet…maybe a bit too quiet. He glanced to his left, where at the far end of the main street he could see his house as well as Brian and Evie's place. Brian had built an addition to the house that he used as an office. He kept three cots there for patients who might need to stay overnight. Lloyd's house was across the street from his own, and Jake was glad he'd left his son out of this. Lloyd deserved some time with Katie.

He lit a cigarette, taking a careful scan of every rooftop, every alley. A farmer from outside of town drove a wagon down the street, nodding to Jake.

"You're up early, Fenton!" Jake called to him.

"Left before the sun was even up," the man called back. "Hope Ruben's feed store is open."

Jake waited, thinking about Randy and how soft and willing she always was early in the morning. He wanted to go home and crawl back into bed with her, but he needed to settle his mind on why Bo Buckley and Gordy Bryant were in town…and who the third man was.

Tobe brought out a huge black gelding, saddled and ready to go. Jake always wondered how the little man managed to handle such big horses, let alone get a saddle on one. "Thanks, Tobe."

The old man grinned a toothless smile. "You take care of yourself, now."

Jake nodded, keeping his cigarette at the corner of his lips. "Did Bo Buckley and his bunch leave some horses with you last night?"

Tobe nodded toward a couple of stalls at the back of the shed. "Yes, sir. Right over there. Got a third one penned up out back."

So, they were still in town.

"I know Gordy Bryant was with Bo. Any idea who the third man was?"

"No, sir. Never seen him before, but he was a younger

man, wore a gun in a way that looked like he knew how to use it, if you know what I mean. Kind of low, like the way you wear yours."

So he *was* a hired gun. How could Buckley have hired someone so fast? Had he hired the man even before Jake brought in his father and the others? "Thanks for the information, Tobe."

Jake shoved his rifle and shotgun into the saddle loops that held them, then mounted Prince. He ducked his head as he rode out of the stable and to the right toward the jailhouse. A little voice told him to go and get Lloyd, but he'd be damned if he'd bother his newlywed son this morning. Besides, he'd sure as hell gone up against more than three men on his own, and he was counting on the fact that they were probably sleeping off a drunk from last night. Bo Buckley was a heavy drinker.

He continued to check rooftops and alleys as he approached the jail, figuring that if things were okay there, he'd check out the saloons in town, see if he could find out where Buckley and the other two men had spent the night.

He passed a saloon, which was still closed, but there sat Jeff Trubridge on a bench in front of it. Jake drew his horse to a halt. "Well, well, I might have known you'd already be up, snooping around."

Jeff jumped up and greeted him. "Morning, Marshal. I figured you'd come by early. I asked around and a couple of people told me you always make really early rounds. I wanted to observe. It's a fine, peaceful morning, isn't it?" He walked up and put out his hand. Jake leaned down to shake it and Jeff lowered his voice.

"Jake, there's a man on the roof of the hardware store across from the jail. And one of those men I saw yesterday—he's inside. I saw him go in earlier and heard a scuffle, but no gunshots. I think they're waiting for you."

Jake kept hold of his hand, squeezing it lightly. "Well then, I'm glad you're an early riser." He let go and casually dismounted, tying his horse. "Don't look around," he told Jeff. "Just go sit back down on that bench. What about the third man you saw yesterday?"

"I don't know. I only saw two."

Jake rubbed at the back of his neck. "Well, when the shooting starts, you get yourself into that alley and behind some cover."

"Yes, sir." Jeff swallowed. "Don't you want me to go get your son?"

Jake tossed his cigarette to the ground and stepped it out. Jeff couldn't imagine how he could act so casual knowing several men with guns were waiting for him.

"No," Jake told him. "It's too late, and I don't want to risk my son getting shot on the first day of his marriage. You just do like I said. And if all goes well today, you've got your story. I'll owe you—plenty."

Jeff nodded. "Thank you, sir." They both stood at the side of Jake's horse opposite the jail so they would be hard to see. "Can I help?" Jeff asked. "I could get your rifle or shotgun off your horse."

Jake actually grinned in spite of the situation he was in. "Jeff, have you ever held or shot a gun in your life?"

Jeff smiled sheepishly. "No, sir."

"Which means you'd be more danger than good, but thanks for the offer."

"Aren't you afraid they'll all just start shooting?"

"No." Jake leaned against a post as though just having a normal, friendly conversation. "They want me to face them down so they can say they shot me in a real gunfight. If they back-shoot me, they can't take credit for being the brave bastards who killed Jake Harkner."

"Hell, Jake, my legs feel like rubber. I'm not even sure I can run into that alley. Maybe I'll die today."

Jake grinned again. "Don't worry. They don't give a

shit about you. It's me they want. You just head for that alley casual-like. I'm going over to the jail."

Jeff took a deep breath. "Yes, sir." *Casual?* Jeff wanted to duck and run. He watched in terror as Jake headed for the jail, crossing the alley and stepping up onto the boardwalk. He stopped before he reached the one small front window of the jail and leaned against the brick wall.

"You in there, Sparky?" he called out.

No reply.

Someone crouched over moved along the rooftop across the street. Whoever it was carefully peeked over the fake front at the top. In almost the same instant, Jake's gun boomed.

Jeff jumped up and ran into the alley, pulling Jake's horse with him. He was amazed at how fast it happened. A second later, a body rolled off the side of the hardware store, then crashed into the alley next to it, his rifle tumbling down and landing near him. A passerby who'd been approaching the store ran inside and slammed the door.

Everything fell silent for a moment except for someone shouting down the street. "Someone's shooting down there!"

"Stay away! Stay away!" another yelled.

"Jake Harkner, you bastard!" someone inside the jail yelled. "How did you know we were in here? Was it that four-eyed shrimp of a reporter who told you?"

Jake recognized Bo Buckley's voice. "No one needed to tell me," Jake yelled back. "I saw your man on that rooftop and figured you might be stupid enough to wait inside for me. You've trapped yourselves, Buckley, so come on out and give up your guns!"

"Fuck you, Harkner! Come in and get us!"

"If I have to come in there, you'll die, Bo. That's a promise. If I go down, you'll go down with me. Is that what you want?"

Someone threw open the jail door, but no one stepped out. "Come on in, Jake! Me and the boys don't mind sharin' a cup of coffee before we blow you to pieces!"

"What have you done with Sparky, Bo?"

"He's okay—just locked up. It ain't Sparky we want to kill!"

"I'll give you one more chance, Bo. You know me. You know I'll get at least two of you before you have a chance to fire your guns. Stop this now and all it means is a little jail time. At least you'll be alive."

"You won't get off one shot before we blow your ass into the street, Harkner."

"You willing to bet on that?"

"Gordy, Ted, Marty, and Stu are with me—all armed."

"Dell didn't come along?"

"My little brother? He's too young to blow a man's head off, but we'll teach him right and proper."

"Who was on the roof?"

"A guy we hired last night in a saloon—said he'd throw his gun in with us. Hell, I don't even remember his name."

"Well then, at least I shot a stranger and not a kid. I don't like having to shoot men as young as Dell. That's why I just smashed Brad's chest in, rather than blow his brains out."

"Well now, ain't that kind of you?"

"I thought it was."

The men inside laughed.

"Jake Harkner, kind and thoughtful toward kids, and a ruthless, murderin' sonofabitch toward everybody else."

"Something like that," Jake answered. "You try anything, or hurt Sparky, and you'll see the ruthless, murdering-sonofabitch side of me."

Five men against one. Jeff wondered how he would manage to find his next breath.

"What about the hired gun, Bo?" Jake yelled. "Who is he?"

"Pierce Henry. He's out in the street somewhere, waiting to shoot your ass if we can't do it. One way or another, you'll die today for killin' Jack, and for what you done to Brad. The kid is hurtin' real bad, Jake. He might not live."

"He made his choice," Jake yelled back. "Now come on out of there, unless you're ready to die! Give it some thought."

It was then that everything changed. A little boy came running down the street on short little legs. "Gampa! Gampa!"

Jeff froze in terror. *My God, it's Jake's grandson!*

"Jesus Christ!" Jake swore.

After that, all hell broke loose. Jeff's eyes widened at the sight of Little Jake Harkner, still in his pajamas, running toward his grandfather. Jake charged off the boardwalk and literally leaped over a hitching post. He ducked and rolled his way toward his grandson while guns blazed from inside the jail. Jake grabbed Little Jake and rolled the both of them toward a large crate sitting on the boardwalk in front of the hardware store. He kept the boy in one arm while firing his six-gun with his other hand.

Someone inside the jail cried out. Jake stood long enough to literally throw Little Jake into the crate. When he did so, a bullet hit his thigh and Jake went down.

"Oh my God!" Jeff muttered.

Little Jake began screaming and kept trying to climb back out of the crate. "You stay in that crate, Little Jake!" Jake roared at him. He was on the ground but had both guns blazing. Two more men ran out of the jail. Jake fired twice more and that's all it took. Both men went down.

"Stop! Stop!" someone called from inside the jail.

By then, Jeff saw Lloyd Harkner running from up the street toward his father, wearing only denim pants—no shirt and no shoes, his hair hanging long and loose instead of tied back the way he usually wore it. He was carrying one six-gun, and another was stuffed into the waist of his pants.

"Pa!" he yelled, noticing Jake on the ground.

"Stay the hell back!" Jake yelled.

Someone threw guns out onto the boardwalk from inside the jail. "We're comin' out, Jake!" someone shouted.

Jake managed to get to his feet while Little Jake continued screaming with tearful, pitiful sobs that Jeff suspected must be tearing at his grandfather's heart.

"Little Jake!" a woman screamed. It was Jake's daughter, Evie.

"Stay the hell back!" Jake yelled. "He's okay!"

Jeff saw Evie's husband, Brian, running up behind her. He grabbed her arm and held her back.

Everything quieted for a moment while the last two men inside the jail slowly stepped out, one wounded, the other still fine. The wounded one had a bleeding arm and wore an eye patch.

Marty Bryant, Jeff noted. He figured the other man to be Stu Forbes.

"Kick those guns off the boardwalk into the street!" Jake ordered, stumbling slightly.

Lloyd moved slowly closer, his other gun drawn and both guns aimed at the two men who'd stepped out of the jail.

"One wrong move, and you'll join the others," Lloyd told them.

"Pierce Henry!" Jake roared, quickly adding bullets to his guns. Blood poured down the side of his denim pants.

Lloyd looked over at his father. "Pa, let me handle the rest of this."

"No!" Jake barked. "There's one more! He's a hired gun, so you let me take care of it!" He put one six-gun back into its holster but kept the other one drawn as he looked around.

"Damn it, Pa, you're wounded!"

Jake paid no attention. "Come on out, Henry!" he roared. "You're supposed to finish me off! Come on out and take care of business like a man! You either shoot me down the cowardly way—from cover—or come out and face me!"

"Shit!" Lloyd grumbled.

Everyone stood still, waiting. Jeff suspected Jake Harkner very much wanted the hired gun to step out. He even slipped his other gun back into its holster and put his arms out, daring the man to face him.

"Come out, Henry!"

Lloyd kept his guns aimed at the two men who'd given themselves up. Still shaking, and his ears ringing something awful from the boom of so many guns, Jeff rose from where he'd been crouched at the corner of the jail.

"Jeff!" Jake shouted to him. Jeff jumped in surprise.

"Sir?"

"Go inside the jail!" Jake ordered, his eyes still scanning the street. "If Sparky is okay, let him out while Lloyd keeps an eye on those two cowards near the door!"

Jeff wiped at sweat on his forehead and cautiously climbed up the steps. He eyed the two men standing near the door. Both of them looked ready to kill, and not far away, Lloyd Harkner stood with guns pointed at them. Jeff realized he could easily get hit in cross fire, especially if there was still someone armed inside. But Jake Harkner had given him an order, and he suspected it was best to follow it. Across the street, Little Jake continued screaming, and Jake moved right into the middle of the street, arms still held out. "Come on out, Henry!" he ordered again. "Let's get this over with!"

Stu Forbes made a move and Jeff ducked as Lloyd's gun exploded. A hole opened in Stu's chest. He stumbled backward and Marty Bryant held his arms high and screamed, "Don't shoot! Don't shoot!"

A terrified Jeff dashed inside and grabbed some keys from the wall, glad to see that Sheriff Sparks was indeed all right. His hands shaking, Jeff unlocked the cell door and the sheriff charged out, grabbing a shotgun on his way to the jail door, aiming it at Marty.

"Get your ass back inside!" he growled.

The man obeyed, and Jeff peered outside the jail door to see Lloyd lower his guns. He started toward his father.

"Stay there!" Jake ordered.

Just then a man stepped out from an alley, wearing a wide-brimmed hat and two fancy guns.

"This is the day you finally die, Harkner," he called, stepping closer. "Today I get the reputation of being the man who drew on Jake Harkner and lived to tell about it."

Lloyd walked past the jail door, a gun in each hand but not aimed.

"Can Jake take him?" Jeff asked quietly.

"Are you kidding?"

"He's wounded—losing a lot of blood."

"He's also in a royal rage about Little Jake ending up in the middle of things," Lloyd answered softly. "You don't mess with my pa when he's this angry."

Pierce Henry walked closer, then stopped.

Jeff watched Jake, who did exactly as he'd told Jeff a man should do. He glared right at Henry's eyes and not his hands. It happened so fast then that Jeff hardly realized guns had been drawn, other than he knew Henry drew first. He'd caught the split-second movement, but before the man's gun was even fully drawn, Jake's was out and fired. Henry stood there a moment, then wilted to the ground, a hole in his forehead.

Jake backed up and everyone in the street froze, not sure if the shooting was over. Jake holstered his guns, but when he turned to go to his still-screaming grandson, the man he'd shot off the roof moved to sit up, not dead yet. Jeff's eyes widened when in a whisper of a second, Jake drew his gun and casually shot the man as he passed him by—no aim, no warning, and no true indication the man meant to shoot back. Just a boom, and the man swooned to the ground.

"Any others?" Jake shouted, turning in a circle. "Lloyd?"

"I think that's all of them, Pa! Sparky is all right."

Jake holstered his gun yet again, heading for the crate, blood flowing at an alarming rate from his right thigh. Evie also ran for the crate, Brian with her and already carrying his doctor's bag. Jake reached the crate first and yanked Little Jake out of it, grabbing him close.

"Daddy, give him to me," Evie asked, running up to her father.

Jake whirled. "What the hell was he doing out here!" he literally roared. "He could have been *killed*! Don't ever let him slip out of the house like that again!"

Evie literally recoiled, stunned. Jeff had a feeling Jake had never raised his voice to his daughter that way. Randy was running up the street by then.

Jake leaned against a hitching post, clinging to Little Jake, who in turn hugged him around the neck, sobbing uncontrollably.

"It's okay," Jake soothed. Brian walked up and tried to get his son away, but Jake refused to let go. "Don't anybody come near me or my grandson!" he ordered.

"Jake, you're hurt," Brian reminded him. "And that's my son you're holding. Give him to me before you end up hurting him yourself."

Jake tried to walk away and began to stagger.

Lloyd handed his guns to Sheriff Sparks, because he wasn't wearing his gun belt. "Hold these!" He ran over to his father. "Pa, you're bleeding bad! Give me Little Jake before you fall on him!"

Jake whirled on him. "He could have been killed today, and it would have been *my* fault!"

"Pa, he's fine, and not everything is your fault. Please give him to me. You're about to pass out."

Blood ran almost in a stream, soaking the right leg of Jake's denim pants. "It's just like with you," Jake told Lloyd, "back in California. You were little like this." His eyes actually teared. "I did everything I could to protect you…bullets flying everywhere…your mother… stabbed…" He started going down. Lloyd grabbed at Little Jake, but Jake still wouldn't let go of him, and the boy kept clinging to his grandfather's neck, still crying. Lloyd hung on to both of them as they went down, struggling to keep his father from falling on top of Little Jake. Even once he was down, Jake continued clinging to the boy.

"Brian, get over here!" Lloyd yelled. "He's bleeding to death!"

Jeff also ran over to the site. "What can I do?"

Lloyd was trying to get Little Jake from his father's grasp. "Take his guns!" he ordered Jeff.

Jeff could hardly believe his ears. "*What?*"

"Take his goddamn guns! He's losing blood and it will affect his brain. He might think we're outlaws trying to get Little Jake from him." He wrestled for Little Jake. "Jesus Christ, how can a fifty-six-year-old man who's lost half his blood still be this strong?" he growled.

Brian straddled Jake's legs and sat on them, doing his best to press on the wound to stop the awful bleeding. "Somebody go get the blacksmith!" he shouted. "*Anybody!* Have him come over here with a hot iron!"

Lloyd struggled to pin Jake and the child in his arms to the ground. "Take his guns, damn it!" he ordered Jeff again.

Terrified, Jeff knelt down and yanked one gun from its holster and threw it aside, then managed to reach over and get hold of the other gun, scared to death one of them would go off and he'd accidentally kill someone. He jumped back, one gun still in his hand.

"Damn it, Pa, settle down before I punch you out!" Lloyd yelled. He finally managed to get Little Jake away. He handed him over to Evie, who was crying. By then, Randy reached them as Jake roared for Lloyd to give Little Jake back to him. He swung at Lloyd, slamming his jaw but weak enough to do no real damage.

"Pa, you're going to bleed to death if you don't settle down and let Brian look at that wound!" He literally laid across Jake's chest then, his own lower lip bleeding from Jake's blow. It clearly took every ounce of strength he had to keep the man down. "Lie still, you sonofabitch! Don't make me hurt you!"

"Jake!" Randy knelt close to him. "Dear God!"

"Get out of the street!" Jake told her, his voice growing weaker. "You'll get shot!"

"Jake, it's over. Little Jake is fine. And *I'm* fine." She leaned closer, placing her hands on either side of his face. "Jake, it's me—Randy. Let Brian help you. You're bleeding to death!"

Just the sound of her voice seemed to help him relax. "Randy? I told you…not to come out here."

"I'm fine, Jake. It's over. Please, please lie still."

"Little Jake…"

"He's okay!"

"Jake saved the boy's life," Jeff spoke up, not even sure why he felt compelled to say it. "I saw the whole thing. He got shot protecting Little Jake."

Jake's eyes closed. "Randy…don't leave."

"Jake?" Randy leaned closer. "Brian, he's passed out! He's bleeding to death! He's *bleeding to death*! *Do* something!"

"I'm trying!" Brian answered. "Where's the black-smith?" he shouted.

"He's coming!" someone yelled back.

Brian ripped open Jake's pant leg with a scalpel. "Damn, the blood is flowing like a fountain!" He looked around. "I need something to tie this off!"

Randy leaned down and kissed Jake's forehead. "Jake? Please wake up!"

A storekeeper ran out with a piece of rope. Brian tied it tightly above the wound. "It's slowing now." He looked up "Where's Pete?" he shouted again.

"Here, Brian." A sweaty, soot-covered, bearded man barged through the crowd yelling for people to watch out for the hot poker he carried. "What do you need?"

Brian quickly cut open the wound more. "There! Press the hot end of that poker right into the wound! I don't know how else to stop it but to cauterize it."

Jake roused again and began struggling.

"Jesus," Lloyd groaned. "Mom, get away! Somebody lay across him with me. I can't hold the stubborn bastard down by myself!"

The storekeeper pulled Randy away as quickly but as gently as he could, then bent down to press on Jake's shoulders while Lloyd continued to lie across his middle, trying to keep Jake from flailing his arms. Jeff moved closer to Randy, just staring.

"Do it!" Brian ordered Pete.

Randy turned away, clinging to Jeff, who stood there not knowing quite what to do. He still held one of Jake's guns but moved his other arm around Randy to comfort her as best he could, wondering if she even realized she was clinging to a complete stranger.

"I knew this would happen," Randy wept. "I *knew* it

would. I felt it when he left the house this morning." She shriveled against him and grasped the front of his jacket at the awful hissing sound. Jake screamed from the pain as Pete burned out the wound. People gasped and some turned and walked away.

"Once more!" Brian ordered the blacksmith.

"Pa, hang on!" Lloyd yelled. "It's the only way to stop the bleeding." He stayed on top of him but grabbed one of Jake's hands and held on tight as the blacksmith again laid the hot iron against the wound.

Jake screamed again.

"Damn it, Pa, why didn't you come and get me first?" Lloyd growled, voice hitching as if he were fighting an urge to cry. There came no reply. Jake had passed out again.

"Let's get him to my office," Brian said then. "I can clean and stitch up the wound there."

Fenton Wales, the farmer who'd driven by earlier, came clattering back in his wagon. "Put him in here!"

Brian, Lloyd, and the storekeeper loaded Jake into the wagon. Pete backed away, shaking his head. Lloyd walked up to Randy and pulled her off of Jeff. "Come on, Mom. I'll help you into the wagon."

Clearly shaken by the pitiful cauterization, Randy stumbled to the wagon and Lloyd lifted her into it, then climbed in with Brian. The wagon driver charged off toward Brian's office, which was adjacent to his house. They passed Evie walking with Little Jake, who was still sobbing. Evie hurried to catch up with the wagon. Katie had reached the scene by then and stood there in a housecoat looking scared and confused. She turned to follow the others back to Brian's office.

Jeff just stared after them for a moment, then turned to pick up the gun he'd thrown aside. He made the mistake of grabbing it by the barrel. "Ouch!" He was surprised at how hot it still was from being fired so many times.

He carefully picked it up by the handle instead, then just stared down at the guns.

I'm holding Jake Harkner's guns, he thought. They had just been used to kill five men, faster than the eye could follow. One of them, the man in the alley who'd dared to stir, had been shot as casually as blinking. He couldn't get over the contrasts in Jake Harkner—a murdering wild man one minute and clinging to his grandson the next.

He had a lot of things to process, and he decided the best thing he could do was to go back to his room and write all this down while it was still fresh in his mind. He headed for the Guthrie Inn, still carrying Jake's guns, which were far heavier than he thought they would be. How did the man draw and fire them so easily, let alone actually hit his targets?

He passed a man standing on the boardwalk and studying the bloody scene in the street. It was the same man Jake had had a few words with on Sunday when he came out of church holding Randy Harkner's arm. The man reached out to stop Jeff.

"Did you see what happened?" he asked.

Jeff looked down the street where the wagon was stopped in front of Brian's house. "Yes." He looked back at the man Jake had called Peter. He had blue eyes and sandy hair that showed a touch of gray at the temples. He was very good-looking for his age, clean shaven, his hair perfectly combed—a man Jeff guessed to be close to Jake's age, maybe a little younger. He wore what Jeff recognized as an expensive suit, the kind normally found only in bigger cities.

"You're Peter…Brown, is it?" Jeff spoke up. "I saw you yesterday after church, when you were talking to Jake."

Brown studied him quietly for a moment, then nodded. "Randy Harkner works for me off and on, mostly when her husband is gone. It keeps her busy. At any rate, I'm good friends with the woman. Is she all right?"

Interesting, Jeff thought. The man seemed far more concerned about Randy than Jake. "She's fine. Badly shaken, but fine."

"Jake?"

"Bad shape. He took a bullet in his right thigh. I guess it went through but it hit a vein or something. He lost a lot of blood and they had to cauterize the wound. It was a pretty ugly thing to see. They took him to the doctor's place to sew up what's left of his skin."

"I'm surprised he even was shot. Harkner is too good in these situations to let himself get hit."

"One of his grandsons ran into the street and got mixed up in the mess out there. That changed everything. Jake ran out into the street to protect him—took a chance getting shot to death doing it."

Brown sighed. "I'm not surprised."

"Actually it could have been a lot worse if I hadn't been up and out earlier. I saw those men go into the jail, and I figured they were up to something, so I told Jake. They were ready to blow him to pieces the minute he walked into the jail this morning. I sure didn't want to see that happen, so I told him they were inside. He actually had the drop on them until Little Jake showed up."

"Well, I'm just glad the kid and Randy are both all right, although I'm sure Randy is beside herself with worry." The man frowned and studied Jeff. "And you know my name, but I don't know yours. You're new in town."

"Jeff Trubridge. I'm a reporter from Chicago, here to write a book about Jake. I'd shake your hand, but I'm holding Jake's guns."

Brown glanced down at the guns. "Rather formidable, aren't they? How in heck did you get hold of them?"

"Jake was out of his mind from loss of blood. I think he's probably mostly in shock. His son yelled at me to take his guns—afraid he'd start shooting randomly, I guess." He looked at the guns. "Feels kind of weird to hold them. These guns are pretty famous."

Brown looked at them again. "Yeah, I suppose so." He rubbed at his neck. "Did you say you were writing a book about Jake?"

"I'd like to."

"Well, good luck with that. It won't be an easy project. After today you'll have a heck of a time getting Jake to talk about anything. He shuts down when anything happens involving his family."

"Oh? You must be pretty close to them to know that."

"I'm not really close to any of them, but Randy has told me a few things. When Jake is gone, I think it makes her feel better to talk about him—and the family in general."

"Yes, she must get pretty lonely. From what I can tell, there were times when Jake was gone from her life for two years or more."

Brown folded his arms. "Well, that was back when the law was after him. Now he *is* the law, so things are a little better, but being a federal marshal still takes him away for longer than Randy would like."

And you feel sorry for her because you're in love with her. "Do you have a wife, Attorney Brown?" Jeff dared to ask.

Brown shook his head. "My wife died three years ago. I came out here from Chicago myself to get away from bad memories. I figured with the land rush there would be a need for lawyers out here. I have no children, so it doesn't matter much where I land myself."

"I see."

Brown kept glancing up the street toward the doctor's office. "I hope Jake will be all right."

Do you? Maybe you'd like to see Randy Harkner become a widow. "Are you worried about Jake's wife?"

Brown frowned with a quick and wary irritation in

his eyes. "I'm worried about *both* Jake and Miranda. And don't be reading something into my concern, Trubridge." He stepped back a little and studied Jeff a moment longer. "Good luck getting your story. I wouldn't want to be the one who had to ask Jake Harkner any personal questions. You never know what will trigger that dark anger inside him. I'd advise you to never ask him about his father. He did kill the man, you know."

"I know that."

"That remark Brad Buckley made yesterday was meant to rile Jake. You saw what happened to Brad."

Jeff nodded. "It must take a lot of anger for a man Jake's age to throw a two-hundred-pound man off the boardwalk like that."

Brown tipped his hat. "That's what I'm talking about. Everything about the man is intimidating. He is a formidable presence. You and I walk into a room and no one notices. But when Jake Harkner walks into a room, he immediately fills it up. Everyone stops talking and turns to look." He glanced down at the guns again. "Don't you wonder how on earth a woman like Randy puts up with the man?"

Jeff nodded. "One can't help but wonder. But there is something special there, I can see that. And I think when he's with his family, and especially his wife, he's a completely different man than what I saw on the street today."

Brown's eyes flickered with what Jeff read as envy and despair. "Randy has said as much. The woman is still crazy about that man, after twenty-six years of hell. Go figure that one out." Brown started to turn.

"Do you care if I use your words in my book?" Jeff asked before he could get away.

"What words?"

"About Jake being a formidable presence and filling up a room when he walks into it. I like that description."

Brown turned away. "Fine with me." He walked off toward his office, and Jeff watched after him, thinking that if the man was trying to hide the fact that he was in love with Jake Harkner's wife, he wasn't doing a very good job of it. Though apparently he knew better than to act on his feelings...so far.

Ten

JEFF STOOD AT THE FRONT DOOR OF JAKE'S HOME, fighting down nerves, when Lloyd opened the door and looked past him cautiously before he let Jeff inside.

"Trubridge," he greeted, nodding.

"Hello, Lloyd." Jeff looked behind him, then back at Lloyd, who looked very tired and disheveled. His hair was still loose but tucked behind his ears. "Were you expecting someone else?"

Lloyd sighed. "Just still a little wary after what happened this morning. There are more Bryants and Buckleys out there—big families, both of them. They aren't going to be happy about what happened this morning." He waved Jeff toward the parlor. "Have a seat."

Jeff felt like a little kid in the presence of the tall, dark, and at the moment, still-dangerous-looking Lloyd. He noticed the younger Harkner had a split lower lip from Jake's blow. His pants were covered with dried blood, but now he wore a shirt. He figured the shirt might be one of Jake's, since it appeared he'd never gone home to clean up and change after his father was hurt.

"I, uh, I didn't come here to bother anyone. I just came to return these." Jeff held up a pillowcase. "Your father's guns are in here. You asked me to take them off him this morning. Having them around makes me nervous. I keep thinking one of them is going to come alive and shoot me for looking at it."

Lloyd grinned and took the pillowcase from him.

"Well, Pa did modify the triggers to pull way easier than the common single-action .44. But no, they won't explode all on their own." He reached inside the pillowcase and pulled out the guns, carrying them to a tray-top table near a stuffed chair, then checked each one. He shook his head. "Empty," he said quietly after opening the first gun and spinning the cartridge chamber. He turned the chamber of the second gun. "Four bullets in this one. I figured that. He'd reloaded one gun for the face-off with that hired gun. That took one bullet, and then he shot that man in the alley. That left four. That's why I asked you to take his guns. Pa was out of his head from such a sudden loss of so much blood. I was afraid he'd grab for them again." He shook out the remaining bullets into his hand and laid both guns back on the table, shoving the bullets into a pocket of his denim pants.

"How is he?" Jeff asked.

"Brian and my mother are in the bedroom with him now." Lloyd shook his head. "Jeff, my pa has been wounded before, but this one—it really put him down. I think this time around was harder on my mother too. This is the closest my dad has come to dying from a gunshot. He's been hurt before, but not like this. If Brian hadn't been right there to move as fast as he did to stop the bleeding, Jake would be dead. But then, this is Jake Harkner we're talking about, so you never know." He smiled sadly, and Jeff detected tears in Lloyd's eyes. "He's pretty much too damn stubborn to die," he added. "Brian says it could take several days, maybe weeks for Pa to get his strength back."

Lloyd sat down in the stuffed chair and waved Jeff over to a paisley-patterned sofa with rolled, stuffed arms. Jeff secretly observed items in the room. The furniture was clean and neat but nothing of extraordinary value—just tidy and well-placed. Doilies graced the side tables and what looked like a hand-embroidered small tablecloth decorated the low cherrywood table that sat between him and Lloyd. A lovely lamp with a colorful stained-glass shade sat on an end table beside the sofa, the only item Jeff knew had to be expensive. A rosewood clock chimed softly from its perch on a mantel over the fireplace.

Lloyd took a cigarette from his shirt pocket. "The hard part will be *keeping* Pa down once he comes out of this. He isn't much for being bedridden."

Jeff felt nervous being in Jake's house. His eyeglasses had slipped down a little, and he pushed them back up his nose as he again apologized for intruding. "I really don't need to stay. I'm sure you don't feel like company right now. I just wanted to return the guns and check on your father."

Lloyd lit his cigarette and drew on it. "No. Stay. Peter Brown stopped by earlier today to see how he was doing. Actually, I suspect he stopped by to see how my *mother* was doing."

Jeff wondered if that remark meant that even Lloyd suspected Peter Brown was in love with Randy Harkner.

"Anyway, Peter told me he talked to you after the shooting and that you'd warned Jake those men were in the jail." He drew on the cigarette again. "I want to thank you. I'm not ready to lose my father, Jeff. I just got him back only a year and a half ago. I still have a lot to make up for, so I need a lot of years to do that. If he didn't know those men were waiting for him inside that jail, he'd have been blown to bits as soon as he opened that door."

Jeff was touched. Earlier today this young man had shot down one of the prisoners with no hesitation, and now he sat here talking about how much he loved his father—a man with a reputation that sent chills down most peoples' spines. "I have to say that in just the three days since I met Jake, I find myself really liking him," he told Lloyd, "although he still scares the hell out of me."

Lloyd grinned again. "You don't need to be afraid of him, after what happened this morning. I'm pretty sure after what you did, he'll let you write that book."

Jeff could hardly hide his excitement. "Well, I hope so, but I can't rejoice in how it all came about. I'm really sorry Jake got hurt." He removed his hat and set it beside him. "I hope Jake told you yesterday after the wedding that I mean to do things right—just the truth—not just about Jake but about the rest of the family...unless of course some of you don't want to be mentioned."

Lloyd smoked quietly, studying Jeff so intently that Jeff swallowed nervously. "Did I say something wrong?"

Lloyd shook his head. "No. I'm just making up my mind." He leaned back in the chair. "In two words, Jeff—how would you describe my father?"

Jeff thought a moment, afraid he'd choose the wrong words and lose his chance at a book. "Well...to be honest with you, I've already contemplated the best words to describe the man. I came up with just *one* word. *Nitroglycerin*."

Lloyd actually laughed lightly. "Nitro!" He laughed again. "That's the best description I've ever heard." He took another drag on his cigarette, and Jeff breathed a sigh of relief. "He's like nitro, all right. Keep him calm, and he's fine. Shake him up, and pow! And even nitro is harder to ignite than my father."

Jeff grinned. "Well, I suspect you run a close second to him as far as personality and temper go."

Lloyd smiled and shook his head. "If you want a comparison, I'm just dynamite. *He* is nitro. I lack my father's meanness. It comes from way deep inside, mostly from his past."

"That first day I saw him, I realized that he can back a man down with just a look. When he's angry, there is fire in those eyes. It's unnerving."

Lloyd nodded. "True." He nodded toward the front

door. "At least outside that door. Oh, he has a few friends, is amiable to most people, but don't cross him and don't mess with his family and don't do something that means he has to come after you. And don't abuse a kid or a woman. That's part of the reason he brought those prisoners back in such bad shape. It wasn't because they robbed a bank. It's because they holed up at a ranch where they raped a fifteen-year-old girl. My dad went nuts."

Jeff dared to ask, "Does it have anything to do with his father?"

Lloyd shot him a dark look that said he'd gone too far. "Probably, but let's not talk about that."

"I'm sorry," Jeff quickly covered. "I should have known better than to ask."

"You're right, and if you ever dare to ask Pa, you'd better pick the right time. Better yet, let *him* bring it up, and then hope he's not in a bad mood when he does." Lloyd leaned forward, studying his cigarette as he spoke. "My dad seldom drinks. I'll bet you are surprised at that."

Jeff frowned with curiosity. "I am."

Lloyd continued to stare at the cigarette. "You want something for that book of yours. That's something. He'll down a beer or two—sometimes a shot of whiskey, but not around my mother or my sister or the grandkids. Only once or twice in my whole life have I seen him actually come close to getting drunk...but even then, he seemed to know when to stop...and those couple of times were only when we were out on the trail. The man is terrified he'll turn into his father if he gets drunk, so you'll never see him pull a cork when he's here at home. He made me promise a long time ago never to drink either. When I ran off on him and tried to defy everything he ever taught me, I drank a lot, but I quit after that." He stopped to smoke. "Jeff, there is a war going on inside Jake Harkner, between his father's cussed mean blood and his mother's goodness. Pa says she was beautiful—and he still wears rosary beads that were hers. There's a beautiful crucifix on the end of the beads."

"Really? That's strange, for a man who won't step foot into church."

Lloyd grinned sadly. "Yeah, well, that's a bone of contention between him and my mother. But I don't think it means he doesn't believe there's a God." He kept the cigarette at the corner of his mouth as he spoke, just as, Jeff noted, Jake would do.

Like father, like son, in looks, actions…

"Pa's mother was Mexican," Lloyd continued, "and her name was Evita. My mother named my sister after her, and Pa says Evie looks a lot like his mother. He loves her more than anything, because *she* always had his back no matter what."

Lloyd set his cigarette in an ashtray and cleared his throat. "I've said way too much—more than he would have wanted me to tell you. Don't let him know. Just let him tell you what he wants, when he wants." He rose. "I'll get you some coffee."

"You really don't have to—"

"It's okay."

Lloyd walked into the kitchen. "Want anything to eat?" he called back to Jeff. "Half the town has stopped by with food."

"No, thank you. I'm fine." Jeff took another look around the very pleasant but small house. Lace curtains graced the windows and front door, wool mosaic rugs decorated the wide-plank hardwood floor, and knickknacks and plants were appropriately placed. He thought how the house did not fit the big, often violent man who lived in it.

Lloyd came back with two cups of coffee, and Jake's gun belt hanging over his arm. He handed a cup to Jeff and laid the gun belt on the sofa, then sat down. "No, I can't just leave it there. You see, Pa worships the ground my sister walks on—calls her his angel. To him, she walks on water, and to her, he is just one step down from Jesus Christ himself. Pa is going to feel awful for yelling at her like he did this morning. He's never once raised his voice to her or Mom or the grandkids. Pa and I have had words—like any father and son, I guess—but I know he loves the hell out of me. Still, Evie is the one who stuck by him when he went to prison. I'll never forgive myself for leaving, but Pa forgave me—"

The bedroom door opened then and Randy stepped out along with Brian. Again, Jeff was struck by how lovely Randy was, though pale and tired-looking now. Her light blue dress was covered with bloodstains, as was Brian's suit.

So, all three of them have been with Jake this whole time, never even changing clothes.

Jeff couldn't help feeling sorry for what Randy Harkner must have been through in her life, yet there she stood, lovely and composed. He jumped up and nodded to her. "Ma'am?"

"You're that reporter, aren't you?" she said, stepping closer and putting out her hands.

"Yes, ma'am." He found himself trying to figure out if her eyes were green or gray. Should he take both her hands? She offered, so he did. She squeezed his hands warmly. Was this lovely creature really married to Jake Harkner? "You grabbed on to me when they were treating Jake out there in the street, Mrs. Harkner. I don't think you even knew who I was."

She shook her head. "I don't even remember that. All I know is that Peter Brown visited earlier and told us about you warning Jake this morning." She smiled softly through eyes that looked slightly puffy from crying. "Jeff Trubridge, right?"

"Yes, ma'am."

"Well, I don't know what to say but thank you, Jeff."

"Ma'am, I was just lucky to see those men before Jake got there."

Brian also stepped forward and shook Jeff's hand. "Thanks for your help."

Lloyd rose. "Is Pa awake?" he asked his mother.

As Randy let go of Jeff's hands, he could see the devastation in her eyes. "No," she answered, turning to face her son. "After all these years, this is the worst I've ever seen, even worse than finding him beaten up and suffering pneumonia in prison." She looked from Lloyd to Brian. "I want both of you to go home to your wives. Brian, poor Evie probably wants to come over here and sit with her father for a while, but she'll just have to wait. Tell her he's still unconscious, and there is nothing she can do. And tell her I know without a doubt that Jake didn't mean to yell at her like he did. He was losing blood and not in his right mind, and he was devastated that Little Jake could have been hurt."

She turned to Lloyd. "And you—please go home to Katie, Lloyd. This has been a terrifying first day of marriage for her."

Lloyd glanced at the bedroom door. "What if he needs me?"

"*Katie* needs you. Take it from a woman who knows what it's like to have her husband in constant danger. She's never experienced something like this before."

"But what if he—"

"Are you listening to me, Lloyd?" Randy spoke the words more firmly. "I know what she's going through right now, and you need to be there. Jake would tell you the same thing. He'll understand if you aren't here when he wakes up. For heaven's sake, that's why he didn't ask for your help this morning. He wanted you to stay with *Katie*."

Lloyd sighed, running a hand through his hair. "You tell him—"

"I know what to tell him, Lloyd, only I won't have to. He'll understand."

Lloyd stepped closer and embraced his mother. Jeff made a mental note. *The outlaw/lawman Jake Harkner, who is often referred to as meaner than a snake, has one of the most loving families I've ever met.*

"Mom, I hate to leave you yet."

"I'm fine—really."

Brian walked up and touched Lloyd's shoulder. "Go ahead, Lloyd. You need to be with Katie right now."

Sighing deeply, Lloyd reluctantly let go of his mother. "Hey, by tomorrow it will be Pa holding you, okay?"

Randy nodded, blinking back tears. "I doubt it will be that soon, but at least he's alive. Brian is more sure now that he'll make it through this, but one more ounce of blood and we would have lost him."

Lloyd still hesitated. "You don't have to always pretend to be so strong, Mom."

"Yes, I *do*. If I truly give in to the terror I feel sometimes, I'd crumble into a raving maniac and be no use to any of you."

"And I have strong shoulders if you need someone to lean on. Pa always jokes about how you like to be hugged, so I'm here for that too."

"You go home and hug *Katie*. Let *her* lean on those shoulders." Randy backed up and pointed to the door. "Go!"

With great reluctance, Lloyd nodded to Jeff and finally left. A very tired-looking Brian gave his mother-in-law a quick embrace. "You clean up and change and get some rest yourself, Mom."

"I will."

Another note: *Her son-in-law also calls her Mom. This woman seems to be everything to everyone.*

"Do you need something to help you sleep?"

"No, Brian. I'll be fine. Please get your own rest."

Brian sighed. "You keep that man still."

"If there is one thing I'm sure of, it's being able to handle Jake Harkner…at least when he's in this house with me. And you said yourself you'd be surprised if he regained consciousness before morning."

Jeff drank some of his coffee while Brian walked into the bedroom to get his doctor's bag.

"Ma'am, if I may ask…how do you do it?" Jeff asked Randy. "How do you manage to put up with all this? You're a mother, a grandmother, and wife to a man who has to be difficult to live with."

Randy glanced at Jake's guns lying on the table. "No one understands my husband the way I do, Jeff. *No* one. I know every detail about his life, including when he was a little boy. I know how he thinks and what his needs are. I know how he suffers silently on the inside. That's how I do it." She wiped at her eyes. "Jake has a good heart. He treats me with total devotion and respect, so no, he's not difficult to live with. We've had some really bad times, a couple of them a big test of our marriage, but deep down I've always known how much Jake Harkner loves and needs me. And sometimes he does the sweetest things for me. That lamp cost him dearly, but he bought it for me once when we went to Denver together in those early years when we were so happy in Colorado."

She seemed to be in another world for the moment. "And years ago, not long after we'd met and then gone our separate ways, thinking it was best because he was a wanted man…Jake rode out of my life and I headed west to find my brother who'd gone out there to look for gold. I got into some trouble—traveled with the wrong people and ended up left behind at a filthy trading post all alone. I was dying from a snakebite. The men there were…awful. I was in terrible pain, sure I was dying, and I was sick and dirty and…and one day I heard Jake's voice, felt him lift me into his arms and promise me he'd never let me out of his sight again. I remember how gentle he was when nursing me back from death, bathing me, feeding me, keeping me warm…and never once did he take advantage of me or touch me wrongly. I knew then all I needed to know about Jake Harkner, and right then I knew it couldn't be true he'd violated that woman when he rode with the Kennedy gang. That was one of the things he was wanted for, but I knew there had to be a mistake. Jake has done a lot of things, but never that. Never that." She met Jeff's eyes, and without one ounce of jealousy in her own eyes or in her words, said, "Jake adores women. He respects all women, even the prostitutes, because there were many times when women like that took him in and protected him. He was just a little boy without a mother." She looked away. "Anyway, I fell totally, deeply, madly in love with the *real* Jake Harkner."

She suddenly stiffened and drew in her breath as she wiped at her eyes. "Oh my. I've said way too much! Jake would have a fit if he knew I told you all that." She forced a smile. "You come back in three or four days, Jeff. He should be awake by then, and I know he'll want to see you. And we need to ask you a few questions before we go any farther with your idea for a book."

"Yes, ma'am."

Randy walked over and picked up Jake's gun belt from the sofa, then reached over and put his guns into the holsters. She carried the belt to a coatrack near the front door and hung them there. "Do you know if these are empty?"

"Yes, ma'am. Your son emptied them."

Randy nodded. "Just making sure."

Jeff wished he could do something for her. "Are you sure you'll be all right?"

She sighed. "People need to stop asking me that." She turned to Jeff. "Thank you again for what you did."

"Well, I just wish I could have done more earlier today. If I'd known how to use a gun, it might have helped."

"Well then, Jake will have to teach you how to shoot, won't he? If you're going to hang around him for your book, you'd better arm yourself."

Jeff breathed deeply against the realization she was probably right. "I never thought of that."

Randy smiled warmly. "Young man, you've set up a tall order for yourself in wanting to write about Jake."

"I suppose I have, but I'm excited about it."

Brian came into the room then and took his hat from the rack where Jake's guns were hanging. "Let's go, Jeff. Randy needs to clean up and get some rest."

"Yes, sir." Jeff nodded to Randy. "Good night, ma'am." He left with Brian, wondering what he'd gotten himself into. *Arm* himself? He'd better wire his father tomorrow and let him know this job would take a lot longer than he'd originally thought.

Eleven

LLOYD PAUSED OUTSIDE HIS HOUSE, LEANING AGAINST the wall and lighting a cigarette. He'd gone to Evie's house first after leaving his mother, figuring Katie and Stephen would be there. They hadn't been. Now he needed time to compose himself before going inside his own house to Katie. He'd seen the terror in his poor new wife's eyes this morning, and she'd been alone to deal with it ever since. He had to be strong for her. She couldn't see tears in his eyes.

What a hell of a way to start a marriage. They hadn't even consummated their marriage yet. Last night was spent talking, planning, and just holding each other. He wanted Katie. She wanted him. Yet his heart was still full of Beth, and hers still ached for a lost husband and baby girl. They shared so much of the same pain that they couldn't quite get past it, and last night had just felt awkward. They were good friends, and Katie had suddenly felt too shy. He'd felt her pulling away, so he'd not pressed the issue. They had a lifetime of love and *making* love ahead of them. All of that would come when the time was right. Still, he wanted to give her the baby she longed for. She deserved to hold a baby again.

Right now his poor wife must feel so alone and confused. Stephen was home, but a six-year-old boy wasn't much comfort. The kid had probably cried himself to sleep, scared for his father and grandfather. On top of that, Lloyd remained shaken himself. When he heard all the gunshots this morning, he thought for sure his father had been killed. He'd never seen so much blood in his life and hoped to never see something like that again—not when it was his father who was bleeding.

He tossed the cigarette to the ground and stepped it out before quietly going inside. He was glad as hell now that he had a woman to come home to, someone to hold and to hold him in return. He hung up his hat and guns in the tiny house that consisted of a living room, a kitchen, and two small bedrooms. Figuring Katie to be asleep already, he quietly entered the bedroom to find her sitting in a rocker beside the bed table, a lantern dimly lit. She looked wide-eyed at him and held a rifle in her lap.

"Katie?"

"I wasn't sure it would be you. There are still some relatives of those men out there somewhere."

He walked up to her and took the rifle away, setting it aside and pulling her into his arms. She was shaking. "Katie, if I thought you were in danger, I wouldn't have stayed over at my pa's place. Besides, I thought you were with Evie. I went there first to look for you." He held her tightly. "You're shaking."

"I'm sorry. I should be strong like your mother."

He felt like an ass. "You *are* strong like my mother." He kissed her hair as she hugged him around the middle. "Katie, it's over. Even though there *are* some Buckleys and Bryants left, they live over a day's ride from here. There hasn't even been time for them to hear about this and get back here. And the ones involved today were the real troublemakers anyway. There is only one left and he's in jail, and in a couple of days a prison wagon will come for him."

"That Brad...he's still alive."

"He's hurting so bad, he's not going anywhere for days, maybe weeks. They can't even move him from the jail to a room somewhere."

"His mother will come looking for him. She'll bring men with her."

"I don't think so. Jessie Buckley is kind of a recluse. She'll send someone else for Brad."

Katie started crying. Lloyd wanted to kick himself for not realizing how traumatic this must have been for her. She'd never been around this kind of violence.

"Baby, everything is okay. God, I'm sorry for leaving you today. It's too bad your folks left yesterday afternoon, or they could have been here for you. I didn't want you to come to my folks' house, because I didn't want Stephen to see his grandpa like that. There was so much blood."

"I know. You still have bloodstains all over you. It's just that...you ran out of here so fast this morning... and then I heard all those gunshots...and I saw your father lying in the street and you down too. At first I thought you were hurt, till I realized you were holding Jake down. And Little Jake was screaming...and all those...bodies..."

"Katie. Katie. Katie." He kissed her hair. "Honey, you should have stayed with Evie."

"I felt like I was going crazy. Stephen wanted to come home and wait for you, and I needed to keep busy, so I came home to clean some more. Heaven knows, with no woman in this house for so long, it needed it." She pulled away. "Oh, Lloyd, I haven't even asked how your father is."

Lloyd led her over to the bed. "You're talking a mile a minute. Calm down." He made her sit down on the bed. "Pa is better. Sit down here while I take off my boots and clothes and clean up. Is Stevie sleeping?"

"Yes." Katie sat down and put her head in her hands. "You must think I'm such a baby. You didn't expect that out of your wife."

Lloyd pulled off his boots and shirt, then his

bloodstained pants. "You are *everything* I expected. I did *not* expect you to take what happened today as though it was nothing. But you have to trust that Pa and I know what we're doing, Katie."

He walked over to pour water from a pitcher into a washbasin, then washed the blood from his chest and hands. "The only reason things went wrong this morning is because Little Jake wandered into it," he continued. "Pa would have been fine otherwise. Believe me, Pa can handle himself, and so can I. I'm just upset that he didn't come and get me, though. I told him Sunday not to do anything without coming to get me first. He figured he shouldn't bother us, but as it turns out, he *did* bother us."

Katie smiled through tears. "He didn't know it would turn out like that." She took a handkerchief from under her pillow. "Oh, Lloyd, I'm so sorry. I just thought maybe I'd be alone here all night. That's the only reason I was scared. And I've just… I have to get used to things like this, I suppose, considering your job."

Lloyd finished washing and turned down the lamp to near darkness. "Come on. Get into bed and let me hold you." Still wearing knee-length long johns, he crawled under the covers and held them open for her. Katie moved into bed beside him and he pulled her close.

"How's your mother?" she asked.

"She's shook up, but not about the gunfight. She's grown kind of hardened to that. It was the way my pa bled that scared her to death. It scared *all* of us."

"Are you sure she's all right?"

Lloyd moved one leg over hers. He kissed her lightly. "Randy Harkner is just as tough as my father, believe me, but Pa has never been hurt in a way that rendered him unconscious and helpless like this. It's just hard to see that in a man like him." He pulled her closer. "I'm not ready to lose him yet, Katie. I realized that full force when I saw him down in the street." He kissed her again. "Soon as he's for sure okay, we'll do something together—go on a picnic or something. We'll take Stevie fishing again. I have to spend more time with that poor kid the next few days."

"Stephen is a Harkner through and through. He understood why you had to be with your father. We said a prayer together for his grandpa. He's such a good boy, Lloyd. He kept asking me if I was okay."

Lloyd stroked her hair. "That makes me proud, and it's sweet of you to think to pray with him." He sighed. "Pa would say that praying for him is useless, because the good Lord isn't too concerned about a man like him. I wish I could make him see that's not true, but Jake is Jake, and he's never been able to dig himself out of his past. I don't know where he'd be without my mother."

They kissed again. "You're a good woman, Katie."

"And I want to be a good *wife*. I hope you like what I've done with the house. You probably didn't even notice, coming back so late and all."

Lloyd toyed with the curls in her hair. "I'll like anything you do. Heaven knows this place needed a woman's touch. We'll stay home all day tomorrow and just be together, and in a couple of days we'll go shopping for whatever you need to fix the place up—material for new curtains, rugs, furniture, whatever you think it needs. It's *your* house now—*our* house. All I have to do the rest of this week is meet the prison wagon when it comes in, and go see my father and make sure he's improving. Sometime this week we'll go out to your folks' too, and get the rest of your personal things." He kissed her eyes. "That sound all right to you?"

"Having you here all week sounds wonderful."

He kissed her gently. "Turn over."

"What?"

"You're stiff as a board with tension. I'll rub your back."

"I should be rubbing *your* back. You're the one who's had a terrible day."

"I've been through worse, Katie, and this is all new to you. You need some attention, and I'm going to give it to you."

Katie turned over. Lloyd studied her lovingly in the dim lamplight, her thick, lustrous hair, the fine line of her build. Even from the back she was beautiful. He began massaging her back and neck, moving his fingers round to lightly massage under her chin, then back to her neck, her shoulders, on down her spine.

"That feels wonderful. How did you learn to do that?"

He grinned, thinking about the prostitute who'd taught him all the right ways to make a woman relax. "You don't want to know. Just enjoy it." He kept working his hands gently, deeply. He felt the tension leaving her, his own desire building to do more than touch. He wanted to taste and explore every part of her body, wanted to love her and be loved in return. He pulled her closer, moved his hand in gentle strokes over her abdomen, her breasts, back to her neck, her shoulders, down her back again.

"I hope you're happy with me, Lloyd. I mean, I've seen how other girls look at you."

Lloyd grinned and kissed her neck. "Katie, when a Harkner man loves his woman, none of the others mean a damn thing."

"It's just that we got married so quick, I'm scared you'll regret it. Maybe you'll wonder if you should have seen about some of the other single women in town."

He massaged her hips. "Katie, listen to me. There isn't another woman in town who attracted me like you did. I gave it time, thought about others, but it always came back to you. I came to your place Saturday because I couldn't get you out of my mind. So never compare yourself to anyone else, okay?"

She grasped his forearm and kissed it. "Okay."

"You just keep in mind that I don't take getting married lightly. If I didn't think you were extra special, why would I have chosen you to be a mother to my son, who I love beyond my own life?" He moved his hand over her breasts, around to her hips and up her back again. "You just relax. That's an order."

"I'm just so scared. That could have been you down in the street today."

"You just remember I'll always be with Jake Harkner when I ride off. A man can't ask for better. We always have each other's back. Pa wouldn't have got hurt if I'd been there and seen Little Jake running down the street." He turned her onto her back. "And I do care for you, Katie. You remember that too." He trailed his hand down over her belly again, moved it under her gown to suggestively massage the inside of her thighs.

She drew in her breath and reached up to trace his eyebrows, his cheeks. "Lloyd…you're my husband now…and you have needs…and…" Her face turned red with the blush he'd come to find sweetly amusing. "I want to be your wife in every way."

"You sure?"

"I'm sure."

He leaned down and kissed her softly, continuing his gentle caresses, waiting for her reaction, figuring that after the way their union got off to such a shocking start, he'd better be careful. It felt a little strange moving from close friends to something more. But she was right. He definitely had needs. And she definitely felt good, every curve, every bit of soft skin…soft lips.

His kiss grew deeper, and as his hand moved over her belly again she opened herself to him, whimpering in that way a woman has of saying she wants more. He gently stroked her, felt the heat, moved a finger into her folds and felt the swelling of that sweet nub that told him she ached for more. His kiss deepened even more when she didn't resist his touch. Now he felt on fire for her.

"I want you, Katie," he groaned. He moved between her legs and pushed her gown higher, leaning down to taste her breasts.

Katie ran her hands into his long hair, over his muscled shoulders, whispering his name. Lloyd savored her breasts more aggressively, needing to satisfy long-buried needs. He toyed with her sweet spot until her body shuddered in response to a long-overdue climax. In the next moment, Lloyd pushed himself deep inside her, making her cry out and arch up to him. She dug her fingers into his shoulders.

"Don't go away again," she whispered. "Not tonight."

"I'm not going anywhere," he told her between kisses, burying himself deep inside of her, wanting to give her a child—hoping to fill the place in her heart and her arms that had been so cruelly emptied when her first baby died. He wanted to give her that and more—his love, his life, his soul.

Her breath came in gasps as he rammed himself deep and rhythmically, in an almost desperate need to prove to himself that everything did indeed turn out all right and they were all here and alive. Finally he could no longer avoid his own climax, spilling his seed deep. Once the pulsations finally ended, he lay there on top of her, kissing her over and over. "I'm so sorry I left you here alone."

"It's all right," she answered between kisses.

"I should have realized."

"I'm all right now, Lloyd." More kisses. "I understand."

"I just thought…" He kissed her with a deep groan.

She grasped his face. "Lloyd, look at me."

He hesitated, meeting her eyes.

"I understand."

His eyes teared. "I ran off on Beth," he told her, "never

knowing she was carrying my son. And I ran off on my mother, my father, my sister…all at a time when they needed me most. I won't ever do that again—not to them—and definitely not to you."

"I know you won't."

He met her mouth again, then moved to kiss her ear, her neck. "Thank you for taking a chance with me, Katie."

"You're a good man, a good father, and a devoted son. I know you'll be a good husband."

He devoured her mouth once more, relishing the taste of her, the feel of her, fighting the lingering feeling that he was somehow cheating on Beth. She'd understand. She would want him to be happy, would want Stephen to have a mother. And he wanted to make Katie happy in return.

It was done now. He'd taken a wife and he'd do right by her. Maybe he didn't love her the same as Beth, but he cared for her, and he knew it could become more. He would learn to put the past behind him, and he needed to stop thinking about today's horror and tend to his new wife.

In moments his long johns and her nightgown were all the way off, and he was moving inside of her again, this time both of them wildly satisfying long-buried needs. This time was closer to purely physical, but he knew the rest would come…the union of hearts…the burning touch of souls.

They had time.

Twelve

EVIE QUIETLY ENTERED THE HOUSE AND APPROACHED the bedroom. It was the evening of the third day since the shooting, and during all her other visits, Jake had been unconscious. The bedroom door was open and she walked in to find Randy carefully shaving Jake.

"Mother, Brian says Daddy finally woke up."

"Oh, he woke up, all right. I'm trying to convince him he has to lie flat for a good two weeks. I'm almost done shaving him. I was scared to death he'd lapse into some kind of fit and I'd accidentally slit his throat."

"You'd be better off," Jake joked lazily.

"I probably would," Randy answered. "You have no idea how tempted I was to let this razor slip. I swear, Jake, sometimes you're like a cur dog, friendly and eating out of someone's hand one minute and biting that hand off the next. I should put you on a leash."

Jake sighed and shifted, grimacing with pain as he did so. "Just so you come to my doghouse…once in a while."

Randy set the razor on a table next to a pan and a cup of shaving soap. She took a wet towel from where she'd hung it over the brass rail of the bed and washed his face.

Evie loved watching the intimate moments between her mother and father, the rare moments when no one would ever think Jake Harkner could harm anyone.

"Daddy, I've been here several times, but you were never awake." She stepped closer. "I'm so sorry. This is all my fault for not keeping track of Little Jake. You could have died."

Jake rubbed at his forehead. "Evie, none of it was your fault." He reached out. "Come over here. I'm so damned sorry for yelling at you like I did. I was hardly aware of anything except protecting Little Jake."

"I know."

Randy got up and carried the pan of water and shaving supplies out to the kitchen, leaving Evie alone with her father. Evie cautiously sat down on the edge of the bed, fighting tears. "Does it hurt bad?"

Jake grasped her hand. "Not all that bad. Your husband probably cut deeper than he needed to just to get back at me for the way I yelled at you. I swear Brian has a secret desire to slug me or something, so he takes it out on how he treats my wounds. Feels like I have about a hundred stitches in my leg."

"Daddy, you know Brian wouldn't do that."

Jake managed a smile. "Well, I wouldn't…blame him if he did."

Evie studied his hand, solid, strong. His right hand had been partially crippled for a while…from hitting the prison wall over and over after a visit from Lloyd. That was when Lloyd thought he hated his father and had said cruel things to him before running off. Desperate at the thought that his son would take the wrong path, Jake had hit Lloyd in an attempt to stop him. He was so upset with himself for striking his son that he'd pounded the prison wall in frustration and self-loathing until he broke several bones in his hand. He'd worked with the hand ever since, managed to get it back to almost full use—certainly enough to draw and fire those famous guns.

"I never should have taken my eyes off Little Jake," Evie told him. "He's such a little devil, always running off and always daring me to stop him from doing something he shouldn't, but he's so crazy about his 'gampa.'"

"He's a Harkner. He can't help being naughty. And I *love* that he's crazy about me." Jake squeezed her hand.

"Evie…you're my sweet and beautiful daughter, and it breaks my heart to think of how I roared at you. That was just that dark, scared part of me that's always afraid I'll lose someone I love because of who I am. You'd all be better off without me around."

"None of us would be better off without you, Daddy, and you know it. You are the strongest, bravest man I've ever known…not just physically, but in spirit. You must know how much we all need you."

Jake smiled sadly. "And you are a daughter who is incapable of finding anything wrong with her father. You are a breath of fresh air, Evie. You stuck by me through the worst of it…and I'm sorry for all the lost years when I gave Lloyd so much attention as he grew up. My goal once he was born was to be a good father to a son. But I never loved him more than you. I just love him…different. Can you understand that?"

Evie nodded, a tear slipping down her cheek. Jake reached up and touched her face, wiping the tear away with his thumb. "You've always been so quiet and undemanding. I truly believe my mother lives inside of you, Evie, like an angel's spirit loving me unconditionally."

She put a hand to his, surprised at the remark. "Do you really believe in angels?"

He closed his eyes. "You'd be surprised what I believe in. And don't be telling your mother. She'll be after me to go to church."

"You *should* go to church, Daddy."

"No. Don't you start on me too. Just know that I love you, Evie. In you I see Evita Ramona Consuella de Jimenez. Her eyes shine right through yours." He moved an arm out and she laid across his chest and rested her head on his shoulder. Jake put an arm around her, stroking her thick, dark hair. "I will never raise my voice to you again," he promised.

"I know."

Jake held her tightly, and Evie grew concerned when she felt him tremble. She started to rise, but he held her fast. "He killed her," he said in a near whisper. His grip seemed almost desperate. "He killed her and my brother right before my eyes."

He shifted and groaned softly. Evie wasn't sure if it was from physical or emotional pain. "Mother told me all of it a long time ago, Daddy. You think Lloyd and I don't know, but we do. Please don't think about it. You'll get upset all over again."

"I was eight years old," he continued, as though not even hearing her. "The sonofabitch took me away with him, and he never talked about them again. Before we left, I stole my mother's rosary beads…and I never let him know it. He would have taken them away from me."

"Daddy, I'm so sorry." Evie wept.

Jake continued to hold her fast.

"God brought my mother back to life in you."

"And he gave me the best father ever."

Jake smiled, breathing in the scent of her hair— seeming to calm again. "That I would argue with. I will agree, though, that he gave you the best *husband* ever. I am so glad you have Brian. He's a good, kind, patient man. He's put up with so much."

"He's good to me," Evie reassured him. "He loves me very much." She sighed deeply. "I'm so tired. I could just stay right here and fall asleep. When I was little, I always felt so safe when you held me."

"And I didn't hold you enough." He grimaced. "Baby girl, right now you'd better go home because I'm kind of…floating in and out of this world…and some other… darker world. I don't trust myself right now, Evie. Just know that I love you, but I'm…so…damn…tired…"

Evie sat up, wiping at tears. Her father looked as though he'd fallen asleep again. Randy walked into the room. "Mother, is he all right? He's just sleeping, isn't he?"

Randy came closer and put a hand on Jake's forehead. "There's no fever. His body is just exhausted from working so hard to build his blood back. I'm making sure he drinks as much water as possible. Brian said that will help. And he said your father could slip in and out for another day or so." She looked at Evie, ached at the tears in her eyes. "Oh, Evie, he'll be fine, I'm sure."

Evie nodded, wiping at more tears. "He said he believes his mother lives inside of me. That makes me so happy. He even told me her full name. I've never even known what it was. All you ever told me was her first name, because you gave it to me."

"I never told you because it hurts him too much to hear it, and he was afraid if you knew it, you'd ask more about her. It's very hard for him to talk about, because it means bringing up his father."

Evie nodded. "He told me what happened. I never thought he'd tell me himself. He didn't know I already knew about it." Evie took a handkerchief from a pocket in her skirt. "Mother, if he'd just open up about things, it would help people truly understand him better. Maybe having that reporter write a book about him will help. It will make him talk about things he normally never talks about. It seems like it's already making *all* of us talk about things we never did before."

"I don't know if that's good or bad. Some things are so deeply hurtful, Evie, that the person hurting has to choose his own time and place to talk about them, if at all." Randy grasped her hands as Evie got up, and they embraced. "You'd better go home now. Tomorrow things will be even better. You can bring Little Jake over so he can see his grandpa is just fine, and Jake in turn can see his imp of a grandson is still in one piece."

Evie nodded. "Are you all right alone with Daddy?

He said he didn't trust himself yet—something about floating between this world and a darker one."

"I can handle Jake, Evie. Surely you know that by now."

Evie leaned down and kissed her father's cheek. "I've never seen him like this."

"After twenty-six years together, I've never seen him quite this bad either."

Evie embraced her once more. "Are you sure you don't want me to send Brian over right now?"

"Yes. I'll be sure to come and get him if I think it's necessary. I think I'd like to be alone with Jake."

"If you say so." Evie left, rather reluctantly. Randy followed her to the door and bolted it. She walked into the kitchen and took down Jake's rifle from the rack, where someone had put it after Tobe took it off Jake's horse and brought it to the house. She checked to see that it was loaded, then carried it to the bedroom, worried about the fact that there were still Buckley and Bryant family members left who would not be happy about what had happened.

She laid the rifle on the floor on her side of the bed, then undressed and pulled on a flannel gown. She felt suddenly exhausted herself. She turned down the oil lamp near the bed and carefully crawled into bed, moving beside Jake and putting an arm over his chest to make sure he was still breathing.

He stirred and moved one hand up to grasp her arm.

"You're awake?" she asked softly.

"Where's Evie?" His voice sounded so weak, so unlike Jake Harkner.

"She went home, Jake. She feels much better after talking to you. Everyone is gone and you need to get more sleep."

He lightly squeezed her arm and managed to open his eyes, turning his head slightly to look at her. He sighed. "If I'm dead, I must be in heaven, because I just saw you and Evie...but how in hell did I make it to heaven?"

"God put you here," Randy answered. "It's his punishment, because in heaven you'll have to listen to my nagging for the rest of your eternal life."

"Never thought of it that way. That...*would* be more like hell." He stirred more. "What time is it?"

"For you, it doesn't matter. Go back to sleep. You must lie still, Jake."

"...*mi querida...esposa*," he mumbled. "*Lo siento. Favor perdóname.*"

Randy leaned closer and kissed his cheek. "What on earth do I need to forgive you for?"

"Everything...everything...for being...who I am."

"I *love* you for who you are, Jake Harkner. Go to sleep." Randy wiped at silent tears, still shaken at coming so close to losing him. *Please, God, not yet. Not yet. I need him so.*

The nagging, intermittent pain deep in her belly was still there, though usually it was gone quicker than this. She was so intent on helping Jake that she'd decided to continue with her secret. Brian was worn-out. She hated burdening others. She thanked God Jake was still with her. He'd predicted once that he would never die of old-age ailments. *I'll go down with guns blazing, or from a bullet in the back. Be ready for it, Randy, because we will never know when it's coming.*

She kissed the strong arm around her, and in his sleep he pulled her even closer.

Thirteen

JEFF MADE A NOTE THAT IT HAD BEEN EIGHT DAYS SINCE the shooting. He'd stayed away from the family, realizing they needed time alone. He knew the prison wagon would arrive today for Marty Bryant, and he wanted to witness the man's departure. The formidable-looking iron wagon sat in front of the jail as he hurried over to watch the proceedings. He noticed Katie Harkner sitting in the seat of a small supply wagon, which was tied across the street in front of the very hardware store where Jake had been shot down. She wore a lovely pink dress.

"Mrs. Harkner," he greeted, tipping his hat. "You look very pretty this morning."

She'd been staring at the jail and seemed startled when he greeted her. "Oh! Mr. Trubridge." Katie glanced back at the jail. "Thank you. Lloyd is in the jail right now, signing some papers. The prison wagon is a few days late, and he has to officially put Marty Bryant on it."

"I'm sure Lloyd will be all right," Jeff told her. "I'll go see what's going on."

"Thank you."

Jeff walked across the street, wondering how the shooting had affected Lloyd's new wife. She'd surely never expected to see her husband in a shoot-out on the first day of their marriage.

As he neared the jail doorway, he heard Marty Bryant cussing a blue streak. "I'm still wounded from when you and that sonofabitch you call a father brung me in," he growled. "I can't ride in that wagon."

Jeff walked inside to see Marty's wrists and ankles were cuffed. He was the one originally brought in seven days ago with a wounded arm. He still wore the filthy clothes he'd had on then, as well as his eye patch. He needed a shave, and his hair hung in oily strands over bloodshot eyes.

"Dr. Stewart said you were good enough to travel," Lloyd told him. He was bent over the sheriff's desk signing papers, and Sheriff Sparks stood holding a shotgun on Marty.

"'Course he'd say that. He's your goddamned brother-in-law!" Marty argued. "Don't put me in that wagon, you asshole!"

Brad Buckley groaned from the jail cell, where he still lay with a cracked breastbone.

"You'll pay for this, kid," Marty threatened. "You and your pa both. You tell him that! My family will figure out a way."

"Yeah, yeah. I've heard it all before, Marty." Lloyd straightened. "Get your ass outside."

Jeff stepped aside, observing quietly.

"How in hell am I supposed to walk with these things on my ankles?" Marty barked.

Lloyd stepped closer. "Let me help you." He turned the man around and kicked him in the rear end, sending him sprawling out the front door and down the steps.

More like something Jake would do, Jeff noted. He cautiously walked to the doorway and watched Lloyd pick Marty up and give him a shove toward the wagon, where two other hapless-looking men sat inside. The wagon guard opened the barred door at the back of the wagon, and Lloyd literally threw Marty inside. The man landed facedown on the floor between the benches on either side of the wagon. He screamed another round of curses, yelling that his eye patch had come off.

Jeff dared to step closer as the wagon guard locked the

wagon doors. He grimaced at the sight of Marty's eye. It bore an ugly scar that was stitched shut, and the socket was caved in, the eyeball completely missing.

"Someone will put it back on when you get where you're going," Lloyd told him, seemingly unaffected by the man's misery. "This is what happens when you put your filthy hands on an innocent young girl, Bryant. You're goddamn lucky Jake didn't shoot your balls off. He doesn't care so much about following federal marshal rules, so be glad you're alive and your privates are still attached and not stuffed in your pockets."

Jeff's eyes widened at the words.

"You just remember, you and your pa are gonna have to go after the Daltons again, boy," Marty yelled. "That will leave your family all alone. I'll get out, Harkner. Somehow I'll escape, and I'll pay Jake back for putting my eye out! And I'll pay *you* back for treatin' me this way!"

"You're going to prison, Marty, probably headed for a hanging. Jake and I can handle the rest of your worthless family."

"You're a *dead* man, Lloyd Harkner! So is your pa. Too bad he didn't bleed to death this time around. I hope it was *my* bullet that hit him!"

Lloyd stepped back and waved at the wagon driver, who nodded to him. "Afternoon, Lloyd. How's your pa?"

"Mean as ever," Lloyd answered.

The driver laughed as the guard climbed up beside him.

"Watch for an ambush, Ken," Lloyd warned. "You can't trust the Buckleys *or* the Bryants."

"Marshal Dexter Lace will meet us in Edmond. We'll be okay." The driver snapped the reins, and the four horses pulling the wagon made off. Lloyd lit a cigarette as he waited for it to disappear around a corner. He turned, just then noticing Jeff. He nodded. "Mr. Trubridge. You going to the house today?"

"If it's okay with you. Brian told me Jake is awake and asked to see me."

"Climb in the back of our wagon. Katie and I are headed for her folks' place, but I can drop you off at Pa's on the way."

Jeff climbed into the back of the wagon, where Stephen sat playing with a wooden gun. "Is Jake still in bed?" Jeff called to Lloyd as Lloyd climbed into the seat beside Katie.

"Yes, but he's already turning into a damn grump about not being able to get up. We're having a hell of a time keeping him there. He'll listen to Brian, though, and Brian has told him that if he gets up and around too soon, he'll just end up back in that bed, for even longer next time. So far, he's staying there."

Jeff grinned, glad to hear Jake was being obstinate. That meant he was definitely better. He hung on to the side of the wagon as it bounced over holes and ruts in the dirt street. "Do you expect trouble from the Buckleys or the Bryants?" Jeff asked.

Lloyd glanced at his wife, who grasped his arm. "I doubt it," he answered, casting a slight scowl at Jeff.

Jeff realized he shouldn't have asked the question in front of Lloyd's new wife. The day of the shooting must have been quite an awakening for her. He looked away, feeling like an ass.

"Men like that talk big, Jeff," Lloyd added. "Marty will be completely out of commission for quite a few years now, and young Brad is still in a bad way. He might be moved to a doctor's office or a boarding-house, but he's in too much pain to stand a wagon ride all the way home. The ones we took down were the worst of the bunch, so I don't think there will be any more trouble."

The hell you don't. "I hope you're right." Jeff suspected what happened at the shoot-out would only make things worse with what was left of the two families. "What happened to Marty Bryant's eye?" he asked.

"Marty got in a bar fight a few months back, and Pa broke it up. Marty went after Pa with a knife, and Pa smashed a beer mug in his face. It shattered and cut into Marty's eye. A doctor had to remove the eye. It wasn't Brian, though. There are quite a few other doctors in town."

Jeff shook his head. "Marty Bryant has more than one reason to want Jake dead, then."

"Well, like I said, men like him are more mouth than action." Lloyd pulled up in front of Jake's house but stayed with Katie on the wagon seat. "Jake will be glad to see you, Jeff."

"Thanks for the ride."

"Sure. Katie and I have already seen Jake this morning, so we're going on out to the Donavans'."

Jeff jumped down and nodded to Stephen. "Have fun, Stephen."

The boy grinned. "I will." He waved at Jeff as Lloyd drove off. Jeff went to the front door and it opened before he even reached it. Randy stood there in a lovely green dress that made her eyes look green too.

"I heard the wagon outside," she told Jeff. "Please, come in. Jake is in the bedroom, and he's been giving me a hard time all morning. I'm glad for the company."

Jeff removed his hat. "Thank you, ma'am."

"You can call me Randy."

"Well, actually, I'm not quite ready to call you by your first name yet. Seems kind of disrespectful."

"Well, it isn't at all, but you do whatever feels right." Randy led Jeff to the bedroom. Jeff felt a bit uncomfortable going into a man and woman's private bedroom, but Jake had to stay in bed, so that was it. To Jeff's surprise, Jake was sitting up, shirtless and smoking a cigarette. On top of that, he was fidgeting with one of his guns.

"Come on in, Jeff," Jake told him. "Pull up a chair."

Jeff had a feeling it didn't bother Jake one bit to be sitting shirtless in his own bed, welcoming someone who was still mostly a stranger. Jake held up the six-gun and seemed to be aiming it at something.

"I wish I could go out and shoot this thing to make sure the barrel is straight after all that gunplay. All that heat sometimes warps a gun."

"Yes, sir. In fact, when I picked one of them up by the barrel the day of the shooting, I burned my hand. I had no idea they got that hot."

Jake set the gun aside. "They get hot, all right," he said rather absently.

Jeff opened his briefcase to take out a tablet. "How are you doing, Jake?"

Jake scowled. "As well as can be expected for a man who has to depend on his wife to feed him like a kid. It's downright humiliating, and I intend to be out of this bed tomorrow."

"You're a man who says exactly what he's thinking, aren't you?"

"You bet. And I'm thinking you pretty much saved my life, Jeff."

Jeff met his eyes, and Jake was smiling a little.

"I owe you. So you've got your book."

Jeff couldn't help a huge grin. "Thank you, but if we could do it over, I wouldn't want to earn that right the way I did. I'd rather you were up and walking around and that this never happened."

"Thank you." Jake smoked quietly. "Why me, Jeff? What's in it for you? You must have some kind of angle. Lord knows there are other outlaws still alive you could write about."

"But I'm not writing about an outlaw. I'm writing about a *man*—complicated and notorious and outspoken and intimidating most of the time, but a man who loves his family. That's not something you can usually say about someone with your kind of reputation."

Jake nodded. "Good answer."

"Besides that, you're a dying breed, Jake. There are few men left with your reputation, few who ever live to tell about it. The world out there is changing, full of laws and courts and jails and advanced machinery and inventions. It's nothing like the world you rode in as an outlaw. That fascinates me. I'm only doing this out of my own personal curiosity and my desire to understand men like you."

"Yeah, well, dying breed was almost a literal description after the other day." Jake drew on the cigarette. "And don't kid yourself, Jeff. Don't make me out to be more than I am. I'm just a man who had about as messed up a childhood as any man could have—one who took the wrong path and committed pretty much every rotten crime imaginable and isn't proud of it. I robbed trains and banks and ran illegal guns during the war. Then I just got lucky and found a woman who changed it all for me." He sighed. "At any rate, I like your choice of words, and I think you're sincere in telling the truth. Just don't *ever* use the word *hero* any place in that book, or I won't let you publish it. I'm no goddamn hero. And don't have me shooting ten men when I only shot five—or whatever."

Only five?

"And don't turn it into one of those ridiculous dime novels."

"I would never do that. I'm not that kind of writer."

Jake reached over and put out his cigarette. He winced as he shifted in bed. "Damn," he muttered. "Feels like somebody stuck a bowie knife in my leg and never took it back out."

"I'm sorry you still have a lot of pain."

"Well, pain means you're still alive, so I guess it's a good thing."

Jeff nodded.

"I don't want to go into much detail today, Jeff. I still get tired when I talk too much. I just want you to know that I want some kind of contract giving me and Randy final say in whether that book gets published, plus we need a trust drawn up, and all that bullshit. Peter Brown can take care of it."

"Yes, sir."

"Meantime, I'd like to know a little more about you," Jake continued. He shifted, and Jeff couldn't help but notice the scars—one at Jake's shoulder, another farther down on his chest, a deep white scar on one arm, another one farther down on his belly.

Jake caught him studying his scars. He pointed to the scar at his shoulder. "Bullet wound—" His chest. "Bullet wound—" His arm. "Knife wound from a bar fight. All from the old days, Jeff. I have a scar down low on my right hip from the bullet I took at the Kennedy shoot-out back in California. I have scars on my back too, but I don't talk about those."

The father?

"This one—" He pointed to the scar low on his belly. "That's where Randy shot me the first day we met."

"So—she really *did* shoot you?"

"She sure did. First time I ever laid eyes on her, I got in a shoot-out in a supply store. She was there. It scared the shit out of her, and she pulled a little gun from her purse and shot me. I couldn't believe it. I just ran out and rode off. Took shelter in what I thought was an abandoned house—figured I'd die there. Next thing I knew, I woke up naked and with the bullet dug out of me, and there stood Miranda Hayes. It was her house. She felt sorry for shooting me, so she turned around and took out the bullet—and hid my guns." He laughed lightly. "I was so mad at her for hiding those guns I could hardly see straight, but I was too weak to do anything about it. She fed me and nursed me and I was mean as hell to her the whole time…mostly because I felt myself falling in love with her, and God knows I had no right loving something like that. And nothing I did or said made her back down."

Jake glanced at Jeff. "That woman has been able to lead me around on a leash since before we fell in love. I guess she saw something in me I didn't know was there." He reached for another cigarette.

"She told me you went your separate ways…told me about the trading post where you found her," Jeff told him.

The darker, more dangerous look moved into Jake's eyes. "Yeah. I thought it was best to ride out of her life, but I got to worrying about her, so I tracked her down. Needless to say, the men who were abusing her at that trading post regretted it. I took her out of there, felt like an ass for leaving her on her own like that. By the time she was well…" He closed his eyes and sighed. "I just knew I couldn't ever leave her alone again. For the first time in my life, I loved a woman for more than…more than what most men want out of a woman. Hell, I'd been with so many women by then that she should have been just another one along the way. But she wasn't… not Randy." He paused, then surprised Jeff with his next candid statement, something a person wouldn't expect to hear from a man like Jake. "People think I'm so strong, but my strength comes from Randy." He lit the cigarette. "Back to you," he said then, obviously wanting to change the subject. "Do you have family? Did you go to some special school to do what you do?"

"Yes…school, I mean. I went to a local college while already working part-time for the *Journal* and worked my way up to senior reporter. I have a married brother back in Chicago, and my father is a bookkeeper. My mother died two years ago. I'm not married. I've worked so hard at what I do that I haven't even had time to look."

Jake grinned and shook his head. "That's too bad. Every man needs a good woman, Jeff. You should take care of that part of your life. Have you even *been* with a woman?"

Jeff blinked. "Sir?"

Jake laughed lightly. "I'm pulling your leg, Jeff. Just trying to figure out if I should set you up with a nice, proper young lady…or with some woman who can teach you what to *do* with a nice, proper young lady when she becomes your wife."

"Well, I…I haven't given any thought to either."

"Sure you have. You're a *man*, aren't you?"

"I, uh, I just want to be a successful writer. That's where I've put all my study and energies."

Jake shook his head. "Jeff, when I get done with you, you'll be thinking about a lot more than just writing. And you should know that when I joke around with someone, it means I like them, and there aren't many people I like."

"Yes, sir."

"Next time Lloyd and I head out, you're going with us."

"Sir?"

"You can't write a good book just from stories all of us tell you. You need to see what life is really like out there beyond this door. When I put on those guns of mine, it's a whole different world, and you're going to join me next time."

"I don't even know how to use a gun."

"I'll teach you. You're going to buy yourself some trail clothes and gear, have Tobe pick out a good horse for you, and you're going to buy yourself a six-shooter. That's an order. But when I say stay out of the way, you'll stay out of the way, got that?"

"Yes, sir."

Jake frowned. "Jeff, please just call me Jake. And for God's sake, relax. Don't be afraid to ask me anything you want."

"Yes, sir."

"*Jake.*"

"Yes, Jake."

"Did Lloyd get Marty Bryant off on that prison wagon okay?"

"Yes. Lloyd and Katie are on their way to visit Katie's folks for the day."

"Good. You spend the next few days getting together the things you'll need to ride out with us. I'm figuring in eight or ten more days, I'll be ready to go."

"You sure? You said just talking wears you out."

"I'll be out of this bed by then. I'm going nuts in here. And I don't like Randy working so hard." He lowered his voice. "I don't think she's well, Jeff, and I'm really worried about her."

"What's wrong?"

"I don't know for certain. I know she's worn-out and went through hell over this shooting, but there is something else, and she's not telling me what it is."

"I hope you're wrong."

A dark worry moved through Jake's eyes. "So do I."

"Can you answer one question for me before I leave?" Jeff asked.

"If it doesn't take a long story."

"No. I just want to know how you would describe Randy if you could only use one or two words."

A look of complete adoration and sorrow moved through Jake's gaze. He quietly smoked, saying nothing at first. "The center of my universe," he finally answered. "And the air I breathe. No man could ask for better."

Jeff scribbled the words. "That's a beautiful way to put it."

"She's a beautiful woman—inside and out. I have absolutely no idea how or why she puts up with me."

"Pardon my forwardness, but I suspect it's because she feels the same way about you, Jake. *You* are the air *she* breathes."

Jake met Jeff's gaze. "I had no right ever touching that woman, but I never wanted anything worse in my life than I wanted her the first time I saw her. Our eyes met and there it was. But the situation…hell, she shot me, and, by God, I wanted her even more. That little slip of a woman had guts." He smiled rather sadly. "And I'm feeling really sleepy again."

"Are you telling me to leave now?"

"I guess I am." Jake put out his hand. "Thank you, Jeff. I'm alive because of your warning." Jeff took his hand. Jake's handshake was firm and genuine. "Don't worry about what might happen out there on the trail. This trip will be pretty routine, other than maybe paying a visit to what's left of the Bryants. I don't want them coming back on us later. At any rate, you'll be with me and Lloyd. We'll make sure nothing happens to you."

"Well, I'm…thank you. I look forward to shooting lessons. Not many men get to brag about Jake Harkner teaching them how to use a gun. I'll be writing my father about this."

Jake grinned and shook his head. "I'm hearing the word *hero* in that statement. Remember what I told you."

"I will, sir."

"*Jake*."

"Yes, sir. I mean…Jake."

"You come back Sunday, Jeff, for dinner. The whole family is always over on Sundays after church. We'll talk some more then. I'll have Randy set something up with Peter Brown, and we'll get some paperwork started."

"All right." Jeff rose. "I should tell you, Jake, that I'm Jewish."

Jake frowned. "So? The last I heard, Jesus Christ himself was a Jew."

Jeff was surprised at the remark. "Well, some people have a problem with someone being Jewish, especially some Christians."

"Jeff, I couldn't care less that you're Jewish, and I guarantee my wife won't care either. And I judge a man only on his honesty and trustworthiness. You're a good man, bright, and I can tell, loyal. That means a lot. Trust is everything to me."

Jeff studied him a moment while Jake still had his eyes closed. "How in heck do you know that stuff—I mean, about Jesus being Jewish and all that?"

"Because for twenty-six years, I've lived with a woman who reads her Bible and who for many of those years read it out loud to our son and daughter. I have ears, Jeff."

"But—you won't go to church."

"Jeff, if you're going to get into things like that, you won't get a story out of me. I don't belong in a church and that's that. Now get going. I'm tired."

Oh, there is so much more to you than you let on, Jake Harkner.

Jeff rose, but before he reached the door, Jake called to Randy. She came into the bedroom.

"What is it?"

"Jeff here is Jewish. Do you have a problem with that?"

Randy shrugged. "He saved your life. Why would I have a problem with his religion?"

Jake threw up his hands. "There's your answer, Jeff. No go home and let me sleep."

Jeff turned to Randy. "Thank you, ma'am."

Randy folded her arms. "I'm serious—call me Randy. And what are *you* thanking *me* for?"

"I…I don't know."

Randy put a hand on his arm. "Jeff Trubridge, my husband is alive thanks to you. You will always be welcome in our home. If Jake trusts you and likes you, then so do I. Nothing else matters."

Jeff nodded. "Well, I'm glad of that." He put on his hat. "I'll stay away a few more days and let Jake get the rest he needs."

"Thank you. You are always welcome to talk to Brian or Evie or Lloyd if you want. I'm not sure what they are willing to talk about, especially Lloyd, but they all know it's all right with Jake. They are all very grateful for you warning Jake the day of the shooting. They know their father expects them to be good to you."

"Thank you, ma'am."

Randy walked him to the door. Once Jeff left, she locked the door and went to check on Jake.

"Did you lock the door?" Jake asked her.

"Yes."

He spun the chamber of one of his guns and looked down the barrel again. "Hang my gun belt on the bedpost here by me, would you? I don't like men knowing I'm not up and around. I can at least have my guns handy."

Randy went out and returned with the belt and a box of cartridges. "Do you want me to load those guns for you?"

"Hell, no. The triggers on these things are too touchy." He studied her lovingly. "You sure you're okay with this book idea?"

Randy folded her arms. "I have my qualms about it, but Jeff seems very sincere."

Jake looked her over. "You look tired, and it's no wonder," he told her.

"Being tired is worth knowing I still have my husband with me."

"Well, I want you to rest once Lloyd and I ride out again," Jake told her. "No scrubbing clothes and doing housework. You find someone else to do it." He began loading the guns. "I mean it, Randy. And I want you to go see Peter Brown and tell him we're coming to see him next Monday about paperwork for that book. We'll have him start working on a contract and a trust." He finished loading both guns while she re-pinned the sides of her hair.

"All right," Randy answered. She turned and he held her gaze with an uncomfortable scrutiny. Randy knew he suspected she wasn't well, but the pain was better now. She still hadn't told him. She wanted him completely well first, and by then maybe she wouldn't have to tell him at all.

Jake finally looked away and winced as he shifted in bed. "Come over here."

Randy stepped closer.

"Come on. Lie down beside me."

She looked at him warily. "Jake Harkner, you aren't ready for anything strenuous."

"Strenuous?" He laughed lightly. "I just want to hold you. Jesus, woman, you've been waiting on me like I'm a damn invalid long enough. It's been hard on you. Don't think I haven't been watching. I thought I saw you bent over like you were in pain a couple of mornings ago. What was that about? You seem strangely out of sorts lately, and it's not just this thing with me."

Randy scrambled for an answer. "It was just indigestion, I guess."

"Was it?" He sighed. "Randy, this is me. Come on over here."

Randy closed the bedroom door. She walked around the other side of the bed and climbed onto it, smiling as she moved closer. "These clothes are staying on."

He put out his arms. "I just want to hold my woman."

She moved into his arms, lying across his chest. Jake embraced her and kissed her hair. "What's wrong, Randy?"

"Nothing. Really. I think I'm just a little worn-out.

I had a funny pain, but it went away and hasn't come back. You know what that's like. You have them all the time."

"And I've been injured enough times to kill a horse. I have an excuse for pain. You, on the other hand, have always been healthy, other than the problems you had when Evie was born. You just make sure you go see Brian if it happens again. Don't brush it off."

"I promise."

Jake kissed her forehead, her eyes. "I've been too sick to tell you how much I love you, but it was there inside me."

"I know." Randy moved her arms around his neck, kissing the side of his face. "Jake, I thought I'd lost you this time."

He pressed her close. "Only the good men die, Randy."

"You *are* a good man."

He found her mouth, kissed her hungrily, then moved his lips to her neck. "Give me a few more days and I'll *show* you how good I am. I'll be good in a very *bad* way. I'll have you wishing I was still too weak to move."

She smiled through tears. "Is that a promise?"

"You bet it is."

"I love you, Jake."

"And I can't live without you, so you tell me if something is wrong, and we'll do something about it. I breathe only because *you're* breathing. Without you, I'm nothing."

She leaned back and traced her fingers over his eyebrows, down his cheek. "Without me you're still a father and a grandfather. You will definitely be someone *others* need if anything happens to me, Jake."

He met her lips again. "You take care of yourself." He kissed her again. "No work while I'm gone next time. I mean it. Not for Peter, and no housework, nothing. Evie and Katie can help you out, and you take the clothes to that laundry service in town. I want to come home to find you rested and well. Understand?"

"Why would I argue with that?"

"Because you're Randy Harkner, and you think you have to be everything to everyone and *do* everything *for* everyone. I love you and I need you to stay well." Another kiss. "Who do you belong to?" he asked.

"Jake Harkner."

"You bet your beautiful body. Now lie down and sleep beside me. You've been sleeping on the sofa so you don't disturb me, but I miss you in my bed. You sleep here tonight."

"Yes, sir." Randy moved to settle in beside him. "I guess I could use a little nap."

Jake grimaced as he turned to his side and managed to pull her into his arms. "Let me hold you. Tomorrow I'm going to start doing things on my own. You've done enough."

"But, Jake, you aren't ready—"

"You've done enough." He leaned down and kissed her once more. "Who did you say you belong to?" he asked again.

"Jake Harkner."

"Every inch of you. Every private place, every nook and cranny, every hair on your head. And from here on, *I'm* taking care of *you* again."

"It's still too soon—"

"Go to sleep, Randy. That's an order."

She closed her eyes and relished the pleasure and relief of being in his arms again.

Fourteen

THEY RODE HARD. THIRTEEN MEN, ALL WITH THE SAME purpose in mind—break Marty Bryant loose and go after Jake Harkner and his son, Lloyd…maybe even their families. Dell Bryant led them, his heart pounding with anticipation. The horses' hooves spewed up sod and sounded like thunder as Dell led the hired men through wooded areas, over hillsides, through creeks and deep gullies…sometimes even right across farmers' fields, not caring if they tore up precious crops. They were bent on taking the shortest route possible in order to cut off the prison wagon. One farmer hollered at them and waved a shotgun. They shot him and kept riding.

Hash and Marty Bryant, along with Jack Buckley, had gathered the men from various places over the past few weeks, starting even before Marty and his cohorts robbed the bank in Edmond. These men weren't a part of that. They had stayed behind at Hash Bryant's place, waiting to be paid for the job they had to do. Their pay was to come from the stolen bank money, but Marty never got back with it, thanks to Jake and Lloyd Harkner tracking them down and arresting them…and killing their good friend, Jack Buckley, in the process.

Dell Bryant felt proud. As the youngest Bryant brother, he'd always been left out of the robberies and mayhem, but now Marty was on his way to prison, and his only other brothers, Gordy and Ted, were both dead by Jake Harkner's guns. And their best friends, Jack Buckley and his son Bo, had also gone down under

Harkner guns. Stu was dead and so was the man they'd hired in town to help with a jail escape. No one knew which Harkner had killed which man.

Now their mission wasn't just to gain a name for themselves by killing Jake and Lloyd Harkner, but pure revenge. The rest of these men wanted the same. They no longer cared about being paid, because they figured once Jake was out of the picture, they could rob every bank from Edmond to Kingfisher to Langston, Guthrie, Cimmaron City, and beyond. They could take sanctuary in No Man's Land because the only marshal who dared go to that lawless place was Jake Harkner...and he'd be dead!

The riffraff riding with Dell were mostly newcomers to Oklahoma Territory, the kind of men who'd come here to hide out from the law elsewhere. Some had murdered, some had raped, most had robbed, and all of them drank, smoked, gambled, and ran with whores. A lot of them had been hired out of Hell's Nest, a settlement northwest of Guthrie where only the lowest of the low had created their own pit of sin and corruption. If a man wanted to hire someone kill, rob, or kidnap somebody, Hell's Nest was the place to find him. It wasn't even an organized town—no laws and no lawmen, no lawyers and no churches.

After the shoot-out that left Jake Harkner unable to snoop around, Dell and his father, Hash, had moved these men closer to Guthrie—camped in the thick woods just outside of town—and waited. From a distance they'd watched the prison wagon leave, and they deliberately waited a few hours before riding out after it. In order not to draw any attention, they didn't take the same road. Instead, they'd taken the shortest route possible to reach a place just a few miles north of Edmond, figuring that if they got there sooner than the wagon, they could launch a surprise attack just before the wagon reached town.

They would make sure it never made it…nor would the men guarding it.

They crested a hill overlooking the roadway, then dismounted to rest their horses…and they waited, all thinking the same thing. Once they freed Marty, they would proceed to take revenge against Jake and Lloyd Harkner.

"We have to get him someplace out in the open," Dell spoke up, as though to read all their thoughts. "And we need a way to lure him there. Taking one of his kin might be the best way to bring him to us. Believe me, he's not a man who will go down easy. He took on seven men once back in California and lived through it. We have just about twice that many. He'll not live through this one, and we'll all be famous—and rich. Banks and merchants and even private homes will be easy prey with Harkner out of the picture."

"So do you have a definite plan?" asked a hefty man whose belly hung over his belt.

Dell loved the attention, loved finally being a leader rather than a follower, or the one left behind when Marty and Ted and Gordy would go out to steal horses or cattle. He drew on his cigarette before answering. "We free Marty. Then we go after Jake's family. We'll figure out a way. And we'll wait until Harkner goes out on more rounds so he won't be there to defend his own. The sheriff in Guthrie is fat and lazy and won't be a problem. Whatever we do, it has to be something to force Jake's hand, something that will be sure to bring him and his son after us. It can't be some other marshal. It has to be Jake, so we have to find a way to make this personal. He'll damn well come, all right."

Less than an hour later, a lookout spotted the prison wagon.

"Here she comes, boys."

"Mount up!" Dell told them.

Everyone scrambled to their horses, and Dell waved

them to follow him in a hard ride down the steep hill toward the road…and the prison wagon. Men would die today, and every lawman in Oklahoma would remember the name Dell Bryant—not just for helping Marty Bryant escape, but even better…for being the man who brought down Jake Harkner.

Fifteen

JEFF'S NEXT VISIT CAME TWELVE DAYS AFTER THE shooting and in the midst of slight bedlam. He came on Sunday, as Jake had asked him to do, and the entire family was there, most of them still in the kitchen, Jake on the sofa with his leg propped up and playing poker with six-year-old Stephen while Little Jake sat beside the sofa playing with blocks.

Lloyd answered the door and ushered Jeff inside, showing him to the stuffed chair across from the sofa, the coffee table between them. "I'm going into the kitchen for some pie," he told Jeff.

"Jeff! Have a seat," Jake told him, dealing cards to Stephen.

Jeff noticed Jake's six-guns were lying in pieces on a tray table at the end of the sofa, apparently taken apart for cleaning. "Are you walking now, Jake?"

"Sure I can walk, but Brian says to keep the leg up when I'm sitting. It's a goddamn nuisance, but I guess I have to do what they say. Tomorrow we'll—"

"Jake Harkner, stop cussing in front of those boys," Randy called from the kitchen.

Jake frowned at Jeff. "Can you figure out how she heard that with all that noise going on in the kitchen?"

"No, sir."

"The woman has ears in every room." He dealt a hand to Stephen while Jeff finally sat down in the chair, noting the stark contrast the Jake of today was to the one who'd shot down five men almost two weeks ago.

Jake wore denim pants but was barefoot. His long-sleeved, button-down shirt was open in front.

"Grampa, is an ace a good card?" Stephen asked.

Jake grinned. "What did I tell you about asking me which cards are good? Now I know you have an ace, and since I don't have a pair or anything close to an ace, I have to fold. The toothpicks are yours."

Stephen jumped up. "Gramma! Gramma! I cheated Grampa! I cheated! I cheated!" He laid his cards in front of Jake. "See? I cheated you! I don't have an ace!"

Jake laid his head back against the arm of the couch and laughed. "Stephen, the word is *bluff*, not cheat. *Bluff!*"

"I cheated you! I cheated you!"

"Pa, are you corrupting my son?" Lloyd called from the kitchen.

"Of course I am," Jake yelled back. "Nobody is better at corrupting someone than I am." Jake covered his face in feigned regret. "Stephen, if you use that word in a real card game, someone will toss you out in the street, or worse," he told the boy. "Take the toothpicks and go eat some pie, you little bluffer."

Stephen reached over and grabbed the toothpicks. He ran into the kitchen, still talking about cheating his grandfather.

"I have no hope," Jake told Jeff, still laughing. "I'm always the bad guy."

Randy walked into the living room, putting her hands on her hips. "What on earth did you show that boy?"

"How to *bluff*, not cheat," Jake answered, still grinning.

Jeff couldn't help his own laughter.

"What am I going to do with you?" Randy told Jake as she gathered the cards together.

Jake winked at Jeff. "Woman, do you really want me to answer that in front of Jeff here?"

Randy broke into a smile, looking slyly at Jake. "I don't think I do." She turned to Jeff. "And welcome. There is so much going on around here you haven't even been properly greeted by the rest of us."

"That's okay, Mrs. Harkner. It's just good to see your family back to normal and Jake doing better."

"Yes, well..." She cast Jake another warning look. "It's debatable if Jake's getting better is a good thing."

Jake took a cigarette from the coffee table and lit it. "You'll find out how much better I am sooner than later."

Randy threw a kitchen towel at him. "You just remember that if you walk around too much—or if you are thinking of any other activity—you could pass out."

"I can't think of a better way of finding out how much I can do."

Randy shoved the cards into their box. "Do you want some coffee?"

Jake drew on the cigarette, still chuckling. "Yes, ma'am. And bring one for Jeff." He looked at Jeff. "Want some apple pie? Randy makes the best."

"That would be nice."

Randy left and Little Jake stood up near the table where Jake's guns lay in pieces. He started reaching for one of the parts.

"Little Jake, don't you dare," Jake warned, catching the movement out of the corner of his eye.

The boy stared at his grandfather with dark eyes round as saucers. "Gampa's guns."

"Yes. And you know you can't touch them."

The boy gave Jake a daring look. He looked at the gun parts and devilishly started to reach for them again.

"What did Grandpa say?" Jake told him, setting his cigarette in an ashtray on the coffee table.

Jeff watched, intrigued. "No slap on the hand?"

Jake completely sobered. "No."

"Gampa's guns," Little Jake said again.

"And don't you touch them."

Little Jake met his grandfather's eyes, and the stare-down was on. "Gampa's guns," he repeated.

Jake just kept watching the boy's eyes. "Little Jake, Grandpa always says to watch a man's eyes when he's about to do something he shouldn't. I'm watching yours. If you make another move toward those guns, you won't get any more hugs from Grandpa. And we won't go on that horseback ride I promised you."

Several more long seconds passed. Little Jake stole another look at the gun parts.

"I mean it, Little Jake."

The child moved his gaze back to his grandfather. "Gampa's guns," he said again, his lips moving into a pout and his eyes tearing.

"Don't pull that trick on me," Jake warned. "Tears won't help. You decide. Touch those guns, and no hugs and no horseback ride."

Little Jake glared at his grandfather another few seconds, then suddenly grinned. "Gampa son-o-biss."

"*What?*" Jake frowned as Jeff put his hat over his face so the boy wouldn't see him quietly laughing.

"Gampa son-o-biss."

Jeff peeked around the brim of his hat to see Jake struggling very hard not to laugh. "Well, Little Jake, a lot of people would agree with you, but when some-body loves you, you don't call them that." He moved a hand over his mouth as though to wipe off a smile and tried to keep a serious look in his eyes. "Do you understand me, Little Jake? That is a bad word that you only use for *bad* people. Do you think Grandpa is bad, just because he won't let you touch those guns?"

The boy just blinked, still pouting.

"I won't let you touch those guns, even though they aren't even put together, because you can't touch

Grandpa's guns *ever*, Little Jake, and that's because Grandpa loves you and doesn't want you to get hurt. So Grandpa's not bad. He just loves you. Do you love Grandpa?"

The boy nodded.

"Then don't use that name, all right? Don't use it for anybody who loves you."

Little Jake nodded again.

"Now—do you want hugs and do you still want to ride on Grandpa's horse?"

The boy nodded again, then jumped into Jake's arms and gave his grandfather several kisses on the cheek. Jake kissed him back, then set him on his feet. "Go play on the swings outside with your *cheating* cousin, Stevie," he told the boy.

Little Jake ran off. Jeff and Jake looked at each other and burst out laughing.

"Oh, Lord, if Evie heard what he said, she'd have a conniption. She is always preaching at me to watch my language around that kid because he picks everything up." Jake laughed again, rubbing at the back of his neck. "Well, as you can see, I've taught one grandson how to cheat at cards and taught the other one how to swear. See what I mean? I'm the bad guy however you look at it."

"You aren't angry with Little Jake for running out in the street the other day? He's the reason you were almost killed."

Jake shook his head. "No. His *love* for me is the reason. That kid didn't do one thing wrong. I don't believe in spankings or slaps on the hand or any other kind of physical scolding for children. I just hope the kid doesn't use that word around Brian and Evie, or I'll get an earful." He chuckled again as he pulled the side table closer. He began moving the gun parts to the coffee table so he could reach them better. "There is no such thing as a bad kid, Jeff. No such thing."

Laughter came from the kitchen, and Jake paused. "You hear that?"

"The laughter?"

"The sound of family. I love that sound. I never got the privilege of just being a kid. I never heard laughter, never felt...safe." Jake paused, putting a few more parts together. "I hit a child of mine only once, but he was grown, and he threw my past in my face like scalding water. I reacted because I saw myself in Lloyd in that moment, and it terrified me. I just wanted to stop him. I punched him. The look on his face hit me in the gut like a sledgehammer. I was in prison. He left, hating me, and I turned around and pounded my right fist into the prison wall until I broke bones in it. I almost crippled myself, but I can use my hand now. Lloyd could have hit me back—he *should* have hit me back. I damn well deserved it, but he didn't slug me. He still loved me but didn't want to admit it. He was too angry and too ashamed at the time. He just left, and he went on a rampage to prove he was just as worthless as his father was. I'd never told him about my past and that was a big mistake, just like Randy always warned me it was. I lost my son for a while, but it all worked out. I got out of prison and he learned the truth and...things are a lot better now. He's a good kid, a devoted son. He's more than I deserve."

Jeff took his notebook from his jacket pocket, sensing a darker mood moving into Jake. Randy returned just then, carrying a tray with two cups of coffee and two plates of pie.

"Jake, where am I supposed to set this, when you have gun parts scattered all over the coffee table and end table too?"

He nodded toward the side table. "You can move some of that stuff aside and set the tray there."

"Honestly, you need to work on those things someplace else. The whole sitting room smells of gun oil. And how can I keep a clean parlor, when you're getting that oil all over my coffee table?"

"Well, when I can move this damn leg, I'll do this in the kitchen. You and Brian are the ones who won't let me up off this sofa."

"You just swore again."

"Yeah, well, I'll work on that." Jake glanced at Jeff. "Is there a married man alive who doesn't have a nagging wife?"

"I…I don't know."

Randy handed Jeff his coffee and pie. "Since you're going to be obstinate, Mr. Harkner, I'll let you get yours when you're ready," she told Jake. "And if you don't stop cussing in this house, I'll quit waiting on you all together."

"Yes, warden." Jake wasn't smiling. The remark was almost cutting.

Randy hesitated. "Jake?"

"I'm okay." He kept working on the guns, refusing to look at her. "And I'm sorry. I didn't mean to sound so ornery."

Randy glanced at Jeff. "What has he been talking about?"

"Leave him alone, Randy. We were just talking about the sounds a real family makes…good sounds… laughter." Jake whirled the chamber of a gun he'd just finished putting together.

Randy moved behind him and began rubbing his shoulders. "Well, maybe since today *is* a good family day, that's all you should talk about—the family you have *now* and how good things are *now*." She looked at Jeff pleadingly, and he could see she wanted him to change the subject.

"Sometimes I think I should call this book *Never a Dull Moment*," he told Randy. "From all the bedlam around here on family day, combined with the kind of life Jake leads as a U.S. Marshal, it's pretty fitting."

Randy smiled. "Well, that's a perfect title for a book

about Jake," she answered. "It's a bit *too* true. There is never a dull moment when Jake is around."

Suddenly Jake felt her fingers dig a little too deeply, and she stopped massaging his shoulders. She let out a tiny whimper. He set down the gun and turned, grasping her wrist. "What's wrong?"

Randy put on a smile, loosening her grip. "Nothing. I think I ate too much pie, that's all." She quickly returned to the kitchen, and Jake watched her the whole way. Frowning, he picked up the gun parts again.

"I don't like what I just saw."

"Sir?"

"She's in pain. I told you the other day that I've seen her do that before, almost bend over in pain. I'm going to talk to Brian about it." He worked quietly and soberly for several minutes, saying nothing. "When I give you that shooting lesson, I'll let you try one of these," he finally spoke up.

"Thank you, sir."

Jake laid a partially assembled gun on the coffee table and eyed Jeff again. "Jeff, you are the most polite young man I've ever come across, but I told you the other day that you don't have to call me sir and you don't have to thank me for everything."

"Yes, sir...Jake."

The kitchen door slammed twice—two grandsons coming in for cookies and then running out again. Lloyd came into the room then. "You doing all right, Pa?"

"I'll live. How's Brad Buckley?"

Lloyd ran a hand through his hair and sat down in a rocker near Jeff. "Still hurting, seeing as you cracked his breastbone."

"I wanted to do a lot worse than that, but I have to remember I'm a marshal. That's pretty hard to do sometimes." Jake took a last drag on his cigarette and put it out in the ashtray. "I suppose the damn kid will give us trouble down the road because I killed his *beloved* father."

Lloyd nodded. "Maybe. I think we should ride out and pay a visit to both families, make sure they understand that if they want to give us any more trouble, they'll regret it."

Jake laid down the second gun, not quite finished yet, and moved his leg back to the sofa. He stretched out against a pillow on the arm of the sofa, suddenly looking tired. He rubbed at his eyes, his mood seeming to change somewhat. "Soon as I can ride we'll go," he told Lloyd. "Jeff can go with us. I told him we'd teach him to shoot and that he could ride with us a time or two, as long as he stays out of the way."

Lloyd shrugged. "Whatever you say, Pa. I did promise Katie I'd stick around a few more days."

"Is she all right?"

"Actually, the shoot-out shook her up pretty bad. She just needs to get used to what I do for a living."

Jake sighed. "She'll *never* get used to it. Your mother never really has. She pretends, but she doesn't fool me." He glanced at Lloyd. "She ever say anything to you about not feeling good—lately, I mean?"

Lloyd frowned. "No. Something wrong?"

Jake put an arm over his eyes, settling deeper into the pillow. "I'm not sure." His voice sounded weaker.

"Pa, are you all right?"

"I'm fine. I've just been lying around too long. Makes a man weaker. Much as I love being with your mother, I've got to get up and around and out of here."

Stephen came running into the sitting room, Katie following behind.

"Hey, you little cheater, where are you going?" Jake asked.

"Home. Katie says I have to help her put away some new china she got."

"That doesn't sound like much fun for a boy," Jake teased.

"It teaches him patience, Jake," Katie answered. "And a respect for fine things."

"That son of mine taking good care of you, Katie?"

Katie reddened as Lloyd rose to walk closer. "Yes, sir. He's been...helping me redecorate the house, and we took Stevie fishing and on a picnic the other day."

"Good." Jake glanced at Lloyd. "You two happy?"

"What do you think?" Lloyd bantered. He moved an arm around Katie.

"Be careful, Lloyd," Jake warned, "about going on picnics and such. There are still some Bryants and Buckleys out there who aren't real happy with us. Don't let yourself be caught off guard."

"Pa, I know what to watch for. In the meantime, you do exactly what Brian tells you to do and don't get up and around sooner than you should." He glanced at Stephen. "Let's go, Son."

Stephen ran up to Jake, leaning down to give him a peck on the cheek.

"Bye, Grampa. I'll beat you again next time."

"I'm sure you will," Jake answered. "By *cheating*!"

Stephen laughed and ran outside.

"Will you please explain to your son the difference between cheating and bluffing?" Jake asked Lloyd.

"I'm not sure I even want him to learn how to play poker," Lloyd answered. "You can't help teaching your grandsons how to get into trouble, can you?"

"They're *already* in trouble. They're *related* to me."

"Yeah, well, God help them," Lloyd joked. "You stay on that sofa, Pa."

"Got no choice. I have to answer to the warden out there in the kitchen."

Lloyd grinned and started to leave.

"Wait for Evie and walk her to her house," Jake told him.

Evie came out from the kitchen then and leaned down to kiss her father's forehead. "Brian should be back soon from delivering Jean Howley's baby. I want to be there when he gets home. Mother gave me some chicken and pie for him."

Jake reached up touched her cheek. "You take care, angel. Lloyd will walk you home."

Little Jake came running up to him then, and Jake grabbed him up and kissed his cheek. "And keep a good eye on this little escape artist," he added, tickling the boy. Little Jake giggled.

Evie left with Little Jake and Lloyd and his family. Randy came into the living room to collect the pie plates and coffee cups. "Jake, you didn't eat your pie."

He closed his eyes, putting an arm over his face again. "Later. I'm all of a sudden tired again."

"Well, you should be. You've done too much today." Randy started to leave the room, but Jake stopped her by calling her name, his arm still over his face.

"Don't forget to see Peter and tell him we'll meet with him tomorrow about ten, if that time suits him. I can walk around good enough for that."

Randy turned away. "If you say so." She untied her apron and removed it, laying it across a chair. "I'm pretty tired myself, so I might as well go now and get it over with." She turned to a mirror near the front door and re-pinned the sides of her hair. "I'm not even sure Peter can see us as soon as tomorrow. He does have other appointments, you know."

Jeff noticed Jake look her over with a possessive gleam in his eyes. "He'll do it...for you."

Randy turned, putting her hands on her hips and giving him a scolding look. "You just get out of that dark mood, Jake Harkner, and stay off that leg while I'm gone, or I'll shoot you in the other leg."

Jake finally grinned a little. "It wouldn't be the first

time you've shot me." He grimaced as he scooted lower on the sofa. "Just make sure we see Peter as soon as possible. We have to get things going with Jeff before Lloyd and I leave again, which will only be another week or so," Jake told her.

"Don't you think that's a little soon for that leg?"

"We have things to do that can't be put off much longer."

Randy watched him closely. "What's wrong?"

"Nothing. Just routine."

Randy sighed. "Well, as soon as Brian gets back, I want him to check your dressings and make sure that wound isn't bleeding on the inside or something."

"Speaking of Brian, it's *you* he should examine. You're in some kind of pain, Randy."

"It's nothing. You worry too much." Randy walked into the bedroom, and Jeff could see Jake tense up.

"You all right, Jake?"

"I'm fine. Meet us at Peter Brown's around ten tomorrow. In fact, come here first and we'll all go to breakfast."

"Sure." Jeff worried there might be a confrontation between Jake and Peter soon. It seemed almost inevitable, with all the tension between the three of them. "I need to get things together for that trip with you and Lloyd—which, believe me, makes me very nervous."

Jake kept his arm over his eyes, his voice sounding weaker. "Jeff, you're braver than you know. If you're put on the spot...you'll come through. That's why I don't mind taking you along with us. And by the time Lloyd and I are done with you...you'll be asking to sign up as a deputy U.S. Marshal."

Jeff grinned. "Thanks, but I'll stick to writing."

Randy came back into the living room, wearing a velvet hat with a flower design crocheted into it. She took a shawl from a coat stand near the door, then came over and leaned down to kiss Jake. "I'm leaving. Promise me you'll stay off that leg."

Jake grasped her arm and leaned up for another kiss. "You *would* tell me if something was wrong...wouldn't you?"

"Wrong?"

"You know what I'm talking about."

She gave him a smile. "I'm all right."

"All the same, I think we should tell Brian. You want him to look at my leg anyway. Tell him about the pains you've been having."

"Jake."

"Don't argue with me about it."

She straightened and sighed. "If it will make you rest easier, I'll bring him over, but not today."

Jake kept hold of her hand. "Today! I love you and I don't intend to lose you because we put something off for too long."

She sighed in resignation. "If you insist."

"I insist. You're always concerned about everybody else and don't pay enough attention to your own health. I should have realized that a long time ago."

Randy sat down on the edge of the sofa and leaned over to kiss him again. "Jake, I'm fine."

"We'll let Brian decide that. Seeing you in pain scares the hell out of me."

"And what do you think *I've* been going through the last couple of weeks?"

"That's different. We know the cause of my pain. We *don't* know the cause of yours. If I lose you, I'm a dead man."

She touched his face. "You aren't going to lose me, Jake."

Jeff made a mental note. *Jake Harkner fears nothing... except losing his wife. I think if that happened, he'd put one of those famous guns to his head and pull the trigger.*

Randy rose and wrapped her shawl tighter around her shoulders.

"And don't stay too long at Peter's place," Jake told her.

She scowled at him. "What's that supposed to mean?"

"It means that if I was Peter, I'd never let you back out the door."

"And risk *you* coming for me? Peter isn't an idiot, Jake." She started for the door.

"Wait!" Jake spoke up. "Have Jeff walk with you. I don't like you walking out there alone."

"I do it all the time when you're gone," she answered, starting for the door again.

"Randy!" There was more authority in his voice this time. Jeff stiffened. "I mean it. Let Jeff go with you. And once Lloyd and I leave, you don't go anywhere alone, understand?"

Randy frowned. "Jake, what are you not telling me?"

"It's just a gut feeling, that's all. Until I know it's really over, don't be running around alone and don't be going anywhere out of town."

Randy looked at Jeff. "The man has spoken."

Jeff swallowed, glancing at Jake. "I don't mind taking her, Jake, but what the heck would somebody like me do if there was trouble?"

"You'll go into the kitchen and take down my ten gauge, that's what you'll do. Anybody can hit anything with a damn shotgun, even if they don't know a thing about shooting. You just raise it and pull the trigger. That thing will blow a man clear across the street. I ought to know." He laid his head back again and closed his eyes. "I've by God sent a man flying more than once with it."

Jeff looked at Randy. She just shrugged. "You heard him. I've used that gun myself. I'll tell you about it sometime."

Taking a deep breath, Jeff walked to the kitchen to retrieve the shotgun.

"Take down the metal box from the top of the icebox," Jake told him. "Get some shells out."

Jeff did as he was told, bringing the shells and the shotgun into the sitting room. Jake sat up. "Hand it over." He opened the shotgun and rammed two shells into it. "I prefer slugs, but for someone who doesn't know anything about where to aim one of these and how they kick, buckshot is better. You're bound to hit *something*."

"Yes, sir."

Jake handed out the gun, and Jeff just stared at it. "It won't bite you, Jeff. And if my wife seems threatened, don't you hesitate. I'm the law here, and I won't arrest you if you screw up."

"What?" Jeff took the gun and saw that Jake was grinning.

"Wait for Randy at Peter's place and walk her back here. You can leave the shotgun here when you get back."

"Yes, sir...I mean, Jake."

"And if Peter tries anything with my wife, use that shotgun on him."

Jeff just blinked. Randy took his arm. "This time I think he's serious," she said with a grin. She took his arm and left with him.

Jake watched them through a side window until they disappeared past the house next door. He laid back down against the pillow. He'd nearly fallen asleep when some-one knocked at the door. Jake roused from the groggy nap and immediately picked up one of the six-guns he'd just put together. Only two cartridges lay nearby and he quickly loaded it, not sure how much time had passed since Randy left.

"Pa, it's just me, and the door is unlocked. Just want you to know I'm coming in."

Jake kept the gun in his hand as Lloyd came inside.

"Why is the door unlocked?"

"Your mother left to go see Peter about a meeting tomorrow. I didn't bother hobbling over there to lock the door." Jake noticed a deep concern in his son's eyes. "What's wrong?"

Lloyd was wearing his guns and looked ready to shoot something. "Sparky brought over a telegram. Marty Bryant escaped."

Jake sat up straighter. "How?"

"They aren't sure. It just says the prison wagon was found between Edmond and Oklahoma City—Marshal Dexter Lace and the driver are both dead, along with the guard. Even the three other prisoners in the wagon with Marty were killed. From the tracks they left, it looks like a lot of men were involved."

Jake closed his eyes. "*Shit!* I *knew* something was wrong. I *felt* it. And Dexter Lace was a good man—a good friend and damn good with a gun."

"It could have been us, Pa. And if enough men came along to shoot up all those men and get Marty out of there, you can bet they have more planned. And we can't count on help right now. Those lawmen who could have helped are off on another pursuit of the Daltons. With Dexter dead, it's just you and me."

Jake reached out and asked Lloyd to help him get up. He grimaced as he rose. "Were any instructions wired to us?"

"Just the obvious—track down Marty Bryant, which I'm sure you already plan to do. Their tracks led on south." He looked his father over. "I can see you're still in pain. You shouldn't be standing, Pa."

"I'm fine!" Jake barked. "And tracks leading south are a decoy. They'll come back this way because they want us—you and me."

Lloyd nodded. "What should we do?"

"Sit tight for now. It's obvious Hash Bryant has rounded up some men and had them go break Marty loose. Maybe it was even Dell who planned it. The kid has been wanting to prove his manhood for a long time now. And that damn prison wagon being late gave him or Hash time to plan this. We have to figure out what they're up to next. I can't go out on the trail yet, but I'll *damn* well get out there soon! And don't you think about going alone! That's an order!"

He limped over to a window and looked out.

"Right now you go catch up with Jeff and your mother. She's at Peter's office by now. You walk her and Jeff back here. Jeff is no match for Marty Bryant if the man is actually around here. Get going, and try not to alarm Katie too much when you get home."

"What should I tell Mom?"

"The truth, I guess. There's no hiding it from her. I damn well hate burdening her with this." He limped back to the sofa. "*Damn it all!*"

"I don't like leaving you here alone, Pa."

"*Me?* Do you realize who you're talking to? Go get my cartridge belt. I just have a couple of screws to tighten, and these guns will be in full working order. You go make sure your mother is safe."

Lloyd nodded and hurried into the kitchen, grabbing a cartridge belt and tossing it onto the end of the sofa. "I'll be back soon."

He left, and Jake felt ready to explode. He picked up a clean ashtray from the side table and threw it against the stone fireplace, smashing it to pieces.

Sixteen

RANDY RETURNED WITH BRIAN, LLOYD, AND JEFF to find Jake loading cartridges into his gun belt. Randy knew what the look in his eyes meant. She glanced at the scattered pieces of glass around the stone fireplace. "Jake, you can't leave yet," she said, quickly removing her shawl.

"Can't I?"

"No," Brian answered for her.

"Pa, you don't even know yet what's going on," Lloyd reminded him. "We already talked about this. Waiting another eight or ten days won't matter, and you'll be a lot healthier. Besides, you wanted Brian to talk to Mom about the pains she's been having."

Jake threw the gun belt to the floor and stood up to pace with a prominent limp. "We should have killed Marty Bryant when we had the chance!"

"This isn't the old days, Pa. You can't just shoot somebody because you want them dead."

Jake looked at him darkly. "If that man harms one hair on the head of one person in this family, I'll damn well kill him even if it means going back to prison! And he won't die easy, because I'll shoot every joint in his body first!"

"Jake, if you mess up that leg again, it will just cost you time going after him," Brian reminded him. "Do you want to be out there within two weeks, or three or *four* weeks?"

Jake paced more. "Goddamn leg," he muttered.

"Jake, *please* sit down," Randy begged. She removed her hat and set it on a chair, then walked up to him, grasping his arm. "Sit!"

He met her gaze. "Did you set up that meeting?"

"Yes. Tomorrow morning at ten, just like you wanted. And don't you dare go there and make Peter wonder if you came to shoot him rather than talk to him. He doesn't deserve to be insulted and threatened, Jake, and the mood you're in, you're likely to do both. If you're going to be like this, I'm not going."

Jake ran a hand through his hair and walked over to plunk down on the sofa.

Jeff turned away to hide his smile. Three men in the room couldn't make Jake sit down, but his wife could.

"Jeff, you can go on back to your hotel," Jake told him. "Be back here tomorrow morning at nine, and we'll go eat before we go to Peter's office."

Jeff tipped his hat to Randy and handed the shotgun to Lloyd, glad to be rid of it. "I'll be back in the morning," he told them before leaving.

Lloyd carried the shotgun into the kitchen and unloaded the shells. "I'm just as angry about this as you are, Pa," he told Jake when he walked back into the sitting room. "But right now there isn't a whole lot we can do. The sonofabitch escaped, and for all we know, he took off for parts unknown so as not to be caught again. You did when you were wanted."

"I wasn't *after* someone. Marty Bryant is, and it's you and *me*! He'll risk being caught again just to get back at us some way, and he could go after anybody in the family."

"Maybe. All we can do is keep our eyes open, and when you're ready, we'll go out there and see what we can find out. I'll go get the Donavans and have them stay here in town with Katie so she won't be alone. And Evie has Brian. Mom can go stay with them or with Katie. If they all stay in town and don't go wandering off alone, they'll be fine while we're gone. They all know the rules."

Jake waved him off. "All right. All right. Go see to Katie. Just don't take her and Stephen out of town for a picnic or fishing or whatever. Keep them in town."

"I think I know how to protect my own family, Pa."

Jake looked up at his tall, strong son, who could use his guns as well as he could. He finally grinned a little. "Lloyd, when Stephen is a man, you'll find that you still see him as a ten-year-old boy." He rubbed at his eyes. "I'm sorry. Of course you know what to do. Go on home. We'll talk later. Brian needs to look at this damn leg, and I want him to see about your mother."

Lloyd looked at Randy. "What *is* going on?"

"I'm sure I'm fine, Lloyd. If something is wrong, I will certainly tell you. Go home to Katie. She's probably worried after learning about that telegram."

Lloyd looked her over. "You take care of yourself. I might be a grown man, but I like knowing both my parents are still around."

Randy smiled as she watched him leave. She walked over and locked the front door while Jake removed his denim pants. He rolled up the right leg of his knee-length long johns so Brian could look at the still-healing wound there.

"I still say you used more stitches than necessary just to be mean," he told Brian.

Brian felt around the wound to make sure there was no swelling underneath. "Of course I did. Doctors have a special talent for torture. Don't you know that?"

"I know it now," Jake joked with him.

"Well, this all looks pretty good, but if you don't listen to me, Jake, you'll mess up my beautiful work and be right back down in bed." He faced Jake. "If you want to get out of here and go look for Marty Bryant, you give that wound a few more days to heal up good and tight and give yourself at least another week to build up your blood or you won't last long on the trail." He looked at Randy. "Now, what's this about you having pains?"

Randy reddened a little. "I'm sure it's nothing. I've just had occasional deep pain really low." She pressed her hands at her groin area. "Almost like a woman feels when...when it's her time...only I haven't had that problem since Evie was born, because they had to remove my...you know. It embarrasses me to talk about it."

"Randy, this is me, and I love you like a mom. They removed your uterus, but I'm guessing not your ovaries."

She nodded.

Brian frowned. "Go lie down on the bed." He glanced at Jake with a look of alarm. "Get dressed," he told Jake. He walked into the bedroom to find Randy sitting on the bed. "Why didn't you mention this to me sooner?" Brian scolded.

"I thought...it might just go away and not come back."

"Well, no more secrets, all right? You're too important to all of us. And take off all your slips. I can't feel anything through all that crinoline. You can leave your dress on. I know this is hard for you. Just lie down on the bed."

Jake came inside the room. "Go hold her hand," Brian told him. "This might hurt."

Jake moved around to the other side of the bed and carefully sat down on it, taking Randy's hand. Brian knelt close and began pressing on Randy's abdomen, asking if it hurt. It didn't until he hit one particular spot. She cried out and gripped Jake's hand.

Jake watched the expression on Brian's face when he pressed the other side and got the same reaction. He didn't like what he saw in Brian's eyes. "What is it?" he demanded.

Brian straightened. "Jake, I can't touch her once and know exactly what's wrong." He leaned closer to Randy. "How long has this been going on?"

She curled up. "I'm not sure. Maybe six months."

Jake felt a black dread. "Why in hell didn't you tell me?"

"Jake, don't get upset. I just wasn't sure if it was anything important, and I don't like worrying you when you have to be out there, watching your back all the time. You have enough on your mind."

"*Worry* me? For God's sake, Randy, I've been giving you things to worry about for twenty-six years, and you don't want to give *me* something to worry about?"

"Jake, why don't you go into the kitchen and see if there is any leftover coffee you can heat up," Brian suggested. "I wouldn't mind more of that pie we had earlier today, if there is any left. I'll give Randy something she can take for pain when it's bad." He turned to Randy. "Mom, I'm not the doctor for this. I think Edward Rogers is the best to examine you more thoroughly. He specializes in these things." He glanced at Jake and spoke with a hint of sarcasm. "I just burn out and sew up knife and bullet wounds."

"You do more than that, Brian," Jake shot back. "You've done lots of surgeries."

"Not on someone as close to me as Randy. If it was Evie we were talking about, I'd send her to Rogers too. This truly isn't my usual doctoring."

"Are you saying I need surgery?" Randy asked.

Brian closed his doctor's bag. "I don't know that at all. I'm just saying someone who knows what they're talking about should examine you, that's all. It might be nothing. Either way, I can tell you're very tired. You've had a long day of cooking and running after grandkids and walking down to Peter's office, and now this news about Marty Bryant." He put some kind of powder into a glass and poured water into it from a pitcher beside the bed. "Drink this. I want you to get some sleep."

"But I have things to do."

"*Drink* it! For crying out loud, you're as bad as Jake when it comes to listening to a doctor's orders."

She sighed and sat up, drinking down the mixture and then making a face. "Tastes awful."

Brian gestured to some peppermint candy lying on the bedside table. "Eat a piece of that candy. That should help. And for heaven's sake, lie down and go to sleep." He glanced at Jake. "You shouldn't leave candy lying around. Little Jake already eats too many sweets."

Jake glanced at Randy and they smiled at each other. "Well, I happen to like peppermint," he told his son-in-law. "Sometimes you need something to freshen your breath real quick."

"Jake!" Randy put her hands over her face.

Jake walked over and pulled the covers over her. He leaned down and kissed her lightly. "Get some sleep. Big day tomorrow." He put a hand to the side of her face. "You'll be all right."

She grasped his wrist. "Stay calm, Jake. Don't leave yet."

"I won't. You'll have me around at least another week, I suppose."

She closed her eyes and Jake watched her a moment. *What would I do without you? How would I breathe?*

Scowling, he got up off the bed and walked out, going to the kitchen, afraid to look at Brian. He took the metal box that held his ammunition from the top of the icebox while Brian poured some coffee.

"You want some coffee?" Brian asked him.

"No." Jake opened the box of ammo and took out two slugs. He picked up the shotgun Lloyd had left on the kitchen table and shoved two slugs into it.

"No buckshot?" Brian asked.

"Slugs do a hell of a lot more damage if there is any distance involved," Jake answered, "and since I never miss, I don't need buckshot."

Brian rubbed the back of his neck. "I'm sure you don't."

Jake slammed the shotgun closed. "What's the verdict?"

"Set that shotgun down and look at me, Jake."

Jake hesitated, then laid the gun on the table, meeting Brian's eyes.

"I love her like my own mother, Jake. You know that."

"Talk to me like a doctor right now, Brian, not a son-in-law."

Brian turned away. "Shit."

Jake felt as though he might pass out. "Just say it, Brian."

Brian didn't answer right away.

"Jesus," Jake whispered. He got up and took a cigarette from where he kept some in a cupboard. He lit it and walked out the back door.

Brian followed him out to the back steps. He waited a moment, giving Jake time to calm down.

"Brian," Jake finally spoke up, standing with his back to his son-in-law. "Before I met Randy, I lived for a while with a prostitute who was…good to me. One day she came down with pains like what Randy is feeling. It ended up being…" He ran a hand through his hair. "Jesus," he muttered.

"Jake, are you saying it was cancer?"

"Yes!" Jake barked, turning to face him. "And it was the most goddamned awful death I ever watched! She was a good woman, and she didn't deserve to die that way! There is no way in hell I could stand back and watch my *Randy* die that way! I'd rather *shoot* her first, and then myself!" He turned away again.

"Jake, you keep in mind that it could very well *not* be cancer. You are absolutely jumping to conclusions.

She could have something on her ovaries, but that doesn't mean it's the worst."

Jake smoked quietly. "Being…intimate…would that hurt her?"

Brian sat down beside him on the steps. "No, it wouldn't make any difference. And if you're looking for some way to blame this on yourself, which you have a bad habit of doing—you had nothing to do with this one, Jake. It is what it is. Though like I said, she needs to be examined by someone who knows more about such things. I understand why you're concerned, but you have to be positive about this."

Jake walked a few feet away again. "What the hell do I do now? I have to go out there and look for Marty Bryant and serve death certificates on Jessie Buckley. I have orders. I'll have to follow those orders or risk going back to prison. Lloyd could do all that for me, but with Marty on the loose, I'm not going to let him go out there alone. How in hell do I leave my wife at a time like this?"

"Jake, what you do is the main reason your wife put off telling you about the pain. She hates for you to be distracted. So you have to think positive now. You can't consider ignoring your job, because the last thing she needs is for that judge to change his mind and put you back in prison. We won't get answers overnight anyway. I assure you that nothing dire is going to happen in the next week or two."

Jake smoked quietly, staring into the darkness.

"Jake, are you listening to me?"

"You're just telling me what you think I want to hear."

"I'm telling you straight. You're one man I wouldn't lie to, Jake. I love that woman too, and I'm going to think positive about this."

Jake stepped out the cigarette and came back to sit down on the steps. He said nothing for several quiet minutes. Brian could tell he was struggling not to break down.

He finally spoke up. "I can't live without that woman, Brian, and I can't see her in pain."

Brian sighed, wanting to weep. "Jake, if worse comes to worst, I can give Randy medicine for the pain—something to help her go peacefully. But if anything happens to both of you, it will kill Evie. My wife would never be the same, and I don't intend to lose her that way. She's a beautiful soul and she worships the ground you walk on, so don't talk about not being able to go on without Randy. Don't you *dare* do that to Evie. Randy wouldn't want that either. And as able and adept as Lloyd is now, he still needs you too. Little Jake is crazy about you, and Stephen thinks you're a hero. You have no right leaving the beautiful family that you have, so you get those thoughts out of your head. We're all here for you and for Randy. I'm a doctor. I will not let her die a horrible death. Trust me on that."

Jake cleared his throat, then swallowed. Brian ached for the man's sorrow.

"Which means you do think she could be dying," Jake said brokenly.

"I'm not going to believe it's cancer unless some other doctor tells me it is. I just think, based on her symptoms, we should hope for the best but…prepare for the worst. And I think that for her sake, you should think *only* the best when you're out there on the trail, Jake, because the last thing she needs is for you to get yourself hurt or killed because you didn't have your mind on what you're doing. You remember that no matter what this is, she'll never get better or have the *incentive* to get better if something happens to you. She's always been the strong one. Now *you* have to be strong—for her. You need to go back in there and let her wake up with you by her side. She needs you just as much as you need her. I've seen how she is when you're away, scared to death you won't come back."

Jake put his head in his hands. "What should I tell her?"

"Just what I said—that I want her to see Dr. Rogers and that she might have cysts on her ovaries that will need to be removed, but that's nothing terribly serious. Don't mention cancer."

"She's not stupid, Brian. And nobody knows me better than Randy. She'll see right through me."

"Then you're going to have to do your best to encourage her to think positively and be supportive. That's all you can do."

The faint sound of piano music coming from a saloon floated over the otherwise quiet night air.

"Do you hear that music, Brian?"

"I hear it."

"Music like that—saloons, drinking, painted women, gunplay, fistfights—all those things once represented who I was...until a slip of a woman named Miranda Hayes barged into my life. That's all it took to make me want to change it all. I never knew what love meant till I met her."

"And you should be glad you had twenty-six years of that love." Brian sighed, getting up from the steps. "I'd better get back to Evie. She's probably really worried. Promise me you'll go back inside. Just hold her the rest of the night, Jake. That's what she needs right now."

Jake grasped a railing and stood up. "Are you going to tell Evie?"

"I'm just going to tell her I want Randy to see another doctor before we jump to any conclusions. Randy will likely wake up in the morning feeling fine because of the medicine I gave her. Take this a day at a time and be grateful for the good days."

Jake turned away. "Yeah. Sure."

"Jake. I'll give you something to help you think more positive."

Jake turned. "What's that?"

"Evie is expecting again. We're going to have another baby, which means another grandchild for you and Randy. Try taking that as a good sign that things will be all right. And tell Randy. That will really brighten her day."

Jake managed a smile. "That's damn good news. You tell Evie I just hope this one doesn't run her ragged the way Little Jake does."

"Well, we're *both* hoping for that."

Jake put out his hand. "If it had been up to me, I couldn't have picked a better husband for my daughter."

Brian grasped his hand. "I suppose I could have picked a saner family to marry into, but being married to Evie makes it all worth it. She's one thing you did completely right, Jake. And she still needs her father. Do you understand what I'm telling you?"

Jake squeezed his hand. "I understand."

Brian let go of his hand. "Go on back inside and hold your wife." He gave Jake a shove. "And once she's awake, do whatever else you want to do with her. You won't hurt her."

Jake smiled sadly and watched Brian walk off. He went back inside and locked the back door, forcing himself to shake off the darkness that enveloped him. His hands moved into fists. *Don't you let her die*, he prayed angrily.

He walked into the bedroom and watched her for a moment, thinking how beautiful she looked with her honey-blond hair spread out on the pillow. He removed his shirt and pants and wiped the bottoms of his feet on a braided rug before easing into bed beside her. He moved an arm around her, and in her sleepy state, she curled against him. He quietly wept.

Seventeen

RANDY STIRRED, FEELING A BIT GROGGY. IT TOOK HER a moment to realize someone had undressed her and she wore only her flannel gown. Jake's arms were around her, and she lay with her back against him. From the slant of the light coming in from the window, she realized it was morning. "Jake?"

He pulled her closer. "I was beginning to wonder if you'd ever wake up." He kissed her behind the ear.

"My gosh. Did *you* undress me?"

"Who the hell else would have?"

She put a hand to her face. "What on earth did Brian give me?"

"I don't know, but whatever it was, you've been out like you went on a drinking binge. You even talked to me, but like a drunk woman. You don't remember?"

"No! I don't remember a thing!" She turned onto her back. "What did you do to me after you undressed me?"

He grinned, kissing her neck. "Unspeakable things. Horrible…shameful…unspeakable things. You don't even want to know. You'd never talk to me again. I'd be out in somebody's doghouse if I told you."

She pushed at him. "You did not."

"Oh, I figured I'd take advantage of the situation, and I did all the things you've always been too embarrassed to let me do. Only the worst prostitute in the worst brothel in Oklahoma would let me do such things."

Randy couldn't help a smile. "And how would you know that?"

"I've seen it all and done it all." He met her mouth in a deep kiss. "It was great."

"You'd better be lying," she told him when he moved his kisses back to her throat.

"I never lie to you. You have been properly ravished, *mi querida*. We had nothing but disrespectful sex last night."

"*Is* there such a thing?"

"You bet. I got to know things about you I never realized in twenty-six years of sleeping with you."

She laughed softly. "You're being mean."

"Mean is what I'm known for."

Randy studied his eyes and saw the hint of fear behind all the joking. "What did Brian tell you?"

His smile faded a little. "He told me it's okay to have sex with you."

Her eyes widened. "You didn't ask him about that!"

He grinned again. "Of course I did. Do you think your son-in-law doesn't know we still frolic in bed?"

"Jake, I will never be able to face him again."

"Mrs. Harkner, who are you married to?"

"Jake Harkner."

"Do you really think those closest to us don't know a man like me still enjoys women?"

"*Women?* As in plural?"

"You know what I mean."

"I'm not sure I do. Did you really just take a bath at that brothel the last time you were gone?" she teased.

"I really did."

"And who helped bathe you?"

"Me, myself, and I."

Randy grinned. "I'm not sure I believe that."

"Who loves you more than his own life?"

"You."

"And there is your answer."

"And those two years on the Outlaw Trail?"

He nuzzled her neck. "That was a very bad time, and I thought you should leave me."

"And are we headed for another bad time? Do you think you're losing me again, Jake?"

He sobered. "I think I love you now more than I ever have—ever. And I will be here for you—all of me. I will never, never hurt you."

He started to kiss her again, but she put her hand over his mouth. "What did Brian tell you? You're avoiding the answer, Jake."

He sighed and kissed her throat again. "He said he wants you to see Ed Rogers, who knows a lot more about these things than Brian does. He thinks you probably have some cysts or something on your ovaries and that they can easily be removed and you'd be fine."

She closed her eyes and thought a moment. "Did he mention cancer?"

"We aren't going to even consider that."

"Jake—"

"Don't you say that word. I mean it. You do *not* have cancer!"

She breathed deeply, fighting her own fears. "Jake, I might need you to be really strong for me. You don't know how to handle something over which you have no control, and this is something you can't hit or shoot or put in jail. You might have to find a different kind of strength, Jake."

He studied her lovingly—the golden hair that still showed no gray, the eyes that changed from gray to green depending on the light, the nearly flawless skin. "I did look at you last night, but not in a bad way. I thought how perfect you still are, a woman any man would still consider desirable. I thought how absolutely unfair it would be if the worst happened because you goddamn well don't deserve it. It should be *me*! This body has been wounded and battered and mistreated my whole life. I once drank too much, and I smoke too much, and I don't eat right, and I'm out risking my life most of the time. I never even should have survived my childhood. I've committed every sin a man can commit, and here I am still alive, and as far as I know, there isn't a damn thing wrong with me. So why should it be *you*?"

She ran her fingers through his thick hair, searching his face as if she could sense his fear. She had to know losing someone in his family, his source of love, was the only thing on earth that frightened him. "Maybe it *isn't* me, Jake. Maybe, like you said, it will turn out all right. Maybe if we make love, we can pretend nothing is wrong. Maybe we should just take a day at a time and enjoy what we have right now." She leaned up and kissed him. "And maybe I'd like to know what disrespectful sex is."

He smiled sadly. "I assure you, you *don't* want to know. You're too good and perfect and beautiful for any man to make love to you in any way but just like that— good and perfect and beautiful."

"It's always been that way with you…good…" She wrapped her arms around his neck. "And perfect…" She arched against his naked body. "And beautiful…" She moved so that he was between her legs. "And you deliberately left off my underwear, didn't you?"

"Of course I did."

He met her mouth in a groaning kiss, wanting her in a different way this time…wanting to brand her because they would see Peter later…wanting to claim her, and to tell whatever was sneaking around inside her body to go away and leave her alone…wanting to make sure he could still do this without hurting her. She didn't seem to want any foreplay. She just wanted her husband inside of her, and he wanted the same.

Nothing was going to take her from him…no man who might love her…no man who might want to hurt her just because she was Jake Harkner's wife…and no disease…nothing…nothing. He raised up on his elbows to keep his weight off of her.

"I don't want to hurt you," he whispered.

"You won't." Randy closed her eyes and sucked in her breath when he entered her. "Nothing hurts. It just feels wonderful." She arched up to him, wanting to know she was alive and still able to please this man who took so much pleasure in return and knew how to enjoy both. Sometimes this was as erotic and fulfilling as all the foreplay and all the different ways there were to do this put together…just the act itself, because it was the utmost form of sharing souls and the most satisfying way of giving and taking and branding and owning. It wasn't for wicked pleasure so much as a sensual, deep, gratifying way to express a love that nothing could destroy…two people so close to each other that they were one.

He pushed her gown up with one hand while moving his other hand under her bottom to press deeper as he tasted one breast. He didn't want to take too long, worried she'd feel pain. Before long, his life spilled into her. He pushed up the other side of her gown and kissed both breasts, her neck—and, hungrily, her mouth.

"All of a sudden I can't get enough of you," he said softly, "but you were hurting. Don't tell me you weren't."

"Jake, I—"

"We're way too connected, Randy." He kissed her eyes. "It's okay to tell me to stop."

"It's a good pain. I don't mind it. It makes me know I'm alive and with you. I wish you didn't have to leave again."

"I have to wait a good week yet."

"I'm scared for you to go this time. Marty Bryant is out there."

"You know I can damn well take care of Marty Bryant."

"And this thing with me...I'm scared, Jake. I want you with me."

"I'm right here."

"Make love to me again. We have time."

"You're in pain."

"I don't care. It's not that bad. I'm scared time might be short and we won't be able—"

He stopped her words with another kiss. "Don't say it," he told her then between more kisses. "It's not going to happen, Randy. We're going to think positive about this and realize we won't know a damn thing until you see that doctor. Things could turn out just fine. God isn't going to take away someone as good and beautiful as my wife." He reached down to guide himself into her again, moving both hands under her hips and pulling her to him.

"Who do you belong to?" he groaned next to her ear.

"Jake Harkner."

"Who?"

"*Jake Harkner.*"

"Every inch of your beautiful body." He met her mouth again, running his tongue deep while invading that sweet place no one else had touched since he took her in a covered wagon somewhere out on the plains on the way to Nevada twenty-six years and a lifetime of heartaches ago. No damn disease was going to take her away from him. He wouldn't let it. There had to be a way to fight this thing. Fighting and killing his enemies was all he knew, and whatever was wrong now, it had become his worst enemy. He would claim her and claim her and make sure that this new enemy knew she belonged only to Jake Harkner, and that *it* could not have her.

Her reaction surprised even him. She kissed him in an almost unfamiliar, wild way. She dug her nails into his back, and after several minutes they climaxed again, together. He kissed her eyes, tasted tears.

"God, Randy, don't cry. It will be okay. I know it will." He pulled her tight against him as he rolled to his side.

"You'll come back, won't you? The next time you go away, you'll come back."

"Of course I will. Why wouldn't I come back? I *always* come back."

"I just don't want to be alone for this, Jake. I'd have Katie and Evie, but that's not the same. I can't do it without you. When you leave again, you can't let this make you careless. If something happened to you now…"

He kissed her over and over. "Nothing will happen."

"But this last thing…when I thought you were dying, I felt like *I* was dying. You think you can't live without me, but I feel the same way, Jake. I feel so safe right here in your arms. Even if it's the worst and I *am* dying, I want to die right here in your arms."

"Don't!" He crushed her against him. "Don't talk that way. It's not like you to give up so easily, Randy Harkner. Brian said to think positive about this, and if I don't, I'll go insane. *You* need to be positive too." He pulled back. "Look at me, *mi querida.*"

She wiped at her tears with a shaking hand and looked at him.

"This is you and me, and we'll fight this together. My God, we've been through so much, Randy. And the way you look, so beautiful and radiant and flawless…that just tells me this isn't something ugly and life threatening. You wouldn't look so healthy and perfect. You keep telling me I need to have more faith, so that's what I'm going to do. If that God of yours brings you through this, I'll even go to church with you. How's that for a promise?"

She seemed to brighten. "You will?"

"I will."

"Oh, Jake, won't that make people turn and stare?"

He smiled for her. "I'm sure it will. The preacher will probably end up speechless and forget his sermon."

That made her smile. "That really might happen."

"This could be really interesting."

She ran a finger over his lips. "I wonder what they would all think about disrespectful sex."

"I'm sure most of them don't even know what that is."

"Well, before you and Lloyd leave again, I want to have disrespectful sex with you."

"I told you I already did that to you last night when you were acting like a wanton drunk."

"But you said you made that up."

He kissed her again. "I guess you'll never know, will you?"

"Well then, was it good?"

"It was the best I've ever had."

"Now we're back to the whores."

"At least I'm a man who knows what the best should feel like." God, how he ached for her. He'd keep her smiling. He had to keep her smiling. "And I have some news for you."

"Oh?"

"You're going to have a third grandchild."

She beamed. "Who? Katie or Evie?"

"Evie. Brian told me last night."

"Oh, I'm glad for them! They've been trying. Brian is so good to her, Jake."

"Well, now we both have something to look forward to, and all the more reason to fight this thing. I'll be right here. Let me be your strength."

"You've always been my strength. You thought I was the strong one, but I am weak without you, Jake Harkner. No woman could love a man more than I love you."

"Then you're a crazy woman, because I have to be the least lovable man on the face of the earth."

"Oh, no. You, Jake Harkner, are easy to love. You might not be easy to *live* with…but you're so easy to love."

"And I'd like to *make* love to you again, but if we don't get up and wash and dress soon, we'll never be ready when Jeff gets here."

She gasped. "Oh my gosh! What time is it?"

"I'm not sure, but I have a feeling we'd better get out of this bed."

"I could stay here all day."

"Do you think I wouldn't enjoy that? I don't know how many years I have left before I'm too old for this."

"*You?* I have trouble picturing you too old for this. That gives me all the more reason to live long enough to see if that's possible."

Their gazes held, each pulling strength from the other. "Thanks to your demanding sexual needs forcing me to ravish you half the night, I'm very hungry now," Jake told her. "Let's go have breakfast, Mrs. Harkner."

She frowned. "Please tell me you really did make all that up."

He got up. "No, ma'am. I'll just let you always wonder."

Randy put her hands over her face. "Oh my God."

Eighteen

JEFF WALKED BEHIND JAKE AND RANDY, WATCHING and listening as numerous townspeople stopped Jake and asked how he was doing. It was the pied piper all over again, people following him down the street, some close, some at a distance.

The morning was cool, and Jake wore his wide-brimmed hat and a duster over denim pants and a blue shirt with the leather vest, his badge hidden under the duster. He wore both of those famous guns and kept an arm around Randy as they walked.

"Jake! By God, other than needing to gain a little weight, you're looking well!" The greeting came from the same man who'd urged Jake to come into church that Sunday morning Jeff sat on the steps.

"He shouldn't be up walking around, Cletus," Randy answered as Jake shook the man's hand.

"Well, I'm glad he's trying," Cletus answered.

Jake thanked him as more people commented on his health.

Jake kept insisting he was fine, but he walked with a limp that suggested a good deal of pain. Jeff sensed something else—something amiss. Maybe it was just the fact that Marty Bryant was on the loose again… or maybe the fact that they were going to see Peter Brown…or maybe something Jeff didn't know about.

All the way to the restaurant, more people followed, both men and women, asking questions, greeting Jake and Randy both. For several days after the shoot-out, the

Guthrie newspaper had been filled with different versions
of the event, some making Jake out to be an emotionless
murderer who killed men as easily as shooting a rabbit.
Jeff decided that was probably true when it came to
men threatening his family. Some stories showed Jake as
the hero of the day, saving the entire town of Guthrie
from peril and tragedy. When papers arrived from other
towns, stories of the shoot-out were in those too, some
grossly exaggerated.

Jeff had also read stories about Marty Bryant's escape
and the murders that took place. Rumors abounded over
where Bryant might be now and what his intentions were.

They went inside a restaurant called Sadie's and sat
down at a table. A woman of perhaps twenty waited on
them. "Glad to see you're all right, Jake," she said, leaning a bit too far over to pour his coffee. One too many
buttons were open on her blouse. After pouring his
coffee, she turned to Randy, giving her a look that told
Randy the girl thought she could seduce Jake anytime
she wanted. "Coffee, Mrs. Harkner?"

Randy, who Jeff thought looked incredibly beautiful this morning in a soft green dress and a matching
velvet hat that drew the green from her eyes, smiled
kindly to her. "Why don't you just pour some coffee
for Jeff here, Mary Ann. You can first pour it down
your blouse, and then you can lean over even farther
than you just did for my husband and let it spill out of
your cleavage into his cup."

Jeff could not control his laughter at the remark, and
Mary Ann straightened and lost her smile. "I'll get you
a cup," she told Jeff, turning and walking away with a
deliberate flounce.

Jeff glanced at Jake, who was obviously struggling
not to laugh out loud. Finally Jake couldn't help a soft
burst of laughter. "Randy, your jealousy is as green as
that dress," he told her.

Randy removed her gloves, eyeing her husband with a sly grin of her own. "The girl couldn't have been more obvious. She might as well have stripped right in front of you."

"I'm sure Jeff wouldn't have objected." Jeff and Jake both laughed again. "And you think *I'm* the mean one?" Jake added to Jeff. "Get this woman's dander up and watch the claws come out. She can handle a rifle and handle *me*. That says a lot."

A different waitress came out then with an extra two cups, one for Randy and one for Jeff. She was slightly older and smiled with genuine friendliness. "Mary Ann says she doesn't want to wait on you anymore. What did you say to that girl, Jake?"

She poured the coffee.

"Right away you blame *me*?"

"Well, I know how you can be with words at times, Jake Harkner," Sadie joked. "I also just happened to see her waiting on you."

"Then you'd better ask what my *wife* said to her." Jake was still grinning and Jeff nearly spit out his first sip of coffee in a need to laugh more.

Sadie gave Randy a sly grin. "I think I have a good idea. And I told Mary Ann to button up that blouse or go home. I don't need my waitresses flaunting themselves around like saloon girls."

Jake removed his duster and let it fall over the back of his wooden chair. "Sadie, you tell Mary Ann that if she wants to flaunt something, have her come back out here and flaunt it in front of Jeff. He's the one who needs a woman. I already have one."

Jeff laughed again as Jake introduced him.

"Sadie, this is Jeff Trubridge, and he's going to write a book about me. What do you think of that?"

Sadie studied Jeff a moment. "You want to write a book about that worthless, no-good outlaw?"

"Yes, ma'am."

"Well, you'd do better writing about his beautiful wife. *She's* got some stories to tell, I'm sure of that. I'll bet she could tell you things that would curl your toes."

Jeff nodded. "I'm sure she could, Sadie. I wouldn't think of writing about Jake without including the woman who has stood by him all these years."

"Well, thank you, Jeff," Randy told him.

"Stood by him?" Sadie frowned. "Have you really *looked* at the man? What woman wouldn't stand by *that*? *I* wouldn't have had any trouble doing it. And that son of his is even *better* looking."

Jake picked up his coffee cup. "Sadie, you're worse than that waitress of yours."

"Yeah? Well, if anything ever happened to this wife of yours, half the women in this town would be showing up at your door with food and anything else you need, and you know it."

Jeff noticed Jake sobered a little too much at the remark. "Well, let's hope that doesn't happen any-time soon, because I'd just as soon keep the woman I've got."

Then Jeff remembered Jake's remark about Randy having some unusual pain of late. Brian was supposed to come and see her yesterday. Had they learned something new?

Sadie laughed and touched Jeff's shoulder. "Mr. Trubridge, you look like a nice young man who just might do a fine job of writing that book. You just be fair about it. Jake isn't as bad as some folks say, and not as bad as *he* pretends to be. Otherwise this beautiful woman with him wouldn't have stuck it out so long, handsome or not."

"I already figured that out," Jeff told her.

"Jeff's breakfast is on me, Sadie," Jake spoke up.

"Jake, you don't have to—"

"Sure I do. I'd be dead if you hadn't warned me those men were waiting for me inside that jail."

"You mean you saved that no-good's life?" Sadie asked Jeff.

Jeff shrugged. "In a way, I guess."

"Well then, your breakfast is on *me*," Sadie told Jeff, patting his shoulder. "What will it be?"

They gave their orders. While they waited, more well-wishers came forward, including Juan, who came inside with a heavyset Mexican woman on his arm.

"Jake!" He walked over and shook Jake's hand, rattling off a conversation in Spanish. Juan's wife reached out to Randy and Randy grasped her hand.

"*Señora*, Jake will be all right now, *sí*?"

"*Sí*, Rosa."

"I am glad. Juan, he thinks Jake walks on water, you know?"

Randy squeezed her hand. "Oh, I can assure you, he *doesn't*." Both women laughed. "Juan is a good friend," Randy added.

"*Sí, señora*."

Their food arrived. Juan and his wife sat down at the table next to them, and Jeff watched the interaction between Jake and a few more townspeople who greeted him as they arrived at the restaurant.

More people like the man than he'll admit, he noted. As intimidating and vicious as he'd been that first day Jeff saw him, as well as the day of the shooting, Jake was now affable and relaxed. They were nearly finished and getting ready to pay when everything changed.

The door opened, and a big man with a beard and a shotgun walked inside. He wore a floppy hat and a wool coat, and he walked right up to Jake's table. Everyone in the restaurant quieted and Jeff lost his smile. The big man nodded to Randy.

"Mrs. Harkner."

Randy looked up at him, and Jeff caught the disdain and dread in her countenance. "Good morning, Hash." She looked at Jake, definite worry in her eyes.

Jeff swallowed. He had a pretty good idea this man was related to the Buckleys or the Bryants. The man turned his attention to Jake.

"Jake," he said in a near growl. "Jessie Buckley sent me to fetch Brad for her." He said the words slowly, deliberately. "I'm told he's got to go home in a wagon because he still can't stand up—on account of you practically killing him all them days ago when you brung in Marty and Jack and the others. You know by now that Marty Bryant escaped, and you can bet you'll pay now for what you've done to both families."

Jake stayed right where he was, glancing at Randy with a look that told her to stay calm. "Those who died deserved what they got, Hash, especially in the shoot-out that took place later." The handsome smile was gone and the darker Jake began to show himself.

"My son didn't deserve to be kicked out of the jail and thrown into that prison wagon the way I'm told he was. Lloyd had no right abusin' him like that."

Jake leaned back, studying his coffee cup. "My son makes his own choices. I wasn't there."

Hash backed up a little, still holding his shotgun but not pointed at anything. "You wasn't there because you was wounded. I hope it was one of *my* boys who did it—one of my poor, *dead* boys!"

Jake sighed. "Hash, why don't you just take Brad home to his family and lay low for a while…till you cool off a little?"

Hash just watched him a moment, as though contemplating what he'd do next. "I'm thinkin' that if you're wounded, this might be a good time to beat the shit out of you, Harkner."

People whispered. One couple got up and left.

"Might be," Jake answered. "I don't doubt you'd have an easy time of it, the condition I'm in right now. Then again, you might be surprised. You saw what happened to Brad, and he's heftier and a whole lot younger than I am. It all depends on how upset I am, Hash, and right now I'm real upset about a *lot* of things." He rose. "Including the fact that your worthless third son helped kill innocent men escaping from that prison wagon and that you probably know where he is."

"I don't know nothin' about it. And you're a lowdown, murderin' bastard, Harkner! Everybody knows it. They smile to your face, but they know you've got no right wearin' a badge. Wasn't long ago you was on the *other* side of a badge, rottin' in prison for robbery, rape, and murder!"

Everyone froze. Jeff had no idea why, but he felt compelled to reach over and take Randy's hand. He was surprised at how hard she gripped it when he did so.

Jake remained casual and chewed on a toothpick as he spoke. "Hash, there are other people in this restaurant, including women and children, who don't need to hear your trash talk. Why don't you just go home?"

Hash Bryant raised the shotgun.

Jake rested his right hand on his gun. "Don't even think about it, Hash," he warned. "Not in here. I don't intend to make a mess of Sadie's restaurant. She's a nice lady."

The restaurant became so silent, Jeff could hear water boiling somewhere. He noticed Randy close her eyes. Her grip on his hand was beginning to hurt.

"I'm thinkin' that when I beat you within an inch of your life, Harkner, I want it to be when you're healed up. A man can't brag about beatin' on somebody who's wounded."

Jake folded his arms. "Well, that's very gentlemanly

of you, Hash. I didn't know the Bryants had a sense of honor, considering what your sons did to that fifteen-year-old girl they holed up with after robbing that bank. I've done pretty much everything people say I've done, but I've never abused a woman, Hash. And after what I saw out there when I arrested your boys, I have no problem with my son abusing *your* son, as you put it."

Hash squinted his eyes, never moving from Jake's gaze. "I've lost *two* sons on account of you! *Two!* Ted and Gordy both, and both by your gun! I'd say that requires some payback. *Your* son is still *livin'*!"

Juan muttered something in Spanish. Jake just glared at Hash Bryant, keeping his arms folded. Jeff had a feeling that if it weren't for his leg, Jake would launch into Hash Bryant right now and drag him out into the street.

"I'd suggest that once you leave town with Brad, you *stay* out of town, Hash. It would be best if I didn't see your face again, understand? If I see you in town anytime soon, I'll throw you in jail just for *being* here."

The water kept boiling, and Jeff could hear a clock ticking on the wall behind him.

"This ain't over, Harkner."

"Maybe not. But your wife has lost two sons because they were thieves and rapists. I'm sure she mourns them anyway, but don't add losing her husband to the picture. Go home and *stay* there. Make any more trouble, and I'll come after every damn one of you. And if anyone in my family gets hurt, I'll kill every last Buckley and Bryant who are left."

Hash Bryant looked around at others in the restaurant. "You hear that? A lawman who executes his prisoners." He turned back to Jake. "Maybe that's somethin' my Marty is willin' to risk."

Jake stiffened even more. "Where is he, Hash? Where is Marty?"

"I got no idea."

"The hell you don't! I'll find him, and if I find you with him, you'll die right along with your son! It would go easier on you if you owned up right now where I can find Marty."

"Find him *yourself*, Harkner," Hash sneered. He glanced sidelong at Randy. "And keep your family in town where it's safer while you're at it."

Jake stormed toward him and ripped the shotgun right out of his hand. "Get out, Hash! You are truly pushing your luck. I am real tempted to change my mind about not leaving body parts all over this restaurant!"

The look in Jake's eyes was enough to make a snake crawl back into its hole.

Hash Bryant backed up. "I'll go, but only because I aim to have it out with you when you're healthy, so's people know who the better man *really* is."

"Fine with me, as long as it's face-to-face and not behind my *back*!"

Jeff heard footsteps on the boardwalk then, someone running. Lloyd came charging through the door.

"Stay there!" Jake ordered. "It's all right."

Hash turned to glance at Lloyd. "Well now, ain't it nice how loyal the son is to the father."

"Pa isn't healed yet, Hash, and there are innocent people in this restaurant, including my *mother*!" Lloyd seethed.

Hash turned his gaze back to Jake. "Oh, I'll leave for now. I'm savin' your pa for when he's better, so's I can rightfully beat the life out of him. I might not be able to take him in a gunfight, boy, or you either...but I damn well can take him another way." He glanced at Randy. "There's plenty of ways to take a man down without a gun." He turned and walked to the door. Lloyd stood in his way.

"Let him leave, Lloyd," Jake told him. "The sooner he's out of my sight, the better."

Reluctantly, Lloyd stepped aside.

"Ain't you just the lovin' son?" Hash sneered at Lloyd before walking out.

Jeff felt Jake's rage. It filled the room.

Jake turned and pulled some money from his pocket and threw it on the table. "Let's go." He took his hat from where he'd laid it on an extra chair and put it on.

"Jake, maybe this isn't a good time to go see Peter," Randy objected, still clinging to Jeff's hand.

"There will never *be* a good time, so let's go before I go after Hash Bryant and bleed to death beating the hell out of him!" He headed for the door, still holding Hash's shotgun. Lloyd followed him out.

Randy finally let go of Jeff's hand. She pulled on her gloves and rose.

Juan grasped her arm. "*Señora*, it is all right. That Hash Bryant, he is a bad *hombre*. Everybody in here, they understand that."

Randy nodded. "His being a bad *hombre* is what worries me." They left the restaurant. Outside, Jake was leaning against a porch post lighting a cigarette while Lloyd paced angrily.

"If I'd known he came into town this morning, I never would have let him look you up, Pa!"

"I know that. I just had better not see his face in town again anytime soon."

"Maybe you'd better go back home and cool down a little," Lloyd suggested.

"No! I have more to talk to Peter Brown about than Jeff's book or a trust fund. I'll be fine."

"You're not fine at all, Pa! I know you. You're so damn mad, you want to hit something, or better yet, go after Hash Bryant. Go home before you open that wound up all over again or do something to get you fired and thrown back into prison."

Jake pushed back his hat and rubbed at his eyes. "I'm

not canceling this appointment. What are you doing here, anyway?"

"I couldn't sleep because of Marty Bryant's escape... and I'm worried about Mom." He glanced at his mother, who remained silent. "I got dressed and went down to the jail and found out Hash had been there, and came looking for you."

A few people came out of the restaurant, moving away from Jake, knowing what he was like when angry. Juan, however, walked right up to him.

"*Señor, Dios se encarga de todas las cosas. Él los protegerá a usted y su familia. Confía en él, señor.*"

Jake nodded and seemed calmer.

Lloyd walked closer to Jake. "What *did* Brian say? Is Mom all right?"

Jake glanced at Randy. "She just might need some surgery, that's all. She'll be fine."

Lloyd looked at his mother. "He's lying, isn't he?"

Jeff just stood there listening in wonder and worry.

"We don't know for sure, Lloyd. I have to see Dr. Rogers first."

Lloyd suddenly looked like a lost little boy.

"Go talk to Brian," Jake told him. "He'll explain."

Lloyd kept watching Randy. "Mom?"

"I'll be all right, Lloyd. Your father is right. Go talk to Brian."

"How long have you been sick?"

"Lloyd, it's most likely something that can be fixed."

Lloyd looked back at Jake. "I'm here for both of you. You know that."

Jake nodded. "I know."

"So is Evie. You keep that in mind. I mean if—"

"Don't say it," Jake warned. "Everything will work out. Let's take one thing at a time. Right now I have an appointment with Peter, so you go do whatever you have to do, and we'll talk later."

Lloyd turned to his mother again. He seemed to be at a terrible loss to know what to say or do. He walked up to her and embraced her. "You get yourself well. I don't want to have to deal with that sonofabitch of a husband of yours if something happens to you."

"I'm sure I'll get better, Lloyd. Do what your father says and just go take care of whatever you need to do today. Jake will be fine."

Lloyd pulled away, glancing at Jake again.

"Go on. We'll talk later." He handed Lloyd Hash's shotgun. "This belongs to Hash. Unload it before you give it to him. I'd prefer it if you just aimed it at him and gave him both barrels, but we have to obey the goddamn law!" He turned to Jeff as Lloyd took the shotgun. "I left my duster in there. Go get it for me, would you? This leg is starting to give me some real pain."

"Sure, Jake." Jeff went back inside to retrieve Jake's coat.

A frustrated Lloyd glanced at Jake once more. "This thing with the Bryants and Buckleys won't end anytime soon, will it?"

Their gazes held. "Probably not. But there is nothing we can do about it today other than make sure Hash leaves with Brad. Go make sure that happens, and remember you're a lawman, Lloyd."

"Yeah. Sure."

Lloyd reluctantly left, and Jake sighed, moving beside Randy and putting an arm about her waist. "Come on. Let's keep that appointment with Peter."

"Be nice."

"I will."

Jeff hurried out after them to see Jake suddenly lift his wife with one arm and carry her across an alley.

"Jake Harkner, put me down! You'll break that leg open."

"My leg is fine." They reached the next boardwalk, and Jake leaned down to give his wife a quick kiss.

You don't fool me, Jake, Jeff thought. *You just don't want your wife to worry. You've got plans for Hash Bryant. Or maybe you're just worried that Hash Bryant has plans for you...or your family.*

He followed them to Peter Brown's office.

Nineteen

JEFF FELT SWEAT BREAKING OUT UNDER HIS SHIRT AS they entered Peter Brown's office. Suddenly his tweed jacket and silk vest seemed too warm in spite of the morning's chill. He entered first to see the very dapper Peter Brown sitting behind his desk, his slightly gray hair perfectly combed, his suit obviously well cut and expensive, his blue eyes fixed on Randy when she entered. The man rose to greet all three of them and put out his hand to Jake.

"Jake, it's good to see you up and walking around."

Jake shook his hand. Jeff watched. A firm handshake, but not the painful one Jake had given Brown after church that first Sunday. "Still a lot of pain, but I'll survive."

"A little laudanum should help. Surely your son-in-law can give you some."

"No, thanks. I don't drink around my wife, and laudanum is even worse. It's just whiskey mixed with opium. I don't intend to find out what *that* mix might do to me. I'm mean enough sober." He glanced at Randy. "Is *that* what Brian gave you last night?"

Randy gave him a warning look but grinned at the same time. "Stop it."

They both laughed lightly, and it was obvious to Jeff they were sharing a very personal joke. He turned his attention to Peter, who watched the two of them with a painful sadness.

"I told your wife we could put this off a few more days," Peter told Jake. "I'm not that busy this week, and I'm guessing you really shouldn't be walking on that leg yet."

"Convincing Jake to stop doing something he shouldn't do is like talking to a wall," Randy commented. "We have a grandson who also does not like to be told no."

Peter looked back at Jake, and Jeff could feel the tension between the two men. "Yes, well, that stubborn little grandson created quite a ruckus…when? It's been over three weeks, I think. You made all the local headlines, Jake, and by now you've probably been featured in stories in newspapers in a lot of other towns, probably even other states. I'm glad you and Little Jake are all right. I mean that. Seeing that kid out in the street had to be awful for you."

"Thanks for your concern," Jake answered, a hint of sarcasm in the remark. "Little Jake is apparently aptly named. He's stubborn and determined." Jake turned to Jeff. "Peter, this is Jeff Trubridge," he added, "the reporter from Chicago."

Peter put out his hand and Jeff shook it.

"Actually, I met Jeff right after the shooting," Peter told Jake. He looked Jake over. "I didn't come on the scene until after the fact, but I saw a tremendous amount of blood still in the street."

Jake removed his hat. "Yeah, well, of all the wounds I've experienced, this one really put me down. It was the loss of blood that nearly did me in this time."

Peter glanced at Randy again. "I think it nearly did your wife in too."

Jake shifted, and Jeff suspected he was holding back an urge to tell Peter Brown not to be so concerned about his wife. "I'm aware of what it did to my wife," he answered. "That's part of the reason I'm here, but we'll get to that later. Right now I want to discuss the book this kid here wants to write. In the short time I've known him, I've grown to like him a lot. I think he'll try to do an honest job of it, which is why I'm letting him follow me around like a damn shadow. This book needs to be from hands-on experience and personal stories, not hearsay. The only way to do that is to let Jeff talk to me and my family. I'm even taking him along the next time Lloyd and I ride out on our rounds."

Peter glanced at Jeff. "Well now, Jeff, *that* will likely be an experience you won't forget. I hope you know how to ride a horse and shoot a gun. You seem like more of a city kid to me. We're both from Chicago, and I know not many men from there ride horseback and carry guns anymore."

Jeff loosened the top button of his shirt. "I *am* a city kid, but I do know how to ride. As far as a gun—well, you saw me the day of the shooting holding Jake's guns. That's the first time I've even touched one. I'm sure Jake can teach me a few things when we head out."

Peter laughed lightly. "Well now, that's an understatement, isn't it?" He glanced at Jake. "You couldn't ask for a better teacher, Jeff, when it comes to using firearms."

"No, sir," Jeff told him, watching the hint of challenge between Jake and Peter. He thought about what a powerful presence Jake was, the way he just filled up a room the minute he stepped into it. A commanding aura seemed to hover around the man. He knew Peter felt it too.

Peter surprised Jeff then with his next statement. "Jake is the best there is when it comes to using those guns." He glanced at Jeff again. "And he's a good man, Jeff, despite some of the things you hear. If he wasn't, you'd see it in his wife's eyes, and she undoubtedly has eyes for only one man. If Jake was all the things others say he is, I doubt an educated, intelligent woman like Randy would still be with him." He'd moved his gaze to Randy on that remark, then looked at Jake. "Put that in your book, Jeff," he said, his eyes still holding Jake's gaze.

Jeff felt perspiration on his forehead. "I've already taken note of that, Mr. Brown. Mrs. Harkner is the strongest, most devoted woman I've ever met."

Peter took up a legal pad and an ink pen. "That she is," he commented, scribbling something on the pad.

"And both of you are embarrassing me," Randy put in, reaching over and grasping Jake's hand.

Jeff wondered if she was afraid Jake would explode into words he shouldn't, but he said nothing. He just kept watching Peter Brown carefully.

"Well now, let's get down to why you're here," Peter told them. "Jake and Randy, you want some kind of agreement with Jeff that indicates you have the last say in whether this book even gets published, right?"

"That's right," Jake told him. He shifted again, wincing with pain. Jeff suspected he was really struggling to keep his mouth shut in front of Randy. "I want to make sure he doesn't exaggerate like they do in those damn dime novels. I'm just a man, like any other, who's a federal marshal because a judge forced him into it. Anything is better than prison, which is where I'd still be otherwise."

Peter kept writing. "You underestimate yourself, Jake."

Jake rubbed at his eyes. "I guess that's something for others to decide after I'm long gone, which I expect will happen sooner than later, with guns blazing."

Peter kept his attention on the tablet. "I'm sure you want this book to justify why you did some of the things you did—"

"No. My past *can't* be justified. It can be explained, but it can't be excused or made right. A man makes his choices, and I made a lot of wrong ones. There's no changing that. I was raised among whores and outlaws, and that's all I knew. Maybe Jeff can explain how it all came about when he writes this book. The fact remains I have a family and grandchildren now who I'd prefer remembered me for the kind of father and grandfather I am. When I'm dead and gone, I don't want my tombstone to say 'Here lies Jake Harkner, notorious outlaw.' I just want it to say 'a good husband and father.'"

Jeff took out his own notebook and began scribbling. Peter looked up from what he'd been writing and held Jake's gaze. He slowly nodded. "And that's what you are." He glanced at Randy, then cleared his throat and looked back at his notes. "I take it you want a trust set up that includes future grandchildren? After all, your son just took a new wife. And your daughter might not be through having children either."

"That's right. Fact is, Evie is carrying again," Jake told him. "This book might not even sell that many copies, but if it does, I don't want any of the proceeds from it. I want it all to go to my grandchildren." Jake shifted again, rubbing at the back of his neck and, Jeff thought, still holding back. "God knows I don't have much else to leave them, other than knowing they carry my blood and will have to live with that—let alone the fact that they carry my *father's* blood. Maybe I got lucky and got rid of most of his blood when I almost bled to death after that last shoot-out."

Randy closed her eyes and grasped his hand again. "Jake, don't go there. Please don't go there."

Jeff could see Jake growing very restless.

"Jake, let's stay with why you're here," Peter told him.

Jake kept hold of Randy's hand. "I just want the truth told."

Peter kept his eyes on the tablet, as though almost afraid to look at Randy again. "Well, let's begin with full names—you, your children, and your grandchildren."

"Jackson Lloyd Harkner and Miranda Sue Harkner,"

Randy answered. "You don't need my maiden name or my first husband's name, do you?"

"No."

"There was a first husband?" Jeff asked, surprised.

"Yes," Randy answered. "He was killed in the Civil War. I was only eighteen. I was married at seventeen, and we had all of two weeks together before he left and never came back." She met Jake's eyes. "I've been terrified ever since that the same thing will happen with Jake. He'll go riding off into No Man's Land and never come back."

Jake shifted yet again. "As long as I know you're here waiting, I'll always come back."

Peter kept writing. "Full names of children and grand-children?" he asked.

"Evita Louise Harkner Stewart," Randy answered again. "Lloyd's full name is Lloyd Jackson Harkner, a reverse of Jake's name. Lloyd's little boy's name is Stephen Lloyd. Evie's little imp is Jackson Lloyd Harkner, like his grandfather."

"In more ways than name," Jake added.

"Dates of birth?"

Randy rattled off all the dates, until she got to Jake's birth date. She looked at Jake. He became very quiet. Peter glanced at him.

"I don't know," he told Peter. "My birthday isn't exactly something that my"—he stopped as though something was stuck in his throat—"my parents... celebrated. I'm sure my mother would have liked to, but she, uh..." He shifted again. "I only know how old she *said* I was. Not long before she"—he cleared his throat, still clinging to Randy's hand—"died, she said I was eight. And for the record, her name was *Evita Ramona Consuella de Jimenez*."

"Jake," Randy said softly, "you're hurting my hand."

He quickly let go. "Jesus," he murmured.

Peter leaned back and rubbed at his temple. "So how old are you now?"

Jake just sat there.

"Jake?" Peter frowned.

"My mother died in 1844. The day she and my little brother"—he cleared his throat—"died...I wrote the year on a piece of paper, and my age. I was eight."

"You had a brother?" Peter asked.

"Mmm-hmm." Jake almost groaned the answer.

"And they both died at the same time?"

"Yes," Jake answered emphatically. "I watched them die. Now let's move on to something else."

The room hung silent. Peter closed his eyes and leaned back in his chair. Jeff waited with bated breath.

"Jake," Randy spoke up softly. "You never told me about any note."

Jake cleared his throat again, straightening and taking a deep breath. "Yeah, well, now you know. I've carried it with me for forty-eight years." Jeff was astounded to see tears in Jake's eyes.

Peter started writing again. "Well then, we'll just make up a birth date and figure the year to be 1836. Surely there are records of your birth. Texas, wasn't it? I have your mother's name, although you'll have to spell it out for me. I'm not fluent in Spanish."

Randy grasped Jake's hand again and he spelled his mother's name for Peter.

"Thanks." He looked at Jake. "Now, if I know the town where you think you were born, and your father's full name—"

"No!" Jake barked. "You make up a date and leave it at that. I don't want my father's name mentioned in *any* way. Not in *any* way! Not in those papers and not in Jeff's book. If his name has to be mentioned, then I'm not doing this at all!"

Peter set down the ink pen and leaned forward. "Jake,

although I am risking you putting a gun to my head for asking, I have to ask it." He paused, weighing his words and swallowing before speaking. "How do you expect Jeff to write this book if he can't settle for once and for all what happened to your father? It's the one thing that hangs over your head...the one question everybody wonders about but is afraid to ask, as I am sure *Jeff* is afraid to ask. The book won't be complete until you clarify that one thing from your past. If that isn't settled, the book won't tell the whole story, and your grandchildren will never understand that part of their grandfather."

Jeff wanted to crawl under the man's desk. Jake sat glaring at Peter, his dark eyes smoldering. The tension inside the small room could have been cut with a knife, and Peter kept a steady eye on Jake. Randy let out a little groan and looked away. Jeff wondered if Jake was going to speak at all, or if maybe he'd just pull a gun any minute and shoot Peter Brown.

"You know I'm right, Jake," Peter told him. "This is man-to-man. I sincerely am not trying to upset you, and God knows I don't like upsetting your wife. I know I'm asking the forbidden question, but you really need to understand that all the other truths about you will do no good if that one little matter isn't cleared up. Everyone knows you killed your own father, but no one knows *why*. The why is all that's necessary to the truth, and you said that's what you want this book to be—the truth."

"The truth is I killed him, plain and simple," Jake nearly shouted. "And for a *damn* good reason! *I'll* be the one to decide if and when I tell Jeff all of it, so right now just let it go!"

The words were spoken with such wrath that Peter literally backed up his chair. Jeff froze in place. He wanted to make notes but was afraid to even move his hand. Peter's secretary tapped on the office door.

"Is everything all right in there, Mr. Brown?"

Peter watched Jake, who glared back at him. "*Is* everything all right, Jake?"

"Jake, you're hurting my hand again," Randy told him.

Again he let go. Randy got up and went to stand behind him, putting her hands on his shoulders. "Everything is fine, Nancy," she called to Peter's secretary.

"If you say so, Mrs. Harkner."

Randy pressed her fingers into Jake's shoulders. "I say so."

Unbelievable, Jeff thought. *If she can control that man when he's like this, she could probably walk into a cage full of tigers and make them all lie down.*

Jake closed his eyes and breathed deeply. He reached up and grasped one of Randy's hands. "Sit down," he told her.

"After you apologize for yelling at Peter. Your past isn't his fault, Jake. He's just doing his job, and you're the one who asked for this meeting."

Jake squeezed her hand. "Sit down, Randy."

She sighed deeply and took her chair. Jake ran a hand through his hair and leaned forward, resting his elbows on his knees. He clasped his hands behind his head, squeezing them together so tight that Jeff noticed his knuckles turn white.

"I'll make a deal with you, Peter. If you can accomplish the other thing I came here for, I'll tell you my father's name and you can do all the research you want. And I had already considered having to tell Jeff…what happened…and owning up to my grandchildren. It's just…I feel like it's no one's goddamn business…but I know I can't die with it either, because then no one will ever know the truth."

"Randy knows," Peter said. "I can tell by the look on her face. And I'll bet Lloyd knows too, doesn't he? But they love you so much that if you tell them never to speak of it, they won't."

"Lloyd doesn't know his full name." Jake stared at the hardwood floor. "Only Randy knows all of it, because I owed her that. For some ungodly reason, she chose to spend her life with me. Before I could let her do that, she needed to know all of it so she could be damn sure she really wanted to live with a wanted man with a madman's blood in him." He took a deep breath, still staring at the floor. "Suffice it to say for now, I was fifteen and...I had no choice."

The room hung silent for what seemed hours.

Jake finally straightened, a dark, intimidating look in his eyes. "I am having a lot of trouble not coming across that desk right now and putting my hands around your throat, Peter, but for my wife's sake, I won't. Besides that, you don't deserve it for asking what you have a right to ask, and for that I do apologize. Maybe I can get you the name later."

Peter nodded. "You don't need to apologize. It's something that's hard to talk about, and I sure as hell don't blame you."

"I had a run-in with Hash Bryant this morning that didn't go too well, and my wife isn't well, and I'm not real happy about coming to you of all people for help—and we both know why *that* is—so combine all of it together, and this is the best job I've ever done of controlling my temper."

"Jake—"

"He knows what I'm talking about, Randy, and so do you."

Jeff still sat frozen in place.

Peter sighed, resting his elbows on his desk and putting his head in his hands. "Jake, please explain then why you *did* come to me. Guthrie is growing by leaps and bounds, and there are at least fifteen or more other lawyers in this town. The only thing growing faster is the number of saloons."

Jake remained quiet again for a moment. "I came to you because I trust you with this. I trust you because whatever you do, it won't be for me. It will be for Randy, because I firmly believe you care about her happiness over your own feelings. Because of *that*, I'm trusting you to try your best to do something else for me...for *us*...Randy and me."

Peter glanced at Randy, who blinked back tears and looked at her lap.

"What is it you want, Jake?" Peter asked.

Jake took a deep breath and cleared his throat. "You know that I'm a federal marshal because a judge *sentenced* me to it, but most federal marshals aren't married men. When I was given this job, I didn't take into consideration how hard it would be on my wife and family, let alone the danger they'd be in for even being related to me. It's bad enough being Jake Harkner, but when you're a United States Marshal, you make a lot of new enemies—something I sure as hell *don't* need. This thing that happened a couple of weeks ago was extra hard on Randy, and my little grandson could have been killed. Lloyd is only doing this because he's a devoted son who insists on staying by my side out of loyalty. I know he'd rather be doing something else, and he has the money to buy a ranch or whatever else he'd like to do. Looking death in the face practically every day is not exactly a fun way to live, Peter, and we're both only human. Someday the right bullet will hit the right spot and that will be the end of it. It almost happened this last time. If Jeff hadn't gotten to that jail before me and warned me he saw Bryant and his men go inside, I'd already be a dead man."

"What are you getting at, Jake?" Randy asked.

Jake glanced sidelong at her, then turned away and rubbed the back of his neck, obviously still very tense. "You and I were happiest those years back when I had that ranch in Colorado, before all hell broke loose and I landed in prison." He faced Peter again. "We loved it there. I want to go back. I want to take Randy to some little mountain town where no one gives a damn who I am and there is hardly any crime. I want to lie in bed with my wife till noon, if we want, with no goddamn reason to get up. I'm in a lot more pain from old wounds than even Randy knows, and I refuse any kind of painkiller because they are all mostly whiskey. I can face ten men with guns, but I'm scared to death that if I drink, I'll end up an alcoholic—the rotten, *mean* kind, like…" He didn't finish. "And I'm damn tired of never being able to step outside the door without wearing guns and wondering when some bastard's stray bullet meant for me will end up hurting or killing someone I love. I want to build us a cabin in the foothills and raise horses again. And on the side, I can clean and repair guns and even customize them for people. I customized my own .44s to shoot smoother and faster."

Randy appeared a bit stunned. Jeff could tell she'd had no idea Jake had been thinking about these things.

Peter finally spoke up. "Jake, what does all this have to do with me?"

"I want you, or some lawyer you know who's good at criminal justice, to petition the judge in St. Louis who sentenced me and ask if my sentence can be reduced. He gave me five years. I've already served close to two. I want to ask for the sentence to be reduced from five years to three. I want to take my whole family and get out of this goddamned, dusty, lawless hellhole of a territory and hang up my guns for good. The only firearms I want to use are my rifle or my shotgun for hunting. I want the whole family to come with us. Randy and I will be buried there, and Lloyd and Evie will take over, and someday they'll lie beside us, and then the grandkids will take over. I want that grave site on a hill under a great big tree, and it will be beautiful and green and peaceful. I want peaceful, Peter—a peaceful life. Will you do that for Randy? She deserves to have some peace at last."

"Jake, I'm fine."

"No, you *aren't* fine. God knows you've had enough stress in your life to kill you off, and now this. Maybe knowing there is light at the end of this tunnel will help you fight whatever is wrong now."

Peter looked at Randy with obvious love and concern. "That's the second time Jake has mentioned something being wrong, Randy. What is it? Is it serious?"

"I…no. I mean, I don't know. It's personal." She looked at Jake. "Jake, you never told me all this before."

Jake sighed and ran a hand through his hair. "You've put up with enough. You've been through too many years of hell, thanks to me."

"I've been loved like most women *wish* they were loved!" Randy answered sternly. "I've been treasured and respected and adored. I've been given two beautiful children and two wonderful, loving grandsons. *You* did that!"

Jake reached for a cigarette from a pocket inside his vest. "I did a *lot* of things."

"Jake, where is all this coming from?"

"You *know* where it's coming from. But this thing about moving to Colorado is something I thought about long before we found out you could be…" He hesitated. "Jesus," he muttered, stopping to light the cigarette.

"Randy?" Peter asked.

"Look, she needs surgery for something that could be cancer," Jake told him. "We won't really know until she sees Ed Rogers."

Peter closed his eyes. "Oh, for God's sake." He leaned back in his chair again. "I'm damn sorry. Damn sorry— for *both* of you. I know what you share, and neither of you deserves this."

Jake looked at Peter as he took his first drag on the cigarette. "Do you think there's a chance I could get this marshal job over with sooner?"

Peter still watched Randy with great concern. He moved his gaze to Jake, and Jeff could see the continuing challenge there. "I can try. I know that you were cleared of what you went to prison for, so what's the excuse the judge used to sentence you to this in the first place? Why didn't he just set you free?"

Jake smoked quietly for a moment. "You name it, I've done it," he finally answered. "Except for abusing women. That never happened. But just the fact that I rode with the Kennedy bunch and they robbed and murdered and they kidnapped and raped a woman once was enough to put me away for life. The judge felt that because I'd gone unpunished for all the other crimes I'd committed, I should still serve some time, but he also saw an opportunity to fill the need for federal marshals in the West. It's a lousy job most men don't want. Since I'd turned my life around and had a family, the judge decided I should be free, but that I should still do time, so he sentenced me to something that would let me be with my family but still use my expertise with guns—for good instead of bad. He figured since I once ran with outlaws, I'd know how to track down the same kind of men."

"Well, he was certainly right about that, wasn't he?" Peter wrote on his tablet again. "Who's the judge?"

"Robert Mitchell. He's in St. Louis."

Peter made a few more notes. "I'll get the paperwork done for the book and the trust, but I'll see about petitioning for a lesser sentence first. That's more important." He glanced at Randy, who was quietly crying. "Are you all right, Randy?"

She nodded. "I just…didn't know Jake was thinking about this. I don't want to get my hopes up about Colorado."

"Giving you some peace is *all* I think about," Jake told Randy. He sighed deeply. "Are we done here?" he asked Peter.

Jeff glanced at Peter, who watched them a moment with obvious pain in his eyes. "I think so—for now. Go ahead and take Randy home. In fact, there is a buggy tied outside with a pinto horse rigged to it. It's mine. I'm leaving soon for a meeting with some people outside of town. Have Jeff use it to drive you two back to your house. It's five blocks away and you need to get off that leg, and your wife needs some rest. Jeff can take you home and bring the buggy back to me."

"Thank you, Peter," Randy said softly, wiping at her eyes.

Jake nodded to him. "I appreciate anything you can do about the sentence. If it means paying a higher fine, I'll pay it. I still have money in a bank in Denver from when I raised horses in Colorado. We used some of it to help support Randy and Evie when I went to prison, but there is enough left to make a new start, and Lloyd has quite a bit of his own money. I know he'll help pay the fine if necessary. And he'll want to go to Colorado with us."

"I'll do my best," Peter told Jake. "I have a few connections that might help."

"Thanks for whatever you can do for Randy."

Peter folded his arms. "Believe it or not, part of me wants to do it for you too, Jake."

Jake looked him over. "I'll let myself believe that, and I thank you for trying. We'll wait to hear from you. Lloyd and I have to head out on rounds in a week or so, and I don't want Randy working for you while I'm gone."

"Jake—" Randy started to protest.

"I'm not saying that to be rude." Jake kept his eyes on Peter. "No offense, but it's because I want Randy to rest and spend time with Evie and Katie and the grandsons."

Peter nodded. "I understand. I have no problem with her taking care of herself. I just hope things turn out for the better rather than worse."

Jake drew on the cigarette and put it out in the ashtray on Peter's desk. "Yeah. Well, I can't live without her, so it *has* to turn out for the better." He rose and took Randy's arm, moving his own arm around her as she walked around her chair to join him. She thanked Peter again and left with Jake.

Jeff looked at Peter Brown. "Do you need anything more from me?" He actually felt sorry for the man. Peter looked devastated, and Jeff realized that helping Jake get out of being a federal marshal so he could move back to Colorado meant Peter would never see Randy Harkner again, something that had to hurt. But the man would do it—for Randy—which showed Jeff just how much Peter loved her. And hearing she was sick had apparently hit him hard.

Peter cleared his throat and straightened, trying to hide his feelings. "You drive those two home first. Then you can come back and give me the particulars on yourself. See if you can get Randy to write down Jake's father's full name and bring it to me. I have no doubt she knows what it is but was afraid to say it out here today."

"Sure." Jeff started out, but Peter called to him. "What do you know about Randy's health…this…surgery she might need?"

Jeff shook his head. "I just heard about it myself this morning. I don't know the details."

Peter frowned. "I know Ed Rogers pretty well. Maybe I can learn something from him."

"Maybe. I'm sick about it myself, Mr. Brown. She's a wonderful woman."

"She certainly is. In all his years of living the outlaw life, Jake struck pure gold when he met Randy. Nothing he ever stole or earned can match what he found in her."

"I have no doubt he is completely aware of that, sir. I think she's real worried about what he would do if he lost her. So is Lloyd."

Peter rubbed at his eyes. "I understand Jake Harkner more than you know, Jeff, and that's the hell of it. The man loves as passionately as he hates, and there is no competing with him." He looked at Jeff sadly. "Do you know what I'm talking about?"

Jeff nodded. "I think I do, sir."

"Yes, well, it's just kind of understood. It's just... there...a fact that I can't deny, and Jake damn well knows it. He has every right to put a gun to my head for thinking like I do, but out of respect for Randy, he won't do that—although I can't be real sure of that if I step over the line. Which I would never do anyway, because I know it's hopeless, plus I respect Randy too much." He eyed Jeff directly. "That's between you and me, not something for that book of yours."

"Yes, sir."

"Go on now and take them home."

"Yes, sir." Jeff walked out, his head spinning with all the angles he could use for his book. This was turning into a far more complex project than he'd dreamed it would be. A love story. A story of the outlaw way. A story about what could cause a young boy to kill his own father. A story of tragedy and triumph and gunfights and secret feelings and stashes of money and everything that made a damn good book.

He hurried out and climbed into the two-seater buggy Peter had told them to use. Jake sat in the backseat with his arm around Randy, who rested her head on his shoulder. Jeff got the horse moving and headed for Jake's house. On the way, they passed a flatbed wagon going the other way. Hash Bryant was driving it, and Brad Buckley lay in the back of the wagon. Hash looked darkly at Jake as the two vehicles passed each other.

No, this thing with the Buckleys and the Bryants is not over, Jeff thought. He glanced at Randy. She had closed her eyes and apparently didn't notice Hash Bryant, but Jake...Jake did.

Twenty

"I DON'T KNOW WHAT TO DO, KATIE. EVERYTHING IS a mess."

Katie curled up against Lloyd, kissing his cheek. "I wish I knew what to tell you. Brian said we have to think positive about this."

Lloyd stroked her hair. "Dr. Rogers verified what Brian figured. She's got some kind of growth. And he isn't even sure he or any doctor in Guthrie can operate on her, so now she and Pa have to decide what to do next. He has to head out the day after tomorrow, so it will have to wait. And that scares all of us, because we don't know how long is *too* long to wait. Dr. Rogers said it's best to operate soon to have a chance of getting it all."

They'd decided to lie in bed together after sending Stephen off to school, knowing they had only today and tomorrow before Lloyd had to leave again.

"I'd go alone this time so Pa can be with my mother, but if the judge finds out he's not doing his job—"

"Lloyd, surely the judge would understand."

"Maybe, but with Pa asking for a reduced sentence, he can't take any chances, and with Marty Bryant out there somewhere with a new bunch of men behind him, Pa would never send me out there without him, and I'm not letting him go without *me*. And with Evie carrying and having to watch after Little Jake, Brian doesn't want to leave her, plus she's had a lot of morning sickness this time, so she's been pretty tired and weak."

"Could there be a doctor in Edmond who could operate? That's not so terribly far, and if you and Jake get back soon enough, Jake could take her there."

"Brian and Ed Rogers are looking into it." Lloyd sighed and pressed her closer. "It isn't just my mother or the timing. It's my pa. I know him, Katie, and I don't even want to think about what he'll be like if my mother dies. If that happens, I'll actually lose *both* of them, because there will be no reaching my father."

Katie kissed him softly. "Whatever happens, I'm here, Lloyd."

Lloyd pulled her close, relishing the feel of her nakedness, the sweet warmth of having just made love. "I wish I didn't have to leave you, Katie. While I'm gone I want you to stay close to town at all times, understand? Your parents will be here tomorrow to stay awhile so you won't have to be alone. Once Pa and I find Marty Bryant, we can relax more."

"How long will you be gone this time?"

"It's hard to say. Some of it will be routine. We do have to serve Jessie Buckley those death certificates and see if we can find out anything about the whereabouts of Marty Bryant. The paperwork is piling up, and if the judge thinks Pa is shirking his duties, he might not even consider a reduced sentence."

"I'd love to move to Colorado with you and get away from all this. I thought I could handle it better than this, but I'm already wondering how long I can live this way."

There it was—the little wedge that kept trying to come between them. Katie was having a hard time accepting the situation, but then, so many unexpected things had come up since they married. It had been difficult to settle into any kind of normal routine. Most women didn't have to worry about their husbands facing constant violence, but Lloyd was having trouble with Katie always being afraid. Something was still amiss.

Deep down Lloyd felt as though she wanted him to choose her…or his father. Beth would never have asked that of him, but then Beth understood better all that had happened after Jake went to prison. She'd been through the worst of it with Lloyd and fully understood his reasons for always wanting to be close to Jake.

He still missed Beth, and he felt so guilty for it. He couldn't blame Katie for that.

"Katie, when I get back I'll tell you all of it—the truth about Pa's past, all right? He doesn't just love me like any normal father loves his kid. He *needs* me. There is a fine line there, between sanity and just…going crazy. That's why I'm so concerned about him losing my mother. She's the anchor that keeps him from drifting away to a really bad place."

"I want to understand, Lloyd…all of it."

"And you have a right to know, so it doesn't keep coming between us." Lloyd stroked her hair. "I promise things will get better once we find Marty Bryant and end all this…and once we move to Colorado." He moved on top of her, kissing her lightly, then stiffened when someone knocked at the door. "*Damn*," he grumbled.

"I knew we shouldn't do this in the middle of the morning!" Katie lamented.

Lloyd moved off the bed and pulled the covers over her. "Stay there." He quickly pulled on a pair of long johns.

The knock came again and he yelled out, "Just a minute!" He grabbed his denim pants and yanked them on. "Whoever it is, I'll tell them you don't feel well. Maybe it's just Pa or my mother." He hurriedly buttoned his pants and grabbed a shirt and started pulling it on as he hurried out and closed the door. "Who is it?" he called.

"Lloyd, it's me—Brian. I have someone with me."

"Jesus God Almighty," Lloyd grumbled. He ran his hands through his disheveled hair and pushed it behind his ears. Evie had recently told him he was starting to look like an Indian, but Katie liked it long and he hated sitting for haircuts, so he just kept letting it grow. He opened the door, his shirt open and his feet bare. He frowned when he saw Peter Brown standing there with Brian.

"I'm sorry, Lloyd, but we need to talk to you," Brian told him.

Lloyd shook his hair back again and stepped aside. "Come in." He closed the door after them. "Come into the kitchen. Katie isn't feeling well and I don't want to bother her."

Brian and Peter followed him into the kitchen.

"Sit down," Lloyd told them. "There is still some coffee on the stove. Either one of you want any?" He poured himself a cup.

"No, thanks," Brian told him. "I'm really sorry to bother you. I know you and Jake have to leave day after tomorrow."

"It's all right." Lloyd set his cup on the table and then took a tin of Lone Jack cigarettes from the top of a cupboard. He took out a cigarette and lit it with a stove match.

"What's going on?" Lloyd asked as he turned a kitchen chair around and straddled it, leaning forward on the chair back.

Brian glanced at Peter, then back to Lloyd. "We just want your opinion about something. Don't fly off the handle. Just listen. If you love your mother, you'll agree we need to do this."

Lloyd stiffened. "Do what?"

Brian rubbed the back of his neck.

"Peter here knows of an excellent surgeon in Oklahoma City. He talked to Ed Rogers about him, and Ed agreed that if your mother has cancer, this man is the best there is. And Peter has to go to Oklahoma City on business. He also knows a lawyer there who would be willing to go on to St. Louis to petition Jake's judge for a reduced sentence. So—"

"He wants to take my mom *with* him to Oklahoma City?" Lloyd immediately stood up. "This is my *dad* we're talking about! Do you really think Jake Harkner is going to let a man who's in love with his wife take her that far away? *Alone?*"

"Lloyd, *think* about it! This can't be put off without possibly endangering your mother's *life*—more each day! Who better to go with her than someone who loves her just as much as your father does?"

The remark brought fire to Lloyd's eyes. He rose, fists clenched. "Did you hear what you just said?"

"Lloyd, you know I'd never suggest this if I didn't love Randy just as much as you do," Brian told him boldly.

"*Nobody* loves my mother as much as *Pa* loves her!"

The room hung silent as Peter laid a long sheet of paper on the table, filled with signatures. "Look at this. I've been going around town for days gathering signatures on this petition. It says your father deserves to have his sentence reduced because of his outstanding service and because he has a family and this is endangering their lives. The petition says he's a good citizen and well liked. I worded it myself, and I've been working night and day on this. I have three hundred signatures, Lloyd. Three *hundred*. That should show you how much I respect Jake and how much a lot of people in this town respect him. I'm doing everything I can to get that reprieve. I want the judge to see this. This should show you my good intentions."

Lloyd studied the signatures, stunned by how many there were. "*You* did this?"

"I thought it would help."

Lloyd turned away. "You want this for my mom, not my dad."

"So what if he does?" Brian asked. "Peter completely respects Randy and what she would want and what *Jake* would want. Do you want Randy to risk surgery for something this important with a doctor who's not totally qualified to do it? Don't you want her to have the best? Wouldn't *Jake* want that?"

Lloyd paced and smoked. "Jesus," he muttered. "I was just telling Katie how torn I am about everything that's going on, and now this! You should have gone straight to Pa, not to me. I'll not be a part of something that he might think is some kind of betrayal."

Peter closed his eyes and sighed. "Lloyd, if you don't want to feel like you're going behind his back, I'll talk to him alone about this."

"*Alone?*" Lloyd shook his head. "Pa isn't exactly in the *best* mood he's ever been in. I won't *let* you go over there alone, because I need to be there to stop him from doing something he shouldn't." He looked at Brian. "Does Evie know about this?"

"Not yet, but she'll want what's best for her mother. You know that."

Lloyd turned away, taking a deep breath. "I appreciate that petition, Peter. I just hate the *real* reason you're doing this."

"Believe it or not, Lloyd, I really want this for your father too."

Lloyd rubbed anxiously at his forehead. "Let me go over there first. For all we know, my parents are—" He turned away. "I just want to make sure they're open to company. We can't just go barging in on them with something like this." He finished buttoning his shirt. "Let me go talk to Katie and finish dressing. Brian, you take Peter back to your house. I'll come and get you once I know it's okay, but I'm warning you, Peter, that you might need my brother-in-law's doctoring when this is over."

"I might need a doctor myself," Brian quipped.

Lloyd smiled sadly and walked out of the kitchen and into the bedroom. "Shit," he grumbled. He did not relish going to Jake Harkner and telling him another man, who was in love with his wife, wanted to take her away for a good two weeks or more…maybe to die…in that man's arms instead of his father's.

Twenty-one

JAKE FINISHED SHOVING CARTRIDGES INTO HIS EXTRA ammunition belt as he watched Randy dry a dish and put it into the cupboard. "I meant it when I said I want you to get help for everything," he told her. "No hard work while I'm gone."

"I know."

"Especially laundry. I don't want you lifting those heavy baskets. You have the laundry service come and pick up our things and deliver them when they're finished. And you stay with Katie or Evie—not alone."

"I will."

"I'll get back as fast as I can."

"Then what? Ed Rogers isn't sure he should operate on me himself, so what do we do? And how long do we wait?"

Jake set the cartridge belt on the table and sighed. "Damn it!" He rose. "We're getting short with each other, and we never do that. I hate this mess we're in."

"Do you think I don't?"

"If it weren't for me and this goddamn job, we wouldn't have these decisions to make."

Randy faced him. "Jake, will you ever stop cussing? And you have to stop blaming yourself for everything that happens. This isn't something you can fix with fists or guns. And you're being short because you have to leave." She turned away. "And I'm being short because I'm scared and I don't want you to go."

He walked up behind her, wrapping his arms around her from behind. "Then I'll stay."

"You can't. I won't let you risk the judge's decision, Jake."

Someone knocked on the back door.

"Who is it?" Jake barked, picking up one of his guns from the kitchen table.

"Lloyd. We need to talk, Pa."

Scowling, Jake opened the door. He set his gun on the table as Lloyd stepped inside and glanced at his mother, who clearly looked upset. She wore a simple housedress and her hair was down, as though she'd dressed quickly in case of company. Jake wore an open shirt. "Is this a bad time?"

"Right now there is no such thing as a *good* time." Jake turned away and Lloyd glanced at the array of weapons and cartridge belts on the kitchen table. "Pa, Brian wants to talk to you and Mom...and Peter Brown is with him."

Jake and Randy looked at each other, then at Lloyd. "About what?" Jake asked.

Lloyd glanced at the guns again, wondering if he should take all of them out of the house first. "I'll let them tell you. I had nothing to do with any of it, except that I agree with them on one thing." He saw the suspicion move into Jake's eyes. "I think you should...listen to what they have to say and I think you should...uh...let this be Mom's decision, not mine or Evie's or Brian's or...even yours. It's her life hanging in the balance, and we all want her to live and be healthy and...that's all that matters."

Jake took a cigarette from a tin on the counter but didn't light it. "What the hell is going on, Lloyd?"

"I'll go tell them to come over." Lloyd put on a look of warning. "You just remember, Pa, that Peter Brown is going to do his best to get your sentence reduced, and that Brian loves Mom like his own mother, plus he's a doctor and he knows what might be best for her...and he's Evie's husband and has been as good to her as you could ask of any man who dared to marry your daughter. So don't you say anything to hurt him."

Lloyd left and Jake looked at Randy. "Do you know what he's talking about?"

"No." She touched her hair. "Jake, my hair is down and I…good Lord, do we look like we just got out of bed?"

"So what if we do? We're married and we've been doing this for twenty-six years." He scowled. "Trouble is, after twenty-six years, something's come between us—and I don't know what the *hell* it is!"

Randy's eyes teared. "The only thing between us is your anger over not knowing what to do about me, and that makes me feel responsible, but I'm *not* responsible, because I didn't ask for this. Please don't stay angry—not when we only have one more day together. You usually leave your anger outside the door, Jake."

He sighed. "I'm just angry at myself." He walked up behind her and grasped some of her hair. "I was okay until Ed Rogers said he didn't want to operate on you. That's when I really started getting scared."

She hung her head.

Jake reached around and grasped the side of her face, making her turn around. He leaned down and met her mouth in a kiss that grew desperate. He pulled her into his arms, then lifted her off her feet and set her on the counter, where the kiss lingered. She wrapped her legs around him, and he wound his fingers more deeply into her hair. He left her mouth and wrapped her tightly into his arms, letting her head rest against his chest.

"I'm sorry," he repeated. "I never get short with you, and you sure as hell don't deserve it right now. I'm angry at whatever is wrong with you, *mi querida*, not at you—angry at myself for not being able to do something about it."

"I know. I just don't want you to *stay* angry—not

when we have so little time together." She reached around his neck. "After they leave, I want to go back to bed, Jake. I want to say good-bye like I always do before you go."

Someone knocked on the front door then, and Jake gave her a quick kiss. "Damn."

"We might as well see what they want, Jake."

Jake lifted her down and Randy put her hands to her face to cool her cheeks. She ran her fingers through her hair and wished she'd had time to pin her hair properly and put on a better dress. "Button your shirt," she told Jake.

He picked up his cigarette and bent down to light it at the stove. "Let them think what they want. We're man and wife and can do what we want in our own house."

"Jake, hear them out. Please, please, hear them out. Apparently Brian and Peter have some idea that might help us through this."

Jake walked to the front door and Randy quietly followed, standing at a window with arms folded, feeling undressed and undone and defensive. Jake opened the door to Lloyd, Brian, and Peter. Randy noticed Peter look Jake over with more than a little trepidation. Then he glanced at her and nodded. Jake moved back and told them all to sit down.

"I'll stand, Pa," Lloyd said, moving closer to Jake. Randy knew immediately that her son was making ready to light into his father and hold him back if he lost his temper. She felt her heart pounding harder.

Jake watched Peter carefully. Neither he nor Brian sat down either. In fact, they both looked as if they were making ready to run if necessary. "What's this about?" Jake asked.

Lloyd moved a little closer.

Peter took a deep breath. "Jake, I know of a doctor who is an expert in the kind of surgery Randy needs. He saved my wife's life once in Chicago, years before she died in a buggy accident. I wired him there and found out he's now in Oklahoma City."

Jake watched him closely. "I'm sorry about your wife, Peter, but what's all this got to do with Randy?"

Peter stiffened. "I have to go to Oklahoma City on business, and that's where a lawyer friend of mine has his office. He's agreed to plead your case in St. Louis because he knows that judge. While I'm there, Randy could see this doctor, if you'll allow it, and if she needs surgery, she could have it there."

Jake just stood there, silent, smoking, staring at Peter. The room hung thick with Jake Harkner's presence. Lloyd watched him closely, not sure exactly what was going through his father's mind.

"Let me get this straight," Jake finally spoke up slowly. "You're suggesting that you take my wife with you to Oklahoma City, you make decisions *I* should be making about her health... *You*, a man who's in love with my *wife*, want to take her away alone for a good two or three weeks, depending on how the surgery goes."

Randy turned away. The fact that Peter Brown loved her had never been put into words until now.

Peter didn't flinch. "Yes."

Jake glared at him. "You must either be very brave or very stupid...or maybe very smart. Don't be thinking I'm some kind of goddamn fool, Peter!"

"*Jake!*" Brian spoke up. "*Think* about it. It could save her *life*! Would I lie to you about something like that? Clara Donavan could go with Randy, but she needs a *man* to go with her—someone who can protect her better than a woman could—someone who can help make the proper legal decisions if she's too sick to. No one can do a better job of making sure everything is handled right than someone like Peter—and he *cares*, Jake, enough to make sure she gets only the best doctor and the best aftercare. He's someone who would look after her with the same concern as—"

"As her own *husband*?" Jake turned away. He glanced at Randy, who continued to avoid facing any of them. He turned back to Peter. "You're someone who can *protect* her? How do you propose to do that?"

"I have a handgun, more than one, in fact, and I know how to use them, Jake. I'm no damned Jake Harkner, but if I have to use a gun to defend Randy, I'll do it."

Lloyd could almost hear thunder in the room. He thought that if looks could kill, the one Jake was giving Peter Brown right now would land the man flat on his back. "And what if she has this surgery…and she's dying and needs someone to *hold* her? I'm sure you'll gladly do *that* too, won't you, Peter Brown?"

Randy remained turned away, not saying a word.

"Pa, this is *Mom* we're talking about," Lloyd reminded him. "She worships the ground you walk on. She'd never look twice at any other man, and you *damn* well know it!"

"She'll be in pain and vulnerable and needing *me*! *Me*! And I can't *be* there for her! And just maybe after all the other times she's needed me and I couldn't be there for her, she'll finally get tired of it and decide to be with someone who *can* always be there for her!"

"Use your head, Jake!" Peter shot back. "Yes, at the risk of you lighting into me, I *do* love Randy. And that's the best reason in the world to let me help her! Help *both* of you! I'll protect her with my goddamn life, and I'll make sure she gets the absolute best care possible— and yes, if she needs holding, I'll by God *hold* her so she's not scared and alone, and you know what? It sure as hell won't be *me* holding her. In her mind, it will be *you*! And no, I'm not stupid, and I sure as hell don't take *you* for a fool. I take Jake Harkner *very* seriously, believe me! Standing in front of you right now, admitting I love your wife, isn't the easiest thing I've ever done, and I'm sweating like hell under this suit at the thought of what you'd like to do to me. I have a feeling that if you tried, even Lloyd wouldn't be able to stop you!"

"Stop it!" Randy suddenly yelled, putting her hands to the sides of her face. "Does anyone care what *I* think of this?"

All four men looked at her. Randy rested her gaze on Jake. "I want to do it."

Lloyd thought Jake looked like he'd just been slapped.

"Jake, when you're gone, I go crazy with worry. This will keep me occupied. And if this means I can have the best care, then that's what I want. I want to come home to my grandbabies and the new one on the way. I want to come home to my son and daughter. And I want to come home, healthy and alive, to my *husband*, and hope he'll be here waiting, and that he'll *also* be healthy and alive…and maybe I'll be able to tell him we're going to Colorado in another year and all this will *end*."

"Pa, Peter has been pounding the boardwalks for days circulating a petition saying you deserve to have your sentence shortened," Lloyd spoke up. "That you've done an outstanding job and that people here think you have paid your dues. He got three hundred signatures, Pa. Three *hundred*! Does that sound like a man who would turn around and betray you? That petition will go a long way toward influencing Judge Mitchell."

Randy covered her mouth in surprise. "Peter! Three hundred signatures?"

Peter kept his eyes on Jake. "Yes. That's how much people in this town care about you, Jake. If you think only your immediate family cares, you're wrong. A *lot* of people care. And a lot of people see through that badge and those guns and your ability to shoot men down with seemingly no feeling, and they see the kind of father and husband and grandfather you are. A lot of people know what you've been through, Jake, and most have a damn good suspicion you had reason to kill—"

Both men never took their eyes from each other during the entire conversation.

"My father?"

Peter closed his eyes then and finally turned away.

"Jake." Randy finally got his attention again. "Three hundred signatures. Peter is your friend, Jake, not your enemy. I've been trying to tell you that." Her voice broke on the last words and she looked ready to pass out. Jake walked up to her and picked her up in his arms. "All of you get out," he told the others. "Just get out and let us talk about this."

Lloyd moved toward Brian and Peter. "Come on. He's right. They should talk about this alone."

Jake and Peter shared a look like two men in a duel before Peter turned away and followed Brian out the door. Lloyd hesitated, eyeing his parents. "I want her to live, Pa, and you do too. I think she should go to Oklahoma City and soon. There really isn't any other choice, is there?"

Lloyd left, quietly closing the door. Jake carried Randy into the bedroom, kicking the door shut and laying her on the bed. He crawled over her and lay down beside her, realizing already that their best and only hope was to do exactly as Peter had suggested. He hated having to admit it. He wanted to think that Randy was right about Peter having nothing but good intentions, but his heart raged with fury over the fact that the man was in love with her...truly in love with her.

They lay there stiffly until Randy took his hand. "Jake, you are always asking me who I belong to. How do I always answer?"

He sighed. "Jake Harkner."

"And as you would put it—you bet your ass."

He continued to just lie there quietly for several more

long seconds. "Why do I feel so far away from you, Randy? I can't stand it."

She lay across him, resting her head on his chest. "You feel far away because you're letting that little boy inside of you run off…far, far away where he can't be hurt. He's scared he *will* be hurt, so he's trying to keep his feelings at a distance and pretend it doesn't matter."

His arms came around her. "I'm scared to feel anything, because it's like getting stabbed in the heart over and over." He rolled her onto her back and moved a leg over her. "*I* should be there to hold you. You went through having Evie all alone, and then that surgery afterward. You've gone through so many things alone."

"I was never alone, Jake. I felt you with me constantly, even those two years you spent in Wyoming while I stayed in California. I knew it wouldn't last, that I was in your mind and heart every minute, and that you'd come back. When you finally found that job in Colorado and sent for me, I was never so happy, and I never asked you about those two years because all that mattered was that we were together again. And that's how I feel about this. I know I'll be all right, and I'll come back and we'll be together again. Even if someone else holds me, it will be you, Jake. It will always be you. Always and always, Jake Harkner. How can you even *consider* it could be any other way?"

He grasped her hair and searched her mouth almost violently. She closed her eyes as he whispered in her ear in Spanish, and she could felt a wetness on her cheek from his tears.

"We have to do this, Jake," she groaned. "I don't want this wall between us. I don't want to go away from you without feeling you inside of me and knowing who owns me and who will be right there with me. I won't be afraid if we do this now and again and again before you go."

"I might hurt you. That's the reason I couldn't make love to you earlier."

"I'm fine today, Jake. Maybe it's just Brian's medicine, but I'm having no pain. I want this, Jake. We both know that this time, more than all others, it's important. Make love to me in the way only you can, because you know everything I love. You made me want you all those years ago in that wagon, and I've wanted you with the same passion ever since."

Somehow their clothes were off again, and the barrier that had been between them melted away so that there was only a wild taking and giving and taking again. He was the outlaw who'd taken her in that wagon years ago and made damn sure she knew who owned her. He moved over her body with hungry desire, tasting every part of her as though he had to remember every private place that belonged only to Jake Harkner. His fingers explored and claimed her depths and brought her to a wicked climax that made her cry out his name and grasp his hair, returning his kisses with wanton desire as he pinned her arms over her head and buried himself deep, with a fierce determination to make sure she knew who was claiming her. He meant to brand her in places no other man would ever touch.

They finished making love…talked…made decisions…made love again. The second time he took her, he asked the inevitable question.

"Who do you belong to?"

"Jake Harkner."

"Who owns this body?"

"Jake Harkner."

He devoured her mouth again with an insatiable need to make sure he remembered how she smelled, how she tasted, how she felt against his fingers, how it felt to be inside this woman who gave him life and a reason for being.

"Are you all right? Please tell me if you're in pain."

"I'm not in pain, Jake—truly." She arched against him, glorying in the fact that this was still so incredibly pleasurable after all their years together. She doubted many men knew all the right moves the way this one did. He rocked her with a gentle rhythm, rubbing against that most pleasant spot, which brought her to another climax. "Don't stop yet," she groaned. "Please don't stop yet."

His kisses again grew hot and demanding as strong arms wrapped her close and his chest pressed against her breasts. She loved it when he took complete control of her. She felt ravished and fulfilled and adored. He kept up the erotic rhythm in a way that made her feel as though she was in an almost constant climax, until finally he could hold back no longer himself. He wilted against her then, damp body against damp body.

"You sure you're okay?" he finally asked.

"I doubt many men can be as forceful yet gentle as you can, my darling husband. I'm fine at the moment."

"That felt so goddamn good, Randy."

"The feeling is mutual."

Jake raised up slightly and kissed her once more. "I'm here to please."

"And you're so good at it."

That brought a grin, but he soon lost his smile and moved off of her, keeping her close. "Don't be afraid, Randy. You know how badly I want to be there for you. And I *will* be there…in spirit. Tell me you'll feel me with you."

"Of course I will. I've always felt you with me when we're apart. I'm not afraid any more, Jake. I'm only afraid for *you* because this might distract you. Please don't let it. You have to come back to me, or I won't care if I come out of this alive or dead. And please don't ever let anything come between us—ever—ever. I hate feeling far away from you when you're here even more than when you're gone."

Jake hated the thought that they had only one more day before they would be separated by a good fifty miles, her to the world of a bigger city and the terror of surgery and a big hospital, with another man who loved her. What if she died and it was Peter Brown who held her in his arms as her life slipped away? It should be him. It should be Jake Harkner. He'd make sure it was…in her mind and in her heart, even though he would be riding off into backcountry with only the ground for his bed and a saddle for a pillow, no cities, not much of anything. Their little house would sit empty this time, the two of them so far apart.

"Do not forsake me, *mi querida esposa*, just as I will never forsake you."

She grasped his hand and kissed it. "Never. I would *never* forsake you."

Twenty-two

RANDY WOKE TO SEE JAKE ALREADY DRESSED. HER PAIN had returned tenfold. All yesterday afternoon and last night, she'd been plagued with it. Now she'd ended up oversleeping from the medication Brian had given her. In a bit of a daze she watched Jake. He was already wearing his gun belt, with a third gun tucked in a holster behind his back and his extra belt of cartridges hung on a hook nearby. He pulled on his leather vest with his badge pinned to it, then picked up his duster and hat.

"Jake Harkner, if I didn't know who you were, I'd be terrified of you. You look like you're ready for an army."

He glanced at her. "There just might *be* something close to an army at the Buckleys or the Bryants, maybe both. I have to take death certificates to Jessie Buckley for her husband and son, both of whom *I* killed, so it will be no picnic. That woman is as formidable as a man."

"Well, if you want to look intimidating, you've done a good job. You'll probably scare your own grandchildren away."

Jake grinned. "Not Little Jake. He'll probably walk up to me and want to touch 'Gampa's guns.' That little devil is the only child I've ever known who truly tempts me to smack his little butt."

"That will be the day."

Jake walked over to her and knelt beside the bed. "You were sleeping so well and you need it so much that I didn't want to wake you until the last minute."

"Well, it's a good thing you intended to wake me.

If you'd left without doing that, I'd never forgive you." She reached out and touched his face. "You're still such a handsome man. I have to say this is how I like you best— guns and badge and looking mean—which is funny, because only I know how *not* mean you are."

He grinned. "I know a few men who would argue that. And you're talking like you're a little drunk."

"And did we do…terrible, disrespectful things…last night?"

Jake's heart ached at her slurred words. "Not this time. We just held each other." He leaned in and kissed her. "Peter Brown is sitting in the porch chair out front," he told her then. "I don't like leaving you in bed and half-drunk with him around," he teased.

She grinned. "He's not my Jake."

"Well, just for insurance, Evie is out there in the sitting room to make sure that man doesn't come in here. She'll help you get dressed."

"Oh, Jake, he wouldn't…and *I* wouldn't… You stop thinking like that. Kiss me again."

He sat on the edge of the bed and gently pulled her into his arms, kissing her softly. "Who do you belong to?" he asked, nuzzling her neck.

"Jake Harkner."

"You bet your ass. *Yo te amo, mi querida.*"

"Tell me this won't be the last time you hold me."

"It won't. You'll come back…and I'll come back… and we'll both be alive and well, and this nightmare will be over."

"It will, Jake. I know it will." She put her arms around his neck. "Hold me another minute. This is the one thing I miss most when you're gone—these arms around me. I feel so safe when you're holding me."

"They're around you, Randy, even when I'm not here." He held her tightly, hating to leave her. "God, I love you."

"I love you more."

With great reluctance Jake let go of her, caressing her hair for a moment before getting up. "I have to go."

"I should have made you breakfast. I always make you breakfast before you leave."

"It's all right. Lloyd and Jeff will probably want to eat anyway. We'll stop at Sadie's."

"To watch Mary Ann pour coffee?"

Jake grinned. "Right out of her cleavage."

"Don't you dare."

"I'll be thinking of *your* cleavage," he joked. Then he sobered, needing to leave, but just standing there watching her. "I meant my promise the other day, Randy. If you come home fine and well, I'll go to church. God might take that as a bribe, and I guess maybe it is, but it's a promise."

"Be careful what you say, Jake. He'll take you up on it."

"That's fine with me if it means having my wife back."

He still just stood there.

"Go, Jake. It has to happen and we can't stop it, so please just go, because I can't stand lying here watching you and wanting to hold you and wanting to beg you to stay. Just go."

He closed his eyes and sighed, then turned and took the extra cartridge belts from the hook. He walked out, wiping at a tear he didn't want her to see. Evie met him in the parlor, reaching out for an embrace.

"She'll be okay, Daddy. I know she will."

"She was in a lot of pain yesterday. Help her get dressed, Evie. I don't want Peter seeing her this way, and she wouldn't want it either."

"I know. And I'll help her pack for her trip." She hugged him once more. "Oh, Daddy, I'll hate having both of you gone! That's never happened before."

"And it won't happen again, baby girl." Jake touched her face. "How are you feeling?"

"A little better. I've just had a lot of morning sickness."

"Well, you let Katie and her mother help around here. Don't do too much."

"I'll be careful. I'm married to a doctor, you know."

Jake grinned. "And I'm glad of it."

Lloyd came inside, wearing just as many weapons as his father. "Can I go see Mom?"

"Go ahead," Jake told him. "She's a little groggy from pain medication."

Lloyd touched Jake's arm. "Say something decent to Peter Brown, will you? He's doing us a big favor, Pa, even though you don't think so."

"I know what he's doing. I just don't care for the *reason* he's doing it."

"It isn't just her, Pa. I honestly think it's partly for you. The man respects that you're her husband. I'm not happy about his feelings either, but he'll take damn good care of Mom."

Jake sighed. "I'm sure he will." He turned back to Evie. "You know the rules, baby girl, and they are more important than ever this time around. All of you stay in town, and stay together as much as you can. Keep a tight rein on the boys and don't go shopping alone. If I could get out of this damn trip, I would, but I can't, and Lloyd won't let me go alone, so you and Katie and the kids and the Donavans stay together. Pat Donavan knows how to use a gun, and Lloyd said Katie isn't bad with a rifle. Her brothers taught her because of rustlers and such out at their ranch, but she hasn't used one in a long time, and a person needs to stay in practice with a—"

"*Daddy!*" Evie interrupted. "You are rattling on like a mother hen. I'm a Harkner, remember? I know the rules."

He reached out and tugged at her hair. "And I'm damn sorry I have to *make* those rules. Once I'm done with all of this, life will be a lot easier."

"And in the meantime, God will take care of all of us like he's always done. Mother is going to be fine, and that means you'll be joining us in church when you get back."

Jake grinned. "I can see neither you nor Randy is going to let me off that hook."

"Certainly not. Now go do what you have to do and get back here so we can all have the extreme pleasure of watching you take off those guns and walk through the church doors. It will be an epic moment."

Jake couldn't help a light laugh. "And lightning will probably strike the steeple, and it will topple right to the ground." He leaned in and kissed her cheek. "And anything that makes you happy makes *me* happy." He gave her a wink. "We'll see about the church thing. Let's concentrate right now on your mother getting well and me getting rid of Marty Bryant so he's no longer a worry."

"Well, the way you look right now, I'd be shaking in my shoes if I was Marty."

He patted her cheek and headed for the door, noticing both grandsons were waiting outside with Brian and Katie to see their grandfather before leaving. Little Jake was running around babbling about "Gampa's guns." Jake just shook his head. He headed out the door, finding Peter leaning against a porch post, watching Brian help Stephen get his foot in a stirrup so he could climb up on Lloyd's horse.

"The older one likes to cheat at cards and the little one is totally wild and unruly, which means the poor things both belong to me," Jake told Peter.

Peter turned, looking Jake over. "You have to be the most intimidating man in this entire territory. Far be it from me to set you off, so don't be worrying about my intentions while you're gone. No man wants to answer to you when you look like that."

"Well then, I've given you proper cause to respect my marriage."

Peter folded his arms. "Jake—"

"Don't say it." Jake pulled a cigarette and a match from inside his duster. "Sometimes she needs holding, Peter, and you damn well know it." He struck the match and lit the cigarette. "And I'm telling you to do the holding if she needs it. She'll be scared of the surgery. And if…" He took a deep drag on the cigarette, hating the fact that he couldn't hide the tears that again stung his eyes. He wasn't used to this. "If they find out the worst, I guess all you can do is tell her and bring her back home to me. I can at least hold her while she's…" He stopped and cleared his throat, then took a drag on the cigarette.

Peter removed his hat and ran a hand through his hair. "Jake, I've lost a wife. I know how it feels. And I know my feelings are partly from just being lonely. I have no bad intentions. I just want to know I did something for her—did my part in helping her. Can you understand that?"

Jake kept the cigarette at the corner of his lips. "I'm trying. She trusts me, and that takes a lot, because I have a very good woman friend out there who runs a brothel—so I guess it's my turn to trust her."

Peter laughed lightly. "Why does the fact that you have friends at a brothel not surprise me?"

Jake grinned but quickly wiped at watery eyes. "Peter, there's a whole lot about me you still don't know." He watched a crowd start to gather. "I'm a little worried about people talking, Peter. I don't want anything bad said about my wife traveling with you."

"I'll set straight anyone who asks. I am your attorney, going to Oklahoma City to see about shortening your sentence. Randy is going with me to help plead your case. I won't mention a doctor, because maybe she doesn't want the whole town to know what's going on. I'll ask her about that."

"I'd appreciate it."

Jake noticed the strap of a shoulder holster under Peter's suit jacket. "Let me see that gun."

Peter took it out and handed it to him. "Not very big, but it will do the job. It's Italian made, but the design is called Chamelot-Delvigne—French gunsmiths. That particular gun was made in '79, and it's a 10.4 millimeter center-fire…double-action, which is rare."

Jake studied the gun, spinning the chamber. "I've heard of these but never saw one. If I wasn't ready to leave, I'd take this out and shoot it."

"I collect foreign-made revolvers."

Jake lowered the gun. "*Do* you now? Why didn't I know this about you?"

Peter shrugged. "I guess I figured someone like you wouldn't be interested in smaller revolvers."

"Like hell!" Jake looked the gun over again. "Someday my living will be as a gunsmith, Peter. I need to see every kind of gun I can get my hands on, and I intend to design some of my own. I've already modified the ones I wear to suit my speed and shoot with a smoother single-action, which is why I can draw and cock and shoot a gun faster than most." He handed the revolver back to Peter. "That's a nice piece. I wouldn't mind seeing what else you have when I get back…if things work out, that is."

"You can come and see them anytime, as long as I don't need to grab one in self-defense when you come over."

A little part of Jake was beginning to like the man. "Yeah, well, we'll see about that." He took one last draw on his cigarette and tossed it. "Look, Peter, I talked to Sparky yesterday. He's going to accompany you and Randy to Edmond, where you can get on a train. He'll deputize and bring along three or four good men. My guess is that Marty Bryant is already up here somewhere planning something, but just in case he's still south of here, I want to take extra precautions. I think once you board a train in Edmond, you'll be safe from there on. The man wants my hide, and he'll have no problem getting it by using my family. You remember that and keep an eye open."

"Whatever you say."

"And before you leave, talk to Juan and ask him to please take care of Randy's roses while she's gone. She loves her roses."

Peter nodded. "I will make sure someone keeps them trimmed and watered."

"Gampa, ride!" Little Jake ran up to him and grabbed his leg. Jake picked him up, still watching Peter. "I promised him a ride on Prince before I leave." He glanced at his bedroom window. "All I really want to do right now is go back inside and be with my wife, but life doesn't always let us do what we really want to do."

"You're telling *me* that?"

Their eyes held in a momentary challenge that couldn't be helped. Jake sighed deeply then and walked off the porch, keeping Little Jake in one arm. Peter noticed he still had a slight limp. He stopped and turned, coming back and, to Peter's surprise, putting out his hand.

"Are you going to break it?"

Jake's look turned serious and a bit commanding. "No."

Peter took his hand.

"I've never put this much trust in a man in my life, except for a man named Jess York. He loved her too. I couldn't be with her then either, and I had to trust Jess to just protect and help her. Seems like it's happening all over again. You take damn good care of my wife and bring her back to me."

"I wouldn't think of doing otherwise."

Their eyes held in mutual understanding. Jake shook

his hand, then turned back to embrace Katie with his other arm before lifting Little Jake onto his horse. He climbed into the saddle and started riding the black gelding up and down the street, giving his rambunctious grandson the horseback ride he'd promised him. Stephen followed, wanting to ride his dad's horse for a few minutes before Lloyd had to leave. Little Jake wiggled up and down, and Jake kicked Prince into a faster gait to satisfy his grandson's excitement.

Peter watched a crowd gather, as always happened when Jake Harkner was getting ready to ride out again. The man was a magnet for excitement. Peter figured he would never quite get over how someone as gentle and poised and graceful as Randy Harkner lived with the man.

Lloyd came outside then, giving Katie a long embrace and a kiss, then reaching up and lifting Stephen down and into his arms for a hug. Jake handed Little Jake down to Brian. "Take good care of my kid here," he told Brian.

"Bye, Grampa," Stephen called to him. "Don't cheat at cards."

"I don't cheat, Stephen. I *bluff*!" Jake laughed, forcing himself not to think too hard about leaving Randy lying in pain, or about how hard a trip to Oklahoma City would be for her, or about the fact that the only person she would have to turn to was Peter Brown. He had to think the best. He had to, or go crazy. He rode closer to Lloyd as he mounted up. "You ready?"

"As I'll ever be. All we need is some food from Sadie's."

It had become Tobe Baker's job to keep Jake's horse and nonperishable supplies ready at all times, so there hadn't been that much packing to do. Most of their fresh food supplies came from Sadie's place, where Sadie kept a tab on what the federal government owed her. Tobe had prepared a packhorse with small tools, horse liniment, brushes for the horses, a supply of tobacco, matches, towels, canned goods, and extra tack.

Lloyd grabbed the reins to the packhorse. "You okay, Pa?"

"No." Jake headed down the street while Little Jake jumped up and down, yelling, "Gampa's guns! Gampa's guns!" He strained to run after Jake, but Brian kept a tight grip on him.

"You didn't fool Mom either," Lloyd told Jake when he caught up to him. "She wants me to keep an eye on you, which I fully intend to do."

Jake cast his son a sly look of warning mixed with humor. "What other orders did my warden give you?"

Lloyd pushed back his hat. "She said to make sure you eat some breakfast when we pick up our supplies at Sadie's, but that you're not supposed to let Mary Ann pour your coffee."

That brought a sudden burst of laughter from Jake, greatly relieving some of Lloyd's worries. He thought what a great laugh his father had and wished he could hear it more often. "I don't think I need to ask what that's supposed to mean," he told Jake.

"Yeah, well, it's a private joke between us." Jake laughed again. He kept grinning as he lit yet another cigarette. "Do me a favor when we get back and tell her I insisted Mary Ann wait on us, and that I enjoyed every damn minute of it."

Lloyd smiled. He'd been "waited on" by Mary Ann himself—even took her up on her offer once, before Katie came along. "Whatever you say. You're the one who has to answer to Mom. I wouldn't want to."

"I can handle Randy Harkner."

"Yeah, well, she says the same thing about you."

"I just let her *think* she's in charge," Jake called back as his horse trotted ahead of Lloyd's again. "Keeps her happy."

"Shit, Pa, everybody knows she's got you lassoed and hog-tied. She corralled you twenty-six years ago, and you still haven't found a way through the fence." He rode faster to catch up again.

Jake didn't answer the remark. "Let's get our supplies and go pick up Jeff. I hope he got himself a decent horse and proper clothing."

So, you're done talking about Mom. He knew his father was torn to shreds on the inside. This was going to be the trip from hell.

Twenty-three

"NOT A BAD VIEW THIS MORNING," LLOYD COMMENTED.

"Mary Ann was thrilled to death that Randy wasn't with me," Jake answered. "Remind me to tell you some time what Randy said to her the last time we were in Sadie's together." He turned to look back at Jeff, who followed behind on an Appaloosa mare. "Get up beside us, Jeff. You're swallowing dust."

Jeff rode closer. He'd bought all the right clothes, but Jake couldn't help thinking he still looked a bit comical, mainly because of his spectacles and the fact that he sat stiff as a board on the horse. "You sure you're an experienced rider?" Jake asked him.

"I said I knew *how* to ride. But I've never ridden for days at a time, and on top of that, I'm not sure what you expect of me, Jake."

"Just observe, Jeff, that's all."

"What if we find Marty Bryant?"

"We *will* find him, and when we do, you stay out of the way. I'll take care of that sonofabitch."

"Yes, sir."

Jake glanced at the six-gun Jeff wore on his hip. "Looks like a Colt .22."

"You can tell that just by the handle?"

"I believe I know a little bit about guns, Jeff."

"Yes, sir. Stupid question."

"Have you tried using that thing yet?"

"No, sir. I got this one because it's a bit smaller and lighter than a .44 and doesn't kick. Takes more strength than I have to pull and shoot what you're wearing."

"We'll stop up ahead in a gully and let you do some shooting where your bullets can't go far," Jake told him. "That way nobody gets hurt."

"Yes, sir."

Jake drew his horse to a halt and swung around to face him. "Jeff, you should know that if I get really ornery with you, I don't want you to take it personally. It will be because I have a lot on my mind." He lit yet another cigarette. "And the reason I'm practically chain-smoking is that I'm trying to keep myself from *drinking*. Randy is leaving tomorrow for Oklahoma City with Peter Brown, of all people. There is a specialist there who is supposed to be extra good at the kind of operation she needs. Peter has to go there anyway to see another attorney about pleading my case, so Randy is going with him."

Jeff raised his eyebrows in surprise. "I didn't know any of this, Jake."

"Yeah, well, it was decided over just the last couple of days, and right now I'd like to drink myself into oblivion, but then God knows what that would do to me, the state I'm in. I just want you to know why I might not be exactly amiable the next few days. I don't know where Marty Bryant is or how many men he has, I don't know if that judge will reduce my sentence, my wife could be dying and I can't be with her, and the man who is taking her to Oklahoma City is in love with her. My mind is flying in ten different directions right now."

Jeff frowned. "I'm sorry, Jake."

"Not as sorry as I am, for a *lot* of things." Jake turned his horse back around and rode ahead of Jeff and Lloyd.

Jeff turned to Lloyd. "Your mother is really headed to Oklahoma City with Peter Brown?"

"She is," Lloyd answered, lighting his own cigarette. "This won't be an easy trip, Jeff. My father is going to go through so many different moods, we won't be able to keep up. I just hope that if the worst happens, my mother doesn't die down there from the surgery or something. If she dies without my dad being with her, it's going to be really, really bad, Jeff. I'm praying she's home when we get back, and by some miracle she's okay."

"Well, I sure hope for the same." Jeff watched Jake riding on ahead alone. "Lloyd, when I asked your father what your mother meant to him, his reply was that she was the center of his universe…the very air he breathed. I thought those were beautiful words, coming from a man like Jake."

"Doesn't surprise me. Pa is going to be one angry, ornery sonofabitch on this trip, so beware. If I were you, I wouldn't ask him a lot of questions. Let him open up to you when he feels like it. Otherwise, leave him alone. He'll put on a good show of being okay. He'll even joke around with you. But right now, he's that nitroglycerin we talked about." He reached into a pocket on his duster and took out a deputy marshal badge. "Here. Pa said to give you one of these."

Jeff's eyebrows raised in surprise. "A *badge*? Hell, I still don't even know how to use a gun!"

"Pa says if you wear this, people will be less likely to mess with you—or shoot you."

Jeff met the young man's eyes and Lloyd winked. "Just pulling your leg, Jeff—but that badge really will make people think twice. And don't worry about the Buckley place. You're with Jake Harkner, remember? And he's in a real shitty mood. You don't take down my dad when he's in a mood like that." He trotted his horse forward, still leading the packhorse. "Put the badge on, Jeff," he called back.

Jeff stared at the six-point badge for a moment, then reluctantly pinned it to his shirt. He straightened, grinning. He couldn't wait to write home about this. *Dear Father and family, I rode with Jake Harkner this week as a deputy U.S. Marshal—badge and all. And Jake Harkner himself gave me shooting lessons.* He kicked the sides of his horse to catch up again.

There was a good hour of light left when Jake made camp in the gully he'd spoken about. They unloaded the horses and let them graze while they spread out bedrolls. Jake built a fire and dumped a can of beans into a black fry pan, then set it right on top of the flames. While waiting for the beans to heat up, he walked several feet away and set the empty can on a log. "Load up that .22, Jeff. Let's see how straight it shoots."

Jeff jumped up from the stump he'd been sitting on and pulled his gun from its holster. The gunsmith from whom he'd bought it had shown him how to open and load it, but he'd left it empty until he learned how to shoot. Now he was nervous and dropped two bullets as he tried to put them into the gun. "Shit," he muttered.

"Don't worry about it," Jake told him, bending down to pick up the bullets. "Jeff—"

Jeff looked up at him. Being with the tall, intimidating father-and-son team made him feel like a ten-year-old. "Sir?"

Jake rolled his eyes at being called sir again. "Are you ever going to stop being nervous around me?"

Jeff shrugged. "I don't think so. I'm okay when it comes to talking about the book, but when it comes to guns..."

Jake grinned and put a hand on his shoulder. "You know, Jeff, if you asked me right now to sit down over there and write a couple of pages about me or Randy or guns or whatever, *I'd* be the nervous wreck, because I'm no writer. I even need Randy to help me with all the damn paperwork that comes with this job. I know *guns* and not much else. *You* are the writer. So don't be embarrassed that you don't know much about guns. *I'd* be embarrassed for you to see how lousy I am at writing, so we're even. Got that? And *don't* call me sir."

Jeff's respect for the man grew every time he was around him. "All right."

"Now load that gun and give it to me for a minute. I want to see whether or not you got cheated when you bought it. It's easy to sell a piece of shit to some- one unawares."

Jeff finished loading it, then handed it to Jake. "Jake, I, uh, I really, really hope your wife will be okay."

Jake studied the gun. "Yeah," was his only reply. Jeff jumped then when Jake suddenly fired five shots at the can in rapid succession, hitting it every time. He studied the gun then. "Not bad. Not bad at all. I think Red St. James gave you a good deal—probably because he knew I'd be the one testing this thing out and I'd have his hide if he sold you a piece of junk. Reload it."

Jake walked out and picked up the can, which now was more or less in shreds but still useful enough for a target. He set it back on the log and walked back to Jeff. "Give it a try. I didn't need to aim, but you will. For a first-time shooter, you're better off using both hands and arms. Don't try it one-handed just yet. You feel the kick more and are less likely to hit anything. Just steady the sight on that can. She shoots true, so if you can keep the gun still, you should hit it. And once you cock that thing, you only need to lightly pull on the trigger. Let the trigger do the shooting, not your finger. The less hard you pull that trigger, the less the gun itself will pull and jump and miss the target. And see this?" Jake noticed that Jeff's left thumb and forefinger were near the firing chamber. "You leave those fingers there and the gasses from shooting will burn them. Wrap your fingers all the way around the butt of the gun and lift your left thumb only for cocking it, then wrap it back over the top of your hand. Keep your trigger finger pressed straight against the side of the gun, right above the trigger guard until you're ready to shoot. Don't ever rest it on the trigger itself. I'll be walking back out there to reset the can. I don't want to get shot in the back by a trigger-happy kid."

"What? For God's sake, Jake—"

"I'm fooling with you, unless you want to be known as the man who shot Jake Harkner."

"Quit it! I'm already a nervous wreck."

Jake grinned. "Shit, just relax and remember what I told you. Now take a shot at that can."

Jeff took a deep breath and raised the gun, keeping his hands wrapped around the butt of the gun the way Jake had taught him. He pulled back the hammer, closed one eye, and aimed.

"Wait a minute." Jake walked behind him and grasped his wrists, pulling his arms out straighter. "Keep your arms straight. You'll hold the gun a lot steadier if you keep your arms stiff and tighten your muscles. You won't hit a damn thing with them half-bent like that, especially when you start shooting with just one hand. You watch me the next time I shoot. My arm is always straight, even if it looks like I'm casually shooting without even aiming."

"Like the guy in the alley across from the jail?"

Jake didn't answer right away, and Jeff feared he shouldn't have brought that up.

"Yeah, something like that," Jake finally told him. "Now keep your arms straight."

Jeff took aim again, and after taking a deep breath, he fired. The can went flying. "Oh my God! I hit it!"

"Sure you did." Jake took a cigarette from his shirt pocket and lit it as he walked out to pick up the can again.

"Like I said, keep your arms straight, keep the sight right where you want it, and don't jerk on the trigger."

"I can't believe I hit it!" Jeff repeated. "This is fun! A man could get used to this."

Jake set up the can again. "Yeah, he can get *real* used to it. But it's just a can, Jeff—not a man. Shooting a man is a whole different thing. And it's not fun." Jake walked back to Jeff, who was a bit surprised at the remark. Did shooting men actually bother Jake? He did it so casually.

"Most men I've shot deserved it," Jake told him, as though reading his mind, "and I sometimes even take great satisfaction in taking certain men out of society. But it's never fun, Jeff, and in the early years I shot men who *didn't* deserve it. They just happened to be in my way. That's not a fun thing to live with."

"Well, I just meant—"

"I know what you meant. I just want you to be ready for the day you actually shoot a human being. It won't feel good, believe me. Try it again, and keep your arm straight."

Jeff took aim again. He missed.

"You got excited and jerked the trigger, and the gun came up on you. Remember to squeeze it. Don't jerk it. Let the trigger do its own thing. And keep your muscles tight. Use up the rest of the bullets. I'm going to get my repeater. Overall, I think you'll be better off using a rifle if we get in trouble, but I still want you to practice with your own pistol every day."

He walked to his bedroll to get his carbine while Jeff kept shooting. Jake reached into his saddlebag and pulled out a fifth of whiskey, uncorking it and taking a swallow.

Lloyd lay with his head against his own saddle. He glanced sidelong at his father and watched him take a drink. "Pa, what the hell are you doing?"

"Leave me alone." Jake corked the whiskey and picked up his carbine, which was fully loaded. He took it over to Jeff and began showing him how to use it. "Your aim will be a lot truer with a rifle, but we'll keep practicing with both guns." He had Jeff fire the rifle several times, which meant practicing how to quickly cock it again before each shot.

"What I like about a rifle is you can put a man down before he gets close enough to use his six-gun, but too often your six-gun is your only choice."

Jeff became a bit concerned at the smell of whiskey on Jake's breath.

"That's why you need to remember to keep your arm straight," Jake continued. "There's no time to let a shot go wild and miss its target."

In a flash, Jake's own six-gun was drawn and fired four times—so quickly that Jeff hardly realized what was happening until it was over with. The can flew all four times until it lay at a distance, finally too shredded to be used for a target. Jake handed him his gun. "My arm was straight the whole time. There are two bullets left in this thing. Do you want to try it?"

Shoot one of Jake Harkner's guns? "I don't know. It's bigger and heavier than my .22, and I swear it's louder than a rifle. My ears hurt."

"You might as well get a feel of it. You never know what will happen out here, Jeff. I might have to toss you one of these to use to help me out. At least get an idea how it feels and how it shoots."

Jeff swallowed. "If you say so."

"Just remember it's a hair trigger, so don't you touch that trigger at all until you're sure you're ready to fire it."

Jeff took the gun that a few weeks ago he'd been so afraid of. He raised it, wondering how in hell Jake could draw and fire it so fast and so well when it weighed so much. He doubted he could even hold it out and aim it with one hand. Using both hands, he held it out, cocked it, and aimed at the shredded mess of a can, then fired.

It boomed and kicked back at his hand, but he hit the can. "I did it!" he exclaimed. "And I barely touched the trigger! You were right about that. Wait till I tell my father about this."

Jake just grinned and took the gun from him to reload it. "The way you keep talking about your father, he must be a pretty good man."

"He is."

An odd sadness moved through Jake's eyes. "Yeah, well, he raised a good kid." He picked up his rifle and headed for his bedroll. "Reload your own weapon, Jeff." He glanced at Lloyd then. "Fix a plate of beans for you and Jeff, and get yourselves a fresh biscuit from that sack Sadie gave us."

"You're not eating?" Lloyd asked.

Jake walked over and uncorked the whiskey again. "No."

"Pa, you know you have to eat. And please don't drink, especially not on an empty stomach. You know damn well that whiskey won't end the pain in your gut, and you know it would kill Mom to know you uncorked that shit."

Jake took another swallow. "She doesn't need to know."

"She damn well *will* know, because I'll tell her myself. She'll be worried and hurt. Is that what you want?"

"What I *want* is to get drunk."

"You said earlier you *wouldn't*, and you know damn well why…but if that's what you want, go ahead. When you get like this, I don't give a rat's ass what you do. Go ahead and behave like your father."

Lloyd instantly regretted the remark. Jake took one last swallow and then corked the bottle, giving Lloyd a look that told him he was lucky he was Jake's son and not a stranger.

"You don't know shit about my father."

"Don't I? I know enough that I don't want you to be like him—*that's* what I know." Lloyd moved to the fire and spooned some beans onto a plate, handing it to Jeff as Jeff walked back to his bedroll. Then Lloyd threw a gunnysack at Jeff. "Grab yourself a biscuit. We'll both eat while we watch my father drink till he turns into a complete asshole."

Jake uncorked the whiskey and took one more swallow as he watched Lloyd spoon himself a plate of beans. Jeff handed back the bag of biscuits, glancing nervously at Jake. Lloyd took a biscuit from the bag and sat down. He glanced at Jake, and Jake saw the hurt and worry in his eyes.

Jake shoved the whiskey back into his saddlebag, then turned to gaze at the fire. "Damn it, Lloyd, if you're going to pout like a spoiled kid who didn't get what he wanted for Christmas, then go ahead and fix me a plate."

Lloyd watched him closely for a moment, then prepared a plate of beans and handed that and a biscuit to Jake. "She'll be okay, Pa."

Jake took the plate. "You didn't see how much pain she was in last night. In all our married life, I've never seen her in that kind of pain. To me that means cancer. I've seen it, Lloyd, on a personal level—a prostitute I was living with before I met your mother."

"Cancer doesn't mean it can't be fixed, Pa. And Beth…I mean, when she had her time of the month, she used to be in almost that much pain. A lot of things can go on inside a woman to cause pain like that, so it might just be something else, just like Brian said. Now eat."

Jake poked at the beans with his fork, wanting nothing more than to go back to Guthrie and scoop his wife into his arms and tell her everything was all right. *That's the one thing I miss the most when you're gone, Jake—these arms around me. I feel so safe when you're holding me.*

They're around you, Randy, even when I'm not here, he thought. His gut tightened and it was all he could do to eat even half the beans. "Eat up and get some rest, Jeff," he said aloud. "Tomorrow we'll pay a visit to the Buckleys."

Jeff set his plate down, glancing at Lloyd.

"You heard the man," Lloyd told him.

Jeff tried to joke. "That's what I was afraid of."

"You'll be all right," Jake assured him. He ate a few more bites and forced himself to swallow the biscuit, then he set the plate aside. "I can't finish."

Lloyd sighed. "I guess some is better than none. I'm glad you put that whiskey back. Jesus, Pa, sometimes *I* feel like the father."

Jake lay back against his saddle and lit another cigarette. "Maybe sometimes that's what I'm looking for. Trying to be a good father to you sometimes made me feel like it was happening the other way around, if that makes any sense. It felt…good. Like with your mother— she'd shake the knots out of me and keep my ass on the straight and narrow, and I let her because it felt good to have somebody care if I was doing things right."

Lloyd took his plate. "Yeah, well, someday you're going to wake up and realize how many people *do* care."

Jeff quickly dug out his writing pad and took some notes. *There is a vulnerable side to Jake Harkner nobody knows about. It's his wife and kids who bring it out.* He skipped a line to make a different note. *Tomorrow we will visit the Buckley family. I am scared to death.* He put down his tablet and picked up his plate of beans. "Jake?"

"What?"

"Thanks for not making fun of my ineptitude with guns."

"Why would I make fun of it? There was a time when even *I* didn't know how to use guns." He smoked quietly again for a moment. "I'll tell you something, Jeff.

Later I'll tell you all of it, but for now suffice it to say that the first time I ever used a gun was...on my own father. That was the very first time. And in a way, every man I've shot since then was him. In my mind, I've killed him over and over...and over."

Jeff looked at Lloyd, who put a finger to his lips, warning Jeff not to say a word. Jeff quietly finished his beans.

Twenty-four

JEFF WAS SURE HE'D FEEL A BULLET IN HIS BACK ANY moment. Leading the packhorse, he rode behind Lloyd, who in turn stayed behind Jake as the three of them followed a narrow road through an open field still full of dried, yellowed cornstalks from the year before. Jake had told him the Buckley farm wasn't all that big, and already Jeff could see a two-story house made of rough, unpainted wood, a poorly built and already-sagging porch running across the entire front of the building. The Buckleys and Bryants were part of the earlier settlers who'd moved into Oklahoma Indian country before it was even legal to do so. Jake wanted to kick them out, but a judge had ruled they had a right to stay because they were peacefully homesteading and hadn't bothered the Indians.

"Peaceful, my ass," Jake had grumbled that morning. "I'm going to write that judge and tell him what I think about his ruling and why he's wrong. Jeff, I might need your help wording the letter properly."

Right now a letter was the last thing on Jeff's mind. He thought he'd seen at least two men lurking in the woods that bordered the cornfield. He figured if he saw them, Jake and Lloyd had probably spotted them also. A barn and shed sat to the right of the house, and Jeff wondered if men were hiding inside, watching them, waiting to gun them down. All kinds of visions danced through his head as they drew closer to the house.

Someone stepped out the front door then,

brandishing a rifle. It looked to Jeff like a woman, but her size and the way she was dressed made it difficult to tell. She was tall and skinny, wearing a man's pants and a plain, homemade cotton shirt that hung outside the pants. Her graying hair was once apparently twisted into a bun but now hung in uncombed strands that had worked their way out of the pins and ribbon that held the rest of it up.

"You stop right there, Jake Harkner," the woman yelled, raising the rifle.

To Jeff's amazement, Jake didn't slow down, but he pushed his duster behind his right gun. Lloyd rode at a faster gait toward the outbuildings.

"Put that thing down, Jessie," Jake called back. "You'd be hanged, woman or not." He rode close to the front porch while Lloyd rode straight into the barn to Jeff's right. Jeff wasn't sure which Harkner to keep an eye on, Jake or Lloyd. He pulled his six-gun just in case he might need it.

"I can draw and shoot before you pull that trigger," Jake was warning Jessie. "You haven't even cocked that rifle yet. Even if you manage to get a shot off, you'll be dead just the same, if not by my gun, then by Lloyd's."

Jeff wondered if they would really shoot a woman. Jessie kept the rifle raised. "Maybe I don't care, Harkner. Maybe I will get the *both* of you, and even that four-eyed little kid behind you."

"Shooting a United States Marshal is definitely a hanging offense, Jessie, and hanging is a terrible way to die."

The woman lowered the rifle just slightly. "It's how *you* should have died years ago, you murderin' bastard! If they'd hanged you for all the crimes you committed, you wouldn't have been alive to kill my husband and my son! The only boy I have left is still in bad pain from what you done to him."

To Jeff's relief, Lloyd rode back out of the barn. He

headed to a shed next, staying on his horse as he kicked the door in, his gun drawn.

"Brad tried to challenge me to a gunfight," Jake explained to Jessie. "Would you rather I'd shot him?"

The woman lowered the rifle even more. "I *hate* you, Jake Harkner, and so do the *Bryants*! They're gatherin' lots of men, and they're gonna come for you."

Lloyd rode around the back of the house, apparently to make sure no one was lurking back there.

"How many men, Jessie?" Jake asked her.

"Why would I tell *you*?"

"Because that way when I bring them all in, you'll get the credit and you won't go to jail right along with them for withholding evidence." Jake took out a cigarette. "I have a couple of death certificates for you, Jessie. Proof your son and husband are dead and buried back in Guthrie. That's why I came here. You should know I made sure the undertaker placed a couple of crosses at their graves."

"Well now, ain't that just real decent of you, puttin' crosses on their graves," Jessie sneered.

Lloyd rode around from the other side of the house and up to Jake. "I didn't find anything, but I saw two men back there in the woods."

"I saw them too," Jake said quietly.

Jessie gritted her teeth. "How in hell can you sit there on that horse, Jake Harkner, and tell me so casually about my son and my man bein' *dead*—and you bein' the one who *killed* them!"

Jake lit the cigarette and waved out the match before dropping it. "I can sit here and tell you casually, because Lloyd and I saw what they did to an innocent fifteen-year-old girl, Jessie—an innocent young girl who'd never been touched by a man till they got through with her. So no—it didn't bother me at all to shoot them both down, and it doesn't bother me to talk about it."

Jessie finally set the gun aside and folded her arms. "They was still my husband and my son. Ain't you got no feelin's about that? *You've* got a son."

"And my son knows that if *he* ever did something like what we found, I'd damn well shoot him *myself* for it! Are you saying it's okay what they did? They not only raped that girl, but they robbed a bank and shot an innocent man who happened to be inside."

Jessie looked away, blinking back tears. "I ain't sayin' that. But you have a lot of nerve ridin' in here like this. Get the hell off my property, Harkner."

"Well, right now, you're still basically a squatter who's here only because a judge is allowing it, which means this part of Oklahoma belongs to the federal government until they open it up for settlement, so I have *every* right to be here, Jessie. And before you claim I have no feelings, I could easily have shot Brad last week, but I didn't. I thought about you losing Bo, so I took Brad down a different way so you'd have one son left."

"Well, ain't that just fucking decent of you!" The words were shouted from near the doorway, and a moment later, Brad appeared, looking much thinner than he had the day Jeff watched Jake throw the kid off the boardwalk in Guthrie. He walked outside, bent over like an old man. "I still can't stand up straight, Harkner! I ain't never had so much pain in my life."

"At least you're alive," Lloyd told him. "Consider yourself lucky, seeing as how it was Jake Harkner who took you down."

"Yeah, well, your old man took me by surprise, else I'd have beat the shit out of him," Brad bragged.

"Well, when you're all healed up, you come on into town and I'll take you on myself," Lloyd answered.

"There's other ways of getting revenge," Brad told him with a sneer.

"Yeah? What's that?"

Brad grinned. "Just ways, that's all. Family is family, Lloyd."

"What's that supposed to mean?"

"Ole Jake here has a family of his own, that's all. He ought to find out what it's like to lose a loved one."

As though sensing its rider's fury, Lloyd's horse whinnied and jerked backward.

"You filthy sonofabitch!" Lloyd spat back. He reined his horse to a standstill and started to dismount.

"Stay on your horse, Lloyd!" Jake warned, eyeing Jessie.

"He threatened the family!" Lloyd growled.

"Killing him won't help!"

"Maybe not, but it would feel real good!" Lloyd glowered at Brad. "I'm real close to coming over there and breaking every rib in your body, you bastard! How does it feel having the shit kicked out of you by a fifty-six-year-old man? Kind of humiliating, isn't it? Next time it will be somebody your own age, and you'll spend a hell of a long time getting on your feet again, if ever!"

"You might not live long enough to try!"

Just then a movement came from Jake's right. In an instant, his gun was out and fired. Jeff's horse skittered sideways at the boom and Jeff hung on tight, also keeping hold of the packhorse as it jerked its head at the sound. A man at the far end of the porch fell with a hole in his chest.

The moment Jake fired the gun, Lloyd was off his horse, his gun drawn. He charged past Brad and into the house. Jeff's eyes darted in every direction, his heart pounding.

"Where in hell did that man come from?" Jake demanded.

"That's Luke Cummings," Brad answered. "He was in the kitchen—must have snuck out the back door after Lloyd came around from behind the house. We didn't give him no orders to shoot. He's just a hired hand."

"And you thought it best not to tell us he was in there?" Jake answered, putting his gun back in its holster.

Jeff stared at the dead body—another man shot as casually as lighting a cigarette.

"Maybe he didn't even mean to shoot you," Brad objected. "How do you know he wasn't just comin' to see what was goin' on?"

Jake sighed as he too dismounted. "Any man who sneaks up on me gets shot, Brad. I can't afford to wait and see what a sneak thief wants. And I didn't miss that he had a gun lifted to fire."

"You got eyes in the sides and the back of your head?"

Jake rummaged in his saddlebag, the cigarette still at the corner of his mouth. "A man like me learns to see everything if he wants to stay healthy."

Jeff could hear Lloyd charging around inside the house, searching for anyone else who might be there. Finally he called down from an upstairs window. "There's nobody else in here, Pa."

Jake brought some papers to the porch and handed them to Jessie. "The death certificates."

The woman wouldn't meet his eyes. She just yanked the papers from his hand. "Get out of my sight."

"Not until you or Brad tells us what's going on at the Bryant place. How many men are they rounding up, and why? Is Marty there?"

"Wouldn't you like to know?" Brad mocked.

Jake turned his attention to Brad. "Yeah, I would. And you can either tell me or wish you had."

"I'm half-crippled. You ain't gonna do nothin', and I don't have to tell you a damn thing. I know my rights."

In an instant, Jake had the young man by the throat. He slammed him against the doorjamb, and Brad screamed with pain. "And I have *my* rights! You just never learn, *do* you?" Jake growled. "I don't have time for your fucking games, Brad!"

Jessie started to reach for her rifle.

"Don't do it, ma'am," Lloyd told her, coming around the side of the house, his six-gun trained in her direction. "Woman or not, I'll pull this trigger."

"I'm not sure how many," Brad choked out, trying with both hands to pry Jake's away from his throat—to no avail. "I just know Hash Bryant said he was gonna"— his face turned redder—"get some men together and figure out a way…to get you…for killin' Ted and… Gordy…and my pa and my…brother…and sendin' Marty…to prison."

"Justice was rightfully served," Jake sneered. "And if you don't want me to punch you right in that breastbone again, you'll tell me how many men Marty has!" he roared. "Have you seen him, or anyone he's riding with?"

"Eight or ten, somethin' around that many," Jessie answered for Brad. "And no, we ain't seen Marty Bryant, but we heard he was the one makin' all the plans. Now leave my son alone."

Jake let go of Brad and grabbed Jessie's rifle out of her hands. "What are they planning?"

"I don't think they even know. It's just all talk." She finally looked up at Jake, glaring at him through eyes narrowed from hatred. "I'm thinkin' Marty might have gone to that no-name town north of here to look for help."

"Hell's Nest?"

"Maybe. I didn't think it had a name at all, but that's a good enough one."

"Who's back there in the woods?" Jake asked her.

"Just an old black man who's been helpin' me out, and my brother, who came to live with us a few weeks back. They ain't no danger. They was just out there gatherin' wood."

"They had rifles."

"*Everybody* carries rifles out here when they go into

the woods. There's always a need for meat, and you never know when you'll see a deer or a rabbit. They ain't gonna go up against the likes of the great and mighty Jake Harkner!"

Jake walked off the porch. He mounted Prince, and Lloyd remounted his own horse beside Jake.

"Those two extra men can help you bury Luke Cummings," Jake told Jessie. "I'll leave your rifle a few yards out as we leave. I don't trust you any more than I trusted your husband, Jessie. I don't intend to get shot in the back."

He turned his horse and rode past Jeff. "Put that six-gun away," he told him without looking at him. "You don't need it." He rode on down the entrance road that led to the woods.

Reluctantly, Jeff put his gun back in its holster as Lloyd rode up beside him. "Let's go."

They left, with Luke Cummings lying dead with a hole in his chest.

Jake stayed ahead of them until they came across the two men working in the woods. The men stood still as Jake approached.

"Hand those rifles to the men behind me," Jake told them.

Eyeing the marshal's badge and intimidated by all of Jake's weapons, they handed the rifles to Jeff and Lloyd as they rode closer.

"Wha'd we do?" the black man asked.

"Nothing—except that you work for Jessie Buckley. You ask *her* why I took your guns. Your rifles and Jessie's rifle here will be found several yards ahead, and I don't want to be able to see either one of you going for them until we're completely out of sight, understand?"

Both men nodded. "You do somethin' to my sister?" the white man asked.

"No. But there is a dead man back there you can help her bury. You just remember what I said. I'll be looking back, and I'd better not be able to see either one of you till I'm too far away to tell. Got that?"

The black man nodded, but Jessie's brother folded his arms and put on a show of not being afraid. "You're that marshal, ain't you? Jake Harkner—the one who half killed my nephew."

"He had it coming."

"Yeah, well, Hash and Marty Bryant are fixin' to kill you, Harkner. They've got upwards of ten men ridin' for them, maybe more than that."

Jake glanced at Lloyd, who just shook his head. Jake looked back at Jessie's brother. "Where did they get that many men?"

The man shrugged. "It ain't hard to find men who want to be a part of killin' Jake Harkner. They've been pickin' them up here and there for over a year, before the robbery and all that's happened since. The men they hired wasn't with the Bryants and Buckleys who robbed that bank. Marty and them boys did that all on their own—did it just to rile you. The bank money was s'posed to be used to pay off the men. Marty figured to kill you when you came after them, but you go down hard, Harkner. They underestimated you and that kid of yours. But this time they're ready for you, with plenty of guns to bring you down. Most of them men stayed on even without the money, on account of they think killin' you is worth hangin' around."

"Where are they now?"

"All over—mostly places where other outlaws and men with no families or jobs hang out. You probably know those places, seein' as how you're no better than they are. Marty's been wantin' to kill you ever since you destroyed his eye in that barroom brawl. Like I said, he helped with that robbery just so's you'd come lookin' for him. Figured him and the men with him could take you down when you came after them."

Jake's horse pranced nervously sideways. "You know how that turned out."

"Then Hash and Marty will just find some other way to get you, Harkner."

Jake pushed back his hat. "Why are you offering this information?"

"Because I don't much like Hash Bryant. He started this whole thing, and now my brother-in-law and one of my nephews is dead. Only trouble my sister's husband got in before this was fistfights and maybe jackin' under the skirt of some other man's wife. I'm tellin' you right now that Jack Buckley didn't have no part in rapin' that young gal. Bo might have, but not Jack. It was the Bryants who did that. I know them."

"Are all of these men Hash and Marty have been hiring at Hash's place now?"

"No. Last time I was there, it was just Hash and two other men. He was braggin' that they all had plans to meet in a couple of weeks and figure out what they'd do to finally get to you. He might have picked up a few up at that hellhole of an outlaw town north of here. He don't want them all in one place on account of he's heard how you have ways of bringin' down a lot of men when they're all together. He heard somethin' once about how you took down twelve or fifteen men up along the Outlaw Trail a couple years back...somethin' about goin' after your kid."

Jeff glanced at Lloyd, who rode closer to Jake.

"So they intend to spread out somehow?" Jake was asking.

"I honest to God don't know." The man looked Jake over, studied his weapons. "I just know I don't want no part of any of it. I heard about the big shoot-out back in California all them years back, and that gunfight in

Guthrie last month. If they want to go up against Jake Harkner, that's their business. But I don't know when or where they're gonna meet, else I'd tell you. I'm just lettin' you know they've got somethin' goin'—maybe rob another bank or somethin' else that would bring you out to them. They'll try for you again—only Hash knows he'll need more men than that first time. That's why he's findin' as many as he can. Cur dogs like to run in packs."

Jake glanced at the black man. "You know anything about this?"

"Only what Frank there done told you."

Jake tipped his hat. "Thanks for the information. Like I said, your rifles will be laying out in the road several yards from here."

"What are you gonna do, Harkner?"

"I don't know, but if I did, I wouldn't tell you. And if you see Hash or any of these men he's hired, you warn them that I was out here and if they want me, they can come and get me. If they want to die too soon, so be it." Jake got Prince into motion and rode off. Jeff and Lloyd followed, Jeff's heart pounding over the fact that any number of men could be waiting and watching, ready to shoot them down.

Lloyd caught up with Jake. "What do we do now, Pa?"

Jake scanned the road ahead. He took his six-gun from its holster and opened it to put a bullet in the empty chamber. "I'd like to go to the Buckley place and shoot every man there," Jake answered, shoving a bullet into the gun and slamming it shut. "But they haven't committed any crimes yet, and we'd probably be riding right into a trap if we go there. It sounds like they aren't all there right now anyway, and I'd like to make sure we have every last one of them. Somehow we have to get a line on where they intend to all meet."

"We'll need more men for that," Lloyd answered.

Jake holstered his gun and lit a cigarette, letting the horses walk casually to rest them. "We'll see what else we can find out about where they are this trip, then go get Sparky and some other men when we have an exact location and rout them out. It's a good thing you told Katie stay close to town, and I'm glad her folks are with her. Evie and Brian already know the rules. They should be safe for now."

A still-restless Prince whinnied and shook his mane. Jake patted the horse's neck.

"Maybe they'll end up all talk and no action," Jeff suggested, hoping he was right.

"Not Marty," Jake grumbled. "He's not going to let this go."

"I don't like any of this," Lloyd fumed. "Let's head for Hell's Nest."

"What's Hell's Nest?" Jeff asked.

Jake drew on the cigarette. "It's a settlement with *no* name. That's just the name I gave it."

"It's a hellhole, Jeff," Lloyd added. "Towns and farms and the like have sprung up all over Oklahoma from the land rushes. Some are nice, like Guthrie and Edmond and Stillwater, but some never quite grew into a full-fledged town. They're just settlements made up of the riffraff who came out in the land rushes just to hide out or find ways to live off of others or gamble and such. We've tracked a few train and bank robbers there, and a few rustlers who herded cattle there to keep a food supply going. Most of the worst of those who've come out here end up closer to No Man's Land because there's hardly any law there, and even Pa and I seldom go there."

"These damn land rushes are a headache," Jake added. "I've heard the government is going to open yet another section of Indian land for settlement. So much for treaties." He rode several yards ahead of them.

"Are we safe?" Jeff asked Lloyd.

Lloyd watched his father. "Hell, no, but there's nothing we can do about it as long as those men are scattered and we don't know what they have planned. Our best bet to find something out is to go to Hell's Nest. We have to take it easy on these horses in case we suddenly need to ride them hard, so we'll make the best time we can without wearing them out."

Lloyd rode to catch up to Jake again, and Jeff took a deep breath for courage, grasping the reins to the packhorse and following behind.

Twenty-five

"Lloyd."

"Yeah?"

"Would you really have shot that woman?"

"If she turned that rifle on my pa? Sure I would. Her kind is no different from a man."

They headed north, and Jeff and Lloyd rode lazily behind Jake, who insisted on staying several yards ahead of them to scout the woods and hills and scrub brush surrounding them. They had only a couple of hours of light left.

"Your mother's a woman, and she shot your father when they first met, but he didn't shoot back."

Lloyd looked at Jeff and grinned. "*Think* about it, Jeff. Surely you're not comparing my mother to someone like Jessie Buckley."

"Well, no, but...it seems like your father would have shot back in self-defense."

Lloyd shook his head. "Jeff, in my mother's case, Jake knew he didn't exactly have to worry about self-defense. She was just a scared young girl who reacted out of surprise and fear...not meanness. Pa knew the minute he faced her that she didn't have a mean bone in her body, or so he tells it."

They rode on in silence while Lloyd smoked.

"What do you know about the big Kennedy shoot-out back in California?" Jeff asked him then.

Lloyd kept the cigarette at the corner of his lips. "You'll have to ask my father about the details. I was the baby in his arms then, younger than Little Jake. That's why it upset Pa like it did. Anyway, I guess he got shot in the hip, and my mother suffered a stab wound. Pa left her again because he knew bounty hunters would hear about the shoot-out and come looking for him. He hid out in Wyoming in Outlaw Trail country for almost two years. My mother gave birth to Evie while he was gone."

Jake continued riding ahead of them.

"Mom suspects, and so do I, that he lived pretty wild for a time…maybe even was with other women as he tried to forget my mother, thinking it was best that way. But he loved her too much to stay away, and she damn well knew that if he could find a way for them to be together again, she'd go to him. He changed his last name and found a job on a ranch in Colorado, and he sent for her…and we had about fifteen years of a good life there. Pa thought he'd finally found a way to live peacefully and not be found, but some soldier who remembered him from his gunrunning days during the war came for him. That was the first time I even knew about his past. He'd never told me. He was scared I'd be ashamed of him."

Lloyd finished his cigarette and threw it down. "The sad part is, I *was* ashamed. I thought my pa was the greatest man who ever walked, and then I found out he was a wanted man. I abandoned him while he was in prison—left for almost four years. I headed out to prove I was just as worthless as my father—learned how to use his guns, got into a lot of trouble. My pa got released and he came for me."

He stopped and eyed the woods around them. "I'll never forget letting them all down for four damn years. I should have been there for my mother and my sister, let alone my pa. I was the man of the family." He shook his head. "Now we're closer than ever, and I'll never abandon or forsake Pa or my mother or Evie again, Jeff. Never. Period."

Jeff tried to put it all together timewise. "Those two years he was gone…your mother forgave him for…you know…?"

Lloyd shrugged. "I think it's just an understanding between them—a bad time that neither of them likes to talk about. Pa tried to pretend he could forget her. He's done that a couple of times, but it never works. Anything he might have done didn't matter, because the man is crazy in love with my mother and always will be. Under normal conditions, he'd never cheat on her. He loves her too much."

Jeff nodded. "From the short time I've known them and seen them together, I can tell there is something really special there. It doesn't take long to see it."

They exited the woods and rode into more open country. Lloyd rode at a faster trot to catch up with Jake.

"We need to make camp soon," Jake told them. "I'm figuring we're close enough to Dixie's place to sleep there tonight if we push the horses a little this time. We wouldn't lose any time and we wouldn't have to sleep on the ground. And Dixie's men can tend the horses there, rub them down, give them good feed, and shelter them in the barn."

"*Dixie's* place? Hell, Pa, I'm a married man now."

Jake gave him a wink. "Jeff isn't."

Lloyd grinned, then laughed. "You wouldn't really do that to him, would you?"

"Why not? The kid needs a lesson in women."

Jeff rode closer. "What's going on?"

Jake grinned. "I just figured that since it's on our way and we need to make camp, we'll sleep at a house called Dixie's Place tonight. We'd have real beds for the night, and we won't lose any time."

Jeff studied Jake's grin. "Wait a minute. Is this Dixie's Place what it sounds like?"

"You bet," Jake told him. "You are going to learn what to do with a woman, Jeff."

"I'm not going to any whorehouse."

"Don't worry about it, Jeff. You'll be just fine," Jake told him, laughing again. "You do plan to get married someday, don't you?"

"Of course I do."

"Don't you want to be the one to know what he's doing on your wedding night?"

Jeff reddened. "I know what to do."

"Jeff, don't pretend you've been with a woman, because I know you haven't. If you're going to travel with me and write a book about me, you're going to learn about that side of my life. And who knows? You just might enjoy it."

Lloyd and Jake both laughed, and Jake kicked Prince into a gentle trot. Lloyd and Jeff kept up.

"You behave yourself while we're there, Pa."

"I always do."

"Yeah, well, Dixie loves your handsome ass, and you're in a bad state."

Jake smiled sadly. "I just need someone like Dixie to talk to. Don't worry about it, Lloyd. And I'll damn well tell your mother, because the woman always knows if I've been there. I don't know how she does it." He sobered. "She'll understand."

They rode quietly for a while.

Jake finally spoke up. "We're just going to have some fun with Jeff."

Lloyd knew his father was sick with worry on the inside. This thing with Jeff gave him something to laugh about. He needed to laugh.

"Your mother knows she can trust me," Jake added. "In the morning, the horses will be well rested and we'll head for Hell's Nest." He gave Lloyd a teasing glance. "Maybe *I'm* the one who should keep an eye on *you*. Like you said, you're a married man now."

"Hell, I've been so busy trying to get Katie pregnant, I'm worn-out."

Jake laughed again, and Lloyd decided that if taking Jeff to Dixie's would keep Jake in a better mood, then it could only be a good thing. Jake had a great laugh, the kind that made everybody else grin, but Lloyd knew there was a deep terror behind the laughter.

Twenty-six

"WELL, IF IT ISN'T THE HANDSOME OUTLAW!"

A voluptuous, rather plump, worn-down woman with painted eyelids walked off the front porch of a tidy two-story brick building.

"Dixie!" Jake called to her as he dismounted and tied Prince to a hitching post.

The woman walked up to him, and Jake put an arm around her bare shoulders. Jeff just watched in wonder, feeling awkward and uncomfortable...and curious.

"Give us a kiss, you worthless sonofabitch," Dixie insisted.

Jake leaned down and gave her a quick kiss. She kept an arm around his waist and looked up at Lloyd. "And you brought the son again. Lord God, I don't know which one of you is the best-lookin'."

Lloyd grinned and dismounted. "Yeah, well, we're *both* unavailable, Dixie," he told her. "I got married a little over a month ago."

"Don't tell me!" She pressed a hand to Jake's stomach. "I'll bet she's beautiful."

"She sure is."

"Well, it's not fair that you two came here just to make us miserable havin' to look and not touch."

Jake laughed and crooked an arm around her neck, pulling her around to see Jeff. "That kid there is Jeff Trubridge, Dixie. He's from Chicago and he's writing a book about me. Maybe you'll even be in it. What do you think of that?"

Dixie wrapped her arms around Jake's middle as she looked Jeff over. "Well now, that depends if he makes me out to be a lady or somethin' *less* than a lady," she answered with a wink.

"And his opinion might depend on your hospitality tonight. The three of us are staying the night here, Dixie. We're on our way to Hell's Nest. Lloyd and I just need a room to ourselves, but Jeff there, I think he ought to have someone to sleep with, don't you?"

"I'm sure we can work somethin' out."

Jeff reddened. "I'm fine with my own room, ma'am."

"Oh, I think Dixie is too full up," Jake teased, giving Dixie a wink. "I think you'll have to share a room with somebody."

"Jake—"

"You'll live, Jeff. Get our gear and let's go inside. Dixie makes great steaks. You can meet some of the other girls."

"Jake—"

"Just get your gear, Jeff. You have a lot of things to write down after our visit to the Buckley place."

Jeff gave up arguing. All three of them unloaded weapons and personals, and Dixie ordered a Mexican man who came from the house to take care of their horses. The man greeted Jake.

"*¿Jake, me imagino que es las primera vez para este niño, ah?*"

"*Sí, Dominic. Necesita la experiencia para cuando tenga esposa.*"

Dominic laughed and took the horses, and Jeff just shook his head, pretty sure the remarks were about him. He understood enough to recognize "necessary" and "experience" and "wife." He followed Jake and Lloyd inside, where three younger women greeted them, one of them not much to look at, the other two decent but with painted faces and low-cut dresses that displayed plenty of bosom.

Dixie led them all to the kitchen, where two other men sat eating steaks and drinking beer. They both looked at Lloyd and Jake warily.

"Boys, this here is Marshal Jake Harkner and Deputy Marshal Lloyd Harkner—his kid, as if you couldn't tell. Jake, this is Hal and Clay. Don't know their last names and don't care. They're new in the territory—fresh in from the last land rush."

Lloyd urged Jeff to sit down at the table, but Jake remained standing. "How new?" he asked, eyeing them carefully.

"New enough, but a person don't have to be from around here to know who you are, Marshal," the one called Hal answered. He was a medium-built man with sandy hair and several missing teeth. Jake noticed neither man wore a gun. Because Hash Bryant was gathering men, who apparently were still scattered throughout the area, he had trouble trusting any stranger he came across.

"How's that?" he asked Hal.

The man shrugged. "Hell, you've been in newspaper headlines and dime novels." The man put out his hand. "I never expected to meet you. This is a real pleasure."

Jake didn't shake his hand. "A *pleasure*?"

"Sure. Hell, you're famous." His hand was still out. Jake shook it warily.

"Whatever you think," he answered. He looked over at Dixie. "While your girls serve Lloyd and Jeff, I want to talk to you, Dixie—in your room."

"Pa—"

"I'm all right, Lloyd." Jake lit a cigarette. "Bring me some coffee, will you?" he asked Dixie. "I'd appreciate it."

"Sure, honey. You know where my room is."

Jeff looked at Lloyd.

"Don't ask," Lloyd told him. He glanced at Jake. "Just don't drink, Pa."

"Just coffee. I need to talk to someone who's not

close to your mother." Jake sobered, eyeing the other two men again. "Either one of you ever heard of a man named Hash Bryant? Or Marty Bryant?" He could tell by their reaction that they hadn't. One thing he'd learned over the years was how to read a man's eyes.

"Don't know him," the one called Clay told him.

"Me neither," Hal added.

Jake glanced at Lloyd. "I'll eat later." He turned to Jeff then. "Kid, this is your chance to learn something. Take advantage of it."

Jake walked out of the room, and Dixie set a steak in front of Lloyd. "What's wrong with your father? He looks thinner than when he was here last time."

"He got hit in a shoot-out in Guthrie. Lost a ton of blood and came close to losing his life."

"Damn," Dixie muttered. "Is there more?"

"Yeah. My mother might have cancer. It's eating him up something awful, Dixie. He's pretending he's okay with it, but you've got your hands full once you get him alone."

Dixie sighed, walking over to pour some coffee. "That's terrible. Just terrible. Your mother is a kind, beautiful woman. It's not fair. I'll see if I can calm him down."

She started out and Lloyd called to her. "Dixie."

"Yeah?"

"Be good, will you?"

She grinned. "Ain't I always?"

"You know what I mean. He's hurting. Don't let him drink. And don't let him think he needs to prove he can handle it if my mother…doesn't make it. He's in a really bad state right now. My mother is on her way to Oklahoma City for surgery, and he can't be with her. It's killing him."

Dixie sobered. "I've been a shoulder to cry on more than once, kid. I'll be good." She looked him over. "But

I gotta say, it's too damn bad *you* got married. You're too easy on the eyes."

Lloyd just grinned and turned to Jeff, then nodded toward a pretty young woman of perhaps twenty or twenty-five. "That dark-haired beauty there, she's real sweet. You ought to get to know her, Jeff. Her name is Rosie O'Toole. You could have a pretty enjoyable night with that one."

"You should know, Lloyd Harkner," the woman answered suggestively. She cast him a fetching smile and brought a beer over for Jeff.

"Really, Lloyd, I don't want to do this," Jeff objected.

Lloyd shook his head. "You'll change your mind."

Jeff drank a little beer. "You sure your mother won't be upset with Jake alone in that woman's room?"

Lloyd cut some of his steak. "It's all part of being married to somebody like Jake, Jeff. He was brought up by women like that. They're the only mother figure he ever had after his own mother was killed. When he needs to talk to somebody like a man might talk to his ma, that's the kind he talks to. I just don't like the state he's in, that's all."

He ate more steak but noticed Jeff only picked at his. "Jeff, we're all a product of how we're raised," Lloyd told him when he was nearly finished eating. "You are the way you are because you grew up loved and educated and probably a bit sheltered. I am a lot like my pa because his blood is in me, but I'll never be completely like him because of my mother. I've got some of her softness, and I was privileged to always *have* a mother—and a father who taught me strength, and taught me how fathers are supposed to raise their sons."

He lit a cigarette. "And Jake is the way he is because of how *he* was raised—no mother for most of his younger years, a father from hell who beat the idea into him that he was worthless, and surrounded by outlaws and prostitutes. I'm guessing there were times when some prostitute, maybe more than one, took him in and protected him from his father. So don't judge him by some of the things he does now. It's all he knows…and my mother understands that." He met Jeff's eyes. "She also knows he'd step in front of her and take a bullet in the gut if it meant saving her life. And if he could take her cancer away by putting it into himself, he'd do it without hesitation. He'll never do anything that would hurt her, her body or her heart."

Jeff slowly nodded.

"That Jake, he's a good man," Rosie said. She sat down near Jeff and pulled off his glasses. "Do you really need these?"

Jeff shrugged. "If I want to see, I do."

"Well, you look cuter without them." She smiled, leaning closer and kissing him. "Sometimes touching is better than seeing, Jeff." She laughed then and tousled his hair.

Lloyd just grinned and got up, walking outside to smoke. *Damn it, Pa, don't do anything stupid.*

❧

Jake removed his boots and weapons belt and guns, hanging the belts over a bedpost where his duster and hat already hung. He sat down on the bed and put his feet up, leaning against the head of the bed.

Dixie walked in with his coffee, bringing it over and setting it on a stand beside the bed. She folded her arms and stood there looking at him. "Lloyd told me about your wife. I'm goddamn sorry, Jake."

Jake looked away, lighting a cigarette. "Dixie, a man like me never deserved her in the first place. I guess I should consider myself lucky to have actually had that woman for twenty-six years."

Dixie walked to her dressing table. She picked up a

handkerchief and began wiping the color off her face, revealing an aging woman who'd seen far too much of her own share of hard living.

"I saw her once in Guthrie."

Jake looked at her in surprise. "How did you know who she was?"

Dixie smiled. "Well, I'd gone into town to stock up on supplies. I was buying some material, and she walked in." She undid her hair and began brushing it out, then faced Jake. "My very first thought was 'Damn, she's one beautiful woman.'"

Jake stared at his cigarette. "That she is."

"She was actually kind to me—nodded to me and greeted me. I'm sure she suspected what I was, because we all have that look about us. I know that. But she was nice to me anyway. Then the store clerk called her by name. 'Good morning, Mrs. Harkner,' he says." She continued brushing her hair. "Well, my jaw about dropped to the floor. 'So, there she is,' I thought. 'That's Jake Harkner's wife, and ain't she just the most beautiful, most gracious thing that ever walked. She's just like Jake described her.' And I kind of put two and two together, her bein' nice to me and all. I think she was nice to me because she knew women like me were once a part of your life and you would *expect* her to be nice to me. And I thought, 'How in hell did Jake Harkner find a woman like that—her bein' so tiny and gorgeous—him bein' so big and mean?' 'Course, when it comes to looks, there ain't nothin' bad about you. No wonder that son of yours is even *better* lookin'—havin' you for a pa and that beautiful woman for a mother. I didn't tell her I knew you, because…well, that's obvious. But I have to wonder if she would have just smiled and asked me to the house or something. That's just how she struck me—as bein' that gracious."

Jake grinned and shook his head. "She probably *would*

have invited you over, but I would have had to answer a whole lot of questions afterward."

Dixie smiled. "That's why I never said anything. But I'm tellin' you this because I think it's damn wrong for a woman like that to die too young, when women like me are still walkin' around free and easy." She set down the brush and walked over to the bed, climbing onto it from the other side. She moved close to him and touched his arm. "Is there any hope?"

Jake didn't answer right away. He finished his cigarette and put it out in an ashtray on the stand. The coffee still sat there, getting cold. "It could just be cysts." He told her all of it, his try for a reduced sentence, Peter, the surgery. "Goddamn it, Dixie, I should be with her and I can't be."

"Well, you must really trust this Peter Brown if you let him take your wife to Oklahoma City and look after her."

Jake took her hand, rubbing the back of it with his thumb. "I *have* to trust him, because he's all I've got. Because this job is a sentence and not by choice, I have to take care of business, and Randy can't wait for that surgery. They said the sooner, the better, because if it is cancer, they might be able to catch it in time."

"Then that's what you have to hope for, Jake."

He closed his eyes. "With *my* luck?"

She squeezed his hand. "You have two beautiful children and two grandsons, and you've had Randy for a lot of years. I'd say that's pretty damn *good* luck for a man with your background."

He smiled sadly, leaning his head back.

"She'll need holding, Dixie, and he'll be the one holding her when she's afraid or hurting. And I'm scared to death she'll die down there without me. I couldn't live with that. Grandkids or not, I couldn't live with that."

"Yes, you could—for *her*. She'd never want you to do

something crazy and not be there for your family, who will need you more than ever, if it's the worst."

"But she'd still be gone."

Dixie didn't answer him. She just sat there beside him and waited. For several minutes he said nothing. Finally he leaned over, wrapping his arms around her middle and resting his head in her lap. He held her tight...and wept.

Twenty-seven

JAKE TIED HIS GEAR ONTO HIS HORSE. "DID JEFF STAY the night with that cute little Rosie?"

Lloyd shoved his shotgun into its boot. "He sure did," he answered with a grin. "And if you'd come to the room we were supposed to share last night, you would have known about it already. I don't want to think the worst, Pa, but I never saw you the rest of the night. And you were awful quiet at breakfast."

Jake rubbed at his eyes. "Don't worry about it, Lloyd. You don't honestly think I'd do anything to hurt your mother, do you—especially now that she's sick? Dixie and I just talked. That's all. You ought to know me better than that."

"I *do* know you, and sometimes you get kind of crazy when you're worried about Mom. I'm not stupid. I know you've done crazy things before when you thought you needed to prove you could live without her."

Jake sighed. "Didn't you notice at breakfast this morning that Dixie was wearing the same damn dress she wore last night?"

"I never thought about that."

"Well, that's because she never took it *off*. Nothing happened, all right? Dixie's a good woman. We talked... a lot. I fell asleep and she let me lay there because she knew I *needed* to sleep. That's all there was to it." He mounted up and rode Prince around the house, calling for Jeff. "Time to go, Jeff, if you can tear yourself away from the cute little gal in your bed!" he shouted.

"Oh my gosh!" The words were heard through an open window of an upstairs bedroom. "Don't leave without me!"

Lloyd laughed and mounted his horse.

"You have no more than ten minutes, Jeff," Jake shouted up to him. "You'd better be down here or we *will* leave without you. We need to make time getting to Hell's Nest!" He rode Prince a few yards from the house to calm the restless horse.

"I'm coming! I'm coming!" Jeff yelled from upstairs.

Dixie came out carrying a burlap bag. She handed it up to Lloyd. "Fresh-baked bread. You make sure your father eats plenty. He never ate last night and not enough this morning."

"Thanks, Dixie. Go tie it onto the packhorse, will you?"

"Sure."

"Dixie. Is he okay?"

"I'm not sure. He did a lot of crying last night, Lloyd, and don't you dare let him know I told you. He needed somebody to talk to, and he knows you're too close to it. So he came to me." She walked over to the packhorse and began tying on the sack of bread.

Jeff came flying out of the house then, still buttoning his shirt and carrying his leather jacket and gun belt on his arm. Rosie came running after him with his hat. She plopped it on his head and leaned in to kiss him. "You come back, sweet boy," she told him.

Jake returned and rode up beside them. "Can you ride, or are you too worn-out?" he teased.

Jeff pulled on his jacket and frowned as he strapped on his gun belt. "I can ride just fine," he answered. He kissed Rosie once more and mounted up. "And if you and Lloyd are going to rub it in all the way till we make camp, I'd just as soon stay behind the two of you."

Jake laughed. "Welcome to my world, Jeff Trubridge." He turned his horse and rode off.

Lloyd rode up beside Jeff and handed him the reins to the packhorse. "You look like you still need some sleep, Jeff." He grinned and followed after Jake.

Jeff looked down at Rosie. "Thank you. You were very…accommodating."

She threw back her head and laughed. "Get going, Jeff. Jake isn't the kind of man who waits around for anybody. But I hope you come back some time."

"I just might do that." Jeff turned his horse and rode off, deciding Jake had been right about learning what to do with a woman. It was definitely enjoyable. In fact, he'd not done any of the writing he'd planned to do. The next time they made camp, he'd have to try to catch up a little with his notes. He kicked his horse into a faster gait to catch up with Lloyd, thinking how he was getting some aches and pains in all the wrong places from so much riding. He'd never in his life been on a horse more than a few hours a month, and this trip was going to last a good eight or ten days, maybe longer. He was determined, however, not to complain. For him, this was a dream come true—actually traveling with Jake Harkner, of all people, and winning his friendship. The man's friendship meant more to him than writing his story. If he never got to publish this book, it didn't matter. He could brag that he once rode with the famous outlaw turned lawman.

He reached Lloyd. "Sorry I was late."

Lloyd just grinned. "I understand."

"Is Jake okay? I mean…I was kind of preoccupied last night, so I never saw him again after he walked out of the kitchen last night with Dixie."

Lloyd didn't answer right away. "I never saw him again either. He told me he just had a good talk with her. I believe him. He slept in her bed, but he was just exhausted from worry. I think he had kind of a breakdown, but don't put anything like that in your book. And don't mention to him that I told you."

"I won't." Jeff adjusted his hat against the angle of the bright sun that was already warming the day. "I've come to really like him, Lloyd."

"Yeah, well, Pa can *be* real likable as long as he senses you're genuine and not out to exploit his reputation or brag that you know him…and not out to kill him."

Jeff grinned. "I have no intention of *that*. I happen to be in very good health and intend to stay that way."

Both men laughed quietly.

"And I've been praying every day that your mother will be all right."

Lloyd nodded. "I thank you for that. I've been doing the same."

"Does Jake ever pray?"

Lloyd took a cigarette from his shirt pocket. "I don't know, Jeff. I honestly don't know. He wears his mother's crucifix, and I think he believes, but I don't know if he prays."

"I talked to him just a little bit about faith on the church steps that Sunday you came back to announce you were marrying Katie. I got this feeling, Lloyd, that a little part of him kind of wanted to go inside. He got quiet a couple of times when he could hear the hymn singing. I'd love to know what was going through his head."

Lloyd smiled. "Can you picture Jake Harkner standing at the pearly gates? God would ask him, 'Jake Harkner, how many men have you killed?' 'Lord, I've lost count.' 'And how many whores have you slept with?' 'Lord, I lost count on that too.' 'Well then, how about cussing?' 'Cussing? Hell, I cuss all the damn time, Lord.' 'And has your heart ever been filled with hate and anger?' 'Lord, my heart is full of hate and anger about twenty-four hours a day, seven days a week.'"

Both men couldn't help laughing at the vision, but then Lloyd sobered. "Then God would ask if he's been a good husband and father. 'I tried to be the best at both, Lord,' he'd have to say. And God would ask him if he ever loved anybody, and he'd have to answer that he loved my mother and his son and his daughter with every fiber of his being—and that he saved my mother's life when he took her from that awful trading post where he found her—and that he saved my life and risked his own doing it when he came for me up along the Outlaw Trail. He'd have to say that he loved his mother and his little brother. 'But you killed your own father,' God might say. And my pa would have to tell him that all he did was try to get rid of Satan himself, because that was who his father was. And I think God would tell my pa that he did a good job of loving his family, and he'd see that my pa has a good heart, and he'd let him through those gates, even though he never stepped foot into a church."

Jeff shook his head. "Maybe I should let you write this book, Lloyd. You have a way with words."

Lloyd shrugged. "When we were growing up, my mother sometimes read poetry to us. I like learning how to express feelings with the right words…pretty words, Pa calls them. He has his own way of expressing himself, as you well know."

They both laughed again. "And it's far from pretty most of the time," Jeff answered. "He's a man who says exactly what he's thinking."

"Maybe so. And he's real good at changing the subject when you start hitting the raw spots."

After three more hours of riding, Lloyd noticed Jake slow his horse. He was watching what looked like a small camp ahead. Lloyd rode closer to take a look. He could see a covered wagon, a few horses and a campfire. Jeff rode up beside him. It was then that Lloyd heard it—a child screaming and crying. From where he and Jeff sat, it looked like a man was whaling on a young boy, with a belt.

Jake charged forward.

"Jesus God Almighty, he'll kill him with his bare hands!" Lloyd kicked his horse into a run, and Jeff hurried behind him.

Twenty-eight

JAKE DUCKED OUT OF HIS EXTRA AMMUNITION BELT, ripping it off his shoulder and throwing it down as he drew closer. Before Prince even came to a halt, he pulled both guns from their holsters and tossed them, then jumped off the horse and slammed into the man who'd been wielding a belt. They landed hard, and Jake hit the left side of his face on the sharp edge of a shovel tied to the wagon bed.

The injury didn't seem to faze him. Jeff and Lloyd watched in shock as Jake wrested the belt from a man almost the same size as he and began whaling on the man with it.

"Jesus!" Lloyd cursed, quickly dismounting. "Go pick up his guns," he ordered Jeff. He hurried over to the young boy, who stood shaking and sobbing as he stared at Jake viciously whacking what Lloyd guessed must be the boy's father.

"Come on, son, get out of the way."

The boy jerked with pain as Lloyd picked him up and moved him back. The child was no older than Lloyd's own son Stephen, and Lloyd ached at seeing a huge white welt on the side of his face. He imagined the rest of the kid's body was a mess. How could any man do this to his own son?

The man lay curled up and screaming as Jake continued wielding the leather belt. Lloyd ran up to him, knowing that when Jake Harkner was raging mad, he had a strength that belied his age—and he was definitely raging mad.

Lloyd dove at Jake's back, trying to grab him around his arms. "Pa, you're killing him!"

Jake shook him off as though he were a bug.

Lloyd bent low and grabbed him about the waist from behind, using all his strength to pull Jake away. "Pa, you'll go back to prison! Stop it! This isn't part of your job!"

Jake whirled, accidentally slamming the belt across Lloyd's shoulder. Lloyd cried out and let go of him.

The minute Jake realized what he'd done, he hesitated, standing there panting and staring at Lloyd. "Shit," he muttered, dropping the belt. "Lloyd, I'm sorry!" He groaned. The man he'd beaten lay writhing with pain, still curled up in defense. Jake stumbled over to Lloyd. "I'm sorry!" he repeated.

Lloyd straightened, rubbing his shoulder. "Now I know how it feels," he commented. He met Jake's gaze, seeing the hatred and terror in the man's eyes. Blood poured down his face and shirt from where he shovel had cut him, and the area around the wound was growing purple.

"Pa, you're hurt."

Jake shook his head. "Doesn't matter. We have to help the boy first." He walked over to where the boy stood, still sobbing. He backed away from Jake. Jake knelt down. "I'm not going to use that belt on you, kid. Let me help you. We can pour water on those welts. That helps. And I have something with me that might help the pain."

The boy continued staring, his tears creating white lines through the dirt on his cheeks. "Did you…kill him?" he asked Jake. "He's…my pa…but I hate him. I hope you killed him." He was trying to stop crying, but his body continued to jerk in silent sobs.

Jake closed his eyes and collapsed to a sitting position. "Come here and take your shirt off."

The boy moved closer and started unbuttoning his shirt. "It hurts...to move my arms."

"I damn well know it hurts." Jake yelled for Jeff to bring over a canteen. He got to his knees and unbuttoned the boy's shirt, gently removing it for him. The sight of the welts on his body brought literal pain to Jake's chest. "What's your name?"

"Ben."

"How old are you?"

"Eight."

Jake struggled against ugly memories as Jeff arrived with the canteen. "Pour water over those welts—gently," Jake ordered Jeff. "Let it trickle over so you don't use up the whole canteen all at once."

Jeff obeyed. Ben jerked and started crying again when the water touched the stinging welts.

"Lloyd, get some laudanum," Jake ordered. He looked at Ben. "I'm a United States Marshal, Ben. There is no law that says I have a right to take you away from that man over there, or that even gives me permission to stop him from beating you. I need to know—do you want to stay with him? If not, I'll take you with me, even if it means losing my job."

The boy closed his eyes against the stinging pain. "He'll...come after me."

"I know he will. When I was about your age, I tried running away from my father too, Ben. But I didn't have a United States Marshal helping me. I'm telling you that if you want to come with us, you can, and I'll make sure that sonofabitch over there never touches you again. You can trust me on that."

The boy glanced at his father again. The man still lay curled up. He looked back at Jake. "Where...would you take me?"

Lloyd walked closer, bringing laudanum for the boy and whiskey to cleanse Jake's wound.

"I'd take you to Guthrie, and I'd find a good family to raise you, Ben. And I am promising you right now that if I can't find decent people for you to live with, I'll damn well raise you myself. I just need to know if you want to leave that man over there. I know he's your father, and I know part of you loves him, but if you stay with him, he'll come close to killing you with that belt. You don't owe him a damn thing, Ben. Where's your mother?"

The boy sniffed and wiped at a runny nose with the back of his hand. "She died havin' a baby. Pa buried her farther back. He said…he shouldn't have to raise me… by himself." The boy's thick, blond hair stuck out every which way, and his blue eyes showed cautious fear when he glanced at his father again. "He gets mad real easy and…gets mean…when he drinks. I think I…want to go with you."

"Then you will."

Ben's eyes widened then, and he stepped back when his father managed to get to a sitting position. The man glowered at Ben and Jake.

"Get the hell away from my son!" he told Jake.

Jake turned his gaze to the man, and Jeff noticed Ben's father's threatening countenance change. The look in Jake's eyes told him he'd better tread lightly. The man grimaced as he tried to get up. "Who the hell…are you?" he asked Jake, and he fell back down.

Lloyd stepped closer to the man, standing over him defensively. "That's Jake Harkner, federal marshal. I'm Deputy Marshal Lloyd Harkner. And you are going to pack up and leave, mister—*now*! You have no idea how lucky you are to be alive."

The man bent over in pain. "Ain't no law…against a man…disciplinin' his son."

"Maybe not. But that was way more than discipline, mister, and there *is* a law against attempted murder. That's what we could arrest you for, and for the most part, a marshal's words are sacred out here. Something tells me you'd rather give up your son than go to prison. That's the choice we're giving you, mister."

"But...you can't—"

"We can. Out here in Oklahoma Territory we're the law—*period*!"

"He's my kid! I've got first rights! How would you feel if somebody came to take your kid from you?"

"I *have* a kid close to the same age as yours, and I don't beat him near to death with a fucking belt! Right now I'm tempted to pick up where my father left off and finish you off, you sonofabitch!" Lloyd walked over to pick up the belt.

"Wait!" the man objected. "You can have him!"

Lloyd turned to the man, and for the first time Jeff saw a dark look very close to what he'd sometimes seen in Jake...this time in Lloyd's eyes.

"What's that?"

"You can have the worthless little bastard!"

Ben covered his face and started crying. Jake got to a kneeling position and put a hand to the side of Ben's face. "Don't listen to him, Ben." He pulled Ben's hands away from his face. "Don't ever listen if somebody calls you worthless, understand?"

"But he's...my pa. He's...s'posed to love me."

"Being a blood father doesn't always mean being the *right* father, Ben. You see this young man standing near us?"

Ben looked up at Jeff. "Yeah."

"And that young man over there?" He nodded toward Lloyd.

"Yeah."

"None of us is your pa, but all three of us already love you. And nobody will ever lay a hand on you again. Do you believe that?"

"You don't even...know me."

Jeff watched in complete wonder and surprise as Jake leaned closer and kissed Ben's forehead. "I know you all too well, Ben. I know every single thing you're feeling. Every single thing."

Lloyd walked up to Jeff, still seething. "Do you have a regular-size pad of paper with you?"

"Sure I do."

"You get it out and you write something up for that man over there to sign—something we can all witness so he can't come back later and try to take his kid."

"Sure. I can do that." Jeff hurried away to search through his supplies, his mind racing with yet another chapter for his book. *Lloyd Harkner is way closer to his dad's temperament than he thinks.*

Lloyd knelt down beside Jake. "We have to take care of that cut on your face, Pa."

Jake shivered, sitting back down and closing his eyes while clinging to Ben's hand. "Jesus, Lloyd, I feel like…I don't know…like I have finally rid myself of that bastard father of mine. I was using that belt on *him*, not that man over there. But I'm damn sorry about hitting you."

"You don't need to be." He sighed. "Stay there and I'll clean up that cut. God knows you lost enough blood back in Guthrie. You don't need to be losing more." He reached for the whiskey he'd brought over earlier.

"Lloyd, do you think the Donavans might take Ben?" Jake asked him.

Lloyd finally smiled. "Are you kidding? Clara Donavan will gush all over that kid when she finds out why we brought him back with us."

Jake nodded. "I was hoping you'd say that."

Lloyd doused a rag with whiskey and pressed it to the cut on his father's face. Jake winced and jerked away.

"This is one ugly cut, Pa. Mom is going to have a fit when she sees this. She'll probably be mad as hell that somebody dared to mess up her handsome husband's face."

Jake smiled sadly. "Yeah, but I get a lot more attention when I come back wounded."

Both men grinned, trying to ignore the seriousness of the situation. Through the whole thing, Jake kept hold of Ben's hand. "Give this kid one sip of laudanum," he told Lloyd. "There isn't a whole lot you can do for this cut. And give me a swallow of that whiskey. Right now it will do me a lot more good inside than outside."

Lloyd gave him a warning look. "One swallow."

Jake jerked the bottle from his hand. "Don't worry." He glanced over at Ben's father as he took a swallow. The man was still having trouble getting to his feet. "I'd rather pick up that belt and beat him unconscious," he told Lloyd.

"I know. You just remember you're trying to get your sentence reduced. You'd have been in trouble if you'd killed that man. We have to turn in some kind of report on this. That's why I had Jeff write something up." He uncorked the laudanum. "Hey, Ben, this stuff tastes something awful, but it will help your pain. You're just a kid, so you take just a little swallow, okay?"

Still sniffling, Ben took the laudanum and swallowed some, his whole face wrinkling up over the bad taste. Lloyd grinned and took the bottle from him.

"Tell you what, Ben. I'll put one of Jeff's shirts on you," Lloyd told him. "We'll have to roll up the sleeves, but otherwise it will hang nice and big on you and hardly touch those welts. We have to keep the sun off them. That okay with you?"

"Yes, sir."

"Do you have extra clothes in the wagon?"

Ben nodded. "In a crate behind the seat."

Lloyd glanced at Jake. "I'll get his clothes." He called over to Jeff, who was still writing. "Bring one of your extra shirts over for Ben," he told him. "He needs something that hangs loose, because of these welts."

Jeff nodded and kept writing. Lloyd walked to the wagon and climbed inside, finding Ben's clothes. There weren't many. He gathered them out of the crate and carried them over to an empty gunnysack on the packhorse, stuffing them inside. Jeff handed him a write-up verifying that Ben's father agreed to give up his son to them. "I left a blank spot for his name," he told Lloyd. "We don't even know what it is."

Lloyd took the paper and carried it over to Ben's father. Jeff took a shirt to Ben and put it on him. It hung past the boy's knees, and Jeff rolled up the sleeves.

"I've felt like a kid myself this whole trip, Ben," Jeff tried joking with him, wanting to get rid of the boy's tears. "I've been traveling between these two big men for a while. Now there is finally somebody smaller than me along, so I feel a little bigger. My name is Jeff Trubridge. What's your last name?"

"Perry." The boy's eyes were already drooping.

Jake got to his feet and brushed the dust from his clothes. "Get his birth date, Jeff. That's important to a man. Write it on that paper."

Jeff remembered the encounter in Peter's office, when Jake had to guess at his birth date. "Sure, Jake."

"Where are my guns?"

"In my gear. You threw them down when you rode up to attack that man," Jeff told him.

"I don't even remember throwing them down. I guess I knew I'd rather beat the hell out of him with that belt than shoot him."

"You tossed your extra gun belt too. I've never seen a man so enraged. It was pretty scary. Lloyd had a hell of a time getting you off that man. Between your age and not being totally healed, I don't know how you can still be so strong."

Jake ran a hand through his hair. "Being mad as hell gives a man a lot of extra strength. And what do you mean by my age? Are you writing me off as an old man?"

"Well, no, not exactly."

Jake grinned but lost his smile when Ben started to swoon. Jake grabbed him up before he could fall. The boy put his head on Jake's shoulder, and Jake carried him over to his horse. "Jeff, come hold him till I mount up—and get my guns."

Jeff hurried over to help out and Jake mounted up. Jeff handed the boy up and Jake set him in front of him on the horse, hanging on to him with one arm. Jeff retrieved the guns and shoved them into Jake's holsters. He hung Jake's extra cartridge belt over Prince's neck.

Lloyd ordered Ben's father to sign the paper, then brought it over so he, Jake, and Jeff could all witness the signature. *Charles Jacob Perry*, it read. *Springfield, Missouri*. Jake handed back the paper. "Go ask him what the kid's birthday is and write it down." He rode off with Ben. "I'll wait for you two farther ahead," he called back. "I need to be alone."

Lloyd winced at the aching sting on his right shoulder and arm. "Jesus," he told Jeff. "The way this one welt hurts, I don't know how he lived through it. I'm glad we had some laudanum for Ben." He sighed, walked back to Ben's father, and asked him Ben's birth date. He walked back to Jeff and wrote the date on the signed paper. He folded the paper and put it in his gear. He mounted up and rode closer to Ben's father. "If I ever see your face again, you're a dead man. That's a promise. It will be the same if my dad sees you." He rode off, more than ever hating the grandfather he'd never known.

Jeff followed. They rode until almost dark, Jake

keeping a passed-out Ben in front of him and saying nothing. He headed his horse into the woods and dismounted, asking Lloyd to spread out a blanket for Ben. Jake laid the boy down, then unloaded all his weapons and spread out his own bedroll, laying all weapons beside it.

Lloyd made a fire. "Pa, that cut on your face is really wicked and turning purple. You okay?"

"I'll live. I've got to change this bloody shirt, though." He rummaged through his saddlebag and pulled out a clean, blue shirt. He removed the bloody shirt as Jeff was coming back with his own gear.

Jeff stopped, forcing back an urge to mutter *My God*. For the first time, he saw the scars on Jake's back. There were a couple that looked like old gunshot wounds, but most of them were white stripes, like from a belt or a whip. Jeff looked away and pretended to have forgotten something, waiting until Jake changed shirts.

"Jeff, get your pencil and tablet," Jake told him.

"I already have them," Jeff answered, coming back with his blanket and a tablet.

"How bad is that welt on your shoulder hurting?" Jake asked Lloyd.

Lloyd lit some kindling under some bigger logs. "I think if you could handle something a lot worse at Ben's age, and now Ben himself is managing, *I* can handle one lash with a belt."

Jeff sat down near Jake. Jake lit a cigarette and smoked quietly for a moment, his shirt still unbuttoned and untucked. He glanced at Jeff. "I'm only going to say this once, Jeff, and I'm doing it now because Ben is asleep and I don't want him hearing it."

"Yes, sir…I mean, Jake."

Jake tossed a twig into the fire. "My father's name was John William Harkner, and he was from Connecticut. You can give Peter that information if he needs it. He left home at a young age and somehow worked his way to Texas, where he got involved in some of the shit going on between Texas and Mexico. I'm not even sure what all he did before I came along. I only know he liked Mexican women, the younger the better, and he drank…a lot. He was big like me. I'm pretty sure he bought my mother off some drunken Mexican man, and I have no idea if he ever really married her. I only know she was very good to me, very loving. But my father… I remember him beating my mother often, and if my brother or I tried to stop him, we got it too…always with that goddamn belt, often with the buckle end of it."

He drew on the cigarette. Lloyd tended the fire, listening quietly.

"When I was eight…he stabbed my mother to death right in front of me, and when my little brother started crying, he slammed a fireplace poker against his head. I kept trying to wake him up, but he was dead too." Jake closed his eyes and took a deep breath. "His name was Tommy. Later my father made me help bury both of them. I had to stand there and throw dirt on their faces."

He spoke matter-of-factly, chain-smoking while doing so. Jeff suspected he was trying to hurry before breaking down. "I tried to run away then, but he caught me and taught me to never try that again. Life was hell for the next seven years—his drinking binges, running with the worst kind of men imaginable, whoring around, and always the beatings. Whores became my mothers and sometimes… When you're twelve or thirteen years old, it's easy for an older woman to entice you, so I learned about women at an age when I should have been playing pretend shoot-outs with other boys my age. Whores were just a part of my life, Jeff."

He tossed the stub of his cigarette into the fire and lit yet another one.

"Somewhere in the back of my mind, I knew there

had to be something better. Every place we went, I saw husbands and wives with their kids, saw normal homes, farms, people living a normal life. Part of me wanted that. When I was fifteen, I befriended a twelve-year-old Mexican girl named…"

Finally he hesitated, the memories getting more difficult. He cleared his throat.

"Santana." He swallowed before continuing. "She looked more like fifteen or sixteen, and she was beautiful. I started getting the idea that maybe when she was a little older, I could get away from my pa and marry her and live like people were supposed to live. We started meeting secretly, but I never touched her, because to me she was special…and too young. And then one day I came home to find my father drunk and…raping Santana."

He cleared his throat again.

"She was…crying and trying to get him off of her… and I tried too. But even though I was already pretty big at fifteen, I still wasn't as strong as he was. He climbed off her and laid into me with that belt until he beat me right to the floor. Then he turned around and put his filthy body on top of Santana again."

Again he smoked for several minutes, saying nothing. Jeff knew he didn't dare say a word.

Jake breathed deeply before finally speaking again. "I spotted my father's handgun hanging on the wall nearby, and I was desperate to stop him from hurting Santana… so I took the gun and put it to his neck…and I pulled the trigger. I didn't even stop to think it could kill him. I just wanted to get him off of Santana. He slumped down and I dragged him off of her…only to see that the bullet had gone through his neck and into Santana's throat."

Jake closed his eyes then and ran a hand through his hair. "She just lay there wide-eyed and scared. I told her I loved her and I'd stop the bleeding…but before I could even grab something to press on the wound…

she was gone. I was scared and confused and...I wanted to scream. I'd killed Santana. I figured they might hang me for murder, thinking I killed her and my pa both because I was jealous or something, maybe even accuse *me* of being the one who raped her. I was young and didn't think things through. I just picked up that gun and saddled a horse and headed north...and thus began the outlaw career of a man who'd killed his own father...and a young girl. I lived like a crazy man for the next ten or twelve years, always running from the law, robbing and killing for money, convinced I was the most worthless sonofabitch who ever lived, because my father made sure to tell me that every day. But always there was that little desire to live like a normal person."

Jeff scribbled notes as fast as he could, because Jake was apparently determined to get the story over with and definitely would not want to repeat it.

Jake angrily wiped at his eyes, staring at the fire the whole time he talked. "Then one day I had a shoot-out in a supply store in Kansas City, and a young woman with honey-blond hair and gray-green eyes witnessed it. She looked at me, scared shitless, and she pulled a little pistol from her handbag and shot me. And that, young Jeff, changed my life. You already know what happened then. That crazy woman has stuck by me through things that would horrify other women and send them running...but not Randy..." He wiped at his eyes again. "Not Randy."

He abruptly changed the subject. "We'll haul ass up to Hell's Nest tomorrow and get there by the day after." The change of subject was so immediate that it took Jeff a moment to realize he was done talking about his father. "If we can't find out anything there, we'll head home. I'm sure Lloyd would like to be with Katie, and we need to do something with young Ben, so let's hope nothing else happens to slow us down."

Jake looked over at Ben and put a blanket over him. He lit yet another cigarette and walked off by himself.

Lloyd looked at Jeff. "Now you know all of it. It's not a pretty picture."

Jeff stared at his notes. "No. It sure isn't."

Twenty-nine

HE TALKS TO LITTLE BEN ALMOST LIKE HE'D TALK TO HIS own grandchildren, Jeff wrote on their fifth morning of travel. He had to hurry to finish his notes. Today they would reach Hell's Nest.

This is not the heartless man some have made him out to be. On the outside, he is tough as nails. I would never want to be on the bad side of Jake Harkner. But on the inside, he is almost like a little boy wanting to be loved and wanting to love in return. I always thought that with human nature, black was black and white was white, but I am changing my mind. There is much more gray in this life than people realize.

Jake left young Ben at a rancher's house three hours behind them. To Jeff's dismay, the rancher was an old ex-outlaw married to a former prostitute, people only someone like Jake would actually trust with a little boy he cared about. Jeff had just about given up understanding the man and how he knew which people he could depend on. He'd promised Ben he would be back for him, and the boy had looked at Jake like a kid would look at his own father. He'd hugged Jake around the neck and cried.

"Look at me, Ben," Jake told him, crouching down so they would be face-to-face.

The boy had reached out and touched Jake's face lovingly.

"I will come back for you," Jake promised him. "Believe that and don't be scared. These are nice people, and I'll only be gone for a few hours—maybe one night— and then I'll be back for you. Do you believe me?"

Ben nodded and Jake hugged him, being careful not to embrace him too tightly because of his still-painful welts. He left instructions with the rancher to take Ben to Guthrie and the Donavans if he didn't return from Hell's Nest.

Now they approached the lawless settlement, and the man riding into town was a far cry from one who'd hugged a crying eight-year-old boy. He was all lawman and probably a lot outlaw, because this place was full of them.

"Do you expect much trouble here, Jake?"

"Can't be sure. It depends on whether any of those men Marty Bryant has been running with are here. Just keep your eyes open and your gun ready. This place is nothing but the worst riffraff who have come to Oklahoma to hide out from the law. The whores are filthy women who will do things for money not even Dixie and her girls would consider. They're the kind of women even *I* would never touch. If Marty Bryant is gathering men, I have a feeling that somebody here will know something about it."

They reached the main street, where Jeff noticed two men lying passed out on the boardwalk. Piano music and laughter seemed to pour out of every saloon, and saloons made up about two-thirds of the buildings and tents in town.

"Hey, it's Marshal Jake Harkner!" The words were shouted by a half-naked prostitute standing on the balcony of the only two-story building in town. "Hey, Jake, are you or that damn good-looking son of yours needing a good lay?"

"I'd be doing *you* a favor, Ida," Jake yelled back, "so I shouldn't need to pay for it."

The woman shrieked with laughter. "Come and do me that favor, honey. I'm still waiting to be able to say I've been had by Jake Harkner."

"Let's go on up to the Land Rush Saloon," Jake told Lloyd. "Jeff, just go along with whatever I do and don't question it."

"I don't see anything particularly out of place, Pa," Lloyd told him. "Same drunks—same lewd women—same smells of urine in the streets."

"Check the horses' rear ends for the Bryant brand. If they're hiring men, they'll be riding Bryant horses, or maybe Buckley horses. One just says Buck—the other is a large *B* with a small *t*. Jeff, you do the same."

"Yes, sir."

"*Jake.*"

"Sorry. I guess I respect you too much to call you Jake."

"Jesus," Jake muttered. "You feeling more confident about using that six-gun?" he said louder.

"A little." Jeff breathed deeply against jangled nerves. They drew their horses up in front of the Land Rush Saloon and tied them. Jeff noticed that Jake shoved his duster behind one gun as he went inside the one-story building. The saloon was small, but several men were inside at the bar, more playing cards at two different tables. Gaudily dressed women hung on some of them. The bartender nodded at Jake. "What'll it be, Marshal?"

"One shot," Jake answered, looking around. "Same for Lloyd here and this other young man with me."

"He don't even look old enough to drink."

"Since when does that matter in this sorry excuse for a town?" Jake bantered with the man.

The bartender grinned as he poured the drinks. "What brings you back to Hellhole?"

"Is that what you're calling it now?"

"Oh, this place has a lot of names. What do you call it, Jake?"

"Hell's Nest, so we aren't too far apart on our opinion of the place."

The bartender laughed. "Somethin' you're needin' besides whiskey? The best whore in town is standing right over there. Her name is Belinda."

Jake lit a cigarette. "I'm only interested in information. Any new men hanging around here? Any talk of a man named Marty Bryant—or Hash Bryant? Maybe talk of taking down Jake Harkner?"

"Oh, hell, lots of men talk about taking you down, Jake, but I haven't seen or heard anything out of the ordinary. Just talk. You ought to ask Belinda. She's reasonably honest." He called out to her. "Get on over here, Belinda."

The blond, blue-eyed woman sauntered their way, her breasts nearly spilling out of a bright red dress. She reeked of cheap perfume, and her thickly powdered face was an obvious attempt to hide a bad complexion. "You men in need?" she asked, eyeing Lloyd especially. "It's not often somebody as good-looking as you comes to a place like this. Lloyd, isn't it?"

"How would you know?"

"Everybody knows the Harkner men." She eyed Jake. "You two come to town and seconds later everybody knows it, and they all start shaking in their boots. And now you stand there just filling up this place. Either one of you can fill *me* up if you want."

"I just want to know if Marty Bryant has been through here," Jake told her. He took his cigarette from his lips and drank down the shot of whiskey.

The woman walked closer, moving her arms around Jake. "What's it worth?"

"How much are you asking?"

"Five bucks...or you in my bed."

Jake reached into his pocket and handed her five dollars. "No time for the other, Belinda, and you'd better have something good for me."

She ran her hands over his chest. "Put that money right here," she told him, pointing to her generous cleavage.

Jeff's eyes widened when Jake obliged her, shoving the money deep between her breasts. "Make it worth it, Belinda."

"I thought just getting a feel might be worth five bucks to you."

"Tell me something I want to hear, or I'll reach back in there and take my five dollars back."

"Well now, that might be worth *not* telling you."

"Could be, but when I take that money back, my cigarette will be between my fingers when I reach down there. I don't think you want that now, do you?"

She stiffened. "You wouldn't do that."

"Try me. I'm not a patient man, Belinda."

She pouted and stepped back. "All I know is that a whore named Trudy Griffith up the street at the Dusty Hollow said something to me about a man named Marty bragging about taking down Jake Harkner for killing half his relatives and sending him to prison."

Jake took another five dollars from his pocket and shoved that between her breasts also. "That's for your promise to keep your mouth shut about this."

She shrugged. "Sure. What else can I promise just to feel Jake Harkner's hands between my breasts?"

"That's all I need, Belinda."

She looked at Lloyd. "How about you?"

Lloyd grinned, leaning down and kissing her cheek. "I just wanted a drink."

All three of them walked out.

"Do you think she's telling the truth, Pa?"

"We'll find out." Jake untied his horse and led it farther up the street to a large tent with a sign out front that read The Dusty Hollow, Lloyd and Jeff following close behind. "I don't want to be too obvious," Jake said as they retied their horses. "Do you play poker, Jeff?"

"Yes."

"Then we're going to sit down to a game and not

even mention Marty Bryant, understand? If this Trudy woman knows something, I have a feeling she'll come to us when she realizes who we are. Sometimes if you ask flat out, they get too scared to offer any information. Belinda didn't hesitate, because she didn't really know anything, but this woman might have a lot more information. Let her give it to us on her own."

"Pa, be careful. Some of the men in there might be part of the gang Marty hired."

"I am well aware of that." Jake started inside.

"Wait!" Lloyd told him. "Look here." He stood beside the horse that was next to his own. "Look at the brand."

Jake walked over to see a capital *B* beside a small *t*. He glanced at Lloyd. "Jackpot." He headed inside again. "Remember what I told you, Jeff."

Jake walked up to a makeshift bar consisting of boards on sawhorses and ordered two bottles of whiskey. Everything got quiet as he turned and set a bottle on one of the tables. "My son, this other deputy, and I are wanting to play some poker," he told the men at both tables. Without asking if he was welcome, he sat down to one of the tables and handed the second bottle of whiskey to Lloyd. "Join the men at that other table," he told him. "Bartender, bring us some shot glasses."

Lloyd took the second bottle and took a chair at the other table, nodding toward one other empty chair. "Have a seat, Jeff."

Trying to hide the fact that he was scared to death, Jeff sat down. The bartender brought over the shot glasses and Lloyd filled two, one for him and one for Jeff. Jake filled his own and downed the whiskey. Lloyd eyed him, a little worried Jake might have to consume a bit too much firewater before he got what he came here for. Whiskey and anger were a poor mix for Jake Harkner.

The entire room grew tense.

"Come on, boys. We're just here to relax a bit before we head on out to some of the settlements," Jake told them.

One of the players at Jake's table dealt a hand. "Marshal, you're after somethin'."

"Just a game of cards," Jake answered. "I've been on the trail awhile and need to rest. I'm tired of all the bullshit of this job. Had to come through Hell's Nest on my way to my next stop, so I figured we'd get in a little card game."

"Is that your name for this place?" another asked.

"Can you think of a better one?"

"Guess not. It's just as good as any." He looked Jake over. "What happened to your face?"

Jake lit a cigarette. "A little run-in with a shovel."

"Did you fight back?"

"Beat it near to death," Jake joked.

"More like whoever *owned* the shovel, I expect."

"Something like that."

Jake drew on the cigarette as he studied the heavyset man across the table from him who'd been asking all the questions.

"You fixin' to give us some of your money?" the man asked.

"Could be," Jake answered. "Last time I played cards it was with my grandson, so I'm a little out of practice with men who know what they're doing."

"You have a *grandson*?" one of them asked.

"Sure. Two of them, in fact, and another on the way." He glanced at Lloyd and grinned. "Maybe *two* more on the way."

"Pretty big family for somebody with a job like yours."

Jake threw down two cards and took two more. "The family came first, the job second. I didn't take it willingly. A judge forced it on me."

"Back when you wasn't no better than the rest of us?"

Jake eyed the fat man again as he poured himself

another shot and drank it down. "I'm *still* not any better than the rest of you." He noticed Lloyd also eyed the man closely. His teeth were brown from chewing tobacco and his eyes a very pale blue. His thinning hair was sticking out in all directions, and his checkered shirt showed sweat stains.

"What's with the kid over there?" the man asked Jake after passing his hand. "He looks twelve years old compared to you and that big, tall son of yours."

"He's old enough to drink, play cards, sleep with whores, and use a gun," Jake answered. "That's good enough for me. Besides that, he's writing a book about me."

"A *book*? About *you*?" The man guffawed. "From everything I've heard about Jake Harkner, that ought to be one hell of a read!"

They all laughed.

"You gonna write about all them whores and all the killin's?" another man asked Jeff.

"That's for you to find out when you read the book," Jeff answered.

Jake laid his cards down. A pair of tens. The fat man had a pair of jacks.

"Thanks for your money, Harkner," he told Jake. "You need to play cards with somebody who knows what he's doin', not a kid."

Jake watched the man pull all the cards together. He handed them to the man sitting next to him. "Your deal." He seemed nervous. They played cards for close to an hour, and Jake tried to make each shot of whiskey last, not wanting to drink so much that his aim might be off or his judgment impaired—yet just enough keep the men around him relaxed and amiable.

"You new in town?" he asked the fat man with the sweat-stained shirt.

"Maybe. What's it to you?"

"I remember people, that's all. I don't remember seeing you here or anyplace else. You new to Oklahoma?"

"Might be."

"Then how did you know about me? You said a book about Jake Harkner would be quite a read." Jake looked at his hand and discarded one card.

"Hell, the whole country knows about Jake Harkner," the fat man answered.

"Then you didn't just hear about me recently—from someone looking to pay you to kill me?"

The room quieted again. Jeff squirmed at the sounds of some kind of wild lovemaking in a curtained-off room at the back of the tent. Obviously a whore was getting, or giving, her money's worth to some man back there. Those sitting at the card tables didn't seem the least bit disturbed by the sounds, including Jake and Lloyd, so Jeff struggled to be casual about it himself.

The fat man eyed Jake closely, still not responding to Jake's last remark. "Hey, kid," he finally called out to Jeff. "When you write that book, maybe you can end it with the name of the man who finally killed Jake Harkner."

"And who would that be?" Jeff asked.

Suddenly there came a boom. The fat man flew backward and his chair fell over. Everyone jumped and backed away, including Jeff. Lloyd never moved.

"Holy sweet Jesus!" one of the players said, looking from the dead fat man, who lay sprawled with a hole in his gut and a pistol still in one hand, to Jake, who slowly set a smoking gun on the table.

"I wouldn't mind playing a few more rounds," Jake said, "unless another one of you is bent on killing me."

Everyone just stared at him, clearly wondering how on earth Jake knew the fat man was aiming to shoot him under the table.

"That was…amazing," Jeff half mumbled.

Jake shared a look with Lloyd, who glanced at the dead man. "Shit, Pa, you just made a mess. That piece of blubber has a hole in his gut six inches across."

"Then somebody had better clean things up," Jake answered casually, his cigarette at the corner of his mouth. He poured himself yet another shot of whiskey, leaving the still-smoking gun on the table. "Whose turn is it to deal?"

The bartender came over and asked another man to help him drag the body outside. Jake drank down the shot of whiskey.

"Trudy, get us some more beer over here," a man at Lloyd's table called out.

Jake and Lloyd both turned to see the woman named Trudy, who'd just come into the barroom from behind the curtain. Her hair was disheveled and her fancy gold dress buttoned wrong. "What the hell happened in here?" she asked.

"Jake Harkner just shot that new guy—Frank Gallus." The man who answered nodded toward Jake, and Trudy sauntered up to Jake. She was perhaps twenty-five or thirty, with long, dark hair and the look of a Mexican about her.

"So, you're Jake Harkner. I've heard about you."

Jake looked her over. "Most folks have."

"What happened to that handsome face?"

"Just a little disagreement with someone."

"Looks like he won."

"I beat the man to a pulp with a belt."

Her eyebrows arched. "Well, there's a novel way of beating on someone."

"Some people make it their *choice* of punishment."

Trudy stood behind him, running her hands over his shoulders and up and down his arms. "I'll bet you'd never treat anyone in your family like that. Fact is, I've heard you have quite a nice family, over in Guthrie."

The words grabbed Jake and Lloyd's attention. "Yeah, I have a nice family. Why would that interest you?" Jake folded his hand.

"Oh, I just thought news about them might be something you'd pay for. And I have some news."

A man came from the back room then, his shirt open and his boots and guns in his hand. He glanced at the fat man being dragged out and then at Jake and the still-smoking gun on the table in front of him. He hurried out the door.

Trudy leaned over and ran her hands down Jake's chest, under his gun belts, and into his pants. "Would you like to know what I heard about your family?"

Jake grabbed his gun and shoved it into its holster. "Trudy, when a man has a woman's hands in his pants, he doesn't generally feel like talking about his family," he told her.

She smiled. "I've always heard you're real familiar with women like me, Jake Harkner. Why don't you come into that back room and show me just how familiar? Your wife is far, far away. She'll never know."

Far away? What did this woman know? Jake felt alarm building. He grasped her wrists and yanked her hands out of his pants, then stood up, winking at the other players. "You boys go on without me. Enjoy my whiskey if you want." He scooped up his money and shoved it into his pocket, glancing at Lloyd. "I'll be back in a bit." He followed Trudy into the back room.

Lloyd glanced at the other men. "Nothing like blowing a man's guts out and then screwing a whore afterward. Pa can go from one to the other without a second thought."

One of the men grinned, and another one appeared uncomfortable.

Once behind the curtain, Trudy pulled Jake to a very messy bed and told him to sit down. She stood in front of him and began removing her clothes. "I'll make a trade with you, Marshal," she told him. "You screw me so I can say I got laid by Jake Harkner, and I'll tell you what I know about your family."

"Fine with me." Jake watched her undress, thinking how different she was compared to Dixie, who would give him any information he needed out of the goodness of her heart. The whore in front of him was the kind he had little use for. He waited until she was completely naked and had climbed onto the bed before acting.

He rolled on top of her then. She smiled, reaching out to unbuckle his gun belt, but Jake forced all his weight on her and grasped her hair almost painfully. "Now you listen and listen good," he seethed. "I've never hurt a woman in my life. Don't make me start with *you*! I've known whores from Texas to Montana, and none I was ever with would do what you're doing! We're talking about my *family* here! You're going to tell me what you know, and I'm not going to have to *fuck* you to find out! Understand?"

She tried in vain to pull his hand away.

"*Understand?*" he repeated.

"Yes!" she hissed. Her eyes teared, and Jake let go of her hair but stayed on top of her.

"You've seen Marty Bryant?"

"I've seen him, all right. He paid me good money to bait you if you came here. He said you like whores and it would be easy to get you in here. I just figured I'd get the famous Jake Harkner in my bed before I told him what I know."

"You figured wrong." Jake rolled off of her. "For the first time in my life, I want to hit a woman, and the state I'm in, I'd advise you to answer my questions."

Trudy scooted away and pulled a filthy blanket over her nakedness. "What do you want to know?"

"*All* of it! How many men does Marty have?"

"I don't know for sure. Maybe ten…twelve…could be even more by now. He left here with two more—said he had just about enough to bring you down."

"Where did he go?"

"Back to his place near Guthrie. He talked about making you come to him by getting to…your family because you killed half of his."

Jake rubbed at his temples. "Jesus," he muttered. "Did he mention a specific plan of some kind?"

She didn't answer right away. Jake turned and got to his knees on the bed, grasping her face in his hands. "I asked you a question!"

"Are you going to kill me?"

"Don't tempt me!" Jake could hardly believe he'd just spoken the words. Desperation was turning him into something worse than he'd ever been. He let go of her and got off the bed. "Jesus, Trudy, this is my *family*. How could you not have told me right away? How could you be so rotten as to try to get me in your bed when every second counts? Of all the women I've known, you're the worst kind." He faced her, wanting to feel sorry for the tears in her eyes, hating the fact that for one quick moment, his father came out of him and raged against a woman. Maybe he hadn't completely beaten the devil out of himself after all. "I'm asking you again. Did Marty Bryant mention a specific plan?"

She nodded. "Promise you won't hurt me when I tell you."

Jake felt sick with dread. "I promise."

Trudy hung her head. "He said…something about you probably looking for him…so you'd be away from your family. He said them being in town wouldn't stop him—said he had it figured out. He said it would be hard to just ride into town and try to kidnap people, so he figured he'd start a fire…grab everyone's attention away from other things. While they were all involved in putting out the fire, he could…"

"Could *what*!"

Trudy got off the bed and backed against a wall. "He could get hold of your daughter, the one you call…an angel…and maybe even the girl your son just married… maybe your grandsons. He said that would bring you to him right quick."

Jake felt as though someone was ripping out his heart. Had he been wrong to think his family would be safe in town? "You filthy slut!" he moaned. "How long ago was Bryant here?"

"About four days ago…"

Rage like nothing Jake had ever known permeated his whole being. He had to do something to keep him from taking his anger out on this woman.

He charged into the main room then, kicking over tables, sending money and beer flying. He shoved aside anyone in his way as he headed for the door. "Let's go!" he ordered Lloyd and Jeff.

Both men jumped up and followed him out.

"He's headed for Guthrie!" Jake shouted. "He'll take Evie! He'll take my Evie! Brian won't be able to stop him, because he won't be expecting it!" He started to mount up—then suddenly turned and vomited.

"Jesus Christ," Lloyd swore. "Pa!" He ran around to his father.

Jake grabbed his arm. "God, Lloyd, they'll take Evie, and maybe Little Jake…maybe Stephen and Katie. We never should have left! Evie! My God, Lloyd, you know what Marty Bryant is like. She's never been touched by anybody but Brian…and she's *pregnant*! Bryant will fucking rape her! He'll rape *both* of them! He might even kill those kids! Trudy said he meant to start a fire in town to distract them."

"Pa—" Lloyd turned away, his own guts tightening

with dread. "Jesus!" he swore again. "Jesus God, protect them." He walked to his horse. "Pa, can you ride?"

"No choice." Jake walked to a watering trough, not caring that horses had drunk from it. He scooped water into his mouth and spit it out to rinse it.

"How did we miss them?" he groaned.

"They must have deliberately taken a different way home," Lloyd surmised.

Jake mounted Prince then and charged away. He felt a blackness moving through him like a raging storm. And he swore he could hear the scream of demons.

Thirty

THEY RODE LIKE MADMEN, STOPPING ONLY TO GET BEN. They left their horses at the ranch and grabbed fresh ones. Jake rode until well after dark, and Ben fell asleep in his arms. The poor child got handed back and forth among all three men as Jake became relentless in getting back to Guthrie, normally a good six-day ride. On the first night Lloyd finally had to stop Jake, convincing him that without sleep he'd be of no use to finding Evie or Katie. He felt crazy himself with the thought of what Katie or Stephen could be suffering. He wanted blood as bad as Jake did, but the pace they were keeping could kill his father…

Still, sleep was impossible. All they could do was rest, but true sleep wouldn't come. Their only goal was to, by some miracle, reach Guthrie before Marty Bryant did. Marty wouldn't be in near the hurry Jake and Lloyd were. "If he took a different way, it will take him longer than normal," Jake hoped aloud once, yelling the words to Lloyd.

Lloyd didn't know what to do or say. They were up before daylight the next day and off again. Lloyd felt ripped apart by worry over his sister, his mother, his wife, his son, his nephew…and his father, who was like a crazy man.

Jeff quietly made camp each night and cooked, finding ways to keep poor Ben occupied and trying to explain to the boy what was going on. He urged Jake and Lloyd to eat something, but the only one who ate much at all was young Ben.

They made it to Dixie's in two and a half days instead of four, changing horses at various ranches and settlements along the way. When they reached Dixie's place, Jake walked up and grabbed her close, clinging to her as he stumbled toward the house.

"Jake, what's going on? Let go before we both go down."

"They're after my Evie, Dixie," he groaned in her ear. "They might already have her and my grandson... my Little Jake! And Katie! Katie and Stephen! My whole goddamned family is in danger, and my wife might be dying, and I...I can't...feel anything. Just rage! Just rage!"

"My God, Jake, cálm down! Calm down!" Dixie managed to push him off of her, then stepped back. "My God, I've never seen that look on your face before, Jake Harkner. For the first time since I've known you, I'm afraid of you!"

Jake turned away and stumbled again. "They'll rape her, Dixie. They'll rape my angel. And she's pregnant and sick! She'll lose the baby! *Se la llevaron! Quiero morirme! Quiero morirme!* And they'll do the same to Katie—maybe kill Stevie and my Little Jake."

There was no controlling him. Dixie looked helplessly at Lloyd, who looked hardly any better than his father.

"Marty Bryant," he explained. "We found out at Hell's Nest that he has a lot of men with him and he's headed for Guthrie to kill or take somebody in the family to get back at me and Jake."

"Oh my God!"

"Dixie, we have to leave a young boy here. It's a long story, but Jake will come back for him once this mess is over with. His name is Ben. We came across the kid's father beating him with a belt, and Jake went kind of crazy. I guess I don't have to explain to you why, and the details don't matter right now."

"Sure, he can stay here. I'll make sure he doesn't see

anything he shouldn't." She touched Lloyd's arm. "My God, Lloyd, you poor thing."

Lloyd grasped his stomach as though in pain. "With my mom down in Oklahoma City, that leaves Katie, Stephen, and Little Jake for Marty's rotten plan. We were told he'd take somebody in the family as a way to get Pa to come to him." He grimaced. "They'll kill Pa. They'll *kill* him if he gives himself up to them. I'm going to lose my whole family!"

"You calm down. The both of you look like you need to eat and rest. If you kill yourselves trying to get to Guthrie, you'll be no good to anybody."

"No!" Jake roared. "We have to leave again. We only stopped to drop Ben off, and I'm doing that because I don't know what we'll find in Guthrie and don't know who will be there to take care of Ben. I trust you, Dixie. You'll take good care of him till we come back for him. And if we don't make it, you take him to Lloyd's in-laws—the Donavans."

"Jake Harkner, you won't *make* it to Guthrie in your condition! If you really love your daughter and want to help her, you need to *rest* before you go any farther. You know I'm right."

"No! I have to go on."

"Jake, you're no good like this. You aren't thinking straight, and riding half the night again could kill you."

"I'm too goddamn thirsty for blood to stop for anything, and I'm too fucking mad and mean to die! If I do, it won't be until *after* I've destroyed Marty Bryant and every last man with him!"

"At least eat something, Jake." She turned to Lloyd. "You too. Let me get you some biscuits and jerky."

"Forget it!"

"Jake—" Dixie grasped his arm, but he half pushed her away. She stumbled slightly and Jake turned away.

"Jesus."

"I know you, Jake Harkner! You're in a rage, but you know goddamn well that if you don't eat something and get some water down your throat and get a couple hours of sleep tonight, you'll *die*! You're going to take some biscuits and jerky with you, and you're going to promise me you'll stop long enough later to sleep a little, you black-hearted sonofabitch! Are you really so stubborn and thirsty to murder those men that you'd risk not even making it there? If you love that daughter of yours and those grandchildren and that new daughter-in-law, you'll do what you need to do to stay alive and get to them! You've always listened to me, Jake Harkner, and you know goddamn well your wife would be telling you the same thing!"

Jake faced her, his eyes still looking like the devil's, but Dixie faced him squarely, her hands on her hips. "You wait right there while we get you fresh horses and some food!" Dixie turned to go into the house, and Jake glanced down at Ben, who stared at him with wide-eyed terror.

"Are you mad at me for making you stop here?" the boy asked Jake.

Jake closed his eyes and turned to lean on a hitching post. "No, Ben, I'm not mad at you, but some very bad men have taken my daughter and my grandsons and maybe Lloyd's wife, and I'm so full of hatred for them that it seems like I hate *everybody*. You have to trust me, Ben. Either I or some really nice people will be along to take you in and give you a damn good life." He looked at the boy. "You'll be loved, no matter what happens to me, understand? I promise you, you'll be loved and cared for. Don't be afraid of how I look right now. I just…I need to be this way to do what I have to do. So you stay here with Dixie. She's a nice lady and she'll be good to you."

Lloyd turned away, feeling helpless and angry and

frustrated and wanting to explode with his own need to get back to Guthrie. He walked up to Jeff. "I don't know what the hell to do, Jeff. There is only one of me, and my mother needs me, my father needs me, my sister probably needs me by now, maybe my wife...or my son...or both."

Jeff dismounted. "Lloyd, Dixie is right. You and Jake need to eat and get some real rest."

"I've got no appetite and neither does Pa." He wiped at tears. "Jesus, I've never seen him this bad, and I've never felt this much...I don't even know what to call it. It's worse than rage. There isn't even a word for it."

"You're your father's son, Lloyd. Right now you're closer to nitroglycerin than dynamite."

Lloyd threw his head back, shaking his hair behind his shoulders. "The trouble is, I can probably take this constant riding and no sleep better than Pa. If he keeps this up, he'll die. If he does, I'll go after Katie and Evie on my own, and there's going to be a bloodbath like you've never seen, because I might not have anything left to live for!"

Dixie came back out with a gunnysack of food. She handed it to Lloyd, then stepped back, seeing the same broiling storm in Lloyd's eyes as the one in his father's. "My God," she muttered. She turned to Jake. "You listen to me, Jake Harkner! You get hold of yourself and you get your thoughts together. You need to plan this. You need to calm down and plan this. And you have to forget you're a marshal and go back to the outlaw inside of you. *That's* how you will do what you have to do. You have to forget your feelings for Evie and those grandbabies and just *act*, Jake. No feelings! Feelings are *killing* you! Use your goddamn good sense and your great skills and those famous guns and go get your daughter and whoever else they might have taken. That's the only way you will be able to help her, Jake. Do you know what I'm saying?"

He met her eyes, and Dixie saw the Jake she'd never really known in his early days, the one she knew dwelled deep inside Jake Harkner the U.S. Marshal—now just a man on a mission of murder and revenge. "I almost hurt a woman back there, Dixie…a whore who wanted me to screw her for information about my own family—information she wasn't going to tell me otherwise. You would never do that."

"Of course I wouldn't. If I knew something like that, I'd ride to hell and back to find and tell you."

"I've never hurt a woman in my life, but I hated her for that. For a minute I wanted to strangle her. It was like…like…"

"Your father? No, it wasn't, Jake. Your father didn't need a reason to hurt a woman. You had a *reason*—and you know down deep inside you never really would have hurt her. It sounds to me like she would have deserved it, but mean as you are, you never would have gone that far. Jake, you have to reach down inside and use that meanness the right way—use it to go find your family and do what you have to do to get them back. You need to be cold, Jake—colder than the man who used to ride with outlaws, colder than the man who killed the whole Kennedy gang and killed all those men when you went after your son." Dixie kept her distance, truly taken aback by his demeanor. "And you have to remember what your son is going through right now, Jake. I know how bad you're hurting over this, but Lloyd's own wife and son might also be involved. That kid is living in hell right now with worry. He's hurting just as much as you are, and you need each other. You can't think this is just your own agony, Jake, because it's Lloyd's too. You need to be strong for each other."

Dominic came outside to tend to the horses. Jeff dismounted and explained what was going on, and the stable hand ranted in Spanish over Jake's dilemma. He took Ben's hand and asked if he would help with the horses. "Jake, I will bring you fresh horses as fast as I can." Dominic headed for the barn with Ben. Jeff followed to help.

Jake sat down on the steps to wait, and Lloyd joined him. Neither spoke for a few minutes. Both smoked.

"Don't let them take you, Pa," Lloyd finally spoke up. "They'll kill you sure as shit, and they won't be quick about it. There has to be a way out of this without you giving yourself up like a goddamn martyr."

"They want you too."

"I fucking know that!" He wiped at his eyes again. "Sweet Jesus, I've had trouble helping Katie face what I do for a living. Now this. If they…" He got up. "Our marriage will never survive this."

"You just remember that those men can't really touch her. Understand? Katie Harkner is *yours*! Just like Evie will always belong to Brian, no matter what happens. If a woman's not willing, she hasn't been touched!" Jake growled the words angrily.

"Well, life still won't be worth living if something happens to my son…and to Little Jake."

Dixie walked closer. "You two keep in mind that if Evie and Katie get through this, and your grandsons are all right, they will need you more than they have ever needed you, so you need to get your heads on straight and not do something that could get you sent to prison. I know you need to reach down inside to the mean snakes that dwell there, but you have to also be smart about this. And, Jake Harkner, it's very possible your wife will come home just fine. And if something terrible has happened to your daughter and grandsons and Katie, she'll need you worse than she ever has her whole life…and you'll need her. Don't do something crazy. Go get your family and get yourself back to Guthrie in one piece."

Jake met her eyes, and Dixie hardly recognized him.

His entire countenance, even his looks, were different. "I see what the old outlaw Jake Harkner must have looked like at one time, Jake," she told him. "How that wife of yours managed to tame you, I'll never figure. But now you have to think about her and what she'd be telling you right now. She'd be telling you to eat…and rest at least a little…and to keep your head on straight and not let rage make you do something foolish. A man doesn't think right when he's in your state, and that won't help your family. Do you understand? Calm down and think this through."

Dominic and Jeff returned with fresh horses, Ben walking beside them. Without another word, Jake mounted up. Dixie hurried up to him and handed up the gunnysack. "Eat," she ordered.

Jake took it. "I'll try. Thanks for the food. And I'm sorry…for that little shove. I didn't mean it, Dixie."

Dixie patted his leg. "I know that. Go get your daughter and Katie, Jake, but use your head. Promise me." She could almost hear thunder and see black clouds hovering over him.

"I'll do what I have to do. I'm not even sure what that is yet, but I'll damn well get them back, and Marty Bryant might as well already count himself as dead."

Jake rode off.

"Bye, Dixie." Lloyd followed, as did Jeff.

Dixie looked at young Ben. "You poor kid." She walked up and touched his hair. "Ben, he's a good, good man—really. He's just gone off to a deep, dark place for now. But he'll get his family back and he'll come for you. I just know he will."

Ben nodded, tears running down his cheeks. "He called me his son."

Dixie smiled for him. "Then that's what you are, Ben, no matter what happens. You're Jake Harkner's son."

Ben watched the three men disappear over the horizon. "I hope he doesn't get killed."

Dixie smiled. "Ben, it takes an awful lot to bring down Jake Harkner." She wanted to sound hopeful for the boy, but the man she'd just seen hardly seemed human. How long his body could keep up with such abuse was what worried her more than the outlaws he was after.

Thirty-one

RANDY!

She saw him...falling...falling into blackness. He reached for her, but only the tips of their fingers touched...and then he slipped away.

And who was that with him? Evie? Why was she with Jake, falling into that black hole?

Gampa's guns! Gampa's guns!

Little Jake? No! She couldn't see him at all. She could only hear his voice. She cried out to them, the family she loved.

Someone grasped her shoulders.

"Jake?" she muttered.

"Randy, wake up."

Randy gasped and started awake to see Peter bent over her. It took her a moment to remember where she was. The dream had been so real, she thought she was back home and Jake was calling for her. She looked around, coming to the reality that she was still in a hospital bed. She looked back at Peter.

"Something's wrong! Something's wrong!"

She reached up and he pulled her into his arms. "Randy, what is it? Are you in pain?"

"No!" She clung to him. "Take me home! Take me home! Something terrible has happened!"

"Randy, you were just dreaming."

"No, it's more than that!" She pulled away and tried to get up.

"Randy, don't get up." Peter held her down. "You

have another week before the stitches come out. Maybe not even then."

"No! He has to take them out now! Today! We have to go home, Peter. Something awful has happened. I feel it! It isn't just the dream. I *feel* it. Jake needs me. They all need me."

"Randy, stop this! You're getting yourself worked up to where you'll just make things worse. If you break open those stitches, you'll have to stay here even longer. I already wired home three days ago that you came through everything okay and that it's not cancer. I haven't heard back that anything is wrong. We'll go home in just another week, and you'll see that everything is fine. I think you're just having nightmares from too much medication."

Randy grasped his arms. "You don't understand! I wouldn't have this feeling if there wasn't something terribly wrong at home. Jake is hurting in some way, Peter. I don't know if it's an emotional hurt or if he's hurt physically. I just know that he's hurt! And Evie might be too. And Little Jake! I heard his voice, Peter. I heard Little Jake talking about 'Gampa's guns.'"

"It's just a mixture of memories and medicine, Randy. Please lie still."

"I can't rest until you go to the sheriff's office or the telegraph office and find out if anyone has sent us a message from Guthrie." She sat up on the edge of the bed, refusing to lie back down. "Please go and see, Peter. I have this awful, awful feeling!" She folded her arms around her middle and rocked back and forth. "Dr. Rogers can take out the stitches after we get back. That way I can leave sooner. I can't wait around here another whole week!"

Peter grasped her shoulders. "I'm not leaving until you lie back down and promise to *stay* down!"

She moved back into bed and Peter pulled the

blankets over her and bent close to kiss her forehead. "I'll see what I can find out. Will you lie still until I get back?"

"Yes. Just go and see! Ask at the front desk first. Maybe someone already brought us a telegram."

Peter straightened with a sigh and picked up his hat from a chair. He put it on and went out, hoping she was wrong about all of this. He hated seeing her so upset. She'd been through so much already.

He started for the front door of the small, brick hospital when a man wearing a badge came through the door. He was decked out with guns much as Jake dressed for the job, and he had a waxed mustache that curled on the ends.

Peter hesitated, listening to the man ask if there was a patient there named Miranda Harkner. Peter's chest tightened. *Good God, please don't say Jake is dead!* He did not want to be the one to give Randy that kind of news. It would kill her!

"That gentleman is a friend of Mrs. Harkner, and is here to watch over her," a nurse told the man with the badge. She nodded toward Peter. "That's Attorney Peter Brown. Perhaps he can help you."

The stocky man of perhaps forty years walked over to Peter and introduced himself. "I'm a U.S. Marshal," he told Peter. "Bill Graham. I, uh, have some rather sad news for Marshal Jake Harkner's wife. I was told she was here."

"She is." Peter felt sick. "You can tell me, and I'll give her the news. She's not completely healed yet. You can't just go in there and blurt out whatever you have to say."

Marshal Graham removed his hat to reveal thinning, sandy-colored hair. His blue eyes revealed a deep sadness. *Not Jake! Not Jake!*

"Mr. Brown, something has happened back in Guthrie. This won't be easy for Mrs. Harkner. I know Jake real well, and I've met his wife. She's a good woman, very devoted to her family."

"And?"

"And, uh, maybe you know that a few weeks ago, a prisoner by the name of Marty Bryant escaped. Jake killed a couple of his brothers, and we all figured he was headed back to get some kind of revenge against Jake. A lot of men, including Jake, have been looking for him, but to no avail."

Peter rubbed at his eyes. "My God," he muttered. "What's happened, Marshal?"

Bill Graham sighed. "Mr. Brown, Marty Bryant and a whole gang of men raided Guthrie, burned some buildings to create a diversion while he took Jake's daughter Evie…and his grandson…the one they call Little Jake."

"No!" A woman behind them nearly screamed the word.

Peter turned to see Randy had come out of her room and heard what the marshal said.

"No! No! No!" She screamed the words over and over as she crumpled to her knees. Peter ran over and grabbed her up, holding her in his arms so she wouldn't fall. "Tell me they've already found Little Jake and my daughter!"

"No, ma'am. It just happened yesterday. A posse went after them, but they all got away, and Sheriff Sparks was shot. He's alive, but not in good enough shape to go after them. Jake wasn't there. I'm sure if he was, he might have stopped it all. He was out looking for Bryant and his men."

"Brian! What about Evie's husband, Brian?"

"I'm told he got knocked unconscious, but he'll be all right. More men want to try looking for Evie and the kid again, but they need someone to lead the way—someone like Jake who knows how to find men like that. But no one is sure how to find him, and he hasn't sent any wires."

"He knows. Jake knows!" Randy clung to Peter. "He'll be there soon, I'm sure of it. Somehow he found out and he'll find Evie." Randy wilted against Peter. "Oh my God. My God! Evie! Poor Evie! Jake will go mad!" She collapsed into sobs. "I'll never see him again. I'll never see Jake or my daughter again! And Little Jake! He's just an innocent child!"

"Randy, Jake will go after them and—"

"They want *him*, Peter. They want *Jake*. He'll do anything for Evie—*anything*! He'll offer himself up like a lamb to slaughter to get her back. They'll kill him, Peter! They'll kill him for sure this time. They might even kill Evie and Little Jake. They're ruthless, Peter!"

Marshal Graham pushed back his hat. "I'm so sorry for this terrible news, Mrs. Harkner. But, ma'am, if I may say so, you ought to know better than most that Jake doesn't go down easy, and if he can find a way out of this and still get your daughter back, he'll do it. Didn't he take on the Kennedy gang all by himself back in California? That's how I heard it, anyway."

Randy dug her fingers into Peter's arm. "Yes." She closed her eyes at the awful memory. "I was there." She looked at Graham. "What about Lloyd's wife, Katie? And my grandson Stephen?"

"Far as I know, they're okay. And, ma'am, remember that Lloyd rides with Jake now. He's a real able man too. I'm thinking they'll be all right. Those two together are quite a force. And I'm sure Jake will be smart enough to take a few more men with him. He's not alone this time, Mrs. Harkner. You ought to take hope in that, and in the fact that…well…like I said, this is Jake Harkner we're talking about, and those men took his little girl. Personally, I wouldn't want to be a part of that gang right now…not with Jake Harkner after me."

Randy straightened a little, but Peter kept hold of her.

"I know all that, Marshal, but you have no idea how much Jake loves his daughter. He'll give himself over to them even if it means being tortured to death. He'll do anything for her."

"Well, maybe he won't have to, ma'am. Maybe he won't have to."

"The man is right, Randy," Peter encouraged. "This is Jake we're talking about. And Lloyd is with him. Your son is just as good as his father with those guns. If they round up a few extra men—"

"Oh, Peter, I have to go home. I have to go *home*! I have to be there for Evie if she lives through this. Let Dr. Rogers take my stitches out. Please, please, take me home. If you don't take me, I'll get dressed and go by myself, I swear it! I should be with Katie and Stephen too. Poor Katie must be beside herself, and Stephen is probably scared to death he'll lose his father and his grandfather."

"Katie's parents are with them, Randy."

"Is there some kind of message you want me to send to Guthrie, Mrs. Harkner?" Marshal Graham asked.

"Just that I'm coming home right away." She pulled away from Peter and covered her face, leaning against a wall. "What will be left of my family when I get there, Peter? I could lose Evie and Little Jake and Lloyd and Jake...all four of them! And Evie is pregnant. Oh my God, poor Brian. Poor Brian!"

"Ma'am, you won't be much good to any of them if you get sicker instead of better," Graham told her. "You need to trust in your husband now. If anybody can get them back, he can."

"He's right, Randy," Peter told her, pulling her back into his arms. "Jake will damn well get her back."

She wept against his chest. "But at what price, Peter? At what price? They will want a trade...Evie and Little Jake...for Jake. They might even make Lloyd part of the bargain, and both of them will give their lives for

Evie in a minute. Lloyd will *never* allow his father to face this alone."

Peter looked at Marshal Graham. "Send a wire to Katie that Randy knows what's happened and is coming home as soon as she can. We'll leave by the day after tomorrow."

"No! Tomorrow!"

"Absolutely not! Your getting home in a couple of days won't make any difference if they already have Evie. Jake and Lloyd will go after them the minute Jake knows, and there won't be a thing you can do until they all get back. And they will *all* come back. You have to believe that, Randy. Jake won't give himself up to those bastards. He'll find a way to bring them all down."

"If I hear anything before you leave, I'll let you know, Mrs. Harkner," Marshal Graham told her.

Randy turned away again. "Thank you." She walked back to her room, feeling as though she were in another world. Evie! Her beautiful, sweet, still-naive Evie.

Peter caught up to her and took her arm.

"Peter, she worships Jake. Evie absolutely thinks he is incapable of some of the things he's done. She's going to see a side of him that will shock her. She sees only the good in him, but I know what this will do to him. If he manages to get her out of this, he will execute every one of those men left alive. I saw what he did to some of the Kennedy gang. And these men...they will rape her, Peter. That will put Jake into a world Evie has never seen. He might even do things that will send him back to prison." She collapsed onto her bed.

"Randy." Peter knelt in front of her. "Evie means everything to him, so maybe he'll do this right—the way he should handle it as a marshal—for her sake. And I'm betting plenty of people are praying for your family, Randy. You remember that Evie, sweet as she is, is also a *Harkner*. She's stronger than you think, because she has two very strong people for parents. I think you're wrong about her not being able to stop Jake from doing something that will get him killed or sent back to prison. All she has to say is that word *Daddy*, and he'll do anything she asks. You know that. I have a feeling that word totally undoes that man—not *Pa*, not *Father*, or *Dad*. She calls him Daddy, and that just turns him into a piece of clay she can mold any way she wants."

Randy managed to smile a little through her tears. "Everyone thinks it's so funny that she still calls him that."

Peter squeezed her hand. "And when she calls him Daddy, it's so endearing."

Randy nodded. "It is, isn't it?" She covered her face. "Evie has no idea the things Jake is capable of."

"And he won't *want* her to know."

"It might not matter—not if they kill him, Peter. Not if they kill him. That will be horrible for Evie. She'll not get over the fact that her father gave his life for her."

Peter pulled the covers over her again. "I'll have the doctor give you something to help you sleep. I'll see if he'll let you leave a few days early and let Dr. Rogers take out the stitches. Then we'll head back to Guthrie, if he gives the go-ahead. But I'm getting you a sleeper car on the train so you can lie down most of the way, and I'll hire a stagecoach that's just for us—no other passengers—so you can have one full seat to lie down on there too. I'll get you home, Randy, but you have to promise me you'll let the doctor give you something to help you sleep tonight and most of tomorrow."

"But we should *leave* tomorrow."

"No. It won't help. One more day, Randy. Even then, we can't leave unless the doctor says it's all right. I'll try to get you home within four or five days."

"I should be there for Jake. He'll need me, Peter. If Evie is badly hurt or killed, he'll go insane. Even I won't be able to help him. The Jake I married will be lost forever."

"And you won't be able to be there for him or Evie or any of them if we don't handle this right. You have got to do what the doctor says, Randy, so you'll be there when they all get back."

When they get back. "They might never come back, Peter. They might never come back."

Thirty-two

THEY STOPPED EVERY FEW MILES WHEREVER THEY could find fresh horses, leaving promissory notes to either return the horses or pay for replacements if necessary. There was no time to dicker with the owners, and seeing the look in Jake's eyes, none argued with him. They rode into dark, rested only four hours, then left again, arriving in Guthrie at sunrise in four days instead of the six or seven it should have taken all the way from Hell's Nest.

They rode past a burned-out barn, and up the street were more burned businesses, some still smoldering. Someone had shot out the windows of Brian and Evie's house, as well as Lloyd and Katie's home...and Jake's. With an aching heart, Jake noticed some of Randy's rosebushes were trampled, and the front door was kicked down. He didn't need to go inside to know the house had been ransacked.

Everything seemed quiet, the rest of the main street eerily empty, even for early morning.

"Jesus," Lloyd muttered. He charged past them and up the street, practically screaming Katie's and Stephen's names. He dismounted and ran into his house, still yelling, but there was no one inside the wrecked dwelling. He came back out and began running up and down the street, as people began emerging from doorways. In the distance, Jake could see someone running from the preacher's house.

"Lloyd!"

It was Katie! She ran toward Lloyd, Stephen close

behind. Jake watched Lloyd wrap his wife and son both into his arms, all of them crying. Jake looked at Jeff, looked back at his house…Brian's house…looked up the street again.

"They took her, all right," he told Jeff, his voice scratchy from grief and too many cigarettes. "They took Evie…and if Little Jake was here, he would already be running out to me, so they took him too. And Randy… if she was here, she'd be waiting at the house for me, even though it's half-destroyed. That means she's not back yet. Maybe she isn't even alive."

Jeff didn't reply.

Jake urged his horse forward. As he approached the jail, he noticed more windows shot out, bullet holes sprayed all over the front of the jail. People began emerging from businesses and homes. Some nodded to Jake but didn't speak. When he looked at them, they stepped back. When Jake neared Sadie's place, Sadie and Mary Ann stepped out, both looking ready to cry. Seeing Mary Ann reminded Jake of the day Randy remarked to the young woman about her cleavage. Randy…his beautiful wife. If she was alive, she'd probably been told about this by now. She was in hell, just as he was. What if she was dying? He should be with her—and he needed to go after Evie. But there was only one of him.

The door to the boardinghouse opened and Brian stepped out, a strip of gauze wrapped around his head, blood showing near his forehead. The devastation in his eyes was painful. Brian…a good, good man…caught unawares and probably thinking he'd failed to protect his family. But how could a man who didn't even own a gun stand up against someone like Marty Bryant and his filthy cohorts in a surprise attack?

More people began assembling to watch. Jake dismounted and walked up to Brian, who closed his eyes and turned, grasping a hitching post to keep from going to his knees.

"They took her. And they took Little Jake."

"I know," Jake said gruffly. "I tried to get here before they did. When did it happen?"

"Three days ago. They burned buildings to distract attention, shot up the town…shot Sparky…made a mess of all three of our homes…shot out all the windows… barged in. There wasn't a damn thing I could do. One of them landed his gun barrel into my head and I…heard Evie screaming as they dragged her off…and Little Jake was crying for his 'gampa.'"

Jake forced back the part of him that wanted to scream…and scream…and scream. If he didn't stay in this dark, angry place, he would be of no use to Evie.

"Get her back, Jake," Brian groaned. "You're the only one who can do it. Get my Evie back."

Jake had to swallow to keep from vomiting. "How many were there?"

"I have no idea…ten…twelve. I think…maybe there were even more, waiting outside of town. There could be close to fifteen of them. Katie got one of them, but he's not talking."

"*Katie?*"

"She managed to get to her rifle, because they came for us first, so she had time. The damn woman barricaded herself in the bedroom and shot the first man who came through the door. I guess that made them give up on her and just take Evie and Little Jake."

"The man she shot is still *alive?*"

Brian nodded. "He's at Dr. Keller's office, under guard."

"Then I guess I'll have to pay him a visit."

He left Brian and walked toward Lloyd and Katie. He lifted Stephen and hugged him tight.

"You'll get them back, won't you, Grampa?" Stephen asked, tears in his eyes.

Jake closed his eyes and held him close, smelling his hair, the familiar scent of his card-cheating grandson. He took one hand and wrapped his fingers into the child's thick, dark, uncombed mane, remembering how Randy hated it when he messed up the boy's hair. He needed to touch him, smell him, remind himself that Stephen was real and alive. "I'll get them back, Stephen. I'll get them back." He turned toward Lloyd and Katie. Lloyd took the boy back into his arms.

"Have you heard anything about Randy?" Jake asked Katie.

Katie nodded as her parents also came out of the boardinghouse. "We got a telegram from Peter Brown," Katie told Jake. "Randy had the surgery, and she's fine. There was no cancer. We got another telegram yesterday saying she would start home today. She knows, Jake. She knows about Evie."

Jake pulled Katie into his arms, holding her tight just to keep from crumbling. "She's really all right? It wasn't cancer?"

Katie hugged him. "That's what the telegram said."

Again Jake struggled against a need to break down. Such wonderful, wonderful news...but his Evie was in the hands of evil men. This was what happened to people who dared to be a part of his life. This was how people suffered for bearing his blood.

"I'm glad you and Stephen are all right," he told Katie.

"Pa, Katie shot one of them! Isn't that the biggest goddamned surprise you ever heard? My Katie shot one and kept them away from Stevie." He moved an arm around Katie.

Jake nodded, managing half a smile for Katie. "Brian told me. You did damn good, Katie, damn good. You're a Harkner now. We have a man left behind that we can question, thanks to you."

"Jake, darlin', what happened to your face?" Clara Donavan asked him.

Jake touched his face, having forgotten all about the wound. "It's a very long story, Clara, and there's no time for it now." He looked down at Katie. "You know Lloyd and I have to leave again, don't you?"

Katie looked at Lloyd. "I know."

"He'll be all right, and he'll come back to you, Katie. I'll make sure of it. But right now there's little time for good-byes. I need Lloyd to go with me to question the man you shot." He looked at Lloyd. "He's at Doc Keller's office."

Lloyd nodded, his own gaze showing a cold darkness seldom seen in the young man's eyes.

He pulled Katie closer. "Baby, I have to go."

"Lloyd…"

He pressed her close. "I love you, Katie, more than I even realized. When I thought they might have taken you too—" He kissed her hair. "I've been selfish with my feelings. And I'm goddamned proud of you for what you did. You might have saved Stephen's life. I've never loved you more. You're braver than I could have ever thought."

"I'm the one who's been selfish, Lloyd, asking you not to ride with your father. Before Evie was taken, we'd had some long talks, and she told me so many things. I understand everything so much better now. Oh, Lloyd, she's such a good person. This is so horrible! You've got to go and get her away from those awful men!"

He leaned down and kissed her. "I hate to leave again, baby." He looked at her parents. "I'm so glad you were here for her and Stevie."

"So are we, Son," Pat told him. "But, by God, it's Katie who did the protectin'! I didn't even have time to load my pistol. I just wasn't ready for this. But it's not over, and sure 'n' you have to go find your sister. We'll pray you come back safe and sound."

"Lloyd!" Katie reached around his neck and leaned up to whisper in his ear. "You *have* to come back. I think I'm pregnant."

Lloyd squeezed her closer again. "Jesus, Katie, we have so much to be thankful for, but now this thing with Evie—I've never felt so torn. I have to go with Pa, Katie. I have to."

"Of course you do."

He kissed her several times over. "I love you, Katie girl. You couldn't have made me more proud, and now a baby."

"I love you so, Lloyd." She kissed his lips. "Go catch up with your father."

He hated leaving her, especially now that he knew she was carrying his child. But he forced back his softer side then and let go of her reluctantly, hurrying after Jake, feeling as though someone were ripping out his heart. Part of him wanted to rejoice over Katie's bravery, rejoice for the good news about his mother…but there was still Evie and Little Jake to feel sick over…and a father on a rampage.

"We need men who know how to use guns!" Jake was shouting to onlookers as he walked. "We need volunteers! We're going after Marty Bryant and the other bastards who took my daughter! Help us form a posse!"

Several men stepped forward and more came out of doorways, some holding a rifle or a shotgun.

"Only men without family—or at least without children," Jake yelled.

Lloyd turned to see Brian hurrying up to him. "I'm going too."

"Brian, you're hurt."

"Not bad enough to not be there for my wife. She'll not only need me as her husband, but she'll need a *doctor*.

She'll probably lose that baby, Lloyd, and God knows how bad they might beat her, maybe even Little Jake…" He turned away in agony. "God, my son!"

"I'll talk to Pa about it," Lloyd promised. "I'm so goddamned sorry, Brian." Lloyd turned to see Jake now storming toward a side street down which was Dr. Keller's office. He ran after him. "Pa!"

"Don't you get in my way, Lloyd. You let me do what I have to do!"

Lloyd could barely keep up with him. A bigger crowd had gathered, yet the air hung oddly silent. Everyone knew instinctively that Jake Harkner was not Marshal Harkner now. He was someone else…perhaps the notorious Jake Harkner they all knew he once was. The handsome smile was gone. The affable man was gone.

Jake walked so fast that Jeff had to ride his horse to catch up to him and Lloyd. Whatever Jake was going to do, he wanted to be there. Right now he missed Jake the family man, the father and grandfather and loving husband, the Jake who'd kidded him about never being with a woman…the Jake who dreamed of going to Colorado and living in peace.

There would be no peace today or for the next several days—however long it took to find Evie and Little Jake. And if they were found dead, the Jake that Jeff had met on the church steps would be gone forever.

"Pa, Brian wants to go with us," Lloyd told him as they approached the doctor's office.

"No!"

Lloyd finally reached him and yanked on his arm. "Goddamn it, Pa, he's Evie's *husband*! He has a *right*! Besides that, he's a doctor, and she'll damn well need one by the time we reach her."

Jake glared at him. "He'll get in the way."

"He *won't*! He'll do whatever you tell him to do, and he's got to be there for Evie. You know I'm right, Pa."

Jake turned away again. "I can't think about that yet. Give me a minute with the man they captured."

"What are you going to do?"

"I'm going to find out where they took Evie!" Jake started walking again. "Don't come in with me if you don't have the stomach for it."

Lloyd followed him up the steps of the doctor's office. "She's my *sister*!" He stepped in front of Jake, glaring at him with fire in his eyes. "And they have Little Jake. I damn well *do* have the stomach for it. This is *my* fight too—and *Brian's*! You listen to me, Pa. Brian needs to go with us!"

Jake rubbed at his eyes, and for a moment he seemed to soften toward his son. "First let's see what this man knows." He pushed past Lloyd and charged into Keller's office, where Sparky lay unconscious on one bed in the corner, and a man Jake had never seen before lay on another. Dr. Keller looked up from a desk. "Jake!"

Jake looked at Juan, the man who'd volunteered to keep an eye on the prisoner. Juan stood there with a shotgun.

"*Señor* Jake! I am so sorry about your daughter."

"Right now you need to leave, Juan. Wait outside."

Juan stepped back, his eyes wide. "*Sí, mi amigo.*" Juan left, and Jake looked at Dr. Keller.

"This the man who was part of Bryant's gang?"

The doctor slowly rose, looking pale. "Yes."

"Who's that?" Bryant's man asked. "Harkner? Jake Harkner? Don't you let him near me! Get him out of here!"

"I want your scalpel, Keller, and then you can leave," Jake told the doctor.

"No!" Bryant's man screamed. "Don't you leave me to that murdering sonofabitch!" He tried to get up. Jake saw a bloody bandage around his middle and one around his arm. He walked up to him and jerked the man out of his bed, deliberately letting him fall to the floor on his back.

Then he took a booted foot and pressed it on the wound at the man's middle. The man began screaming for help.

Jeff cautiously stepped inside, his eyes widening.

"Your scalpel!" Jake ordered Keller.

"Jake—" The doctor made a weak protest.

"Give me the goddamn scalpel, Keller! I don't want to hurt you too!"

Keller went to his desk and opened his doctor's bag, taking out his scalpel. He handed it to Jake, his hand shaking. Jeff just stood there, frozen in place.

"No! Don't do this!" Bryant's man screamed again.

"How is Sparky?" Jake asked Keller.

"He'll be all right. He took a bullet in the chest, but it missed his heart. He'll have lung problems for a while, but he'll recover. He's dead out on laudanum."

"Good. Now leave!"

Keller glanced down at the prisoner. "You made a big mistake being a part of harming this man's daughter," he told Bryant's man. He looked at Jake again. "He calls himself Dooley. Just Dooley." He glanced at Jake and Lloyd and shivered. Then Keller walked out.

Jake looked down at Dooley. "Where did they take her?"

"I...I don't know."

Jake pressed on his wound with his boot, and the man screamed in agony. "Where did they take her?"

"They'll kill me!"

"*I'll* kill you if you don't talk! And I won't be fast about it! Where did they *take* her?" Jake pressed harder on the man's belly.

"I'm not familiar with Oklahoma." The man started to cry, his face covered with perspiration. "They said... something about...hollow...some hollow."

Jake took his foot away and knelt close to him then, running the scalpel over the man's face. "Do you know how easily these things can cut a man's eye out?"

Jeff felt ill but forced himself to watch, understanding Jake's wrath but torn by his ideas of what was right and wrong to do to a man.

"Where do you want me to start, Dooley? An ear? Your nose? Maybe I should go ahead and cut out an eye!"

"That's all I know!" the man groaned. "Some hollow."

"I want you to think real hard. There are three places in this territory that I know of that end with the word *hollow*, and I'm not going to waste precious time visiting every one of them to find out where my daughter and grandson are. *Which one is it*, Dooley?"

"I don't know! I don't remember!"

Dooley wore only his long underwear. Jake reached down and jerked the underwear down to the man's knees.

"What the hell are you doing!"

"Considering what those men have in mind for my daughter…and you willing to be a part of it if you hadn't been caught…maybe I should use this scalpel to cut off your *dick*."

"No, wait! Wait! Name the hollows. Maybe I'll remember if you name them!"

Jake looked up at Lloyd. "Hold him down, Son."

Father and son's gazes held for a moment while Dooley screamed for help. No one came to his aid. Lloyd turned and straddled the man, sitting on his chest and facing him.

"Gurney's Hollow?" he asked Dooley.

"No! No, that's not it!"

Jake sat on the man's legs and grabbed his privates.

"Don't let him do it! Don't let him do it!" Dooley screamed.

"Apple Hollow?" Lloyd asked.

Dooley shook his head. Tears poured out of his eyes.

"Dune Hollow?" Lloyd asked.

Dooley's eyes widened and he managed to nod his head. Lloyd got up, but he turned and held Dooley's shoulders against the floor. Dooley managed enough breath to speak gruffly. "That's it! Dune Hollow! I swear to God, that's it! Please let me go!"

Jake let go of his privates. "Well now, I appreciate your cooperation, Dooley. But I need to make sure you don't get away. My very brave daughter-in-law put that bullet in your gut, and I'm goddamn proud of her for it, but you look like you're recovering, and we can't have that. Sparky over there isn't in any condition to jail you, and I don't have time, so I'll make sure Juan does it for me. But I think your recovery has been too quick, and I need to make sure you don't go anywhere."

"What...what do you mean?"

Jake jerked him up, the man's long johns still around his feet. He ripped off the bandages around his middle, then slammed a booted foot into the man's wound. Dooley screamed bloody murder as Jake ground his boot hard. Then Jake turned and left, glancing at Dr. Keller. "He broke open his stitches. You'll have to sew him up again." He charged away, Lloyd at his side.

"Pa, Dune Hollow is a good two-day ride east."

"I know where it is." Jake called to Juan, "Make sure that man sits in jail as soon as he's able to walk."

"*Sí, Señor* Jake. You go and get your precious daughter. *Que Dios te acompañe.*"

Jake kept walking as he talked to Lloyd. "You tell Brian that if he wants to go with us, he needs to get some things together fast. Have Tobe fix up a horse for him and borrow a rifle from someone for Brian to take." He walked fast as he talked. "Jeff!" he barked.

Jeff hurried to catch up again, leading his horse with him. "Yes, sir."

"I'm going to my house. Tell the preacher to come over there."

"The preacher?"

"The preacher."

"Yes, sir." Jeff hurried away.

"Lloyd, you go say your good-byes to Katie and Stephen." Jake stopped walking and faced his son. "I'm glad as hell they're okay, Lloyd. Katie did good, real good. You take damn good care of that woman."

"You know I will. I love her more than ever, Pa. What she did—that sealed it."

"And that news about your mother…" Jake pressed his lips together tightly.

"I know, Pa. I want to celebrate that too, but there's no time to think about it now. Just think about the fact that when we get back, she'll be here, and she'll be well. She'll be here to greet you, like always."

Jake turned away. "I've never needed her this bad."

"She's already with you, Pa. She's already with Evie too. And Evie is stronger than you think." They kept walking as they talked. "And she won't be scared, Pa, because she knows you'll come. She knows we'll *both* come. And Mom will be counting on us to bring Evie back, but she'll also be counting on *you* coming back, so don't go offering yourself up to Marty Bryant too quick. I know that's what you'll do if you have to, but there has to be another way."

Jake swallowed. "Maybe." He reached back and Lloyd grasped his hand. "Go talk to Tobe and then get Brian."

"I will. I'll round up some extra men too."

Jake let go of his hand.

"Pa—"

Jake faced his son.

"Katie's pregnant. That's a good sign things will work out. I'm sure of it."

Jake nodded. "Good. That's good. I'm happy for both of you." He turned and walked back to where he'd left his horse. People stared and backed away.

Jake mounted up and rode his horse to the house, his heart aching at the sight of the damage…the trampled roses, bullet holes all over the front of the house, windows shot out, the door beat down. He dismounted and walked inside, wanting to weep at the destruction there, as though a tornado had ripped through it. The lamp Randy loved lay smashed to pieces on the floor.

He walked to the bedroom and pushed open the door. To his surprise, everything there was intact. If only Randy were standing there, waiting for him. He could hear her voice, remembered when she was changing clothes and complaining about not fitting into her camisole. If anything happened to her, how could he ever walk into this room again, or ever sleep here again?

He walked over to the bed and picked up a pillow, breathing deeply of the rose scent. He remembered how passionately they'd made love before he left. She was alive! And there was no cancer! What a wonderful day this would be if it weren't for his Evie being taken, and his precious Little Jake's life in danger. Would they hurt or kill a little boy? Could they be that cruel?

He squeezed the pillow tight, burying his face in it. "Randy…Randy," he groaned. He sat down on the edge of the bed and rocked with the pillow in his arms.

Sometimes all I need is your arms around me. He could hear her saying it, feel her in his arms right now, smell her on the pillow.

"Jake?"

He looked up to see the tall, gangly Preacher Zilke standing in the doorway, looking a bit hesitant.

"You sent for me, but from the looks of you, I'm not sure I should come in."

"Don't worry. My anger isn't at you." Jake laid the pillow on the bed. "Sometimes all you need is to breathe in someone's scent to feel close to them."

The preacher nodded wordlessly.

Jake glanced at one of Randy's nightgowns hanging on a hook on the wall before addressing the preacher.

"I felt like I should tell you that I promised Randy that if she got through her surgery and it wasn't cancer, I'd go to church. But before this is over, Zilke, I'll have done things that will mean walking into a church is impossible. I already threatened to hurt a woman to get information out of her. I've never hurt a woman before, but this one would have risked my family's lives if I didn't—" He looked away. "And I just tortured a man to find out where they took my Evie." He shifted, and the bed squeaked a little. The memory of how sometimes it squeaked a little too much when he and Randy were making love stabbed at his heart like a sword. "Right now, I'm not sure there is a God after all, Zilke. Why would he let this happen to my daughter and that wonderful little grandson of mine?"

"Jake, I know Evie well, and she is the sweetest thing who ever walked. I believe God gave her to you just to show you that there is good in you. It's not all Randy that has made her the way she is. It's also you. She feels your love, sees through that outer crust. I am telling you now that whatever has happened to her, evil has *not* touched her, Jake. Evil *can't* touch that young woman, but evil can *use* her to bring out the evil in *you*. This could be a reckoning, Jake, a chance for you to once and for all cast out that evil."

Jake put his head in his hands. "I don't understand."

"I think you do. Evie thinks you walk on water. And when you find her—and you will—she will see whatever you decide to do to those men, and you will have to remember that and think about what that would do to *her*. She fully understands you kill men and you visit whores and smoke and cuss…but she doesn't see any of that. She sees a man who would willingly give his life for her if he had to. She sees a man who, in spite of the whores, has been faithful to and loves her mother as much as any man can love. She sees a man devoted to his children and grandchildren, a man who would gladly stop living this way if the law would let him…and she knows why you killed your father…and it doesn't matter to her because she understands the reasons."

Jake looked at him in surprise.

"She told me, Jake. I know far more about you than you think. And when you go after those men, you have to remember to let God deal his own justice. You can't do to them what I'm sure you'd *like* to do to them, because Evie will be there."

"Sometimes God's justice isn't enough."

"They will burn in hell, Jake."

"Yeah, well, I'll be right down there with them."

The preacher shook his head. "Oh, no, you won't. You are far too good for that, and God knows it. When you approach those pearly gates, Jake, God isn't going to see Jake the gunfighter, or Jake the avenger, or the Jake who associates with prostitutes and was once a wanted outlaw. God is going to see Jake the little boy who had to help bury his murdered mother, Jake the little boy who suffered so terribly at the hands of a madman. He'll see the little boy who wants so damn badly to just be loved—the Jake who has learned all about how to love back because of the family he once never dreamed he would have. And God will welcome that little boy into his kingdom with open arms."

Jake shook his head. "You don't know what all I've done."

"The only thing you've done wrong, Jake, is you've never forgiven yourself for your father's death—and you've never forgiven your *father*. You don't know anything about *his* past. Have you ever considered that? Maybe there was something there that made him what he was, or something mentally wrong that he couldn't help. You can't be free of your demons until you forgive him…and yourself. God completely understands you and will welcome you into his kingdom one day, and here on earth everyone at my church will welcome you with open arms when you come through those doors."

Jake kept his head in his hands. "I'll kill more men. I can't get to Evie without killing more men."

"Of course you will. But the only thing that will be wrong is what you might want to do to those left alive *after* you get Evie back. That's the big test, Jake. If you think your father still lives in you, then this is the time to get rid of him. You have to leave *justice* to *God*, Jake. He's given you the talent necessary to help people. You should use it for your job and to protect those you love, but not for wielding your own form of revenge. When you get out there, you remember the kind of man Evie thinks you are. You be *that* man. Do you understand?"

Jake ran his hands through his hair. "I, uh, I called you over here to ask if people from the church can clean up this place—maybe replace the windows that are broken. I don't want Randy to come home to this."

"We've already had a meeting about it, and Katie and her mother are taking charge. Everyone has their assignment. Young people are coming over to sweep up broken glass, and women are making curtains. Some of the men in town are going to replace the windows. They might not all be done by the time Randy gets back or you get back, but it will get done."

Jake reached for a cigarette on the night table and lit it. "Katie's a good girl, and brave. She's good for Lloyd."

"Yes, she is." The preacher just stood there a moment. "Do you want to pray with me, Jake?"

Jake drew on the cigarette, shaking his head.

The preacher sighed. "Don't tell me you don't pray, Jake. You wear a crucifix. You pray, all right. You just won't admit it. Can't let your guard down, can you?"

"Not right now. I don't dare let the hurt get to me.

Feelings get in the way of what I have to do. Feelings can come later."

"Then God be with you, Jake...and with Lloyd...and most certainly with Evie and Little Jake. They're waiting for you, Jake, so go and get them."

Jake met his eyes, a little surprised at the remark.

"I think you have God's permission to do what you have to do, Jake. Just remember what I told you about what happens *after* you get Evie back. And remember that you are always welcome at church. You are worthy in God's eyes, and now you have a promise to keep. Randy is coming home, alive and well. Remember that. God is working in your favor. He will be with you when you ride out after Evie."

Jake nodded. "I hope you're right."

"I *am* right. God bless you, Jake Harkner."

Zilke left. "God be with *Evie* and my grandson," Jake muttered. "And he'd better help me do this right."

Thirty-three

No one talked. They just rode at a steady pace, fast enough to try to reach Dune Hollow in three days instead of four, slow enough to keep from killing their horses. Jake, Lloyd, Brian, Jeff, and four men from town—feed-store owner Ruben Tate, whose children were all grown; farmer Fenton Wales, whose wife had died and who had no children; hardware-store owner Harry Wilkes, who had one nearly grown daughter; and gunsmith Red St. James, who did have family but was adept with handgun and rifle. Ruben, Fenton, and Harry knew rifles well enough to hunt with them, but this time they would hunt men. Brian carried a repeating rifle loaned to him by Lloyd. Jake had deputized all of them.

Jake and his son are side-by-side, and right now it's hard to tell them apart—not just in looks and ability, but also in their demeanor. Never has Lloyd more fully taken on the outlaw side of his father. If it weren't for his long hair, it would be even harder to tell them apart. Jeff made notes in his head and wondered if he would live to tell his story. *There are eight of us, but we figure up to fifteen men are with Marty Bryant. That's two men each, if a person wanted to conveniently divide us up that way, but there will be nothing convenient about this, and I suspect that between Jake and Lloyd, few will be left for the rest of us to worry about.*

But even that wasn't much of a comfort.

They took roads, sometimes took shortcuts, waded through creeks, wove through heavy woods, climbed hills, wound through brush. Jake knew the country, and he was taking the shortest route to Dune Hollow. Every man along was afraid to talk to him—even afraid to talk to Lloyd, who adored Evie as his sister as much as Jake adored her as his daughter. Jeff had no doubt part of Lloyd's devotion was because he'd never forgiven himself for abandoning his mother and Evie both when Jake went to prison. He felt as though he'd failed Evie then. He would not fail her now.

They stopped at noon again the second day, rested their horses, quietly ate biscuits, and drank coffee heated over a small fire.

"All of you listen up," Jake said then, surprising them that he spoke at all. "All of you know what those men have likely done to my daughter. If any one of you ever talks like she should be ashamed, you'd better hope I don't know about it. She's the sweetest, purest woman who ever walked, so you will treat her as such, no matter what has happened. Plain and simple. Evie is a lady, through and through."

After a moment of silence Red spoke up. "Ain't a man here who doesn't respect Evie, Jake."

"If we thought any different, we wouldn't have volunteered for this," Ruben offered. "Anyone who knows Evie thinks of her as the kindest woman in Guthrie. She teaches Sunday school, knows her Bible, helps people in need, and she's helped nurse a lot of us when we were bedded down sick or wounded at Brian's place. We'll find her, and she'll be just as sweet and good when we get her back home."

Jake smoked quietly, taking a few seconds to answer. "I like the fact that you said *we*," Jake told Ruben. "You men are risking your lives here, and that says a lot for how you feel about my daughter. I'm grateful, and I know Lloyd and Brian are too. And if Lloyd and I do this right, we'll be the ones taking the brunt of this thing and hopefully keep any of the rest of you from getting hurt. We'll head out again soon. I know it's a bitch riding this hard, but time is important. My plan is to ride *around* where they're camped. They expect us to ride straight at them from the west, but that's all open country, and they figure they'll have a good view and we'll have little protection."

Jake knelt down and pulled an unburned stick from the fire, drawing in the dirt. "Here's Dune Hollow. If we ride hard the rest of today, we can reach it late tonight. It's called that because it sits in kind of a dip. From our direction, it doesn't drop down that much." He drew around the other side of the X he'd made. "But over here on the east edge is a pretty high ridge. We'll go around to that so we can come up that ridge and be on top of them. They won't expect that, because they know my temper, which means they figure I'll come riding in hell-bent for blood, without thinking this out. I'm betting they figure I'll charge right into that hollow from the west, not wanting to lose any time. That would leave me wide open for their guns, and they'll figure once I'm in the hollow, I'll be trapped because of that ridge to the east. Besides that, I'm banking on them thinking that it's going to take me longer than this to find them, so they won't be as alert as they would be a couple more days from now. They probably figure the man they left behind is dead. They don't know he told me exactly where they were holed up. Our last bit of luck is that Marty Bryant doesn't have the brains of a hummingbird." The others laughed lightly.

"That's for damn sure," Red put in.

Jake made some squiggles along the line he'd drawn to indicate the ridge. "If we get around here and come up this ridge come morning, the sun will be at our backs as it rises…and it will be in their faces. We'll have a big advantage. It's hard to shoot uphill at a man, but it's damn easy to be at the top of that hill shooting down at them. We'll hit them the minute the sun breaks over that ridge. A rising sun can practically blind a man. It will be really hard for them to see us at all, so if we're lucky, we can bring down half of them before they even know what's going on. Then Lloyd and I can move in and blow the rest of them away. We'll use those fucking sonsofbitches for target practice. Any man who touches my daughter or my little grandson is going to find out he made the biggest mistake of his life." Jake rose from the fire then. "Ten minutes and we leave again." He walked off alone.

The rest of them sat there, looking at each other.

"The man has spoken," Fenton Wales said.

"This is gonna be a whole lot more satisfying than killing a deer," Ruben Tate offered. "A deer, I respect. These men shouldn't be allowed to exist."

"I can't think of a better man to be risking our lives with than Jake Harkner," Harry Wilkes said quietly. "And you, Lloyd," he added, nodding toward Lloyd. "Lord knows you're as dependable with those guns as your pa is."

Lloyd sighed and tossed his cigarette into the fire. "Maybe, but he's the best, Harry. And when he's this upset, you can bet he'll use those guns till they melt in his hands. I'm just praying I don't watch my pa get shot to pieces tomorrow. If that's what it takes to get to Evie and Little Jake out of there, he'll do it."

Brian sighed deeply and rubbed the back of his neck, hanging his head in obvious agony.

"Brian, your wife is the nicest woman I ever met," Red spoke up. "We'll get her out of there, or some of us will die tryin' to. That's a promise."

Every man there knew the hell Brian Stewart had to be in right now. He stared at the fire, obviously struggling with his emotions. "I'm grateful," he managed to answer, his voice gruff from grief.

Everyone quieted again until Jake returned and poured his remaining coffee on the fire, then kicked dirt on it. "Let's ride," he told them.

No arguments. They all mounted up and rode again... and rode, and rode...once in a while slowing down to ease up on the horses, twice getting off their mounts and walking with them for a while, stopping to let them drink, but never actually stopping altogether for more than five minutes.

Every man here, including me, knows the danger we are heading into, Jeff mentally noted, *but two things keep us going—a deep respect for Evie Harkner Stewart and her husband, and the knowledge that we are led by a man who knows exactly what he is doing.*

Even as a writer, Jeff couldn't imagine what must be going through Jake Harkner's mind. What a joyful time they could be having, waiting for Randy to get home, knowing she was well, if not for this ugly thing with Evie. The future of Jake's entire family lay with what would happen when they reached Dune Hollow, yet now he seemed so much calmer. Jeff wondered if it was something the preacher had told him.

They rode until it was almost too dark to see. Jake pulled up then and trotted his horse in a circle around the rest of them, talking quietly. "We're around the back side of Dune Hollow right now. I took the longer way around, so if they have scouts watching, they didn't see us. We'll move deeper into the woods to the left and make camp there. No fire. If they have scouts up on that ridge, they'll see it. Sorry, boys, but just biscuits and water tonight. Pour some water into your hats for the horses, and each man keep his horse right beside him to keep it from any alarm that might make it whinny. And no smoking. The lit end of a cigarette can show up for a mile or more. Everybody get out your bedrolls and stay in a tight circle. I need to talk to all of you again, and I don't want to have to yell."

They all did as they were told. Once their eyes adjusted to the light of the half-moon, they could actually see each other well enough to know who was who. Everyone ate quietly and took care of personal business farther out in the trees. The woods came alive with the sound of crickets and an occasional owl.

"If we're close, why can't we hear anything?" Jeff asked Lloyd softly. It was the first time he'd spoken to the young man since leaving Guthrie.

"They're on the other side of the ridge. A ground barrier like that completely cuts off all sounds from the other side of it. Didn't you ever hear that's why men close by never heard what was happening to Custer when he and his men were massacred?"

"No."

"In Montana there are huge, almost mountainous ridges that create sound barriers. The way I heard it, army scouts at one time were right on the other side from where up to ten thousand Indians were camped, and they never knew it."

Jeff nodded. "I never heard that." Both men sat quietly for a moment. "You okay, Lloyd?"

"No. I'm dynamite, remember? But Pa, he's nitroglycerin. That thing he did to Dooley back there in Guthrie—I don't think I could have done that, but it didn't bother me to watch *Pa* do it. There's the difference between us."

"Jake seems calmer," Jeff mentioned.

"I know. I think it's partly from learning my mother is all right. He takes so much strength from her, and he knows she'd be telling him not to go off half-cocked here. She'd tell him to stay calm and use his head. She'd remind him that he doesn't think straight when he's raging mad. I expect he feels her with him. That's all it takes for him to settle down."

Jake joined them, gathering everyone close.

"Tomorrow we'll make our way up this ridge—leave the horses here. I am hoping two things will give us an edge. Because I was gone when those men raided Guthrie, they have no idea when I got back, so they don't know for sure when I'll come looking for them. So I highly doubt they expect me to reach them so soon. And they don't know I've already had a little chat with the man Katie shot back in Guthrie and I know exactly where they are. They think they have a lot of time to have their enjoyment with my daughter and drink and take it easy and talk about all the ways they intend to torture me before they kill me. But before we go in there shooting, I'll need to weigh the options. I can't do that till we get up on that ridge tomorrow and get a look at the layout down there, so I don't want any man here to just start shooting without my orders. I'll tell you when to shoot and *who* to shoot so there are no wasted bullets. And it could be Lloyd and I have to go into that camp with guns blazing, so you men pick your targets and make sure one of us doesn't end up with a bullet in our own back by accident. You're all good with those rifles, so aim at a man and imagine he's just a deer or a bear. He's not a man. Understand? You can't let doubt or feelings get in the way. If you have qualms about it, leave now. I'll understand."

Ruben Tate spoke up. "That woman down there is loved by a lot of people, Jake. She's not just your daughter—she's Lloyd's sister and Brian's wife. And we all have no use for any man who'd abuse a woman or a little kid. There's not a man here who'll hesitate to put a bullet in any one of those men."

"All right then, get some rest." Jake stepped closer to Brian. "Come with me, Brian. Leave your rifle here."

His head still bandaged, Brian got up and followed his father-in-law farther into the woods. Jake sat down on a log and told Brian to sit down beside him. Both just sat there quietly for a moment, resting their elbows on their knees, listening to the crickets.

"Brian, you know about that time I went looking for Randy back before I married her, when she went alone to find her brother in Nevada...and how I found her at that trading post...so sick and weak she could barely move. Those men..." He sighed. "They didn't actually...do the worst...but they took liberties. They defiled and humiliated her. I took care of them my own way, and I got her out of there...and I nursed her back to health. And I saw her only as the beautiful woman I was falling in love with, and nothing those men did made any difference. I felt like she was mine, before I even touched her that way. And she was someone to be treasured and loved."

Jake sighed thoughtfully before continuing.

"And that's what Evie is to you...yours...to be treasured and loved. As her husband, you're the only one who can erase all the ugliness of this. The preacher told me something this morning that I'd never considered before." He paused, listening to an owl. "He said that evil can't touch Evie. He said evil could *use* her to get to me, but it couldn't touch her, and I believe that. She's carrying your baby—*your* baby—if she hasn't lost it. Even if she's lost it, you're the one who planted that baby in her belly, out of pure, innocent love, which is the only kind Evie knows. So there isn't a man down in that hollow who has really touched her at all, and only you can make her understand that. Do you know what I'm saying?"

Brian nodded, fighting the tears that wanted to come. "She was only eighteen when I met her. I'm the only man she's ever been with, the only one who owns her heart and soul, just as she owns mine. This changes none of that, and I'll damn well help her see that." He choked in a sob. "What hurts the most is that I failed to protect her." He rubbed at tear-filled eyes. "A man is supposed to be the protector. I mean—look what Katie did. I should have done something like that."

"You were taken by surprise. And *I'm* the one who failed to protect her, Brian. I took it for granted you would all be safe if you stayed in town. And you *have* protected her, your whole married life. You've sheltered her from everything mean and ugly out there, loved her with gentleness and respect. You've given her a good life. She's never known a raised voice or a physical threat, and you have the kind of job that lets you be with her almost constantly. That's the kind of husband she needed. She wouldn't have been strong enough to be married to some gruff, gun-toting lawman or hunter or blacksmith, or some man who likes to drink in taverns. Hell, you don't even smoke." He put an arm around Brian's shoulders.

"You're more of a man than I am in a lot of ways, Brian. You care about people and you save lives. I *take* lives." He took a deep breath, fighting another urge to vomit over the thought of men abusing Evie. "If you'd ever hurt Evie, I probably would have thrashed you within an inch of your life and kicked you out. But never once have I seen Evie upset or unhappy. She's always… smiling…and I can see the love in her eyes. I thank you for that."

Brian breathed deeply for self-control. "Hell, I can't take a whole lot of credit, because she's so easy to love. I take hope in the fact that she's her father's daughter, which means she has a silent, inner strength that I don't think even you are aware of, Jake. I've seen it, mostly when you were still in prison and she was as stubborn as Randy about refusing to be told she couldn't visit you or that I couldn't give you a doctor's attention when you were dying in there. She has helped me with surgeries, and she can handle blood and guts just fine for someone

so soft and innocent in other ways. Don't underestimate
her strength, Jake. And Little Jake—God knows how
stubborn *he* can be. He's probably making all those men
nervous, babbling about how 'Gampa' will come and
hurt them with his guns."

Jake managed a faint smile. He decided not to voice
his fear that they would hurt Little Jake just to be mean.
Brian had enough to grieve over. He sighed and rose.
"Brian, I need you to promise me something."

"Anything."

"If I don't survive tomorrow, and if Lloyd doesn't
either, there's a little eight-year-old boy at a brothel
called Dixie's Place, a bit northwest of Guthrie. I left him
there with a promise I'd come back for him. I need you
to promise you'll go and get him and welcome him into
your home or see that the Donavans get him."

Brian shook his head. "Only you would leave a
homeless eight-year-old boy at a whorehouse to be
cared for."

Jake came and sat down beside him again. "Hell, I
was raised in whorehouses, and look how I turned out."

Brian managed a smile. "That doesn't give that kid
much hope."

"Yeah, well, that kid is the reason for this wound on
my face. We found him on our way to a crappy settlement I call Hell's Nest. His father was beating him with
a belt."

Brian closed his eyes. "Good God. I can just imagine
your reaction."

Jake cleared his throat. "No imagination required
there. As I was lighting into his father, I hit my face on
the edge of a shovel tied to the side of the man's wagon.
I took that belt from him and used it on him until Lloyd
managed to stop me from beating him to death. I made
him sign a paper to give up the boy—actually, he signed
voluntarily, like the kid was nothing more than a pet

dog. I kept him with us and promised him a good home. If the Donavans don't take him, I'll damn well raise him myself, because he's *me*, Brian. He's *me*. So if I don't live through tomorrow, I need you to go and get him for me. The woman who runs the place has a good heart…a good heart. A lot of those women have good hearts, and women like that raised me, so it doesn't bother me at all leaving Ben there. Don't ever think less of them, especially Dixie. She's good people."

Brian nodded. "I'll go and get him."

"I'd appreciate it. And I want a couple more things from you."

Brian sniffed and wiped at his eyes. "What?"

"I don't want you using that rifle, for one thing. Have you ever fired a gun in your life?"

Brian swallowed. "No, but I sure as hell can pick one up and aim it."

"Maybe so, but you're a man born to save lives, not take them, and I can't afford to have bullets flying in the wrong directions, especially if Lloyd and I are down there in the thick of it and not knowing where Little Jake is—and they'll probably have Evie right out front as a way to keep us from shooting at them. You stay at the top of the ridge and use that rifle only if one of those bastards is coming toward you. Wait till he's close and then shoot him, and don't think twice about it. We'll likely need you more as a doctor than a shooter, so keep yourself healthy."

"What's the second thing you want?"

Jake picked up a piece of tall grass to chew on it, longing for a cigarette. "If I live through this, I'll likely get down there first. Give me five minutes alone with Evie before you come for her. Just five minutes. It will take you that long to get down that ridge anyway. You first tend to any of those men with us who might get hurt, especially if it's Lloyd. You find Little Jake and make sure he's all right. I just want five minutes with Evie."

Brian rose with a deep, pitiful sigh. "She'll want to know you're all right anyway. In fact, the only thing that comforts me is that she knows her father will come for her. That will give her courage." Brian ran a hand through his hair. "Get her out of there, Jake. Just get her out of there. I'll damn well take care of the rest."

Jake listened to the owl again, thinking how quiet it was tonight, and how tomorrow the air would be filled with the sounds of gunfire. "I'll get her out of there, even if it means my life. That's a promise." He rose and walked over to put an arm around Brian. "Try to rest. You'll need your wits about you tomorrow."

Brian nodded and they walked back to camp. His own body aching from lack of sleep, Jake laid out his bedroll next to Lloyd's.

"Try to stay calm tomorrow, Son, no matter what we see down there. If we do this right, we'll get your sister back."

Lloyd stared at the night stars. "Pa?"

"What?"

"I love you. I don't say it often enough."

Jake thought about his own father. How he would have loved to be able to say those words to the man, and to hear them back. He sat there quietly for a moment. "I love you too, Lloyd. You'll never know how much."

"I think I do. You told me to stay calm tomorrow. You have to do the same. I'm not ready to lose you, and if something happens to you, it will kill Evie. She'll fall into a million pieces and never recover from this. You remember that, and don't be too ready to hand yourself over to them. If Evie has to suffer a little more in order for you to find another way, she'll gladly do it. Don't underestimate her. She's the one who was strong when you went to prison. I ran off. I'll never be able to make up for that."

"You've more than made up for it. Do you realize

what it means to a man like me to hear his son say he loves him? That alone makes up for everything else. A man couldn't ask for a better son."

Lloyd sighed. "Or a better daughter," he added.

Both remained quiet for a moment. Jake pulled his hat down over his face.

"Pa?"

"What?" Jake kept the hat over his face.

"We've had some wild times together, haven't we?"

"That we have."

"You can be a damn lot of fun sometimes...when times are good. We've had each other's backs for quite a while now. I'd die for you. You know that, don't you?"

Jake remained quiet for a moment, forcing back emotions that might get in the way tomorrow. "I damn well know it."

Thirty-four

EVIE AWOKE TO THE STILL-DIM LIGHT OF DAWN. Everything hurt, and she curled up against the ugliness of what the two men who lay on either side of her had done to her over the past six days.

Morning sickness engulfed her, made worse by the smell of perspiration and men's filth. She sat up and deliberately leaned over Hash as vomit spewed forth. The man cried out and cursed, slamming a hand across her face. The incident woke Marty, who followed suit and threw Evie to the floor. He then jumped up and grabbed a pitcher of water, throwing some of it into Evie's face, then tossing the rest over Hash.

"Shit! Go outside and clean up in the horse trough," he ordered Hash. He looked at Evie. "You bitch!" He crashed the pitcher against a wall, then threw a shirt at her naked body. "Put this on and make us somethin' to eat! And make sure that kid of yours don't do any cryin' again today."

Evie picked up the shirt with shaking hands and pulled it on. It, too, smelled of perspiration, but at least she could use it to cover her nakedness. She was inwardly pleased she'd vomited all over Hash. Her sickness would keep both men away from her.

She wondered how long the sight of Marty's face, with its sewn-up eye socket, would haunt her. *Your pa done this to me, so you can damn well look into this face while I take what's his!* the man had sneered. *And you can thank your pa for what you're goin' through now, missy.*

The only thing that kept her going was drawing on the strength she knew her father would have. She was Jake Harkner's daughter, and she'd rely on that strength until he came for her...and that was one thing she did not doubt. Her father *would* find her.

She managed to get to her feet, quietly thanking God that she'd so far managed to hang on to her baby. Little Jake, normally a totally happy, rambunctious child, lay in a corner of the ramshackle cabin Marty had brought them to, just watching his mother but saying nothing. She buttoned the shirt and went to him, kneeling down and smoothing back his dark hair.

"It's okay, Little Jake. Grandpa will come for us."

"Hurt," the boy said sadly.

"I know, my precious."

"Gampa's guns hurt that son-o-biss."

Evie would normally scold him for using the word, but not now, not now. "Yes, Grandpa's guns will hurt them. Grandpa will come and help us, Little Jake, you'll see."

She'd no more gotten the words out than she heard it...a whistle.

Daddy! Her heart pounded. Jake Harkner would surely prefer the element of surprise, but he probably couldn't wait to reassure her he was here.

Little Jake bolted upright. "Gampa's guns!" he said, brightening.

Evie put a finger to her lips. She had to think of something to keep Little Jake quiet and in one place so he wouldn't get hurt in the shooting that would surely follow. "Hush, Little Jake. Remember to stay very still. Grandpa won't come unless you stay right here and don't move."

"What's going on?" another man in the cabin asked. "What was that whistle?"

"Harkner!" Marty exclaimed.

Evie rose. "You're going to die today, Marty Bryant! My father must be pretty sure he has you trapped, or he wouldn't have let you know he's here!"

"Shut up, bitch!"

"He's out there somewhere," Evie goaded, feeling empowered by just the thought.

"There ain't no way Jake has got here yet," Marty answered, going to a window. "Even if he has, *he's* the one who will die today!"

"Think what you want. After today you will be roasting in hell," she said calmly. "Jake Harkner will see to it."

Marty went to the door. "Hash, did you hear that whistle?"

Hash splashed water over his face. "I heard it, but I ain't worried. Let him come. It's what we've been waitin' for, ain't it?"

"But there's no way he could have found us this quick."

Evie sensed the fear in Marty's voice.

The others inside scrambled, pulling on pants, loading guns. Marty stuck his head a little farther out the door. "You men out there!" he yelled. "Make ready! That's Jake Harkner who just whistled!"

"Shit!" someone cursed.

"I'm tellin' you, Marty, the man would be comin' in from the west, not over that ridge to the east," Hash argued.

Evie stepped outside the door, studying the top of the ridge, trying to see something…anything…but she saw no sign of life. Yet she knew her father was up there, and most certainly her brother too. She fought the sick fear that Brian might have been killed when Marty Bryant had slammed a gun into his head. *Dear Jesus, let Brian be alive. And be with my father and brother. Help them.*

How would Brian feel about her now? Eight men. Eight men had defiled her in the worst way. If Jake had taken longer to find her, she was sure the other men would have decided to take their turns with her too.

She couldn't bear any more of this hideous abuse, or to watch Little Jake suffer. She rubbed at her belly, praying she would keep this baby because he or she, and Little Jake, might be all she had left of the sweet love she'd shared with her beloved husband. She turned to go back inside…and that was when she heard the gunshot. Just one…a loud crack in the crisp morning air. In the same instant, Hash Bryant fell forward into the watering trough, blood reddening the water.

Yes, Jake Harkner was definitely up on that ridge.

After that, all hell broke loose. Four men came running from behind the cabin and started shooting toward the ridge. A bevy of gunshots spit from behind brush on the hill, and all four men went down. Marty tackled Evie to the ground and dragged her kicking and screaming back into the cabin. She'd hoped to keep him outside where he would be an easier target, but he managed to get her into the cabin and slammed the door shut.

Jake watched Marty drag Evie into the cabin, her screams ripping at his insides.

"Fucking bastard!" Lloyd groaned. "She was trying to keep him outside, Pa, so we could get a shot at him."

"I know."

"She's smart. Sweet as she is, she's got the Harkner fight in her."

Jake put more cartridges into his rifle. He couldn't think about what he'd just seen. "We got five of them before they scattered for cover like roaches."

"Marty sure as hell knows we're here now," Harry Wilkes said excitedly.

"I *want* him to know," Jake told him. "Marty scares

easy. You boys did a good job picking your targets. I'll have Marty Bryant shaking like a tortured puppy before this is over."

"Jake, we can't be sure how many more there are inside that cabin, or anywhere else," Fenton Wales commented.

A covered wagon below rocked from the movement of men inside, and more had run into a barn. Someone opened a wooden shutter that had covered the cabin window. "That you, Jake?" Marty yelled from below. His voice seemed to echo in the morning air.

"You should be wishing it wasn't, Marty!" Jake yelled back, keeping behind brush cover near the top of the ridge.

"How'd you get here so fast?" came Marty's reply. "What are you doin' up on that ridge?"

"You didn't plan this out very well, Marty. I have the advantage now, so send my daughter and grandson out, or you won't live to see the sun set!"

"I ain't never comin' out! You come on down here instead."

"Is Dell with you, Marty? Do you want to see your little brother get killed today?"

"Dell is a man now. He done learned with your daughter! And he's the one who attacked that stagecoach and freed me!"

"Yeah, Jake!" It was Dell who shouted then. It sounded like his voice came from the barn. "Your daughter's a sweet one, that's for sure!"

"Jesus Christ," Lloyd groaned. "I can't wait to kill that little sonofabitch."

"Hold it!" Someone below shouted the words. A man came running out of the barn. "Let me leave, Harkner! I never touched your daughter! It was the *rest* of 'em! Not me!"

Brian put his head down on his arm. "Sweet Jesus," he muttered. "I can't take much more of this."

The man who'd come out of the barn put his hands in the air. "I'm unarmed!"

"That's my sister down there! Did you try to help her?" Lloyd yelled.

"I...no... I was outnumbered!"

"He didn't try to help on account of he was havin' at her like everybody else!" Dell shouted, followed by laughter.

Lloyd rose, taking aim with his rifle.

"Get down!" Jake ordered.

"Sonsofbitches! I'll kill every one of them!" Lloyd swore.

"Lloyd, he's giving himself up," Jake warned.

Lloyd crouched back down and looked at Jake with a dark, hateful glare. In that moment, Jake saw himself, the old Jake, the outlaw Jake. "Don't do it, Son."

"Do what?"

"You *know* what! Don't do it! I've *been* there, and that hatred and thirst to kill will destroy you. Remember that Evie is watching us."

"You heard what they said!"

"I want to kill every one of them as much as you do," Jake growled. "But you start shooting the ones giving themselves up, and Marty might shoot Evie just for spite, and we could *both* end up in prison if we don't handle this right!"

Lloyd rubbed at his eyes and turned his attention back to the hollow. Just then, the man who'd decided to give himself up started running.

"*Now*, Pa?"

"Hell, yes."

Lloyd aimed and pulled the trigger. His rifle shot cracked through the air and the man went down.

Men below began cursing a blue streak.

"Murderin' bastard!" one man shouted.

"It was you that shot him, wasn't it, Lloyd Harkner? You're as bad as your pa!"

"I take that as a compliment," Lloyd shouted back.

"That was my brother," another man shouted. "He wasn't even armed!"

"The way I saw it, he was running from the law," Lloyd shouted back, actually grinning. "It's not my fault the sonofabitch gave me an excuse to shoot him. The rest of you would be wise to give yourselves up right now!"

"So you can shoot us when we put down our guns?" Dell shouted. "You and your pa ain't no better than vigilantes."

Jake looked over at Red and the others. "What do you think, boys? Are we all vigilantes?"

"Hell, yes," Red answered. "Once this is over, you can hang every one of them that's left as far as we're concerned, Jake."

Jake turned his attention back to the hollow, where men remained hidden. "I'd sure like to, but Evie's down there," he told Red. "I have a feeling she'd be mighty upset by that, in spite of what she's been through. We can't let her see us string up a bunch of men."

"Then we'll just have to shoot them all before we get down there," Lloyd suggested.

A rant of curses came out of Marty's mouth then, ending with a promise to "get Lloyd" for kicking him into the street and throwing him into the prison wagon and making him lose his eye patch.

"Keep them talking," Jake told Lloyd. "I'm trying to spot Marty in a window."

"Things will be a lot worse for you once we come down there!" Lloyd goaded, feeling a wicked pleasure at shooting the unarmed man. He lowered his voice. "They're scared shitless, Pa. We've got the lowdown on them damn good." He yelled again, "You really screwed up this time, Marty! There's no getting out of this one!"

Jake watched the cabin window, but he couldn't get a good view of Marty and wasn't sure if Evie might be standing right beside him.

"Gampa! Gampa!" Little Jake screamed the words from inside the cabin. It tore at Jake's heart.

"Show yourself, Harkner, or I'll shoot the kid and turn his ma over to the other five men in this cabin!" Marty yelled.

"Five plus Marty," Lloyd muttered. "That's six in the cabin. We took down four plus Hash. With the man I just shot, that makes twelve in all accounted for. There must be more in that wagon and more in the barn."

"We need to get Marty outside," Jake told Lloyd and the others. "If I can take him down, the others will try to run off. That's when we get every last one of them." He aimed his rifle again. "Marty!" he shouted.

"I'm listenin'!"

"I want to see my daughter again, and my grandson! You bring them out, and I'll come down."

"No, Daddy, don't you come down here!" Evie screamed out the window.

Someone jerked her away. More screams. Little Jake kept crying for his "gampa."

"Jesus, I have to go down there," Jake told Lloyd.

"No! Every man there will take a shot at you, Pa. You'll be riddled with bullets before you ever reach bottom. Every damn one of them wants to say he killed Jake Harkner."

"I don't have any choice."

"Try once more to get him to come out. The man is *stupid*, Pa. We can flush him out."

More screams.

"My God, they're hurting her," Brian agonized.

Jake struggled not to give in to his own personal horror. "Stay calm, Brian." He fired into the wagon and someone cried out. Things quieted again after that, and it sounded like men were arguing inside the cabin.

"They're starting to get real scared, Brian," Jake told his son-in-law. "A scared man makes stupid mistakes, and he won't take the time to mess with a woman. He'll be more concerned with how to save his neck."

Little Jake had stopped crying, which worried Jake.

"Bring them out now, Marty, and I'll come down!" Jake shouted. "That's a promise! You'll never get me down there otherwise, no matter what!"

"I'll kill her right now if you don't come down!"

"No you won't!" Jake answered. "You kill her or my grandson, and you know for a *fact* that you're a dead man! I'll starve you out of that cabin, and then I'll do things to you that you can't even imagine before I kill you! Understand?"

"Holy shit," Red remarked.

"Bring them out, Marty! You're *trapped* in there! If you want me down there, I need to see my daughter and grandson first!"

Things quieted again. Finally, the cabin door opened.

"Get ready, boys," Jake told the others. "Remember what I told you about choosing your man."

One man jumped out of the wagon and started running.

"I've got him," Red St. James declared. He fired his buffalo gun. The man's head literally disappeared.

"Red, I think you should keep that deputy's badge," Jake told him.

Red grinned. "I just might do that."

"You goddamn murderin' outlaw!" Marty screamed.

"That one was on Red St. James!" Jake yelled back. "I have plenty of help up here, Marty, but I told these men up here to save *you* for *me*!"

"You ain't gonna do *nothin'*," Marty all but screamed. "I'm gonna take your daughter with me for protection! I'm bringin' her out, Harkner, and she's stayin' right with me till I get to my horse. The rest of my men will cover me. You let me go and I'll drop her off a few miles north of here." He dragged Evie outside. She wore only a man's shirt. It kept falling open because the buttons had been ripped away.

A furious Brian started to charge down the hill, but Lloyd leaped up and managed to tackle him to the ground as bullets flew their way.

"Damn it, Brian, we'll get her away from there! You have to stay calm!"

Brian fought him, and Lloyd ordered Harry Wilkes and Ruben Tate to come and hold him down.

"Brian, we can't do our job if you don't stay put!" Jake told him.

Brian turned away, staying on his knees. The other two men let go of him.

"Brian, we need to be able to use our guns to help Jake. We can't be spendin' time holdin' you down," Harry told him.

Brian nodded, grasping his middle and bending over.

Jake watched as a second man came out of the cabin holding a wiggling Little Jake in front of him.

Marty started dragging Evie toward the barn. "Cover me, boys!"

"I *have* to go down there. It's the only thing that will distract him," Jake told Lloyd.

"No! Pa, *look* at Evie! She keeps moving her head to the side. She thinks you can take him, Pa. She's trying to keep her head out of the way!"

Jake followed Marty with his rifle.

"See? She's not fighting him."

"But she's tall and Marty is short, so their heads are even. One jerk the wrong way and I've killed my own daughter!" Jake lamented.

"Bullshit! You can do it, Pa! And I can take the other one. Little Jake is too small to give the man decent cover."

"Look how he's wiggling," Jake answered. "Jesus, Lloyd, you could kill Little Jake."

"I won't! I can take that man, Pa, and you damn well can take Marty."

Jake blinked back tears. "Jesus God, if it was anybody else but Evie…"

"*Do* it, Pa! She's counting on it! She's a Harkner. She's giving you a target!"

"It could be like with Santana all over again. I can't do it, Lloyd."

"Yes, you *can*, goddamn it! *Shoot* him!"

Jake struggled against tears. "God help me," he whispered, raising his carbine and taking aim.

Thirty-five

"I'm takin' her, Jake!" Marty screamed, his voice ringing in Evie's ears. "If you want her back, you'll have to come and get her, and there's eleven other men down here with me who will blow you to pieces!"

Don't do it, Daddy! Don't come down here! At first Evie tried to strain against Marty's tight grip around her chest and arms, then realized that fighting him meant making it harder for Jake to shoot him. She felt ill at the smell of Marty's foul breath, refused to look at his ugly eye. She kept her head turned away as far as possible.

"Hold your fire, Jake, else you'll kill your own daughter!" Marty continued screaming. "You'll never—"

Evie felt it then, an odd buzzing sound so close to her ear that it hurt. Instantly Marty's hold on her loosened. He fell, taking her down with him. At almost the same time, the man holding Little Jake slumped to the ground. Evie couldn't even remember hearing gunshots. She grabbed Little Jake then as the air exploded with gunfire, so much of it that it was painful to her ears. The shots became muffled then, her ears shutting down on her.

After that, everything seemed to happen like a strange dream. She saw men pour out of the cabin, the wagon, the barn...running past her...shooting...shooting... shooting! She stayed on the ground, keeping a tight hold on Little Jake, who struggled to get away and run to his grandfather. The boy covered his ears.

Then she saw them. She recognized their size, and Lloyd had lost his hat. His long hair was flying behind

him like an Indian's as he charged down the hill as if
he was some kind of warrior, making quick stops to
shoot his rifle. The tall man beside him in a black shirt
and hat was unmistakably her father. They deliberately
made difficult targets as they ducked and wove behind
and around shrubs and small trees. Evie felt the terror of
possibly seeing her father and brother both shot down
before her eyes. She managed to crawl behind a barrel,
looking around the side of it to see fire spitting from the
ends of her brother's and her father's six-guns, which
they now used instead of rifles. She noticed more puffs
of blue smoke coming from up on the ridge…more men
who must have come to help Jake.

They had all seen her mostly naked. She leaned
over Little Jake, sick with humiliation, devastated that
her own brother and father had seen her this way. She
opened her eyes then to see Lloyd go down.

"No! No!" She thought she was screaming the words,
but couldn't hear herself. "Lloyd!" Then Jake went
down. "Oh, God, Daddy!"

Jake rolled over and got up again and kept shooting
both guns. Evie couldn't tell for sure exactly where
he'd been shot. She saw Lloyd get to his knees, a
bloodstain at his lower left side. He, too, kept shooting. More men came down the ridge then, and bodies
lay strewn everywhere.

Evie couldn't be sure how long the shooting went
on before suddenly, like magic, everything quieted. She
thought she heard men shouting orders but was afraid
to raise her head and look—afraid she'd see her father
and brother dead. In the next instant, someone grabbed
her and Little Jake. Evie instantly recognized those arms.
"Daddy!" she screamed. She wrapped her arms around
his neck, clinging tightly. "You're hurt!"

"I'm all right. I'm all right." His voice sounded so far
away.

Evie curled against him, and Jake held her tight while Little Jake wiggled free and hugged his grandpa around the neck from behind.

"Gampa kill the son-o-bisses!" he yelled, grinning and squeezing Jake's neck.

"Little Jake, go find your uncle Lloyd," Jake told him as he clung to Evie.

The boy ran off, still shouting that "Gampa's guns hurt the son-o-bisses." Jake ordered someone to see if there was a blanket in the wagon, and in the next moment a blanket came around her. Jake leaned against the barrel and sat all the way down, holding her close. He kissed her forehead and grasped her hair, pressing her head against his chest.

"Jesus, Evie." He kissed the top of her head, and Evie felt instantly calmer...safe...loved...

"I knew you'd come," she sobbed.

"I never should have left town."

"Daddy, you're hurt..."

"Don't worry about it. It's hardly more than a cut on my arm." He held her close. "My God, Evie, I'm so sorry! I failed you! I failed the most precious person in my life."

"You couldn't have known. You came for me. That's all that matters." Evie heard a voice in the distance then.

"Brian! Lloyd is back down! Come and help him!"

Evie turned her head to see Brian coming down the hill. "He's alive? Brian is alive?"

"He's fine. He came with us so he could be with you right away."

"Lloyd!" She tried to pull away.

Jake hung on tight. "Stay still, Evie. Brian will take care of him."

"I should go to both of them, but I can't. I can't look at Lloyd again...and Brian..." She covered her head with the blanket. "He can't see me like this! Their filth is all over me."

"It's all right, baby. We'll take care of that." Jake watched Brian bend over Lloyd. *Lloyd! Not Lloyd! God, don't take my son!* He sat there torn in a thousand pieces... Evie's devastation, Lloyd possibly dying, Randy...was she home yet? What was going through her mind? God, how he needed to hold his wife!

"Daddy, I'm going to be sick again—" In the next instant, she leaned away from him and vomited. Jake fought tears as he held her hair away from her face.

"Jeff, bring me a canteen!" he yelled.

"Don't let him see me."

Jeff ripped a canteen from a horse that lay dead near the cabin and ran it over to Jake, aching at the look in Jake's eyes. He uncorked the canteen and held it out.

"Thanks. You'd better go after Little Jake before the kid picks up somebody's gun and starts trying to shoot it," Jake told Jeff. "Brian brought clothes, so take Little Jake up the ridge and bring Brian's horse down here. Keep that little hellion occupied."

"Sure, Jake." Jeff didn't know what to say to Jake or to Evie, so he left to corral Little Jake, who still ran around with just a little shirt on, pretending to shoot the men who were already dead.

Jake helped Evie rinse her mouth. "That damn kid thinks this is all a game," he tried to joke, secretly wanting to cry with joy that Little Jake was alive and all right. He reached into his shirt pocket and took out a piece of peppermint. "Chew on this."

"Daddy, you always have peppermint with you." She gratefully sucked on the candy. Jake thought about how he and Randy liked to use it in the mornings, and he couldn't help wondering if they would get that chance again. Randy seemed so far away.

"I'm such a mess! I'm such a mess!" Evie lamented. "How can you stand to hold me?"

Jake closed his eyes and kissed her hair. "Baby girl,

you have never looked more beautiful. You're alive, and that's all that matters. I'm just so sorry! I never thought they would raid the town like that. I should never have left. If I'd been there—"

"Daddy, please stop blaming yourself. I was just so scared you'd come down and they would kill my father in front of my eyes—and maybe Lloyd too."

"Lloyd will be all right. I see him moving around right now. He's trying to sit up." He held her tight, never wanting to let go and thanking God Lloyd was moving. "Evie, tell me you haven't lost the baby."

"No, but only because...oh, God, I just lay there and didn't fight them, because I was afraid they would beat me more and I *would* lose the baby." She curled into an even tighter ball. "Was I wrong to do that? Does that make me bad?"

Jake wanted to scream in rage. "Jesus, no, Evie. It makes you damn smart and damn strong."

"It was so ugly...so ugly..."

"Hush, Evie. Brian loves you more than ever, and you have to *let* him love you, understand? You remember what you and Brian have. Your baby is just a symbol of how right and good it can be between a man and a woman. No man but Brian has ever touched you. Do you understand what I'm saying?"

"But he'll wonder—"

"He *won't* wonder!" He squeezed her tighter. "You listen to me, because I've seen every ugly thing a man could possibly see in a lifetime, and I sure as hell know men. They don't come any better than Brian. He's a good and patient man who loves you deeply and can make it all beautiful for you again. Let him do that for you, Evie. All he wants is his wife back and that baby you're carrying."

She clung to his shirt, crying. Jake put his cheek against Evie's hair as he watched Brian wrap gauze around Lloyd's midsection. "He's okay, Evie. Lloyd is moving around more. He's okay. Brian is going to come over here soon, and you go to him, all right? And don't you *dare* show any shame, because you don't have one goddamn thing to be ashamed of. Understand?"

She wiped at her tears, smearing the dirt on her face. "I understand that you'll never stop cussing, no matter how much mother and I ask you to. Some of those awful words are already coming out of Little Jake's mouth. You should have heard some of the things he said to those men, Daddy. Once he pouted those little lips and called them goddamn fucking bastards. A little three-year-old!"

Jake almost laughed at the vision of Little Jake talking back to such vile men. "Evie, I hope the baby you're carrying turns out to be a sweet, quiet little girl, because if you have another kid like Little Jake, you'll end up in a madhouse."

The remark brought the intended tiny laugh. "He's tough, like his grandpa. You have to stay alive for a long time, Daddy, just to help me raise him. He hangs on everything you tell him. So does Stephen."

Brian rose from helping Lloyd and walked over to where Jake sat with Evie. "You'd better let me look at that arm, Jake."

"Not now. It's just a flesh wound, and the bleeding is already slowing. I can take care of it. What about Lloyd?"

"He'll make it. A bullet went right through the flesh at his left side—knocked him sideways and took his breath away, but the bleeding has slowed. The pain will be worse than what the actual wound is."

"I told Jeff to take Little Jake to get the horses. I was afraid he'd pick up a *real* gun and start shooting it in all directions. Jeff will get him some clothes. I swear that kid thinks this was all fun and games."

"They hurt Little Jake to make him shut up," Evie lamented, her face still buried against her father's neck.

"But he only cried for a minute, and I swear he got that same dark, angry look in his eyes you get sometimes, Daddy. He wasn't scared at all."

Brian met Jake's eyes, and Jake saw the agony Brian felt at the thought, and at Evie's condition. "He might be my son, Jake, but when it comes to not giving up on anything, Little Jake is definitely a Harkner." He reached out and caressed Evie's thick, dark hair, leaning closer to kiss her forehead. "And so is this daughter of yours." He pushed some hair behind Evie's ear. "I brought clothes, Evie, in case you would…need them. Jeff will bring them down."

Evie kept the blanket over most of her face when she turned to look at her husband. "I was so scared they'd killed you and I'd never see you again…but now…"

"I am very much alive, Evie. Come, let me hold you. I'll clean you up and you can get dressed. Let's just go home, honey."

"I can't."

"Yes, you can. Are you still carrying our baby?"

Evie pulled the blanket back over her face. "Yes. I didn't fight them, Brian. I didn't fight them because I was afraid they'd beat me more and I'd lose the baby. And if I screamed and fought, Little Jake would try to defend me, and then they'd hurt him, so I stayed still." She broke into tears of shame and horror again.

Brian closed his eyes and looked away for a moment, struggling against the worst rage he'd ever known. This was the first time as a doctor that he wanted to kill men rather than help them. He touched her hair again. "Evie, you were protecting our son and that baby inside you. You *survived*! God means for you to have this baby, honey. It's a symbol of what we have…you and *me* and nobody else." He pulled the blanket away from her face. "You and me, Evie. Absolutely nothing has changed about how much I love you and that baby you're carrying. Those men couldn't take that away, could they?"

Jake urged her to let go. "Let your husband hold you, Evie. Let's all go home to your mother. She's home by now and waiting for us and probably out of her mind with worry."

"She's okay, Daddy. Before this happened—"

"I know. I heard. So we have a lot to be thankful for, don't we?"

"Evie, let me help you." Brian's eyes teared at the bruises on her face. "My God." He leaned close and kissed her cheek, and she finally let go of Jake and threw her arms around Brian's neck.

Jake tucked the blanket around her as Brian picked her up. He put a hand on Brian's shoulder. "Go take care of her. I have some business to settle with those men over there who are still alive." He began reloading one of his guns.

"What?" Evie caught him loading the gun.

"You go with Brian, baby girl. When I'm through, there won't be a man left alive to talk about you or—"

"No!"

The darkness moved back into Jake's eyes. "Evie, I can't let this go."

"No! No! Don't kill them!" Evie clung to Brian as she looked pleadingly at her father. "It's murder! You're *better* than that. You killed so many men today, but only because they were trying to kill *you*. Don't turn around and just murder the rest of them," she sobbed. "That's what it would be. *Murder!*"

Jake closed his eyes and turned away. "Evie, they need to *pay*."

"Most of them already have, by your guns, and Lloyd's. Don't go beyond the law, Daddy. I know Lloyd shot that man on purpose after he gave himself up. Don't let him turn into someone lawless too! Killing those men would be like the *old* Jake, the one who led you and mother to so much heartache. And you'll make Lloyd a killer too! *Please* don't kill those men! I'll never get over this if you do. I'll feel responsible!"

"Jake, listen to her," Brian told him.

Jake turned and met his eyes.

"Don't put this on her conscience, Jake."

"Promise me, Daddy. Judging them is up to God himself, not you. I forgive them. I *have* to forgive them to keep my sanity."

Jake looked at his bruised, violated daughter. *Evil can't touch her.* The preacher was right. Why else would she plead for the lives of men who'd done such awful things to her?

"Don't go over there and execute the rest of them, Jake," Brian pleaded. "Not in front of Evie."

Evil can use her to bring out the evil in you...this could be a reckoning...a chance to once and for all cast out that evil. Jake felt a war going on in his heart. *Whatever you decide to do to those men, Evie will be watching...*

"Evie—"

"I *know*, Daddy. I know a lot more about you than you think. I'm not blind, but I know part of you doesn't want to be like that anymore. Don't make *me* the reason you go back to prison. And I don't want Little Jake to see that kind of revenge. You're wearing your mother's crucifix," she reminded him. "I know that means more to you than you let on. And Little Jake needs to know Grandpa's guns are for good, not for evil—not for revenge. Your own mother wouldn't want that."

"Jake, Marty and Hash Bryant are both dead," Brian reminded him. "Let it go now. I'm taking Evie around back to help her clean up and get dressed. Don't let her hear any more gunshots."

Jake reached out and put the back of his hand to Evie's bruised cheek, then turned away, holstering his gun but struggling with a need to make every last man pay for touching his daughter. Brian turned and carried Evie around a side of the house where others couldn't see them.

Evil can't touch her.

Jake kept hearing the preacher's words. Not only could evil not touch her, but because of her, he realized evil couldn't touch him either. No longer could his father's blood influence that dark part of him that was always looking for revenge...for every man he killed *was* his father, over and over and over again.

His throat hurt as he walked over to Lloyd, who still sat on the ground. Jake slumped down beside him, suddenly weary and realizing that for the last seven days he'd slept the equivalent of perhaps two nights, if that much. He touched Lloyd's shoulder.

"When I saw you go down too, I thought I'd lost you," he told Lloyd. "I never want to know that feeling again."

"You won't lose me, Pa. I have to be around to keep your ass out of trouble. That's become my major occupation, you know." Their gazes held. "How is she?"

Jake let go of him and ran a hand through his hair, realizing he'd lost his hat at some point. "I'm not sure. It's going to take time, Lloyd, but she has Brian, and she couldn't ask for a better man to get her through this. And she hasn't lost the baby."

Lloyd wiped at sudden tears. "I just...I want to kill every man left."

"Evie knows that. She asked us not to. She said she'd feel responsible, that she forgives them, and we shouldn't take any more revenge."

Lloyd looked over at the remaining five men, who were being treated by Red and Ruben as best they could.

"Ain't no way Doc Stewart is going to help any of you bastards," Red was telling them, "after what you did to his wife. You can just *suffer!*"

"Only Evie would ask us not to make the rest of them pay," Lloyd said quietly. "How can she forgive them?"

Jake sighed, looking down at the drying blood on his sleeve. "Because it's not her place or ours to either condemn *or* forgive them. She said that's God's decision." He met Lloyd's gaze again. "And she doesn't want me to lead *you* down that pathway. That's exactly where you were going when you shot that unarmed man, Lloyd. I don't want that for you, and neither does Evie. After what she's been through, she's thinking about *us*." He looked away. "We have to honor what she wants."

"I suppose," Lloyd answered with a sigh. "I saw Dell's dead body. I hope it was my bullet that got him."

They sat there quietly for a moment, then looked at each other.

"She only asked me not to *kill* them," Jake added. "She didn't say anything about not kicking the shit out of them."

Lloyd nodded. "A man needs to unleash his anger over something like this, but I'm hurting pretty bad right now, Pa."

Jake looked toward the cabin. "Evie can't see them right now." He grimaced as he rose.

"You need to take care of that arm, Pa."

Jake lit a cigarette. "I'll have Jeff do it after I tend to business." He walked over to the remaining men, who all looked terrified.

"Pa, maybe you'd better not," Lloyd called to him. "Remember what you just told me. It's the same for you."

Jake kept walking.

"Pa, you could go to prison too, easier than I would!"

Four of the men sat hog-tied, one bleeding badly from a crease to his neck. A fifth man lay on his back, groaning from a bullet to the belly. Jake realized he didn't know any of them.

"Don't do it, Harkner," one of them begged as Jake

drew his gun. "You're a marshal now. Marshals can't execute people."

Jake knelt down and pushed the gun under the man's nose. "Can't they?" He pushed upward painfully. "I'd like to shove the barrel of this gun into your mouth and pull the trigger, you worthless bastard! I've done it before. But my daughter actually forgave all of you. Can you believe that? She *forgave* you sonsofbitches! And that's her right. But it's *my* right *not* to forgive! I promised her I wouldn't blow your fucking brains out, but I didn't promise I wouldn't make you suffer."

Jake's men stood back.

Jake slammed his gun across the first man's face, then stood up and rammed a booted foot into his privates. He kicked another one under the chin.

"Pa, don't!" Lloyd yelled. "Somebody stop him."

Red and Ruben each grabbed hold of Jake.

"Jake, you'll just kill them another way!" Red told him, both men struggling to keep hold of him. "Your daughter will *see* them! She'll *know*! *Stop* this—for Evie's sake!"

Jake hesitated, then shook them off, tears in his eyes. "Nobody knows what she means to me!"

"Pa, you have to stop," Lloyd called to him from where he still sat. He grimaced as he tried to get to his feet, then sat back down again. "Just...stop..."

Jake looked at the man with the belly wound. The man started crying when Jake approached where he lay. "I'm gut shot," he whined.

Jake just shook his head. "Did my *daughter* beg and cry like you're doing now?"

The man just looked at him and sobbed.

Judging them is up to God, Daddy. I forgive them.

Jake wished he knew how to forgive.

You have to forgive yourself, Jake, and your father. You'll never be free until you can do that.

They were his father...all of them...every man who'd

died by his guns. Jake realized it was done now. Done. He felt strangely relieved.

He turned away.

"Not one man here says a word about this," he warned. "Or about Lloyd shooting that man earlier."

"Ain't a man here who blames either of you," Red told him.

"Jake, every one of us would like to kill these men, but we just can't do it, and neither should you," Ruben told him. "There's laws now about things like this, and you know it."

Jake rubbed at the back of his neck. "Yeah...I know. And I'm forever grateful to all of you," he told them.

Jeff came back with Brian's horse, a now-dressed Little Jake sitting in front of him. Harry Wilkes followed with Jake's horse. Jake stumbled to the animal and grasped the pommel, resting his head against the saddle.

Jeff led Brian's horse around the side of the cabin. Moments later he rode back to where Lloyd still sat and dismounted, lifting Little Jake down. The child immediately ran to his grandfather.

Jeff knelt in front of Lloyd. "You all right?"

"I will be. Flesh wound, but it knocked me down good. It hurts like hell."

Jeff watched Jake lift Little Jake with his good arm, and the child hugged his grandfather around the neck and kissed his cheek several times over. "This will bother him for a long time, won't it?" Jeff commented to Lloyd.

"Pa?" Lloyd smiled sadly. "You never know for sure what's going through that man's head. Yeah, it will bother him. He wants real bad to flat-out kill the rest of those men, but he'll respect what Evie wants. I'd like to kill them too, but that would break Evie's heart. The hard part for Pa in all of this is Pa figures this is all because of who *he* is, but being able to hold Little Jake and knowing my sister has a man like Brian to help her... That helps, but he won't really be okay until he gets home to my mom. *She's* his medicine. I guarantee he's thinking about her right now. Thank God she'll be all right." He winced and pressed his hand to his side, then reached up with his other arm. "Help me up, Jeff."

Jeff took his hand and let Lloyd use him to get to his feet. "Speaking of your mother, Lloyd, I think Jake promised her he'd go to church if she came through her surgery without cancer. Do you think he'll really go?"

Lloyd smiled more fully, the humor of that promise lightening his mood. "Well, you don't promise something like that to my mother without keeping the promise. She'll hold him to it." He grinned at Jeff. "That will be something to see, won't it?"

"I think it will be how I end the book…Jake Harkner, notorious outlaw, feared lawman, a man who smokes and cusses and spends time at brothels…taking his guns off and walking into church. Hell of an ending, isn't it?"

Lloyd smiled sadly. "It sure is. I'll bet it's already eating at him that he made that promise. He'll try to figure a way out of it, but my mom will absolutely hold him to it." He looked toward the cabin. "And Evie—it will help her a lot to see Jake walk into church. Hell, she holds him right up there next to God to begin with."

Both men grinned.

"That's a hell of a comparison," Jeff remarked.

Jake yelled at Jeff to come and help him wrap his arm.

"I'm not sure it's safe to go over there," Jeff quipped.

"I'll go with you." They both walked toward Jake, Lloyd leaning on Jeff's shoulders and grimacing with pain.

"Lloyd, you said once that Jake fills up a room when he walks into it, but sometimes he fills up the whole damn country," Jeff quipped. He glanced up at Lloyd. "You do know you're just like him, don't you?" Jeff added.

Lloyd stopped walking. "I know. I have to watch myself because I'm too *much* like him."

"Lloyd, you shot that one man down after he gave up his guns."

Lloyd gave him a dark look. "It's done, and the other men here have agreed not to talk about it," he told Jeff. "Don't you write about it. And I shot him because he didn't help my sister, plain and simple."

"And I'm guessing that's exactly the kind of thing Jake would have done in his early days."

Jeff walked off to help Jake, and Lloyd hesitated, watching after him. He studied Jake as he took gauze from his supplies, and all the while Little Jake stood there with his arms wrapped around his grandpa's leg. The kid was nuts about Jake. So was Stephen.

He glanced at the prisoners. One of those still hogtied glared back at him. "Which one of you bastards shot my brother while his hands were in the air?" he asked.

Lloyd put a hand to his side and walked closer. "*I* did," he sneered. "The sonofabitch didn't try to help my sister."

"And you're just like your pa—a ruthless, no good sonofabitch! My brother was unarmed!"

"So was my *sister*!"

"You must be *Lloyd* Harkner."

"I must be."

"I'll remember that name. Someday I'll come for you, Lloyd Harkner."

Lloyd just smiled. "Be my guest. I'd like nothing more than a chance to kill you right here and now, but I can't. You come back at me with a gun and I'll have my excuse to blow you away."

"Yeah? Well, if they don't hang me, I *will* come back. You can count on it."

Lloyd nodded. "What's your name?"

"Holt. Mike Holt. Remember it."

"I'll do that." Lloyd looked back at Jake. Jeff was helping wrap his arm, and Little Jake still clung to his leg. He thought about Mike Holt saying he was just like his ruthless, no-good sonofabitch father. Jeff had made the comparison also, but not in such derogatory words.

"Well, if I'm just like Jake Harkner, I guess I don't mind so much," he muttered. "Mean and all."

Thirty-six

RANDY BRUSHED HER HAIR, THINKING HOW JAKE LIKED it long and loose. She'd been home two days and still no word. The constant worry over whether Jake and Lloyd and Evie and Little Jake were alive stabbed at her constantly, leaving her unable to sleep. Everything seemed unreal, and loneliness engulfed her.

Someone lightly knocked at her bedroom door. "Randy? It's Peter. Can I come in?"

She wrapped her robe tighter around herself. "Yes."

He opened the door and left it open as he stepped inside, folding his arms. "I know you'd rather I didn't come into this room, but Katie and Stephen went back across the street to help her parents with more cleaning at her house, and there is a woman here who wants to see you. Now, mind you, I'm not real familiar with her type, but I'm pretty sure she's a prostitute."

Randy rose, drawing in her breath. "Then she knows Jake! Maybe she's seen him!"

Peter shook his head. "Why am I not surprised?"

"Let her in, Peter! Have her come in here and close the door." Randy retied her robe.

Peter looked her over with a frown. "Randy, she's a harlot."

"And she has news of Jake—I'm sure of it. And don't look down on her, Peter. Jake wouldn't."

"And that doesn't bother you?"

"Of course not. It's probably Dixie James. They're good friends."

Peter's eyebrows raised in disbelief. "And *that* doesn't bother you?"

"Not at all. It's all right, Peter. This is Jake we're talking about."

Peter dropped his arms and then put his hands out as though to give up. "Of course. What was I thinking?"

Her eyes teared. "Peter, she knows something important, or she wouldn't be here. Whatever it is, I need to know too. Maybe…maybe Jake's dead and she knows it."

He reached out and touched her arm. "Don't think that way. And by the way, she has a kid with her—maybe eight or nine years old, blond hair, kind of shy. Do you know who he is?"

Randy frowned. "No. Maybe he belongs to Dixie."

Peter sighed and left. Moments later he ushered in a plump woman with faded blond hair that was pulled into a twist at the nape of her neck. She showed subtle signs of having once been pretty. She'd left off the heavy paint such women usually used, other than a little face powder and lips demurely painted with a soft pink color. She wore tiny diamond earrings and a prim, close-fitting dress and straw hat with a blue ribbon that brought out the blue in her eyes. She turned to the boy with her.

"You stay out there with that nice man, Ben, till I talk to Jake's wife, all right?"

The boy glanced at Randy. "She's real pretty. I knew she would be 'cuz Jake said so."

Randy frowned in confusion as the boy turned away, and the woman came inside and closed the door.

"You're Dixie James," Randy said matter-of-factly.

"Yes, ma'am. How did you know?"

"Jake tells me everything." Randy blinked back tears. "Please tell me you haven't come here to tell me he's dead."

Dixie shook her head. "No, ma'am. I don't know myself what has happened to him. I only came here to tell you about the kid out there...and I was hoping Jake was back by now so I'd know he's okay." Her own eyes filled with tears. "I care a lot about that man, Mrs. Harkner, and the last time I saw him he was a mess...a real dark, menacing, angry, starving, sleep-deprived mess."

Randy covered her face. "My God," she groaned.

"He'd just found out about your daughter, ma'am. He was headed to Guthrie to find out for sure, but somehow he already knew she'd been taken." She shook her head. "I've never seen him like that, Mrs. Harkner, and I hope to never see it again. Never since I've known him has he scared me, but he scared me that day. And he was real upset over wanting to kill some...some loose woman up at Hell's Nest who knew about Evie but didn't tell him right away. She wanted...well, when he found out she knew and didn't say anything, he told me that was the first time he wanted to hurt a woman, but he didn't. He was just...my God, he had the darkest look in his eyes I've ever seen in a man, like Satan himself was boiling right up inside of him."

"Dear God," Randy whispered, putting a hand to her eyes. "I knew it would be bad. He needed me in the worst way."

"I wasn't sure if you'd be upset that he stopped at my place. I mean, he only stopped to change horses. I gave him some fresh food and made him promise to eat and try to sleep a little bit more. The man was killing himself trying to get to Guthrie. I came here hoping he was back and everything was okay. I'm just real worried maybe he rescued his daughter but got sick and died afterward from the way he was abusing himself. Then again, Jake's a mighty tough man. He's survived an awful lot in his life. And he had that son of yours with him. Still, I'm not sure which one of them was worse off. Poor Lloyd was beside himself too, thinking they'd taken his wife and son. I tried real hard to get them to stay a bit, maybe sleep for a while, but Jake wouldn't have it. He insisted on going on."

Randy turned. "Dixie, I'm sure you helped both of them as much as you could. I couldn't be there for them, and I just ache over that. I know Jake sometimes stops at your place. He likes to tease me about it. You're a good friend, and you are always welcome in this house."

Dixie looked her over. "I saw you once in town. You probably don't remember…"

"I *do* remember—your face, anyway. I didn't know who you were, but I knew…well…"

"Yeah, we all have that look about us." Dixie sighed. "I was so impressed by how beautiful and gracious you were. Jake said if I'd told you who I was, you probably would have invited me over, but he said he'd have a lot of explaining to do afterward."

Randy managed a smile. "Jake is Jake, Dixie. Nothing you could tell me would upset me."

"Well, then… I mean, you should probably know that he stopped by on the way to Hell's Nest. That was before all of this other happened—before he knew about Evie. He was a real mess then too. He…I…he kind of broke down over you, thinking you could be dying. I held him half the night. I thought you should know. I swear to God it was just holding, that's all. He needed someone to cry on, someone not close to him like family is. I think he just didn't want anybody in the family to see that, especially not Lloyd. He was so damn scared for you. I'm glad to see you looking so well. And I hope you understand. He'll probably tell you himself. I just want you to know nothing wrong happened."

Randy turned away. "I understand him much better than you think, Dixie. I know how he was raised. And

I know the kind of people he turns to in times like this. Don't fret about it. I know Jake inside and out. I believe you." Her eyes teared at how much she loved him, how she missed him. "He teases me constantly about stopping there," she added. "It's kind of a running joke with us. He can be so exasperating sometimes, goading me about things like that. I think part of what he loves about me is that I understand."

Dixie smiled. "It's easy for me to picture that. He teases me too. When Jake is in a good mood, he's so handsome and likable and has that great sense of humor. He really cares about people. Really cares. You have no idea how much that means. I'm not just some prostitute who's worth nothing more than—well, I'm a friend. Not many people, especially men, call me that." She sighed. "Anyway, I hope he's found your daughter and grandson by now. You just remember that this is Jake Harkner. If anybody can get them out of this and live through it, it's Jake. I told him that to be strong and think straight he had to be the *old* Jake, the mean one, the one with no feelings. I said he couldn't let feelings get in the way, and believe me, when he left, the feelings were buried way down deep and he was some other man I'd never met before."

Randy nodded. "I've seen that Jake." She turned away and went to sit down on the bed. Dixie stared at the bed, feeling suddenly uncomfortable. So, this was Jake's bedroom.

"Mrs. Harkner, I have to ask…how did your surgery go?"

Randy wiped at tears. "Good. I'm fine. There was no cancer."

Dixie breathed a sigh of relief. "Oh, I'm so glad! Jake would be so lost without you. If anything happened to you, I'm not sure he wouldn't turn one of those guns on himself. It just broke my heart to see how bad he was hurting that night he came to me. Can you beat that? He can face down fifteen men with those guns and it doesn't scare him a bit…but losing you? That terrifies him. And I gotta say, for a man who grew up unloved, he sure knows how to love back. That little boy I brought here with me, Jake already loves him…treats him like his own kid. I brought him here to tell you about him so's you'd be prepared. Whether Jake comes back or not, he'd expect you to take and love that boy."

Randy motioned for her to sit down in a nearby rocker. "Who is he? Why would Jake expect me to take him in?"

Dixie sat down, removing her gloves. "I won't need to explain once I tell you how he found him." She looked Randy over. "Are you all right? I mean, am I wearing you out? You can lie down if you want. I don't mind. Maybe I should leave now."

"No. Please stay. I'm fine. In two more days I'll have stitches taken out, and everything is healing well. I just still get tired easily. Tell me about that boy out there."

"His name is Ben Perry. After Jake left my place and headed for Hell's Nest, he came upon the kid being… beat…with a belt."

Randy closed her eyes. "Dear God."

"Yeah, you can imagine what that must have done to him. Jake dropped him off at my place on his way to Guthrie, and he was in such a hurry he didn't have time to explain much more than that. But I've talked with Ben since then, and the kid told me that Lloyd had a hell of a time stopping Jake from beating the kid's pa to death with the same belt once he got it away from him. It was pretty bad, I guess, and Jake fell against a shovel and cut that handsome face pretty bad. I saw the cut. I have a feeling that once it's totally healed, it won't much mess up his looks, but it looked real bad the day he stopped at my place. Lord knows men don't come much more handsome than Jake...except maybe that son of yours."

Randy wiped at her eyes. "It must have been horrible for him...seeing that man beating on the boy."

"Well, the way little Ben tells it, his pa said for Jake to go ahead and take him...said he didn't want him. Jake—he knows that feeling of not being wanted, I reckon'. It must have broke his heart, so he took the boy. Apparently he wants to keep him, Mrs. Harkner, raise him as his own and love him like he ought to be loved. The boy was a real mess when Jake dropped him off— terrible welts all over his body. He's a real good boy, very polite, kind of lost. He's scared Jake won't come back. I told him I figured you were kind enough that if you can't keep him yourself, you'd make sure he was with real good people who would love him."

Randy pulled a handkerchief from the pocket of her robe and blew her nose, then wiped at her eyes. "Of course I will." She sighed and stood up, walking to a window. "I'm glad you came, Dixie, so I'd know what to expect. If Jake makes it through this, it's still going to be hard for him. He's very good at blaming himself for everything bad that happens to his family." She turned to meet Dixie's gaze. "But Evie—she will find a way to help him. No matter what has happened to her, she'll be concerned about Jake instead of herself. She'll never let Jake take the blame for any of this."

Dixie nodded. "I hope she can manage that, and I hope with all my heart he makes it back, Mrs. Harkner, all in one piece, with your daughter and grandson in tow, as well as your son, of course. I saw a lovely redheaded woman headed across the street earlier—came from this house. Might that be Lloyd's new wife?"

"Yes. Her name is Katie. And she's a strong, brave young woman. She has already lost one husband and a child. Stephen has taken to her like the mother he needs, and she's going to be a perfect wife for Lloyd. She even held off some of those outlaws when they raided the town. When one of them came through the bedroom door, she shot him with a rifle. Isn't that something?"

"It sure is! She's the kind of wife Lloyd needs, just like you're the kind of wife Jake needs. He told me once that you shot a couple of men yourself, back when you went with Jake to rescue Lloyd from some gang of outlaws up in outlaw country in Wyoming. I'm surprised he took you with him."

"I wouldn't take no for an answer. I wanted to find my son."

Dixie nodded. "And whatever Randy Harkner wants, she gets, I'll bet."

Randy smiled more. "I know how to handle Jake Harkner."

Dixie grinned. "I'll bet you do—but I won't ever tell him you said that."

"Please don't." Their gazes held, and Randy realized this woman loved Jake in that distant, untouchable way that Peter Brown loved her. "Life can be so strange can't it, Dixie?"

"It surely can, Mrs. Harkner." She rose to leave then. "I just thought you should know all these things before Jake gets back...and he *will* come back any day now, I'm sure."

"I'm hoping he'll make it here in just another day or two," Randy told her. "It will depend on Evie's condition and if they have to stop somewhere with her first. She could...lose her baby."

"She won't. I just know this will work out, Mrs. Harkner. God is looking down on your family, and this whole thing will somehow help Jake. He'll realize prayer can be answered."

The remark surprised Randy, coming from a woman who likely had never set foot in a church in her life.

But then neither had Jake...yet he was a good man who loved with every fiber of his being. "Do you want to know something that might cheer you up, Dixie?"

Dixie smiled. "Sure."

"Jake made me a promise that if I came home cancer-free, he'd go to church."

Dixie raised her eyebrows in surprise. "Jake?"

"Yes."

"In *church*?"

"Yes."

Dixie burst out laughing. She waved Randy off. "Oh, I'm so sorry, but that *does* give me something to laugh about. Jake Harkner in church!" She laughed again. "Oh my, I am going to stick around—not just to make sure Jake gets back okay, but to watch him walk into church." She looked at Randy kindly. "Ma'am, it is absolutely amazing how tightly you have that man roped to your side. He's wild and wicked and mean as a hungry bobcat sometimes, but when it comes to you... he just melts right down. I've met that Jeff kid—the one who wants to write a book about Jake—and he said he couldn't do it without you being a big part of the story, and he's right about that." Her smile faded. "You're an angel of a woman, Mrs. Harkner. Jake is the luckiest man who ever walked, and he damn well knows it."

Randy walked back to the window. "Thank you. What he doesn't know is that I feel like *I'm* the lucky one, Dixie. Not many women are loved the way I am loved, in spite of the wild shoot-outs and the brothels and the rough life he lives. When we're together it's nothing like that."

"Oh, I can see that." Dixie rose and walked toward the door. "I'd better get out of here before Lloyd's wife gets back. She might not be so understanding about her husband visiting my place."

"Katie will need to learn patience, because Lloyd is a lot like Jake, and believe me, Jake isn't always easy to live with." Randy blinked back more tears. "But the way he loves someone…that makes it easier. He treasures the people he loves." She took a deep breath, struggling to keep from breaking down completely. "And you don't live with a man like Jake for twenty-six years and not trust him, because Jake is the kind of man who just blurts out everything he's been up to…right out in the open… no bones about it." She faced Dixie.

"That's Jake, all right," Dixie answered with a sly smile. "You know, Mrs. Harkner, Lloyd told me once that Jake said a man can have all the women in the world, but they don't mean a damn thing compared to having that one special woman that's just his alone and who loves him inside and out."

Who do you belong to?
Jake Harkner.
Who owns every inch of this body?
Jake Harkner.
Yo te amo, mi querida.

"I hope to hell he's alive, Mrs. Harkner," Dixie told her, interrupting Randy's thoughts, "and your son and daughter are all right."

"They *have* to be, Dixie. They *have* to be. What will I do if they aren't?"

Dixie shook her head. "Ma'am, I'm going to stay right here in town till I know, too, that he's all right. And I can keep the boy with me if you want, till Jake gets here. Then you can talk about it with him. You don't need the extra burden right now. I just wanted you to know about him. I brought him here because the boy was getting anxious to know if Jake got back yet. That kid already thinks the world of Jake." She turned to go.

"Dixie—" She turned back around, and Randy

surprised her by walking up to embrace her. "Thank you for being there for him when I couldn't be. I feel so much better knowing that. You might have saved his life."

Dixie patted her back. "He's a good man, and a good friend. He respects women like me, and that means a lot." She pulled away.

Randy wiped at her eyes with a handkerchief. "I guess I had better go have a talk with Ben."

"Well, I don't want him to be a burden to you right now. You need to take care of yourself. Like I said, Ben can stay with me at the hotel, or with Katie's folks for a while. I don't know them, but that's who Jake thought would take him in if it's too much for you. Lloyd told me what good people they are, and you still need time to heal, Mrs. Harkner. And when Jake gets back, you two will need some time alone. Ben will understand if you explain it right."

"Well, if Jake loves this child, then I do too. How old is he?"

"Eight."

"That's the same age Jake was when—" Randy closed her eyes. "Maybe little Ben out there can help heal his wounds, Dixie...the unseen wounds deep inside. I think God sent that boy to him."

Dixie nodded. "I'm thinking the same." She turned. "I'll leave you to your rest now. I really have to get going before people know I'm here, Mrs. Harkner. They might talk."

"I couldn't care less if people see you here. My husband is Jake Harkner, and Lord knows the rumors that abound about that man. And from now on, if we meet again, call me Randy."

Dixie pressed her arms. "Thank you. And I'll be praying Jake comes back."

"The whole town is praying." Randy opened the

bedroom door. "Thank you again, Dixie. Let's talk to Ben together."

They walked into the parlor, where bullet holes still showed in the walls. One window remained boarded up. Randy's heart ached at the empty table where her beautiful lamp used to sit. She remembered when Jake bought it for her, on a trip together to Denver...a lifetime ago.

Peter frowned, meeting Randy's gaze. "This boy here told me how he met Jake...says Jake has adopted him. That true?"

Randy glanced at Ben, who looked at her with wide, hope-filled blue eyes. "Yes. It's true." She imagined Jake at eight years old, terrified and alone and horribly abused. How could she not take this little boy and love him?

"So you'll take him in...just like that?" Peter asked.

Randy watched the hope in the child's blue eyes. She nodded. "Just like that."

Thirty-seven

"Do you want more coffee?"

"No. How do I look?"

"Randy, Jake will be so glad to see you, it won't matter how you look. In his eyes you are always beautiful." Peter studied her lustrous hair, brushed out long because Jake liked it that way…her pale-yellow dress, Jake's favorite color…the tiny diamond earrings she wore that Jake had bought for her years ago when he asked her to come to him after two years away doing only God knew what…the slim figure of a woman she was, determined to stay that way for…who else? Jake.

All men find you beautiful. Peter watched her pace, watched her go to the door again, hoping this was the day Jake would finally come home, still worried he wouldn't come home at all.

"Randy, please sit down. You should be resting."

"I can't. It's been eight days since he rode after Evie. I'm so worried about her, what my precious daughter has been through. And poor little Ben is so scared."

"It's amazing how attached he apparently became to Jake, when he's known him such a short time."

Randy watched the quiet street. "I'm not surprised. They share the same soul." *Please come home, Jake! Bring our Evie back.* "Peter, what if he's dead? What if they killed him? Maybe Lloyd too. Maybe they even killed Evie."

"He didn't go after Evie alone, Randy. He had Lloyd and Brian and Jeff and four men from town who are good with guns. He probably could have gone after them alone and *still* made it back."

Randy smoothed her dress and looked at herself in a mirror. "Sparky said it takes close to four days to reach Dune Hollow. Knowing Jake, he probably made it in three. By the fourth day, he would go after her. He'll probably take it slower coming home, for Evie's sake."

She walked to the front door again. "And he'll probably ask Red St. James and those other men to stay behind and bury however many men need burying and let them bring in whoever is left alive. That will save him time so he can get Evie and Little Jake back here sooner."

She faced Peter again, her mind running in circles with various scenarios that could influence when Jake might get home...*if* he got home. "He might stop somewhere to clean up first."

Peter laughed lightly. "He's coming home to *you* and knows you're all right, plus he's been through the depths of hell. He won't stop to clean up first this time. He'll be bent on getting to you as fast as he can." He stood up and grasped her arms. "Randy, I wish you would just sit down. I need to talk to you."

She met his eyes...saw the love there. "I'm sorry." She embraced him. "Peter, I am so grateful for everything you've done. You're such a good man, and having someone with me who cares so much means a lot." She pulled away. "But even if something happened to Jake—"

"I know." He sighed and took hold of her hands. "I just want to tell you that I hope Evie and Lloyd and Little Jake all make it back alive and well, and I hope he gets that reprieve and that you can all move to Colorado. I won't forget you...ever...but I know when something is hopeless, and you, my darling Randy, are hopelessly in love with Jake Harkner. When he dies, you will be in love with his *ghost*. There will never be another man for you, and what you feel for him is the most beautiful thing I've ever witnessed." He leaned forward and kissed her cheek. "What I feel for you is partly because I want my wife back with me, but I can't have her, so I guess I'd better start looking around...elsewhere. I feel honored just to have been able to hold you when you needed holding, and my only comfort is that I'm pretty sure Jake appreciates what he has in you. He doesn't just love you. He *adores* you."

Her eyes teared. "Thank you so much, Peter."

"For helping a woman I love? That takes no thanks." Randy slowly turned away and went back to the door.

"He should get here today," she repeated. "I feel it." She rested her forehead against the oval window in the door. That's when she heard the familiar whistle, somewhere in the distance. "It's him! It's him!" She started to open the door.

"Wait!" Peter hurried over, taking her arm. "Wait and see who's with him. You need to prepare yourself, Randy. And you sure as heck shouldn't be running down the street in your condition. Don't go tearing something open and put yourself back in the hospital."

They stepped out onto the porch together. Randy glanced at all the bullet holes that still pocked the outside of the house. So many! That meant a lot of men. It sickened her to think of Evie with them...and Little Jake.

They finally appeared at the end of the street. "Three! There are only three of them!" Randy held a hand to her mouth, sucking in her breath. "Peter, just three!"

"Don't panic," Peter warned. "At least that looks like Jake and Lloyd. I think that's Jeff with them." They came closer. "Jake has Little Jake with him."

"Where's Evie? Where's Evie and Brian?"

With a pounding heart, Randy watched Katie run out of the house and toward Lloyd, who dismounted and limped up to her. "He's hurt, Peter! Lloyd's hurt!" She started off the porch, but Peter kept hold of her. "He's embracing Katie. He's all right, Randy." The Donavans came out with Stephen and Ben. Stephen ran up to his father, and Lloyd embraced both his wife and son.

Ben ran to Jake, who reached down and tousled his hair. Ben grasped his hand with both of his and Jake lifted him with one hand onto his horse. He put his arms around Ben and said something to him. Ben threw his arms around Jake's neck, and Randy could see the boy was crying. Jake talked to him a moment longer, then lifted him down, saying something more to him. Ben nodded and walked back to the Donavans.

As always, townspeople were beginning to gather behind Jake.

"Jake, where's Evie?" a man asked.

"She and Brian came in the back way. They're already at their house. I don't want one person going over there, understand? They need to be alone."

"Oh, Peter, that means…" Randy turned away and wept. Peter put an arm around her.

"She's alive, Randy. She and Brian are alive, and Brian is a good man. They love each other and they will get through this."

"The baby. If she lost the baby, it will be harder for her to ever recover from this."

Randy took a handkerchief from her dress pocket and wiped at her eyes. Peter could see that at the moment, he didn't even exist as far as Randy was concerned. Her gaze remained riveted on her husband. He went inside and picked up his hat, quietly leaving out the back door.

Jake said something to the Donavans. Lloyd and Katie were still clinging to each other.

Jake looked toward the house then, and Randy stepped into the street. Ignoring more questions, Jake kicked his horse into a faster lope, heading toward her.

Thin! So much thinner, Randy thought as he came

closer. *And so, so tired. He's been to hell and back!* She could hardly believe he was real and alive, and she saw in his eyes for a flicker of a moment the darker Jake, the outlaw Jake, the Jake who was suffering over what had happened to their daughter. But his gaze changed to the loving Jake as in seconds he was off his horse and hurrying up to her.

Neither spoke at first as he swept her into his arms. Never, ever, ever had those arms felt so good around her. She wrapped her own arms around his neck as he picked her up off her feet, whirling her around.

"Sweet Jesus," he groaned. "I can't believe it's you and you're all right."

Randy buried her face against him, breathing in his scent—tobacco, leather, sweat, the lingering scent of gun smoke and even his horse. It didn't matter that he needed a bath and a shave. It only mattered that she was in his arms.

"I thought I'd never see you again," she sobbed.

"It's true?" he asked. "No cancer?"

"Yes. Oh, Jake, don't let go! Don't let go!"

"Never. My God, baby, you feel so good…smell so good…" His voice was gruff. He sounded so achingly tired, yet here he was, holding her as though she weighed nothing. "How tight can I hold you? I don't want to hurt something."

"You won't hurt anything. You can't hold me tight enough."

He kissed at her neck, her hair, her cheek, keeping her pressed close. "I wasn't sure we'd ever hold each other again. When I first got back to Guthrie, I was crazy with rage over Evie. The only thing that kept me sane was finding out you were okay and on your way home."

"When I heard what happened, I was afraid you'd hand yourself over to them just to free Evie."

"She's okay, Randy. She's okay."

"I should go to her."

"No. Leave them alone. Brian and Evie need some time together." He began kissing her, over and over. She smelled peppermint on his breath, felt the rough stubble on his chin. "I asked the Donavans to take Stephen and Little Jake and Ben to their place so Brian and Evie can just be with each other—and Lloyd and Katie need time too. Lloyd is hurt, but he'll be all right."

"Oh, Jake! What happened to him?"

"Just a flesh wound. Thank God Brian was with us."

"Evie! Poor Evie!"

"She still has that baby. And she has Brian. She just needs time, Randy." He found her mouth and savored it hungrily again. "God, I'm such a mess," he groaned, "and you're so beautiful and clean and soft, and I want you so bad, but I need a bath and a shave and I'm so goddamn tired, Randy. I don't remember the last time I slept. Even after we got her back, I couldn't eat for thinking about what happened." He continued holding her with her feet off the ground.

"She's alive, Jake, and so is Little Jake. That's all that matters right now. You, my darling Jake, found them. God only knows how many men you had to go through to get them. And now you're here and alive, and there is no one like my Jake. No one." They kissed over and over.

"It's you that got me through it…knowing you were all right."

Randy finally leaned back to take a better look at him, touching the scar at the side of his face. "Oh, Jake, Dixie told me what happened to your face. She brought Ben here, and I already love him, Jake."

"*Dixie?* She came here?"

"Yes. She's probably off someplace watching us right now. She wanted to wait and make sure you got back alive. She told me about Ben, and what shape you were in after you found out about Evie. All of it had to be so horrible for you. If only I could have been there for you. It must have been so terrible!"

He groaned as he kissed her again, then nuzzled her neck. "There is so much to tell you, *mi querida esposa*. I'm so sorry, but if I don't go inside and lie down, I'll pass out right here in the street. It's all catching up with me." He kissed her again. "I want you so bad," he whispered, "but I'm so goddamn tired, baby."

"Of course you are."

"Tell me you're still just mine."

"You know I am."

"Who do you belong to?"

"Jake Harkner—always and forever."

He kissed her again. "God, you look so beautiful and you smell so good. I'm such a mess, Randy," he again repeated.

"I don't care! I never knew a man could look and smell so good when he needed a bath and a shave."

"How are you? How are you really?"

"I'm all right, now that you're here and I know Evie and Little Jake are alive. But I have more scars, Jake."

"Do you think I give a damn about that?" He kissed her again. "When I'm better, I'll kiss the scars away." They kissed again.

"Little Jake. Did they hurt him?"

"He's fine now. Please don't ask me to talk about it yet. I can't, Randy. I can't think about it. Just know that they are all fine. And I don't want to let go of you, but we have to go inside. I just want to lie down beside you in that bed that smells like roses."

Randy forced herself to let go, just enough to step back and take another look at him. "Oh, Jake, it had to be such hell for you. I'm so sorry for what you've surely been through. And you've lost so much weight."

Jake moved an arm around her, and they helped each other up the steps to go inside. "You can fatten me up with that bread you make," he told her, his voice sounding weaker and weaker. Randy thought about Dixie's concern that Jake would ride himself to death to get to his Evie. Apparently he'd nearly done just that.

As they stepped across the threshold, Jake began apologizing for the house, the broken lamp, her trampled roses.

"They can all be replaced, Jake. Right now it's enough that I have you and Evie and Little Jake and our son back home."

She helped him remove his coat, hat, boots, cartridge belts, and guns, shaking her head at all the armor he wore. His vest came off, his shirt. She grimaced at the bloodstained gauze on his upper left arm...the still-red scar on his cheek where his beard didn't grow.

"I can do this," he told her. "You shouldn't help. You're still healing."

"It feels good to touch you, to know you're alive."

He sat down on the bed. "I should have been with you for all you went through," he lamented. "Are you in pain?"

"No. I just got my stitches out yesterday. I'm fine, Jake, just still sore. And I still get tired easily, but right now having you sitting here in front of me gives me new energy." She knelt in front of him and started to unbuckle his belt.

"You were going through some pretty terrible things yourself," she told him.

"Randy, let me do this, please. I don't want you overdoing things." He stood up and finished unbuckling, removing his denim pants.

"What if you *had* been with me?" Randy continued, studying the magnificent man he still was, even though so much thinner. "It would have taken you three times longer to find Evie. God had his reasons for making you stay behind, Jake. He has worked so many miracles for us."

Jake sat back down in a way that told her he couldn't have stayed on his feet even if he wanted to. He literally collapsed onto the bed, and Randy remembered that morning—oh, so many years ago—when she came home to find the outlaw Jake Harkner passed out on her bed back in Kansas. She'd stripped him and washed him and shaved him then, and she'd nervously removed the bullet from his side that she'd put there herself. Jake mumbled something about Evie, then rolled to his side.

"My sweet, beautiful angel," he groaned.

Randy moved around the other side of the bed and crawled in beside him, still dressed. She realized he was quietly crying. "Jake, come here."

He moved his arms around her. "I wanted to…kill all of the ones left alive, Randy, but she wouldn't let me. She forgave them, Randy. She *forgave* them. Preacher Zilke said evil couldn't touch her, and he was right. He was right."

Randy wiped tears from his cheeks. "When on earth did you talk to the *preacher*?" Randy asked.

"Before I left." He pulled her tightly against him. "There is so much to talk about, Randy. I picked up a little boy along the way. I want to raise him, Randy. His name is Ben, but he's me. He's *me*."

Randy kissed his hair. "Jake, I told you I already know about Ben. Dixie brought him to town to explain, just in case you didn't make it back."

"Don't be upset about Dixie. I stayed with her one night after we left. I held her and held her and I wanted it to be you. I cried like a goddamn kid. I was sure I was losing you."

"Jake, I'm not upset. Dixie told me about that. She's a good woman, and she was there when I couldn't be. I'm only concerned about what seeing that boy get beat with a belt did to you."

"Where is he? Where is Ben?"

"Jake, you are so tired you don't even remember you already asked the Donavans to keep him for a while."

"She helped me, Randy. Dixie…kept me from killing myself."

Randy closed her eyes and sighed. "Jake, you're rambling and not making any sense. Just sleep now."

He met her mouth in a hungry kiss. "Over a week," he mumbled then, "since I slept. I want…to make love to you…and know you're really here and alive…but I'm so damn tired, Randy."

"My God, of course you are. Just *sleep*, Jake. All that matters is that you're back and it's over. There will be lots of time for everything else. All that matters is you're here! You're here in our house and in our bed and in my arms."

"I was so afraid…of losing you."

"I'm going to be fine. I was just as scared you would never make it back. Let's just lie here and enjoy the feel of each other's arms." Randy realized how devastatingly tired he must be, because of his repeated ramblings. He finally stopped talking and soon fell into a deep sleep.

Randy carefully pulled away and got up. She covered him, then went and locked the front door. Jeff would take care of things out in the street, and the other men would probably be here tomorrow with what was left of those who'd done such awful things to Evie. She determined she would go and see Evie tomorrow. Her beautiful, precious, forgiving daughter would need a lot of talking to. Thank God for Evie's patient, loving husband. And Little Jake, her wild, naughty, brave, cussing grandson. He was all Jake. She didn't even know yet what had happened to him. If Jake didn't want to talk about it, then that meant those men *had* hurt the child in some way, but she'd seen him run to the Donavans as though nothing was wrong. It made her smile. He was all Harkner through and through. Put him down and he got right back up. He was tough like his grandfather… and like the little boy Jake who'd lived through so much pain, both physically and emotionally.

She walked back to the bedroom and undressed. She pulled on her flannel gown, then walked around the bed and climbed into it from the other side, snuggling against Jake. "Thank you, Jesus," she whispered.

Jake moved his arms around her, but his eyes were closed. "Bed…still smells like…roses." He moved a leg over hers and breathed against her neck. "*Mi esposa. Yo te quiero…mi vida*," he whispered.

Randy kissed his wounded arm, his eyes, his hair. What had he been through? How many men had he killed this time? He'd never fooled her. Killing so many men weighed on him. "And I love you, Jake," she said softly. "Forever and forever…and forever."

She remembered his remark about Evie forgiving the men who'd abused her and telling Jake he should do the same.

Evie, my darling Evie, you taught your father more in that one gesture than all our love and preaching over the years could have taught him.

In his sleep Jake pulled her even closer. She drank in the pleasure of his embrace, nestled in the sweet feeling of love…and the safety of his arms. She could still feel the strength of those arms in spite of his being thinner and so terribly worn-out. When he was awake again and rested, she'd help him bathe and shave, and she'd fatten him up with that bread he loved. She had five loaves of it in the kitchen. She'd kneaded and baked it all just to keep busy, praying with every warm, sweet-smelling loaf that he'd come home to eat it. A neighbor had let her cut some roses, and she'd filled the bedroom with vases of them. Jake always teased her about how this room—and she—always smelled like roses. She'd wanted the familiar smell in the room when he got home…and here he was…home.

She felt the tears come then. He was really here and alive. How could she have gone on if he'd never come back? How awful that they both could have died… separately…away from each other. She couldn't think of anything worse. There was so much to be thankful for.

She kissed him over and over, his unwashed hair, his stubble of a beard, his eyes closed in exhausted sleep, his familiar lips. She nuzzled her face into his neck, realizing that no matter how clean or dirty he was, he always smelled good there, a specific, familiar smell that never seemed to change, that distinctive little area that held an identifying scent. And Jake's was simply man. Just man.

Thirty-eight

RANDY AWOKE TO A TAPPING NEAR HER MOUTH. SHE turned into Jake's arms to see him with one end of a peppermint stick in his mouth.

"Oh, no you don't," she told him.

"Why not?"

"Because we're going to church today, remember?"

He rolled the peppermint stick into the corner of his mouth. "So?"

"So we can't make love and then go to church."

Jake frowned. "Well, if that's the case, then I'm not going. I don't like that rule."

"Jake Harkner, you've been fighting that promise for a month now. Your excuse has been that you won't go until Evie is ready to go, and she is. Our lovely, healing daughter is finally ready to get out and see people again, and the main reason she agreed to do so was because you promised her you would go to church with all of us today. It's time to keep your promise. You are out of excuses."

He bit off a piece of the peppermint and ran the other end of it over her lips. "What's that got to do with making love before we go?"

"It just doesn't seem right, that's all. We've waited this long so I'd be completely healed and we were both stronger. What are a few more hours going to matter?"

"Randy, do you realize who you're talking to? This is a record for me. We haven't gone this long without sex unless I was gone and we couldn't be together."

"Jake—"

"What if I promise to keep it respectful?"

Randy smiled. "You don't know *how* to make love respectfully."

"And you enjoy it."

"Jake, I am absolutely not going to have sex before I go to church."

She started to get up but he pulled her back down. "We're married, so it's not sinful, if that's what you're saying. And, hell, the Bible is full of stories about lust and whores and men tasting the fruits of women's breasts and murder and mayhem and all the damn things I've already done, so maybe I'll fit right in when I walk into that church."

"Jake Harkner, you just used the words *hell*, *lust*, *whores*, *breasts*, and *damn* all in the same sentence as the word *Bible*. You are the most hopeless child of God I have ever known."

He moved a hand over her breasts, caressing them through the soft flannel gown. "All I know is that God made man and woman to fit together just right, and for a reason. They're supposed to mate, and you're my mate." He moved his hand down to the hem of her nightgown and up underneath it, along her thigh. "And I've waited because I wanted you to be completely healed. I can't take this torture any longer."

"So you pick a Sunday morning before church to stop and make love after all this time?"

"Seems like a great way to start a Sunday morning. You're the one who says God saved both of us. I think he saved us for this."

"Not many people would think God saved someone so they could have sex again."

Jake grinned, the old familiar, handsome grin that always undid her. "Come on, woman, take off the underwear and bite on this peppermint stick."

"Why do you have a way of always making this seem sinful?"

"Because it's more fun that way."

"What if Ben wakes up?"

"That kid sleeps like a bear in hibernation."

"I'm only going to let you do this if you promise not to use one cuss word today when everyone comes for dinner. Evie is right. Your grandsons are starting to talk like barroom brawlers, and Ben will be doing the same thing if you don't stop. And be careful in church if the preacher talks to you afterward. I know how easily those words fall out of your mouth without you even being aware of it."

"Take off the underwear and I promise not to cuss."

Randy smiled, her eyes full of doubt. She bit the other end of the peppermint stick, and they ate it down until their lips met. Once they did, she had no argument left in her. The underwear came off. Not only that, so did the gown, and Randy found herself allowing the man to ravish her in what she considered was surely the most sinful way of all.

But it had been so long. So long. Her weak protest was whispered and not very firm as his kisses trailed from her breasts, over her belly, where he licked and kissed at her scars. He moved down to her thighs. She sucked in her breath when he found her sweetness and groaned with the pleasure of tasting her in the most intimate way she once never dreamed she'd let a man do to her. But this was Jake, and she doubted there was anything he *didn't* know about how to please a woman. She grasped his hair and offered herself to him, taking wicked pleasure in the way he had of making love to that secret place that belonged only to him. She cried out with an intense climax, almost painful from that deep, reawakened need for this man. He moved his tongue back up over her belly and savored her breasts as he grasped her bottom with both hands and filled her with manly passion. She tasted her own sweetness on his lips as he devoured her mouth in that way he had of bringing out not just desire but pure *lust*—lust that made her arch up to his thrusts, all of it made so keenly perfect because she was well and there was no more fear of what might have been. This was sweet, soft, warm morning sex—their favorite time to make love.

As always, he commanded her every response, making the oh-so-familiar act seem like the first time, as only Jake Harkner could do. And after so long without this, it did almost feel like the first time…like that wild night of lovemaking when he really did do this to her in the back of a wagon…somewhere. They moved in perfect rhythm as he filled her over and over again with all that was Jake, until she felt his pulsating release. Saying nothing, he nuzzled her neck and leaned down then to taste each breast yet again with relish, and she knew he wanted to do it all over again. And she *wanted* him to take her again. She felt his swelling desire for her, and again he moved inside her, hard and deep, as though he couldn't get enough of her…and she wanted as much of him as she could get. He deliberately moved in all the right ways, rubbing against that special spot with such expertise that she found herself gasping with a second climax. It felt so good to be physically able to make love again in all the best ways.

"Jake—"

"You okay?"

"It feels wonderful."

He smiled as he spoke between kisses. "Then enjoy it," he whispered in her ear. "You're well now, *mi amor*. I feel you pulling me into you."

He kept burying himself deep to fulfill the need she had, and to satisfy his own need to claim his woman again, to prove to himself she was still his and only his.

"Who do you belong to?"

"Jake Harkner."

"You bet your ass. I own every beautiful inch of you."

"And I own *you*, Jake Harkner. You remember that when other women tempt you."

He kissed her harder, pushed himself harder. "You're the only woman I can't resist."

"It's the same for me."

The words were spoken amid hungry kisses and sweet, rhythmic thrusts that made Randy wonder if it was even possible for him to go any deeper. When Jake Harkner claimed her, she was branded for life. And she didn't mind at all.

His life spilled into her then, and finally he relaxed, lying there on top of her for a while, both of them listening to birds outside the window. He kissed her again, more kisses, over and over. He raised to his knees then, running his hands over her breasts, her belly, her private places. With a mischievous glint in his eyes and a teasing grin he took a deep sigh of satisfaction and said the words that made her burst into laughter.

"*Now* we can go to church," he told her.

Thirty-nine

JEFF WATCHED THE PROCESSION, MUCH LIKE THE ONE he'd watched that first Sunday when he'd sat on the church steps with a Jake Harkner who'd refused to go inside. He'd left the whole family alone this last month, knowing they all needed some healing time—time he'd used to work on all his notes and get them in order for the book about Jake Harkner. It wouldn't be easy. Jake was the most complicated man he'd ever met. How did one describe a man who could be so incredibly ruthless and seemingly unfeeling, yet such a loving family man? The one walking toward the church now couldn't possibly be the same man who'd blown another man's guts out from under a card table.

He watched Evie walking with Brian's arm around her and Little Jake holding her hand, and he felt like crying at how lovely she looked. Lloyd and Katie walked with them, arm in arm, Stephen holding his father's other hand. They all greeted Jeff warmly.

"Are you coming to Mother's for dinner after church?" Evie asked Jeff. "I made peach pie. It's Daddy's favorite."

"Oh, I'll be there, all right," Jeff answered. "Jake and I have a lot to talk about. And thank you for the invite." He studied her with deep admiration. "You look really beautiful today, Evie."

Brian pulled her closer. "A woman who is expecting always looks extra beautiful," he told Jeff.

Evie smiled, moving her arms around Brian. "This man is spoiling me something awful," she told Jeff.

Little Jake ran off then, right toward Jake and Randy, who approached them with young Ben in tow. Jeff curiously studied the guns Jake wore, visible under a black suit coat. He wore a white shirt and a string tie and black cotton pants. It was the first time Jeff had seen him wearing a suit, and he looked strikingly handsome. Still, he wore those guns. Jeff knew Randy would never allow him to wear them into church. Had he changed his mind?

Evie leaned up and kissed Brian's cheek, then left him to greet her father, who wrapped her into his arms and kissed her hair. "Daddy, you look wonderful!"

Jake looked her over. "So do you, baby girl. You getting along all right with that worthless husband of yours?"

"It's terrible! He's so good to me it makes me feel guilty. You've got to tell him to let me do things on my own, Daddy. He's wearing himself out trying to do *everything*. Will you talk to him?"

"Hell, no! Why would I ask a man to stop treating my daughter like she's some kind of princess?"

Evie pushed at him. "You know what I mean, and Daddy, you just said a cuss word right before walking into church. I am *praying* Little Jake doesn't blurt out some kind of horrible swearword during the service." She looked him over. "Why are you wearing those guns? Don't you dare walk into church with those on."

Jake kept an arm around her as he led her back to Brian. "You get more like your mother every day. I hear enough preaching from her."

"You *are* coming inside, aren't you?"

Others walked past them, some stopping to greet Jake and the rest of his family. Jeff figured most of them probably did not realize Jake intended to actually step inside church today.

"I'll be there," Jake told Evie.

"Without the guns?"

"Without the guns."

Brian moved his arm around Evie and nodded to Jake. "Jake, you have never looked more dapper."

"Dapper? I'm not sure I like that word. I'm not the 'dapper' type."

Brian smiled, a hint of sadness in his eyes.

"She doing okay?" Jake asked, sobering.

"She's doing fine." Brian pulled Evie closer and kissed her cheek. "This is one strong woman."

"Forgiving people can be healing, Daddy," Evie told him.

Jake didn't answer. He turned away and noticed Peter approaching with a rolled-up piece of paper in his hand. He walked closer to greet Jake and Randy, eyeing Randy with an obvious appreciation for how beautiful and well she looked today—wearing, of course, a yellow dress. He nodded to Jake, then handed out the rolled-up paper.

"In six months you will have served a full three years, Jake. Then you can head for Colorado if you still want to go," he told him.

Randy gasped as Jake unrolled the document and read it. "My God," he muttered, sobering. He looked at Randy. "In six months I'll be a truly free man."

"I think that petition everyone signed helped," Peter told him.

Randy's eyes instantly teared. She threw her arms around Peter. "Oh, thank you! Thank you, Peter!"

Peter glanced at Jake as he embraced her in return, giving him a look of helplessness. "You're very welcome," he told Randy before gently pushing her away. "And don't just thank me. Thank the whole town, because all those signatures made an impression on the judge, or so I'm told." He looked at Jake. "A lot of the people in that church signed it, Jake. I hope you understand how welcome you will be in there."

Jake put out his hand and Peter shook it. "Thanks for everything," Jake told him, true sincerity in his eyes.

"You are very welcome. I'll be heading back to Chicago soon. I was just waiting for this order to come through."

Jake nodded. "I hope you find someone again, maybe in Chicago."

"Yes, well, maybe so. But you, my friend, have the best of them all."

They squeezed hands. "I am well aware of that," Jake told him.

Peter let go of his hand and tipped his hat to Randy, then glanced at Jake again. "Come and see my gun collection sometime before I leave."

"I'll do that."

Peter turned and walked up the church steps.

Randy could barely see for the tears in her eyes. "Oh, Jake, we can go to Colorado!"

Jake held up the rolled-up order. "Lloyd and Evie, get over here," he called. The whole family gathered around him, and Jake held out the paper. "My reprieve. We're all going to Colorado next spring."

"Oh, Daddy!" Evie burst into tears and hugged her father. The rest of them took turns reading the reprieve, hugging Jake one at a time.

"We'll find the prettiest spot in the foothills and run the biggest ranch in the state," Lloyd told his father. "No more violence, Pa. You and Mom and the rest of us can finally have some peace."

Jake hugged Randy close. A little part of him worried that peace was impossible. He kissed Randy's hair. "And no more being apart," he told her.

A very joyful but tearful Harkner clan all headed for the church. Stephen and Ben, already friends, shoved each other back and forth playfully, and Lloyd warned Stephen not to get his clothes dirty. He watched Ben take Katie's hand and head for the church steps. Lloyd hesitated, then turned and walked back to Jake. "You sure you can handle this?" he asked.

"Handle what?"

"Church." Lloyd grinned.

Jake gave him a shove. "Get in there with Katie. She doing okay?"

Lloyd nodded. "Her belly is already getting bigger. And don't you go teasing her about it. She embarrasses so easy."

"And I'm sure you have your own ways of embarrassing her. Maybe I'll ask her about that. I'd like to see if her face gets as red as that hair."

"Don't you dare do that to her, you mean sonofabitch."

"I promise to try to hold my tongue."

Lloyd pointed a finger at him, then walked back to Katie and gave her a quick kiss before walking into church with her.

Randy took Jake's arm. "The time has come," she told him teasingly.

"You make it sound like a hanging," Jake quipped.

"To you it probably *does* feel like a hanging. Now take those guns off and come inside, Jake."

Jake went up the steps, where Jeff stood leaning against the railing—grinning. "Want me to hold those guns for you?"

Jake looked at Randy. "Go on inside. I promise on my honor that I'm coming."

Randy put her hands on her hips. "Your *honor*?"

"Hell, I can be honorable sometimes."

Randy closed her eyes and shook her head. "Don't you dare disappoint Evie. She's here because of *you*, Jake."

Jake looked her over lovingly. "I'd rather shoot myself than break a promise to Evie. I'll come inside in a few minutes."

Randy glanced at Jeff. "Make sure he does."

"Sure. Jake does anything I tell him to do," he joked.

Before Randy turned to go inside, she and Jake shared one more look, one Jeff thought burst with absolute, sublime love. She finally went inside, and Jake turned to Jeff.

"That woman has been trying to change me for twenty-six years. You'd think she'd give up by now."

Jeff grinned. "You both look very handsome and very happy. I take it Randy is completely well now."

Jake grinned as he lit a cigarette. "Jeff, you don't know the half."

"I have a feeling I do."

Jake drew on the cigarette. "Yeah, well, she's one hell of a woman." He began untying the holsters from around his thighs, then unbuckled his gun belt, handing out to Jeff. "Watch these for me."

Jeff took the gun belt, shaking his head. "You're really going to do it?"

Jake took another drag on the cigarette. "Got no choice. Between Randy and Evie, I'm hopelessly hog-tied." He frowned. "By the way, you can hang those guns over the railing if you want. I doubt anyone is crazy enough to try to steal my guns. Come on into church with us."

Jeff grinned. "Jake, I'm Jewish, remember?"

"Well, Jeff, I highly doubt anyone is going to attack you in there and force you to convert."

Jeff shook his head, laughing. "Only you would put it that way. Just go on in. I'll keep an eye on these guns. For all you know, Little Jake will come running out looking for them."

Jake shook his head. "That kid is fully back to his old daring, fearless self." He looked past Jeff then to see Dixie standing under a nearby tree. "Well, I'll be damned." He hurried down the steps, and Dixie stepped closer.

"You come see me soon as you can, Jake, and tell me all about everything."

Jake tipped his hat to her. "I'll do that, pretty lady."

"I thought I'd come and watch you walk into that church, you mean-spirited, black-hearted sinner. This is going to be right entertaining."

Jake grinned, leaning down to kiss her lightly on the forehead. "Thanks for all of it, Dixie." He told her about the reprieve.

Her eyes teared. "You just come visit a few times before you move away. I'll miss you like hell, Jake."

He nodded. "I'll miss you too, Dixie. And we can't go till next spring, so I'll be by a few times yet."

She stepped back. "You'd better get your worthless hide into that church."

Jake gave her a smile. "You can come too."

Dixie laughed. "Please! If we *both* walked in there, the entire congregation would faint dead away. Just seeing you will be enough of a shock." She gave him a shove. "Go on with you now."

Jake reached out and squeezed her hand before turning away and heading back up the church steps. "There stands one fine woman, Jeff."

"Yes, sir, I agree with you."

"You coming to see us in Colorado?"

"I'll have to. I won't have this book done until next spring, and you need to see it first."

"Well, we might not leave till spring anyway. Winter isn't exactly the best time to head for the mountains, and that's where six months lands us. By the time we head for Colorado, I'll have four grandchildren instead of two, and an extra son. How's that for a worthless bastard like me?"

"You're a lucky man, Jake."

Jake nodded. "Damn lucky." He sighed, staring at the doors as those inside started singing. *Just as I am, without one plea, but that thy blood was shed for me.*

Jake put a hand on Jeff's shoulder. "Jeff, I am going to

make you a bet." He squeezed his shoulder, then stood back and took one last drag on his cigarette.

"What's that?" Jeff asked.

Jake tossed the cigarette into the dirt at the bottom of the steps. People inside the church continued singing. *But that thy blood was shed for me.* "I am betting you that when I walk into that church, people's mouths will drop open in shock, and they will be so surprised that within one minute, all singing will stop. Five bucks says I'm right."

Jeff took a watch from his jacket pocket. "All right. As soon as you go through that door, I'll watch this thing. If all singing doesn't stop within sixty seconds, you owe me five dollars."

Jake nodded. "It's a deal." He took a deep breath as the hymn continued. *Oh, Lamb of God, I come...I come.* "Lord, I'd rather face ten men with guns than walk into that church," he told Jeff.

"There's no turning back now, Jake."

Jake rubbed at the back of his neck. "I guess not." After one more deep breath, he glanced at Dixie and tipped his hat, then removed the hat and walked inside.

Jeff watched the second hand on his pocket watch. After twenty seconds, he could tell fewer people were singing. After another twenty-five seconds, only a couple of people still sang. And just before the full sixty seconds, the singing stopped.

Jeff shook his head, smiling. "Jake Harkner, you sonofabitch." He sat down on the steps to wait, his smile turning to a surprising urge to cry. He glanced at Dixie. She smiled and nodded, then walked away. Jeff sighed, wondering...hoping that Jake, and Lloyd, for that matter, would really find peace at last in Colorado. With men like that, who knew? He couldn't stop thinking about the day they'd rescued Evie and how the man called Mike Holt had threatened Lloyd for shooting Mike's brother. But Holt was on his way to prison. Maybe he would even hang. Jeff hoped for the latter.

Inside the church, the singing renewed, twice as joyful as before. Jeff quietly laughed. Right now Jake Harkner was going through pain worse than a gunshot wound. It was worth his five bucks just to picture it.

Epilogue

JUNE OF 1893 FOUND A FAMILY HEADING WEST ACROSS the eastern Colorado plains...three men, three women, two older boys who chased each other around on horseback, one four-year-old boy who rode on his grandfather's horse, three large wagons, several horses and a few cattle...and two babies, both little girls, one with auburn hair and very dark eyes, one with light hair and gray-green eyes that seemed to change with the light.

Back in Guthrie, Oklahoma, a young couple walked past rosebushes that had sprung up in regrowth from the summer before. They stepped into a little yellow house, excited that they had purchased the former home of the notorious Jake Harkner.

"What's that lovely smell?" the young man asked.

The young woman breathed deeply. "Roses. It smells like roses in here." She walked into the main bedroom, where someone had left a little vase of yellow roses, now drying up, but their aroma still strong.

Acknowledgments

Many thanks to:

Jeff Quinn of Gunblast.com, for advice on firearms of the late 1800s.

My editor, Mary Altman, for a great job of making my books the best they can be.

Dana Alma, for her help with the use of Spanish in this story.

The many devoted fans who urged me to write this book and kept me going.

My agent, Maura Kye-Casella, for helping close the deal on a story that means so much to me.

Reference books:

Calhoun, Frederick S. *The Lawmen: United States Marshals and Their Deputies*. Washington: Smithsonian Institution Press, 1990.

Strickland, Rennard. *The Indians in Oklahoma*. Norman: University of Oklahoma Press, 1980.

Read on for an excerpt from

Love's Sweet Revenge

From the author…

When I wrote *Outlaw Hearts* over twenty years ago, I never forgot my beloved Jake Harkner. Writing its sequel, *Do Not Forsake Me*, was a dream come true. I never felt Jake's story was truly finished with that first book, and when Sourcebooks asked for a sequel, the story just poured out of me, mainly because I'd been totally in love with Jake for over twenty years, and I lived with this story. And then when I finished Book 2…well…we have Jake and Randy and the whole family heading for Colorado. Since I was still in love with Jake, I just had to follow them, because even I, the author, wanted to know what would happen when they reached the place where they thought that finally they would find peace.

And they do find that peace…for a while…but the Harkner name just seems to bid trouble, and trouble isn't yet finished with Jake and his son Lloyd. In Colorado they face new challenges that test Jake and Randy's deep love for one another, and challenges that bring Lloyd and Jake to a new reckoning—a final coming together of the Harkner family that leads Lloyd and Evie and the grandchildren into a new era of law and order…and peace at last.

Following is Chapter 4 and part of Chapter 5 of Book 3, *Love's Sweet Revenge*. I am using this chapter because although this story opens with a beautiful moment of serenity and lovemaking between Jake and Randy, and the following two chapters help the reader see that this family is strong and together but trouble is coming, Chapter 4 shows you both the continuing sweet relationship between Jake and Randy, and it also shows you that Jake is still…well…*Jake*, when it comes to facing his adversaries. I might add here that dealing with rustlers is just the beginning of what is ahead for this family. The *real* trouble hasn't even started yet! Be sure to watch for the continuing story of the Harkners in Book 3, *Love's Sweet Revenge*!

Four

"YOU GETTING SORE IN ALL THE WRONG PLACES FROM too much riding?" Jake asked Miranda, turning his horse to face her.

"It's not the *riding* that's got me sore in all the wrong places," she quipped, taking up the reins of their packhorse.

Jake laughed in that teasing way he had, making her feel embarrassed.

"On a trip like this, a man your age should be too tired for frivolity, Mr. Harkner."

"Don't underestimate what a man my age is capable of, Mrs. Harkner." Jake winked at her as he lit a cigarette.

"In your case, I don't underestimate *any*thing," Randy shot back.

Jake grinned and turned his horse again, heading down a pathway toward the valley below. Randy followed behind him, pulling the packhorse along. "Just don't be underestimating *me*, dear husband. I've been just fine on this trip. I'd rather put up with the hard ground and lack of home comforts than to be home worrying about what's happening when you're gone for too long at a time. We went through enough of that back in Oklahoma."

"Well, I'm sure as hell not bringing you along every time, so don't be thinking that's going to happen. It's been nice, and we needed the time together, but out here a lot of things can go wrong. Even so, being a marshal back in Oklahoma proved more dangerous than all the grizzlies and bobcats and renegade Indians and rustlers put together out here."

"Are you giving me orders, Jake Harkner?" she called out.

He kept the cigarette at the corner of his mouth when he glanced back at her. "You mean by telling you you can't come with me next time?"

"I mean exactly that."

He turned away. "Then I am giving you orders. What if something goes wrong? You're a distraction. I might not be as alert as I should be."

Randy smiled. "I *like* being a distraction. That means you're still attracted to me. A woman my age needs to know that."

"Easy, Midnight." Jake pulled up on the reins to the black gelding he favored over the other horses he owned. The path had suddenly banked steeper, and small rocks tumbled as Midnight whinnied and stepped lightly to his master's command. "Stay there!" he told Randy.

Randy slowed her horse, a gentler gray gelding called Shortbread. She watched Jake and Midnight half slide down to a flatter pathway. Jake dismounted and tied his horse, then grasped at trees and rocks and anything else he could to keep from slipping as he climbed back up to where Randy waited. She noticed how worn-looking his leather boots were in spite of being fairly new. That's what ranch life did to a man's clothing. She wore leather boots herself, and a split riding skirt. She shivered under the extra sheepskin jacket Jake had made her bring along, and she was glad for his advice. Mountain mornings could be very cold, even when the weather was warming in the valleys.

Jake reached her and took a last drag on his cigarette, then threw it down and stepped it out. "Get down. We'll walk down using the trees to keep from falling and let Shortbread and the packhorse make their own way down.

They aren't as sure-footed as Midnight, so I want you off Shortbread. The last thing I need is for you and that horse to take a fall out here where there's no help." He reached up and grasped her about the waist, helping her down.

"I do have help," she teased. "*You're* here."

"Yeah, well, I'm no damn doctor." He leaned down and gave her a quick kiss. "And why on earth would you think I'm not still attracted to you, after the two days we spent up in that cabin?"

Randy smiled, wrapping her arms around his waist. "I just like hearing you say it, that's all."

He yanked her wide-brimmed hat farther down on her head when she looked up at him again. "See?" he told her. "You're distracting me again. And there's Shortbread and the packhorse, already headed down. Come on." He kept hold of her arm as they made their way down the escarpment, Randy voicing little squeals at a few slips on the steep hill. Jake's strong grip kept her from tumbling down like a loose rock.

"What a relief!" she said when they reached the flatter pathway.

"Must have washed out in that rain we had last night." Jake helped her remount and handed her the reins to the packhorse again. He untied and mounted Midnight, and they headed farther along, ever downward until they reached the vast expanse of green valley below the cabin.

Randy glanced up at the line shack, feeling a little sad at wondering if and when they would go back again. Their last two days there were the sweetest, most peaceful, most satisfying days they had ever spent together. It was as though all the bad things they'd ever faced together never happened, as though he was thirty again and she was twenty and they were starting over. "Jake?"

"Yeah?" He kept riding ahead of her, heading even farther down into the valley, where they would turn south and head closer to home.

"I really enjoyed the last couple of days. We can go back again sometime, can't we? Maybe after roundup?"

"Sure we can. It's just that I can't take you with me every time I leave the house. I have my ranch work, and you have work to share with Evie and Katie—and the grandkids would have a fit if Grandma was gone all the time. They are probably already asking about you."

"Oh, I know that. I wouldn't *want* to be gone all the time. It's just that this time together seemed so special. I'm glad I came along."

Jake slowed his horse and let her catch up. He looked her over lovingly. "I'm glad too. But I love you and I want you to be safe."

"I'm always safe when I'm with you."

He smiled and shook his head. "Well, out here it's the unexpected things that even I can't stop that worry me. And I like you at home, because after days of mending fence and herding and branding cattle and seeing nothing but the ass end of cows and horses, I look forward to coming home to something that looks a lot better."

Randy laughed. "It's nice to know you think I look better than a cow's hind end."

"Woman, your own hind end is the prettiest thing I've ever seen." He rode off again. "And if we don't stop this kind of talk, I'll end up dragging you back up to that cabin."

I wouldn't mind, she thought, feeling strangely sad at having to leave their little hideaway.

"And if you don't stay home next time I leave, how can I come home to you all warm and comfortable and rested and baking that great homemade bread?" he called out.

He rode a little faster then, and Randy nudged Shortbread into a trot to keep up. What a contrast he was to the angry, mean, unhappy wanted outlaw he was when they met. It had been a long time since she'd seen that dark, brooding side of her husband, the look that came to his eyes when something happened to threaten anyone he loved, or something came along to wake up ugly memories. He was a man capable of extreme gentleness for his size and demeanor—and also capable of extreme violence, though only against anyone who threatened those he cared about.

"Have I told you how you fit this land?" she told him, urging Shortbread up beside him. "When I watch you from behind, I see a big, tall man on a big horse handling a big ranch in big, big country. You fit this land, Jake. It's like Jeff said in his book."

Randy loved Jeff's description of Jake, saying that he had a way of filling up a room with his bold presence… that sometimes it seemed he filled up the whole land.

Jake turned and bridled closer, then reached out and pulled her off her horse and onto his in front of him. "Ma'am, if you don't quit your flirting, we'll never make it home. I'll end up making camp early and we'll be cavorting right out in the open. Some of my men could show up and catch us in a very compromising position."

Randy laughed and sat sideways, removing her hat and resting her head on his chest as he kept his horse at a slow walk. Jake reached over and grasped Shortbread's bridle, pulling the horse close enough to grab the reins. "Here."

Randy wrapped the strings of her hat around the saddle horn on Shortbread, then took the horse's reins. Jake urged Midnight around so he could grab hold of the packhorse. "Hell, between hanging on to the pack-horse and handling my own reins, I can't put my arms around you."

Randy wrapped her own arms around his waist, still clinging to Shortbreads reins. "I'll just hang on. I know we can't ride like this for long, but I like it."

Jake kissed her hair. "So do I."

"I love you, Jake."

He didn't answer right away. "To this day, after

almost thirty years, I still have trouble figuring out why. I've put you through so much."

"You've loved me and that's all that matters. After all those thirty years I feel like we're not just husband and wife, but lovers. Does that make any sense?"

He laughed lightly. "You are determined to make this ride difficult for me, aren't you?"

She leaned up and kissed him. "You're fun to be with when you're like this, all relaxed and happy. And you didn't answer when I said I love you."

He kissed her hair again. "That's because *I love you* isn't good enough for the likes of you. I was trying to think of something better than that."

She threw her head back and looked up at him. "Worship? Adore?"

"Something like that."

They both laughed and she hugged him again. But even without looking at him, she felt the sudden change. He halted his horse, and she felt his whole body stiffen. She leaned back again and saw the darker look of the old, defensive Jake Harkner, the wanted man always on the alert. He was looking past her.

"Jake?"

"Rustlers. Hang on to Shortbread." He turned Midnight toward the foothills. "We're heading for those rocks to the west!" He urged the horses into a faster lope, heading into an outcropping of rocks that looked as though they'd tumbled there from nowhere. "Get down and hide the horses!" he told her when they reached cover. He hung on to her arm as she slid off his horse. Jake dismounted. "Tie them farther into the trees." He yanked his rifle from its boot. "I think they've already seen us, but I'm not sure."

Randy pulled the horses into the trees, her heart pounding. In moments like this, she trusted her husband to know what to do. She obeyed every order.

Jake ducked behind a huge boulder. "Get the shotgun and my leather pack with the extra cartridges and buck-shot," he told her, cocking his repeating rifle.

Randy took the shotgun and ammunition pack from the packhorse and carried them over to him.

Jake set both rifle and shotgun against the rock while he checked his Colt .44s, the guns that had brought him so much notoriety...and often too much heartache. "You stay down, and I mean *down*," he told her.

Randy knelt beside him and peeked through an opening between the boulder and another rock. In the distant valley a good six or seven men were herding a fair number of cattle south.

"How do you know it's not Pepper and some of the other men?"

"None of my men would be riding in bunches like that this time of year. They're spread out, a couple here, a couple there. And we aren't rounding up yet. We're just checking things out. There's counting and branding to do before we start herding any cattle." He rested on one knee, picking up the Winchester and positioning it in the same opening to watch. "They're still a little too far away, damn it!"

"Jake, please don't take them on by yourself."

"I don't think I'll have any choice. Take the shotgun and keep it handy. If anything happens to me, *use* it!" He handed her one of his six-guns. "And then shoot the rest of them with this."

Shoot the rest of them? "Jake, why not just let them ride on?"

"Because it's *my* cattle they're stealing, and besides that, they're already coming this way. Don't touch the trigger on my .44 till you have to. You know how touchy they are. You'll end up shooting me or yourself. Just set it aside for now but be ready to use that shotgun."

Randy carefully laid the six-gun on a flat rock, closing

her eyes and praying she wouldn't have to use it, worried that all the sweet and wonderful things she and Jake had shared the last few days could end in disaster here and now. Crouched on her knees, she peeked around the other side of the second boulder to see five men drawing closer, all very well armed. Two more were making their way around either side of the boulders where she and Jake were holed up. Her only consolation was that if any one man could take on six or more against him, it was Jake Harkner.

Five

"JAKE, TWO OF THEM ARE TRYING TO WORK THEIR WAY behind us."

"I know. You just stay low, understand? Keep an eye behind us, but you let me do the shooting unless something happens so I can't."

The whole time he spoke, he kept a keen eye on the five men cautiously approaching. Randy jumped when he suddenly fired his Winchester, cocked, and fired again.

"Jesus Christ!" someone yelled.

Jake fired again. A man cried out. "My leg! My fuckin' leg!"

"The other three are down in the tall grass," Jake told Randy. "Keep watching our backs."

Randy struggled against tears, remembering another gunfight back in Guthrie, when she almost lost her husband to nearly unstoppable bleeding…another gunfight, back in California years ago, when he took a bullet to the hip…another huge gunfight when they both saved Lloyd from a gang of outlaws out to kill him.

"Who's there?" one of the rustlers called out.

"Jake Harkner! And those are my cattle you're stealing, you sonofabitch!"

Things got quiet for a moment.

"Shit!" someone swore. "*The* Jake Harkner?"

"I've never come across another man by the same name!"

"Goddamn it, Harkner, we didn't know it was *your* cattle we were stealin'."

"Doesn't matter. Stealing is stealing!"

"You did your share of it once yourself, you damned outlaw!"

"Long time ago—and a different man, mister!" Jake shouted. "I'll give you one chance to ride off, long as you head north and not south and you leave my cattle behind. Nobody has ever got away with rustling off the J&L, and I intend to keep it that way!"

"Jake, behind you!" Randy gasped.

Jake whirled, his six-gun out, and fired in the blink of an eye. It boomed much louder than the Winchester, and the man sneaking up on them flew into the air with a scream, a huge hole in his chest.

"Billy, there's a woman with him!" a second man somewhere behind them called out.

"Lie down flat!" Jake ordered Miranda.

Randy did as he told her, just as a bullet pinged against the rock right where she'd been sitting. She felt Jake's weight on her when he laid himself over her to protect her. Randy squinted and covered her ears when he fired his .44 five more times.

Randy heard a man screaming. It sounded like he was running toward them. "That was my father, you bastard!" he was yelling. She felt Jake move, realized he was reaching for the six-gun she'd left lying on the flat rock. More shots rang out, pinging against the rocks and ricocheting in all directions.

She felt Jake's body jerk. "Jesus!" he grunted. He fired the second .44 twice. Another man cried out.

"Jake, are you hit?" Randy screamed from under him.

"Just grazed. I think it was a bullet that bounced off a rock."

"Come on out, Harkner!" one of the men in the grass yelled. "You can't stay there forever. The minute you up and run, we've got you on account of we'll take your woman down first. If you don't want her to suffer, you ought to come on out of there."

"You two are all that's left!" Jake shouted. He remained on top of Randy. "Do you really think I can't take you both down, even out in the open? Let's make it a fair gunfight! You two against me!"

"Jake, no! You're hurt, aren't you? You're hurt!"

He moved off her, staying low. "Load my other six-gun...quick!" he told her. "And stay low like I told you."

Staying on her belly, Randy reached out with a shaking hand and grabbed the empty gun he'd left near her. She reached for the bag of cartridges nearby and dumped them on the ground, picking out the right ones for his .44s. She nervously began loading the gun while the man Jake had shot in the leg lay groaning and crying. "My leg! My leg!" he kept hollering. Suddenly he raised up and pointed his gun at Jake.

Jake fired again.

"You bastard!" one of the others swore. "He was wounded!"

"So am I! He should have stayed down!"

"The poor guy was confused from pain, you murderin' sonofabitch!" the first man answered.

"I've been called worse!" Jake turned to Randy, still keeping his head down. "Keep your fingers away from that trigger," he reminded her.

"I know." Randy noticed the back of his jacket was soaked with blood. "Jake, you're bleeding!"

"Doesn't matter. I can't let them get to you. Finish loading that thing and give it to me."

Randy slammed the cartridge chamber closed and handed him the gun. One of the men behind them groaned.

"Jake, one of those men back there is still alive."

"He isn't in any shape to do us any harm," Jake answered, shoving his six-gun into its holster. "How about it, mister!" Jake yelled louder. "An even gunfight, me against the both of you!"

Randy realized he was using his only option at flushing them out once and for all.

"You'll lose, Harkner, and then your wife will be all ours, or at least at the mercy of which one of us is left!"

"Hank, that's Jake Harkner you're talkin' to," the other man yelled. "You shouldn't have threatened his wife. He's taken on a lot more than just two men on his own. Let's just get out of here!"

"I'm not leaving without taking that sonofabitch down," the first man growled. "He killed Kenny! Kenny was already wounded."

"That's the whole point! He don't miss! You know his reputation! Let's just go!"

"Too late, boys! You get up on those horses and you're dead! I said you could ride off, but I've changed my mind. You shouldn't have threatened my wife! Your only chance now is to face me down fair and square."

There came a long silence. Randy noticed Jake grimace with pain, and perspiration began to bathe his face. "Jake, don't do it! You're hurt!"

"Not bad enough to let either one of those bastards get to you. Remember what I said about that shotgun!" He shimmied up to the crack in the rock to keep an eye on the men lying beyond in the grass. "Make up your minds!" he growled. "Sure death—or a tiny chance at living!"

"This ain't fair! You're Jake Harkner."

"And you made the decision to steal my cattle!"

"We didn't know this was your spread."

"Well, you know it now!"

"Billy!" the second man shouted. "Somebody is riding toward us from the north. Let's get out of here!"

"Harkner ain't gonna let us leave." The one called Billy dared to stand up, his hands in the air but six-gun still in hand. "I'm callin' you, Harkner! Fair fight, like you said, with Cal here a part of it."

"I ain't drawin' on no Jake Harkner!" Cal answered.

"We have no choice, Cal! Put your gun in its holster. Let's get this over with!"

Jake slowly rose, holstering his guns.

"Jake, don't!" Randy begged.

"Stay put," he told her. He walked from behind the boulder, noticing riders in the distance. He could tell it was Lloyd because of how his long hair flew out behind him in the wind.

The one called Cal slowly got to his feet. He carefully holstered his gun, as did Billy. They held their hands away from their holsters.

Jake staggered slightly.

"He's hurt!" Billy sneered. "I *told* you. We've got a chance, Cal."

"Then let's get this over with. More men are comin'!" Cal answered. He went for his gun. Billy went for his at the same time, but before either of them could clear their holsters, Jake's guns were blazing and they both went down.

Randy started to rise, not noticing until then that the man left alive behind them had gotten to his feet. She grabbed up the shotgun and fired.

Jake whirled at the boom. Randy was sitting on the ground, still clinging to the shotgun. "Jesus!" He holstered his guns and knelt beside her. "Randy?"

"I'm okay. The shotgun knocked me down."

Jake helped her to her feet, pulling her close. He wrapped his arms around her. "You sure you're okay?"

"I'm fine." She glanced toward the man she'd shot at. "I think I missed. The shotgun kicked up when I fired it."

Jake kissed hair. "Stay put." He gave her another squeeze, then walked over to check out the man she'd shot at. "He's dead," he called out, "but not from any buckshot." He came back and pulled her close again, hugging her so tightly she could barely breathe. "That's it. You're not coming with me again."

"Jake, you can't judge by this." Randy hated realizing the spell was broken. The trip had been so beautiful, until now.

The approaching riders finally reached them.

"Pa! You okay?" Lloyd charged up to them and dismounted before his horse came to a complete stop.

"We're all right," Jake told him, still clinging to Randy. "A bullet ricocheted off the rocks and ripped across my back, but there's no bullet in me that I can tell. I think it's just a gash."

Lloyd touched Randy's hair. "You all right, Mom?"

She closed her eyes and pulled away from Jake, embracing Lloyd. "I'm just a little shaken up, and that shotgun slammed pretty hard against my shoulder. I have a feeling it will be bruised by morning." She couldn't help the tears then. "It's just that I never know when this is the time I'll lose your father for sure."

Lloyd squeezed her a little tighter. "Hell, you know that mean sonofabitch doesn't go down easy." He leaned down and kissed her cheek and turned to Jake.

"Thanks for the kind names you call me," Jake quipped.

"Just saying it like it is," Lloyd told him. Lloyd gently pushed his mother away and walked around to see the blood on the back of Jake's sheepskin jacket. "Take off your jacket and let me look at that wound."

"Leave it. I'm fine."

"You're bleeding worse than you think, damn it! I saw enough blood after that gunfight back in Guthrie. I don't need to see you nearly bleed to death again. For all you know, you need stitches."

"And who will do that? *You?*"

"Hell yes. I would take great pleasure in yanking a needle through that wound and hearing you yell."

Jake scowled at him as he removed the jacket. "I'll just bet you would."

"Let me at least maybe put some whiskey on the wound."

Jake sighed. "Thanks for coming," he told Lloyd, sincerity moving into his eyes then. "If something had gone wrong, they would have got your mother." He winced when Lloyd tore open the back of his shirt. "You men start going through those men's clothing and gear and see if you can find some identification," Jake called out to Pepper and Cole.

"The bleeding is already slowing," Lloyd told him. "I'll splash some whiskey on it for safekeeping." He walked over to his horse and took a flask from his saddle-bag, along with a roll of gauze.

Jake glanced at a shaken Randy. "You really all right? You're not hurt anywhere?"

She walked up to him and leaned against his chest as he moved an arm around her. "I'm fine."

Lloyd returned with the supplies and Randy felt Jake jerk when Lloyd pressed the gauze against the wound, then splashed some whiskey on the deep cut.

"I'd rather *drink* some of that," Jake told him.

"I expect you would."

"I suppose I've added another scar my back," Jake grumbled.

Lloyd glanced at his mother. She saw the pain in his eyes at knowing the scars on his father's back were from Jake's own father, put there by the buckle end of a belt when Jake was just a little boy. "I suppose so," he answered quietly, "but I don't think it will have to be stitched up. We'll let Brian look at it when we get back."

"God knows it's a good thing your sister married a doctor," Jake tried to joke. "He doesn't need a practice of his own. His own family keeps him busy enough."

Lloyd smiled sadly. "Yeah, well, if you'd learn to stay out of trouble, we wouldn't need him so much."

"Hey, Jake!" Cole called out as he rummaged through the clothing on one of the bodies. "Do you ever leave a man alive when you get into something like this?"

"Sometimes," Jake answered, taking a cigarette from a pocket on the front of his shirt and lighting it.

"Well, remind me to always stay on your good side."

"Just don't try rustling any of my cattle," Jake told him, taking a deep drag on his cigarette. "When I start shooting, I generally don't have time to be careful where I put the bullet. I figure it's best to plant it where I can make sure the man shooting at me can't shoot back any more."

Lloyd made ready to wrap some gauze around the wound.

"Leave it," Jake told him. "I'm more concerned about your mother. Just give me my jacket and one swallow of that whiskey."

"I'm just fine, Jake," Randy reminded him.

"No, you aren't. You might have messed up that shoulder, and I know what something like this does to you emotionally."

Lloyd handed his father the jacket and the flask. Jake took a deep swallow of the whiskey, which told Randy he was in pain because he never drank otherwise, at least not around her. She glanced at Lloyd and knew he'd realized the same.

Jake handed Lloyd the flask and grimaced as he pulled on his jacket. He pulled Randy close then, and she couldn't help breaking into tears as she hugged him around the middle.

"I'm goddamn sorry," Jake told her. "We had such a nice morning."

"You didn't ask for this."

Lloyd lit his own cigarette. "Yeah, well, this didn't just interrupt you and Mom," he grumbled to Jake. "I'd just got back from several days out riding the east side to find Katie waiting for me," he told Jake. "Then some of the men came to tell me there could be rustlers out this way. I'm as angry over this as you two are."

Jake grinned. "Can't blame you there, Son."

"Yeah, well, don't you tease Katie about it. You know how easily she gets embarrassed."

"That's why teasing her is so much fun."

"I mean it, Pa. I know you."

"I'll try my best to be good." Jake kept Randy close as he watched Cole and Pepper rifle through the pockets and saddlebags of the dead men. "How in hell did you know there might be trouble?" he asked Lloyd.

"That courier from Denver, Jason Hale, saw them from Echo Ridge. He was on his way to us with some news, and he knew we wouldn't likely be herding cattle to Denver this early in the season. When we heard there might be rustlers out here, we rode half the night trying to catch up with them, or with you—whichever came first. I was hoping you'd miss them all together, but no such luck."

"Hale never comes out in the middle of the week like this," Jake commented. He kept an arm around Randy as he took another drag on his cigarette. "What did he want?"

Lloyd seemed hesitant. He sighed before answering. "It's not exactly good news. Jeff Trubridge wired us about something he thought we should know right away. Trouble is, Jason gave the note to Evie and it upset her. Brian is home now, though, so she'll be all right. He always knows how to reassure her."

Jake came instantly alert and Randy felt a sick alarm as the both faced Lloyd. "What's wrong?" Jake asked.

"Lloyd, is Evie okay?" Randy pressed. "She's going to have another baby and shouldn't get upset."

"*Baby?* Sis is pregnant again?"

"Yes, though don't let on that you know. She's going to tell us at Sunday dinner. I already told your father to act surprised."

"What the hell is wrong?" Jake asked, raising his voice more. "Why is Evie upset?"

Lloyd rubbed at his eyes. "Shit. I didn't know she was pregnant again. That just makes things worse."

"Makes *what* worse?" Jake asked.

Lloyd pulled the note from his pocket and handed it to Jake, then looked at his mother. "Mike Holt is out of prison—won some kind of appeal. He'll come after me as sure as the sun shines every day." He turned to Jake then. "The past just keeps on rearing its ugly head, doesn't it?"

Jake closed his eyes and ran a hand through his hair. "Thanks to me."

"I didn't mean it that way, Pa. This one is my fault too, for shooting Holt's brother in the back. But after what happened to Evie—"

Randy saw it then—that little flame of Jake Harkner that lived in her son. The dark, vengeful side. She always hated seeing it because Lloyd was raised in love. He never knew the horrific childhood his father grew up with, and he was far more forgiving than Jake, but he had the ability to wreak revenge if warranted, the ability to shoot a man with no regrets if that man dared to harm one of his own.

"I just don't want that man to suddenly show his face to Evie," Lloyd told Jake. "I don't think she could handle it if she saw even one of those men again."

"We should have killed every last one of them when we had the chance," Jake stewed.

"We couldn't just execute the ones left alive, Pa, much as we would have liked to. But you would have ended up back in prison, and Evie would have never lived that down. We couldn't let her see her father and brother deliberately murder those men. And maybe she was able to forgive them, but having to face any of them again…who knows what that would do to her? If she's having another baby, that's a damn good sign her and Brian's marriage is healed. I'm just trying to figure out if we should discuss this with her or just leave it alone and hope the bastard doesn't show up."

"I'll decide when the time is right to talk to her

about it," Randy told them. "She might even bring it up herself."

"Let me talk to Brian first," Jake told her.

"Katie will be none too happy about this either," Lloyd told them. "This will scare her to death after all that happened back in Guthrie. I left her in the barn and took off without even explaining anything, but she'll find out before I get back and she'll be upset."

"You probably should have stayed with her and let the other men come out here," Jake told him.

"When my parents could both be in trouble?" He tried to make light of the situation as he gave his mother a teasing grin. "I figured I'd better try to keep this old man from getting himself into more trouble. Sometimes I'm the only one who can do that."

Jake scowled at him. "I could make you sorry for calling me an old man, but I wouldn't want to mess up that pretty face for Katie."

Lloyd grinned. "That'll be the day."

Jake held his gaze, the look in his eyes softening. "It'll be okay, Son. We have good men working for us. We just have to be extra alert for a while. For all we know, Holt will want to stay out of trouble and he won't show up at all."

"Yeah, and fish don't need water. Stay here with Mom," he told Jake. "The other men and I will get these men buried. You go wielding a shovel and you'll start that cut bleeding all over again."

"Be sure to save all their belongings. We'll have one of the men take them to Denver and report this." He saw the worry in Lloyd's eyes at the remark. Lloyd and pretty much everyone else in the family always feared something could happen to land Jake back in prison. "I was in the right, Lloyd. Cattle thieves are the same as horse thieves. If I hadn't shot them, they would have been hanged. There won't be any trouble over this."

Lloyd nodded. "I know. It's just—"

"The name. I know."

Lloyd smiled sadly. "I'm glad we found you and Mom okay. I sure as hell know this was something you could handle, Pa, but there's always that little worry that something could go wrong this time, and I didn't like thinking Mom could be left out here alone."

"So, you came back because of *her*, not me"

"Of course I did. I knew damn well you'd be okay on your own." Lloyd grinned and Jake couldn't help his own smile then.

"Well, you did right," he told his son. "Let's get these men buried and get home. There's a lot of rounding up and branding to do." Jake called out to the other men, "Any of you recognize any of those men? Did you find something with their names on it?"

"Got names off of five of them," Cole answered, "but I don't know any of them. Pepper doesn't either."

Jake watched Cole Decker limp over to his horse. He had an old leg wound from the war, and that was all Jake knew about his background. Cole was of slender build but strong as a horse, and he tended to drink too much, but he was a happy drinker, not a mean one, so that was okay with Jake. He suspected some pretty shady doings in the man's past, not much different from Jake himself, but he knew by a man's eyes if he could be trusted, and Cole could be trusted. *All* his men could be trusted, or he wouldn't allow them anywhere near his family.

He turned and pulled Randy close again. "Okay, woman, you're right. I don't just love you. I *adore* you. I *worship* you." He hugged her even tighter. "And I'm glad as hell you're all right."

"I will accept those words," she answered, her face buried into his sheepskin jacket. She breathed deeply of his familiar scent, then looked up at him. "Let's go home to the grandchildren. Suddenly I want very much to see them and get back to a normal routine. It helps me handle things like this."

Jake leaned down to kiss her. Randy thought how few women could have a moment like this with their husbands while surrounded by six men he'd just shot dead. She hugged him tighter. "Oh, Jake, don't let go for a while."

"I never let go of you, even when we aren't together." Jake watched the other men start digging graves closer to the trees. "I suppose you'll want to pray over those no-goods," he told Randy.

"It's the right thing to do."

"If it was up to me, I'd strip them down and leave them for the buzzards."

Randy laughed through her tears, needing the relief from the tense drama of what had just happened. His remark was so typical of Jake Harkner. "Oh, Jake, God is going to have a time with you when you get to heaven," she teased, her ears still ringing from the boom of her husband's guns.

"Yeah, well, I think he and I will have a whole lot to talk about. Let's just hope that conversation takes place a good ten or twenty years from now."

Randy hugged him tighter, unable to begin to imagine life without this man. Always there was the worry that the next gunfight would be his last. "I love you, Jake."

He sighed, rocking her slightly in his arms. "We'll go back to that cabin again before summer is out. I promise."

"Can we stay even longer next time?"

"Sure we can."

"Jake, I'm scared for Lloyd."

"Nothing will happen to Lloyd or anybody else in this family. I won't let it."

That's what worries me even more. Randy looked up at him, felt his lips on hers in an oh-so familiar kiss.

But even now she had a sick feeling this was just the beginning of new troubles for the Harkner family.

Read on for an excerpt from Anna Schmidt's

Last Chance Cowboys: The Drifter

From the author...

As with every book I write, the story came first and then came the realization of the true meaning of that story. With the Last Chance Cowboys, every story is about how life changes in unexpected ways and at the most inconvenient times—usually just at the time we think everything is going so well! In the first story, Floridian Chet Hunter is *The Drifter*—a man who has traveled across the country headed for California and a little peace. And while he's riding those lonely, dusty trails toward what he does not yet know is his destiny, Maria Porterfield is thrust into the role of "head of family" when her father dies and her older brother takes off for greener pastures. Their worlds collide when Chet rides up to the Porterfield ranch seeking only a meal and a chance to rest his horse. The connection is immediate and confusing for both Maria and Chet. And when Chet agrees to stay on—"for a while"—what each of them thought was their future shifts...in such a good way!

In my life, I've had to face a number of those unexpected and inconvenient changes—as have you, dear reader. My own battle with uterine cancer and the death of my beloved a few years ago casting me into a world and life I could not have imagined and felt ill-prepared to face are just two of my life-changing moments. What I know for sure is that change comes for a reason, and in the end, change will either make us stronger (and perhaps better people) or it will destroy us and any chance we might have at a different sort of peace and happiness. May all your challenges be small ones and may you—like Maria—fall madly in love with *The Drifter*…

Two

CHET HAD GOTTEN NEXT TO NO SLEEP AND HIS EYES
were bleary, making it hard to focus. He could see that it
was raining in the distance—probably at the Porterfield
ranch, but he was miles from there and the sky was clear.
The dust that the wind was whipping up kept him from
seeing more than a foot in front of his horse's nose, and
the fact was that the missing cows were almost the same
color as the landscape. According to Bunker's best guess,
a steer and two calves were still missing. Bunker and the
other hands seemed willing to accept the losses as normal,
apparently satisfied that they had rounded up most of the
herd and the damage was not too great. But Chet didn't
like leaving even one animal behind. Not knowing their
fate ate at him.

Cracker scouted ahead, then ran back, tail wagging.
She knew the drill but not the territory and she was
being extra cautious. After an hour with no luck, Chet
turned away from the river and the terrain changed from
parched grassland to barren dry rock formations that
jutted up out of the land as if they'd exploded. Chet
thought he heard something and Cracker turned and
sniffed the air to their left.

There it was again. The bleating cry told Chet this
was one of the calves and he gently kneed his horse's
sides, at the same time signaling Cracker to approach
with caution. They wound their way around an outcropping of jagged rocks and there stood the calf—none
the worse for his adventure but obviously scared and

confused. Chet loosed his rope from the back of his saddle and dismounted.

"Hey there, young man," he said, keeping his voice low and soft and forming his noose as he approached. The calf backed away and let out another loud bleat for help. "Your mama's probably back at the ranch by now. How 'bout we go find her?" He swung the rope once and let it fall right over the calf's head and neck. The calf startled and turned to run, but Cracker was right there. Chet hung on, planting his boot heels in the dirt. "Whoa there, my little friend."

It took less than five minutes for him to gain control of the calf and mount up again to continue the search. He doubted that the steer would go along as easily…if he even found it.

Another hour, then two. The sun had reached its peak and Chet drained the last of his water. He hadn't bothered to refill it before turning away from the river. In fact, he'd not filled it last night before turning in—distracted by the way the day had gone. He'd been more concentrated on brushing down his horse and ridding Cracker of the dust and dirt of their journey. Then he'd washed up and put on a clean shirt, thinking all the time about how he might best approach Maria Porterfield, who seemed—in spite of her gender and the fact that she couldn't be more than twenty, if that—to be in charge of the ranch.

He had to figure out the right way to speak to her so she might offer him a job. From the minute he stumbled across the fenced land of the Tipton Brothers Company, he'd begun to have his doubts about working for that outfit. He tended to be a live-and-let-live kind of guy. Judging by all that barbed wire, those who ran Tipton Brothers liked being in control. There would be a lot of rules and probably not much pay. Men who owned big companies like that could be pretty tightfisted when it came to sharing the profits. If he could work at a smaller spread like the Porterfield ranch, that would probably be a better fit.

Eduardo had come to the barn while Chet was washing up. Chet hadn't been fooled for one minute when the Mexican babbled on about needing to stay out there for the night. Something about a coyote coming after the chickens. Truth was that he was glad for the company. Eduardo seemed inclined to talk and that suited Chet just fine. It had been Eduardo who had advised him to wait until morning before trying to talk to "Miss Maria."

"She's been having a pretty hard time of it these last few months. My Juanita says she hasn't even grieved properly for her papa."

Over the course of the evening, he'd learned all about Mr. Porterfield's tragic death, the fact that the eldest son had taken his inheritance out in cash and headed east, and the details of how the ranch's foreman had just that morning quit and left with three of the ranch's most experienced hands. What he hadn't been able to get Eduardo to talk about was the women of the house—especially the fair-haired beauty the men called *Miss Maria* in a tone that bordered on reverence. As he rode on searching for the other missing animals, he realized that as much as he wanted to find out what had happened to those strays, he wanted more than anything to return them to *Miss Maria*. He wondered if that might even make her smile. She struck him as someone who did not smile nearly enough.

༄

It was late afternoon when Maria saw Roger Turnbull's mustang gallop into the courtyard. He slid from the saddle and ran toward her as if he had just discovered that the house was on fire and he was needed to rescue its occupants.

"Maria, are you all right? Is everyone all right?"

It occurred to Maria that there had been a time before her father died that he would never have been so familiar—Miss Maria, yes. Just Maria? Certainly not.

As she had feared, the rain had come and gone and done about as much good as someone spitting on a patch of dirt and hoping grass would grow. The ground was so hard packed that the rain had simply run off the surface. But at least when she'd gone to wash clothes, she'd been thankful to see that the stream that ran through their property had risen some. She continued to hang clothes on the line that stretched across the yard while she spoke to Roger around a wooden clothespin she held between her teeth—a clothespin that would bear the mark of those teeth. The minute she had seen him galloping up to the gate, she had bitten down hard.

"We are fine."

Roger tipped his hat back and surveyed the area. "How many did we lose?"

His proprietary tone was her breaking point. "We? We! You left yesterday if you recall, taking three of my men with you. Why do you care how many of the herd I lost?"

"Now, Maria, just calm down. I am here now and..."

Just then Maria became aware of a ruckus near the corral.

"Well, will you look at that?" she heard Bunker bellow, followed by whistles and cheers from the other men.

"Who the devil is that?" Roger growled as he watched the drifter ride up to the corral leading a calf and a steer with another smaller calf draped across the saddle in front of him.

Maria slowly removed the clothespin from her mouth. With her eyes riveted on Chet Hunter as he and the other men carried the wounded calf out of the heat and into the barn, she started walking away from Roger.

"Maria? Who is that?" he demanded as he caught up to her, matching her stride for stride.

She smiled and said, "That is our new foreman."

Roger let out a derisive laugh. "That cowboy? How do you know him?"

"I don't, but as you can see, he appears to have already earned the respect of the men. Where the others were satisfied with a loss of three animals—as you would have been; as you taught them to be—he did not give up. So in answer to your question about how many we lost? The answer is apparently not one single animal." Maria turned and strode away.

By the time she reached the barn, she heard Bunker saying, "I have to hand it to you, Florida, you did one fine job saving this little guy."

"Thank you for that, but could we get one thing straight? My name is either Chet or Hunter."

The circle of men froze. No one—not even Turnbull—crossed Bunker. But then Bunker let out a laugh and clapped the drifter on the back. "Got it," he said. "Tell you what. How about you teach me and the other boys here a little something about the way you use that whip and we'll count you as one of us?"

Someone spotted Maria and nudged Bunker and the men fell silent as they whipped off their hats in a gesture of respect. Maria was well aware that while their deference was partly because she was their boss, more likely it was born of habit. Hired help had a long and unbreakable tradition of showing special respect for their boss's female family members. They might court the daughter of a neighboring rancher, but she knew that not a man among them would think of showing that kind of interest in either her or Amanda. *No man except Roger*, she thought. But then Roger did not consider himself one of the men. She walked directly to the drifter and looked up at him.

"Mr. Hunter, I would like to thank you. You certainly did not need to go out of your way to find these strays, but I am truly grateful that you did."

"You're welcome, ma'am."

He ducked his head, and with all the shadows in the barn, she could not see if Amanda's assessment of his eyes was correct. "I wonder if I might speak to you after you've finished here," she added.

"I expect these men know a good deal more than I do about how to save this little guy, ma'am." With his hat he gestured toward the doors and waited for her to lead the way. The problem was that Roger was between them and the door, observing every move she made—as usual. So she turned in the opposite direction, moving deeper into the shadows. The drifter hesitated, then followed her, and thankfully the rest of the men turned their attention back to the injured calf, discussing treatments and whether or not the little guy would make it.

"I believe you mentioned that you are looking for work, Mr. Hunter?"

He was still holding his hat, and he cocked his head to one side as he looked down at her. "You don't call the others 'mister.' Why me?"

Rattled by his sudden switch in topic, Maria felt her cheeks flush and was glad for the protection of the shadows. From the corner of her eye she saw that Roger had moved closer and was now standing on the edge of the circle of men, pretending to give his advice on the calf, but Maria was not fooled. She decided to ignore the stranger's question and get to the point.

"I would like to offer you the position of foreman for the Clear Springs Ranch, Mister...Chet."

"You're offering me work?"

"I am offering you the position of *foreman*."

He leaned against a stall and crossed his arms over his chest. "And if I say I don't want to be your foreman, what then?"

"Why would you turn me down?"

The late afternoon sun was coming in through gaps in

the rafters and the light settled on his face. He grinned, and the way that smile relaxed his features made her look away. Amanda was right—sparkling eyes or not, this was one good-looking cowboy.

"Because, Miss Porterfield, I don't want to be the boss of these men. Besides, they know what they need to do. They are all good at their jobs from what I've seen."

"But they need direction."

He uncrossed his arms and ran a hand through his thick hair. "Well now, from what I've been hearing, miss, that would be your job. You are in charge since your father died, right?" He glanced back toward the men—toward Roger. "On the other hand, maybe that guy has realized his mistake in leaving. Looks to me like he's gotten right back into that saddle."

He had a point. Roger was ordering the men around, raising his voice when they didn't react with the speed he expected. "Excuse me a moment, Chet." She headed back to where Roger stood over the calf. The other hands had scattered to do his bidding. "Exactly what do you think you're doing, Mr. Turnbull?"

"Taking charge. Looks to me like somebody needs to." This last he aimed directly at Chet.

"I am in charge," she said quietly. Behind her, she heard Chet clear his throat and had the oddest feeling that he was offering his support—or perhaps his admiration. Either way, that gave her the strength she needed to stand her ground. In spite of her uncertainty about how she was going to keep this place that had been her father's legacy from going bankrupt like so many other small neighboring ranches already had, she would not back down.

Roger cupped her cheek, and behind her she heard the drifter take a step in their direction. "Just go, Roger," she said, lowering her voice so the others would not hear. Then she stepped away from him, breaking the contact. "You made your choice. Now please just go," she repeated and walked past him and out into the yard. She hoped that neither man was aware that her knees were shaking so badly that walking was a new adventure.

✦

She was quite a woman, this Maria Porterfield, Chet thought as he watched her walk across the yard and resume the task of hanging the wash. First she had stood up to him and then the guy who seemed to think his job as foreman carried with it certain side benefits when it came to his former boss's daughter. Now that the boss's daughter was in charge, that probably didn't sit well with a man like Turnbull. From what Chet had observed, this was a man who was used to having his way.

Turnbull was watching *him* now, sizing him up. Neither man moved. Neither man blinked. It was a contest to see who would speak first. As far as Chet was concerned, it was not worth his time to play this game. He was tired and hungry. He jammed his hat in place and walked past Turnbull, nodding once before continuing on his way. Once he reached the yard, he wondered if he ought not to just keep on walking.

His horse's reins were looped over the corral fence and Cracker was waiting as always for him to make a decision about what they would do next. That dog was the closest thing he had to a best friend, someone he could talk to and trust. Whatever decision he made, he had to do right by her. He had pretty much decided that whether he stayed or went, Cracker deserved her dinner and the horse could use a good brushing. He led the animal to one side of the stable. Some time later he was just finishing the grooming when he turned to find Maria clutching a bundle of laundry she'd evidently collected from the clothesline. The setting sun was behind him, and he knew she was having trouble seeing him clearly.

"Something you need, ma'am?"

"I believe I offered you a position. I need your decision."

He swallowed, taking his time, hoping he wasn't about to make a big mistake. "I'll take the work—as a hand, not as your foreman."

"I don't understand why you wouldn't want to take a position that will pay more."

He thought about everything that Eduardo had told him the night before. "It's not my place to offer you advice, miss, but seems to me that Mr. Turnbull wants to come back. Don't you think it might work out better for you having him here than over working for the Tiptons?"

Her eyes narrowed as she studied him. "Mr. Turnbull is none of your business. The question is will you stay on."

He shrugged. "For a while."

"I need people I can depend on, Chet."

"Yes, ma'am."

She scowled up at him. "Does that mean I can trust you to be here when we need you?"

He allowed himself the pleasure of looking her over for a long moment. "Can't say, ma'am. Only you can decide if you trust me or not. It means I'll work hard for as long as I'm here." He realized he was wearing his hat and snatched it off his head. "I do thank you for the chance to work, Miss Porterfield. I won't let you down."

She studied him for a long moment, squinting up into his eyes as if trying to decide whether or not to believe him. Then she brushed past him on her way back to the house. "We'll see about that," she muttered.

He slowly began to smile as he watched her go.

Outlaw Hearts

The beloved classic, marvelously reissued
by Rosanne Bittner

USA Today bestselling author

—◆—

At twenty, Miranda Hayes has been widowed by the Civil War and orphaned by a vicious band of rebel raiders. Alone on the harsh, unyielding frontier, Miranda is surprised to run into the notorious gunslinger Jake Harkner, a hard-hearted loner with a price on his head. Suddenly Miranda finds within herself a deep well of courage…and powerful feelings of desire she's never known.

Hunted by lawmen and haunted by his brutal past, Jake has spent a lifetime on the dusty trail and on the run…until he meets a vibrant, honey-haired beauty who is determined to change his violent ways. But does she love him enough to risk her life to be his woman—an outlaw's woman?

—◆—

Praise for Rosanne Bittner:

"Bittner has a knack for writing strong, believable characters who truly seem to jump off the pages." —*Historical Novel Review*

"Fans of such authors as Jodi Thomas and Georgina Gentry will enjoy Bittner's thrilling tale." —*Booklist Online*

For more Rosanne Bittner, visit:
www.sourcebooks.com

Desperate Hearts

by Rosanne Bittner

USA Today bestselling author

— ✤ —

She's a woman with a secret

Elizabeth Wainright is on the run. Accused of a murder she didn't commit, she has no choice but to cut ties with her old life and flee west. The last thing she wants is attention, but when her stagecoach is attacked, she suddenly finds herself under the fierce protection of one of Montana's famed vigilantes…whether she likes it or not.

He's a man with a code

Lawman Mitch Brady is sworn to uphold justice in the wild lands of 1860s Montana. He's never met a man he's feared, and he's never met a woman more desperately in need of his help. Something's shaken the secretive Elizabeth, but as he gets to know the beautiful city belle, he finds the only thing he wants more than her safety…is her trust.

— ✤ —

Praise for Rosanne Bittner:

"One of the most powerful voices in Western romance." —*RT Book Reviews*

For more Rosanne Bittner, visit:

www.sourcebooks.com

Paradise Valley
by Rosanne Bittner

❦

Maggie Tucker has just gone through hell. Outlaws murdered her husband, looted their camp, and terrorized Maggie before leaving her lost and alone in the wilds of Wyoming. She isn't about to let another strange man get close enough to harm her.

Sage Lightfoot, owner of Paradise Valley ranch, is hunting for the men who killed his best ranch hand. But what he finds is a beautiful, bedraggled woman digging a grave. And pointing a pistol at his heart.

From that moment on, Sage will do anything to protect the strong-yet-vulnerable Maggie. Together, they'll embark on a life-changing journey along the dangerous Outlaw Trail, risking their lives…and their love.

❦

Praise for Rosanne Bittner:

For more Rosanne Bittner, visit:
www.sourcebooks.com

About the Author

Award-winning novelist Rosanne Bittner is highly acclaimed for her thrilling love stories and historical authenticity. Her epic romances span the West—from Canada to Mexico, Missouri to California—and are often based on personal visits to each setting. She lives in Michigan with her husband Larry and near her two sons Brock and Brian, and three grandsons, Brennan, Connor, and Blake. You can learn much more about Rosanne and her books through her website at www.rosannebittner.com and her blog at www.rosannebittner.blogspot.com. Be sure to visit Rosanne on Facebook and Twitter!